DEAD ALIVE

A Novel

LISA SLATER

DEAD ALIVE

2021

This book is a work of fiction; a product of the author's imagination. Names, characters, places, and incidents are the product of the author's imagination or are used fictitiously. Any resemblance to actual events, persons, living or dead, is coincidental.

All rights reserved.

Copyright © 2021 by Lisa Slater

ISBN (print)   ISBN (ebook)

Requests for permission to make copies of any part of the book can be submitted to:

Lisa Slater

infolisaauthor@yahoo.com

DEAD ALIVE

A Novel

PART ONE

Chapter One

Korengal Valley, Afghanistan
"Valley of Death"

1

The early spring morning was cold enough to chill Specialist Scott Young's fingers right through his gloves as he and his squad stalked into Aliabad under the cover of darkness. The Army-issued M4 he held in his hands felt more like a chunk of ice that he ought to toss into a stiff drink than a rifle. At twenty-three, he could be sitting on some stool celebrating with a whiskey—neat, like he'd prefer this morning, or with whiskey stones, like he'd prefer later this afternoon. Instead, he was tramping through the Korengal Valley in Afghanistan, holding a rifle designed to shoot 5.56-millimeter rounds and 40-millimeter grenades from the attached M203 beneath the barrel. When it came time to use it – and his gut was whispering that he would – the weapon would warm soon enough.

As Young walked carefully through the eerily silent village, the sun slowly began to rise, flickering across his sharply-edged face and dark shadow of a beard that remained even after a fresh shave. The warmth started driving away the chill, giving him a brief, and severely false, sense of home. If he closed his eyes, he would be able to smell Texas – which as odds would have it was roughly the same size as all of Afghanistan. Although Texas boasts of many beautiful mountains, such as Guadalupe Peak at 8,751 feet above sea level, none of them come close to the enormous mountain range stretching through Afghanistan. Its highest point reaches over twenty-five thousand feet into the thin air. In many places, the elevations made helicoptering soldiers up and over just as dangerous as the rocket propelled grenades (RPGs) trying to shoot them back down.

Young's smoky brown eyes remained open, and Texas faded. The town of Aliabad endured. The village was a meager collection of stone houses, small lowly livestock sheds, and an occasional hungry barking dog, whose sole function was to act as an alarm system. The area was civilian, so although Firebase Phoenix could cover their movement, no firepower could be hailed down on known residences. This enchanting old-world village was situated just east from the harshly unglamorous and southernmost post, Observation Post Dallas.

OP Dallas was where Young and his comrades took shifts behind guns or sleeping under a sandbagged ledge. Their rotation, like every platoon's, consisted of thirteen months of seemingly never-ending stretches of boring drudgery, spiked with flashes of electric battle thrill. Was it just Young, or was battle the only thrill around here? That is, if he didn't count the masterful machine-gun view, the stench of unshowered men, and shitting in a barrel. Better have a buddy take a picture, lest one forget the spinetingling elation of emptying that same barrel. Only Private First Class Brandon Bennett counted such things as unbiased entertainment.

Bennett was lumbering on Young's left, carrying an M4 and a rack of thirty-round magazines. Nicknamed "the Tree," standing slouched at six feet, four inches, and thick with muscle, he tended to move with about as much grace as a tree. As a farm boy from Iowa, he stood out, looking more like a Scottish Viking. As a child he'd made his name amongst the smaller, faster boys by moving machinery with his bare hands. In the military, he was known for both his Viking-like strength and bully-like banter.

"Giving you a hard on yet?" Bennett asked Corporal Anthony Ramirez, a twenty-two-year-old brown-haired Puerto Rican, who not only took pride in carrying his M-249 Squad Automatic Weapon (SAW) but relished it. The SAW is a bad-ass belt-fed thrower of rounds at just a touch of the trigger. Bennett claimed it gave Ramirez a hard-on. Unsurprisingly, Ramirez never disputed the charge. He just grinned and let everyone stare and silently speculate.

"I bet it feels like your sister when it gets all fired up, don't it?" Bennett teased. "All hot and bothered. Hot like the sun, I bet."

"Like the sun," Ramirez repeated thoughtfully in his heavy Puerto Rican accent. "As long as my sister is a million miles away from the likes of you, yes, we'll go with that."

Ramirez was the unruffled type, which gave Bennett cause to continue trying to tousle his even temperament. "The sun is like sixty million miles away, Ramirez," Bennett lectured. "So far it actually makes your sister feel kinda close, don't it?" Bennett waggled his large rear and smiled. "In fact, I think I can feel her tits in my pants."

"That's just your fingers," said Ramirez, calmly shifting the weight of his SAW.

Bennett glanced down and yanked his fingers out of his belt, surprised. "Hot damn."

"The sun is closer to a *hundred* million miles away, boys" said Doc Linus Winehouse from the back of the pack.

Doc, at age twenty-four, was older than everyone except Staff Sergeant Knight. He was surprisingly short and exceedingly thin with dark hair and beautifully tanned skin. Could have been a magazine model if he hadn't pledged his life to the Army. Probably for the best. Doc had a different core mission than the rest of them. He took care of people. Particularly his soldiers. He was like their soldier mother. If the day came that he couldn't take care of them, his face would likely be one of the last faces they stared into. They might have ribbed Doc about his height, but one just doesn't comment on the physical stature of a man like that.

"Nah, no feckin' way, Doc," argued Bennett.

"Yeah, it is," Doc insisted.

Bennett wasn't one to go down without a fight. "I paid attention in science. The teacher was hot. I'm sure it's sixty million."

"I'd put an extra package of crackers on that you were paying attention to the wrong parts of class," commented Ramirez.

"You're on," said Bennett. "Hit me."

"What's the one thing you remember most vividly about the classroom?" asked Ramirez.

Bennett was silent for a few seconds. "There was a classroom?"

Laughter filled the quiet morning air.

"Sixty million," Bennett said assuredly. "I'm sure."

"How sure?" chimed in Specialist Jerome Holden, their twenty-two-year-old RTO—radio telephone operator. Holden was walking near Staff Sergeant Knight so he could relay anything the Sarge needed via radio. He'd been a California surf instructor before joining the military. He wore rainbow-colored sunglasses and had a cigarette hanging from either his mouth or his fingers whenever possible. "Bet a roll in your hay barn with your sister? Didn't you say you had *two* sisters?"

Bennett's head snapped. "What the hell? My sisters are classier than hay rolling. At least use the back seat of your—"

"Movement in the window straight ahead," Young said, squatting a little. Everyone fell quiet. Young's focus narrowed in on the window, and he forced himself to glance right and left.

Houses lined up on the left. A crumbling house and a stone wall intended to keep in the goats at night on the right. Although not uncommon for this time of the day, there were no livestock – which theoretically could be easily explained. The herdsmen could have already taken them into the hills to graze. But where were the women in their bright garb and the playful children? Where were the old men with their orange-dyed beards, muttering in Pashto?

The dwelling straight ahead was marked by intel to check for a weapons cache. No one was supposed to know they were coming, but lately nearly every major patrol resulted in a fight. Young couldn't help but suspect a leak to the insurgency by a local inhabitant.

"Sarge, trouble."

"Split. We don't want to be in a funnel," Sergeant Zach Knight ordered.

Small bullets from an AK cracked over their heads.

Young crouched and provided Alpha team with suppressive fire as they alternated between firing and bounding for cover. Bennett and Doc ducked behind a stone house on the left, followed by Young. Ramirez, Knight, and Holden threw themselves behind the stone wall on the right. Together, they punched more rounds through the window as Bravo team hustled as quickly as they could, heavy with at least twenty pounds of gear. More AK gunfire exploded from both sides of the street, kicking up dirt and chipping at stone. Bravo team dove for cover. By some miracle, no one was hit.

Korengal Valley is called the Valley of Death. It's located in eastern Afghanistan, in the Konar Province, just a hair-raising breath away from the Pakistan border, sanctuary of the well-funded Taliban. The area spans over six miles long and just over half a mile wide of steep lethal mountains caked with loose shale and scattered holly trees. Countless military men have been shot (or narrowly missed being shot) by an intrusive bullet snapping by their heads or ripping through a uniform sleeve while squatting over a shit hole or sleeping on a stale cot inside of their barrack tent, killing nothing but time.

Time, now that was something a civilian could relate to better than a combat soldier stationed in Afghanistan. Back home, there was a reason to keep time. Stateside friends had jobs that they could clock in and out of for every shift. Young pretty much kept track of the hour only for ambush patrols, where they made their rounds in efforts to obstruct insurgent forces from setting traps for further patrols. At any rate, the only way his shift would end here was if he were wounded and sent home kicking and screaming, his thirteen-month tour over, or he'd "clocked out" for good.

"Clocking out" wasn't so scary. Young understood there were scarier things to fear than death. Still, it went without saying, he understood there was a mighty thin line between life—and the end of it. For a combat soldier, it could be instantaneous, or a matter of a few minutes. Hours or days, if you were up for a good challenge. Years, if you were the son-of-a-bitch who returned stateside to find civilian life mundane and without purpose or loyalty. And then there was the never-ending terror and discomfort of memories that weren't memories at all but daily internal wars with the worst enemy of all. Yourself. Medical folks call it PTSD.

In a nutshell, for a soldier in combat, life meant you were able to continue the job—protecting your brothers next to you. Death? Well hell, that just meant you'd done it already.

Aside from protecting the brothers next to you, today's job was to act on the never-ending insurgent radio chatter, always hinting at large weapon caches hidden somewhere inside the village. They never knew where it would be stashed or who was doing the stashing. It could be almost anyone. Many were joining the insurgency because they wanted the Americans gone more than they wanted the Taliban gone. The Taliban, after all, paid wages for stashed weapons and shooters, and assisted with the exporting of the illegal timber trade. But, if the patrol squad was lucky, they'd walk and ask questions until a villager would risk their life by talking to them, in hopes of bringing peace. Or, they'd walk until someone took a shot with an AK or a mortar. Usually the latter.

Bennett shouted across the street, "Sarge! I think there's weapons in there!"

"No shit," Doc said, rifle up.

Sergeant Knight shouted, "Bennett! The friggin' sun is ninety-two million miles away!"

Bennett grunted. "How does he know that?"

Doc laughed.

From under Young's Kevlar helmet, a drop of sweat beaded down his forehead. The earth had warmed dramatically in the last few minutes. Just as he had predicted, his rifle had warmed too. "I think the sun gets a mite closer in the Korengal valley," he mumbled.

"Nah," said Doc. "That's just hell, seeping up from the dirt."

2

Afghanistan is no stranger to fierce conflict and terrible loss. There had been many conquests: Alexander the Great, Islamic, the Mongol Empire (repeatedly). There were three Anglo-Afghan wars, a ten-year span of constant combat during the Soviet Occupation—until the Soviet's defeat in 1989—and numerous civil wars, which in 1996 resulted in the Taliban's catastrophic and violent capture of Kabul.

Fast-forward another few years. Al-Qaeda, Bin Laden's army of three thousand soldiers, and fifteen thousand Taliban (comprised of both willing followers and terrorized civilians) merged into one group. On September 9, 2001, it was this merged group that assassinated the powerful hero and Northern Alliance commander—and ally of the United States of America—Ahmad Shah Massoud. The same group struck American soil two days later, setting into motion a plan to blast the Taliban out of the country.

The American's intentions were to assist the country in assembling a strong Afghan army and creating critical constructions, such as military outposts, hospitals, schools, and roads. The intentions became reality, but as time clicked by in the count of years, increasing numbers of American and Afghan soldiers were dying. Many were beginning to feel the well-laid plan was becoming more futile by the day.

Technological advancements did, at first, rock the fierce bands of rebel fighters entrenched deep in the hills and mountains. Bombs poured down upon them in waves of unstoppable wreckage, while brave Afghan fighters rode in by horse and sword, pushing the Taliban boundaries back further and further. It had been working. However, the growing confidence of an overly sophisticated plan may have underestimated several pieces of the less modern country. It didn't take long for the involvement of the rugged terrain and bordering countries to take a massive toll. To make matters worse, the Korengalis' familiarity with decades of death and destruction by war made the suffering of the Taliban's merciless conviction to press them under the strict thumb of Islamic law almost customary.

Talib is Arabic for student. The Taliban were great students. They quickly learned the American rules of war and engagement, discovering for themselves when and why the Americans pounced. More importantly, when and why they didn't. It took little effort to exploit those rules as American weaknesses at every opportunity. Thus began the games of "hit and run." The Taliban would set up land mines or simply shoot from a hilltop and then disappear behind it, later pretending to be goat herders. No one could argue otherwise. Other times they openly utilized "civilian camouflage," audaciously standing on rooftops, bearing all sorts of weapons but effectively surrounding themselves with women and children—known non-targets. Where the Americans valued human life, the Taliban did not. Especially women and children.

"Another few feet and we'd have been trimmed down to size," Bennett said, laughing, as he threw his back against a stone house with Doc and Young.

"Speak for yourself," Doc said, squatting low, allowing Young to take the high aim by standing over him. "You've got size to trim."

Young glared angrily around the bullet-chipped corner of someone's marred home. "It was a trap." A bullet whizzed over the top of his head, biting high into the stone, adding another chip. He, and Ramirez from across the street with his SAW, returned the gesture with a burst of their own.

"I wonder which son-of-a-bitch we have to thank for giving away their position too early," Bennett half yelled. "Feckin' moron. I think I'll shake his hand."

Just then, a large object flew out of the window and landed in the dirt, creating a billow of dust around it. Young looked down his sights at the crumpled outline, ready to fire, finger quivering with anticipation. The others were doing the same, he could feel it.

"Hold your fire!" Sarge's voice boomed despite not a shot having been fired. But they were ready.

"What the—?" Young muttered under his breath.

"It's a kid," said Doc, sounding surprised.

Bennett stuck his curious head around the corner. "What kind of kid?"

"The short kind," Young answered.

Someone from inside the window yelled, and the boy stood. Even from a distance he appeared to be shaking. Young scrutinized every part of the boy's small body looking for a sign of a weapon of any kind. It was not beneath the enemy to use children as shields, or on suicide missions. The boy appeared clean.

Appearances were deceiving.

The kid took one shaky step, and fell.

AK rounds spit from the window before Young could register that the small boy's face had slammed against the ground. Young's team returned fire. Damn it, they weren't hitting the shooter. Young wanted to load a grenade into his M203, but without knowing whether the boy was a pawn or threat, dead or alive, he didn't dare risk missing the tiny window opening and hitting a child. Maybe that was why they'd thrown him out—a pathetic defense against harder artillery.

As the shooting continued, it seemed that the Taliban crowding in around them was multiplying by the second.

"This is feckin' bad!" Bennett yelled. Young agreed. "We need air support, now! Where's our air support?"

"They're radioing for it," Young advised, but he knew it was going to take a while. It always did. There were time-consuming steps to be followed that rarely benefited the men and women on the ground or in the air.

Military Kiowa Warriors were a ground soldier's saving grace a thousand times out of a thousand—so long as they were present. This single-engine, double-bladed helicopter could zoom in and provide reconnaissance, target acquisition, quick communications, missile, rocket, and machine gun support. On occasions when fire support capabilities couldn't be utilized, a Kiowa pilot could operate as back up by using their light armor, flying only tens of feet above the ground.

The boy, splayed and belly down in the dirt, glanced up. He was alive. Blood from a beating he'd likely undergone and terror fouled his face. Rounds continued pouring in, digging into the ground, producing splashes of dirt. A muzzle appeared outside the glassless window for the first time and angled toward the ground where the boy lay.

"They're aiming for the kid," advised Young.

Doc stormed the window with 5.56-millimeter bullets, buying Young time as he loaded a grenade into his 203 attached under the barrel of his rifle. Doc was watching him from the corner of his eye. Young knew what he was thinking. He was thinking it himself. Though an enemy position, there could be civilians hunkered down in there as well.

The boy looked up, making eye contact with Young. It was as though they were both functioning on the same silent circuit. This could possibly be Young's one and only opening. He beckoned wildly for the kid to dart right.

The kid jumped to his feet, dodged right, then ran as fast as his bare feet could take him— straight down the enemy funnel, towards Young, Doc, and Bennett.

"He's coming this way!" Doc yelled needlessly—they all saw it.

"Feck me," Bennett muttered down the stock of his rifle.

The firefight exploded to levels that Young's ears could barely stand. They were growing accustomed to being deafened so his ears could just suck it up. As the child desperately pulled himself nearer and nearer, rounds embedding into the dirt around him, Young studied the kid's open, flinging hands.

Damn it. Was there a weapon? It was difficult to tell between the dust being kicked up around the kid's feet and the sweat and grit in

Young's eyes. The bloody-faced boy was sprinting. For his life? For an afterlife reward? Young couldn't be certain. Young's team was trusting Young to make the right call. Young coiled to jump on the boy the moment he made a knife or grenade.

The boy tried to dart past Young and slide behind the wall but was immediately greeted by Young's arm and a hard yank that swept the child off his feet. A loud screech escaped the tiny mouth, mucked by old blood from his nose. Surely, he was wondering if he'd jumped from the pot and into a fire. However, he had taken the risk of running. So maybe, for him, it was out of the fire and into a pot. Nonetheless, to Young's relief, he found no knife and no grenade. Young released the boy's arm, expecting him to bolt and run off.

Despite shaking from fear and adrenaline, the dirty, malnourished kid not only didn't run off, but refused to leave, even when Young shoved him.

"Get!" Young commanded, eager to be rid of him, and back to the fight.

The kid stared at Young and grinned the tiniest grin.

"Why the feck is he smiling at you?" asked Bennett.

"Because he's alive, I suspect," answered Doc.

The boy squatted and took turns staring at each of them.

"He's creepy," replied Bennett between shots. "Who the hell does he think he is?"

Young smiled at the kid and shoved the lightweight up next to Bennett. "He's the son-of-a-bitch that gave away the enemy's position too early. Shake his hand."

Bennett glanced at the kid suspiciously over his rifle stock, then nodded his big head. "Okay kid," he said, and stuck out a large white hand. "Put her there, little asshole."

Little Asshole smiled, revealing a fallen out lateral incisor.

"Can't be much more than eight," Doc advised.

And yet, they owed him their lives.

Chapter Two

1

Doc carefully cleaned the face of the kid and stuck some gauze up his nose to stem the flow of blood. "If he knows what's good for him, he'll get as far away from us as possible. Go find his parents."

"We need a translator," said Young. "Sarge!" Young hollered towards the other side of the small street. "Can you spare a translator!"

Sarge's voice boomed over, "I'll send you the shittiest one I've got. Prepare for a grazing."

A few seconds later, Holden sprinted over, low and fast as the others made a barrage of sweeping bullets. "Shittiest one he's got… I'm the *best* translator he's got."

Young could tell by the way Holden swiped his uniform sleeve across his face that he was hankering for a cigarette. "You're the *only* one he's got right now."

"Yeah, that too." He wiped his face again. "Well, now you've got me, what are you going to do with me? I won't mention that I was crossing my fingers for a pretty blonde instead of you."

Young shrugged. "Sorry about that. Bennett is sort of blonde."

"Pass," Holden said then looked down at the scruff of a boy. "What's he got to say for himself?"

"I don't know. Why don't you ask him?"

"All right, I will."

Holden and the boy exchanged rough conversation using what little Pashto Holden'd picked up from the locals. He wasn't a trained, or designated, translator but that didn't stop him from picking up the language almost as easily as any of the rest of them could pick up change from a sidewalk. A little effort, and bam, words in the pocket. It came in handy.

Occasionally, as bullets were exchanged and casings were scattered, the Korengali boy cowered, but he never darted away. To Young's annoyance, the little thing tried to stay as close as possible.

Between shots Young snapped at Holden, "What's he saying? Ask him if there are civilians in the building?"

In the current scenario, they couldn't reach the building to clear it without losing someone, and they couldn't take it down from above not having it cleared of civilian hostages. They were in a pickle to say the least. What made matters worse was, in the last few minutes, there had been a shifting in the enemy's positions. They were quickly infiltrating from surrounding areas, in an attempt to flank the squad, thus blocking a retreat. This ambush was better orchestrated than typical village insurgents taking a couple of pop shots at the American soldiers as they were leaving. The Taliban was definitely here, in full force, and was looking to play for blood. Lots of it.

"No living civilians," Holden replied, earning him hard glances from Young and Doc. Holden's face didn't change, but his voice dropped an octave. "The kid lost his parents when they didn't cooperate."

Sand and rock kicked up in Young's face and he grimaced. "Why not the kid?" he demanded, anger building at both the stinging in his eyes, and the stinging in his heart.

Holden's head jerked. "Maybe they thought they could turn him into a weapon? Sell him?"

Young glanced at the boy and then away again, returning his focus to the battle. He'd learned that it was common practice for persons in the Afghan military and police force to keep catamites—young boys to service their needs. For male Afghan adults to undertake in homosexuality, that was punishable by death. But prepubescent children, well, they were up for grabs. Sick bastards.

Young punched a bullet through the head of man who'd stuck it up a bit too high in order to hail down a heavy attack of 39-millimeter rounds. The Taliban's Russian-made AKs were well noted for their lightweight and mechanically simple advantage. Yet, on the other hand, its recoil is brutal on the shoulder and terribly inaccurate at distance, unlike the M4. The standard-issue M4 is lighter than the M16, with an effective ability to reach distances up to six hundred meters at nine hundred and fifty rounds per minute.

Turning back to Holden, who was still conversing with the boy, Young asked, "How about these other buildings?"

"Empty. Boy says the other villagers left. They didn't want to be caught in the battle. Only shooters remain now."

Young nodded, satisfied.

"I've got to get back to Sarge," Holden said. "Tell the kid to scram. Cover me, Doc." Holden was out in the open and sprinting for the other side like some kind of crazy hero man, hurdling the stone wall, and disappearing before anything else could be said.

"Show-off," Bennett commented, with a strong bit of respect in his voice. Shots rang out on their left diverting his attention. With very little movement, he transferred his sights to an area just below a small puff of dust. "Found you," he sang.

At the precise moment Bennett pulled the trigger on the exposed shooter, Young pulled the trigger on his M203, aimed for the little window that'd been troubling them. The grenade slid through the small opening like an overzealous dick, followed by an immediate booming explosion that rocked the ground.

"Yeah baby!" Holden's voice rose excitedly from across the street. A few others from B squad joined in.

The celebration stopped short when an opposing RPG hit the stone wall where Ramirez, Knight, and Holden were taking cover. Stone and dirt flew in every direction, peppering the block. The haunting sound of Knight hollering "medic!" curdled Young's blood.

Doc answered the call immediately and without hesitation. He dashed for what was left of the broken wall before Young and Bennett could provide suppressive fire to degrade the enemy's opportunity of inserting a bullet into his ass.

"Feck!" Bennett hollered as he and Young popped up and began grazing known, and unknown, shooting positions as best they could. "Who's hit? Who's hit?" he yelled.

"I don't know!" Young shouted back.

They heard Holden howl a long string of obscenities and both found themselves sighing a little right before another explosion pierced the air, followed by Sergeant Alvin Green from B squad yelling for his men to relocate for cover.

Specialist Akachi Chibuzo, a hugely-built African American, whose proud family originated from a small village in Nigeria, was dragging Private First-Class Kendrick Smith behind him. Smith was cussing and kicking frantically for Chibuzo to let him go so he could get back on his feet—only, one of his feet were missing. Chibuzo ignored the idiotic argument and continued towing him with one arm and shooting with his other until he reached an old clapped-out Afghan truck—a Toyota once painted in bright colors and immodestly decorated with bells.

"What the hell, man?" Smith screamed up at Chibuzo once his back was against a deflated tire. His helmet had flown off, revealing his bushy, strawberry-blond hair and eyebrows.

Chibuzo kneeled at Smith's feet – foot – and dug out his tourniquet and pressure pads. He applied the tourniquet above the knee, causing Smith to scream and cuss furiously. Smith attempted to kick Chibuzo with his missing foot.

"Get off me you—" Smith got a good look at what Chibuzo was making such a fuss over. His face paled. "What'd you do to my foot, Akachi?" he screamed accusingly.

Chibuzo pressed the pads to the blood-gushing stump with all his might. "I didn't do it! Sit still!"

"Like hell you didn't! It wasn't like that before! I know what my foot looked like, and it wasn't missing!"

"Well, it's missing now. You can mope about it later." The bandages were soaked through and dripping. "I've got to tighten it more."

Just as Chibuzo reached for the tourniquet—and Smith had opened his mouth to cuss at him some more—a hole seemed to magically appear in Smith's neck. It gushed blood, soaking the front of Smith's dusty uniform shirt. Smith's face contorted into an expression of shock as his hands reflexively covered the spurting hole and then paled to that of wilting daisy. His body went limp as he looked at his friend in disbelief.

Chibuzo's eyes widened, and he called anxiously, "Medic!" Slamming his own large, dark hands over Smith's neck, he looked around, feverishly calling again, "Medic! Doc!"

Young immediately sprinted for the truck to provide defense for their highly exposed position. With every stroke of his boots, guilt for not getting to them sooner drove in deeper and deeper. It was his fault. Damn it. He should have been there sooner.

What about Bennett? You left Bennett, the back of his mind reminded him. There was no winning on a battlefield. There was only the last loser.

Young's knees hit the ground hard as he slid in behind the "jingle truck" next to Smith and Chibuzo. He knew, even then, he deserved the pain. A moment later something crashed into the back of his legs. He whipped around not knowing at all what to expect. It was the kid.

"No!" Young screamed at him. "Get out of here!"

The kid didn't budge. He just huddled as close as he could. Young couldn't push him away or he'd surely take a bullet, if he didn't take one right where he was. *Fine, stay put. Die the way you choose.*

Doc dove behind the truck like a baserunner sliding, head first, into homeplate.

Chibuzo was straddling Smith, his big arms bracing his hands against Smith's neck and also supporting Smith's drooping head.

Beneath the covering of Chibuzo's sleeves, Young knew those arms were covered with tattoos, from the wrists up. Many were beautiful, but the simplest tattoo was just words, written in bold black. Akachi, "the hand of God," Chibuzo, "God give me directions."

Doc dug in straightaway, allowing Chibuzo to shift to his friend's side in order to gently support his weight and head. Doc held bandages over the wound while at the same time injecting him with morphine.

Chibuzo was a strong, intimidating man, from his shaved head to his six-pack abs. But under the skin of this great and mighty warrior, his heart was constructed of booming laughter and encouragement to all those around him. He was the first to force you to dig deeper, try harder, and he was the first to jump in and help you accomplish it.

Young hoped God was giving both Chibuzo and Doc directions right now.

"I…don't want…to die alone," Smith gasped.

Chibuzo, holding his dying friend, cooed soothingly, "You're not alone, my brother. I'm here. I've got you."

While Young desperately searched for the shooter who had an angle on them, he heard Ricky gurgle the words, "Okay, brother… okay," and then nothing.

A moment later, a short, pained groan escaped Chibuzo, followed by the slamming of a powerful fist into the side of the truck. Over and over and over. Young felt the kid flinch against his legs the first time Chibuzo's fist shook the truck, but after that the small boy remained absolutely motionless.

Ricky was gone. Ricky had escaped this fight. Escaped from Afghanistan. Escaped from this nightmare. In a way, Ricky had been the lucky one.

2

Both squads were completely flanked in now. While whichever Taliban asshole was in possession of the rocket may have been late out of the gate, he was here now. Grenades were raining in. From the sound of the return short firing bursts, Young knew that, like himself, the men were preserving ammunition. Stuck in this well-devised surprise hell hole, they were going to eventually run out of ammo. It was only a matter of time. If the last bullet was expended, they'd all be dead shortly after.

Even from his position at the broken-down jingle truck, Young sensed Knight on the radio arguing the importance of immediate air cover and evacuation of wounded. Doc had rejoined Holden, finishing with helping Holden wrap a bandage around his head to cover where debris had splattered his face. The first grenade that had exploded next to them had left protruding grenade splinters beneath Holden's left brow and in the globe of his right eye.

Specialist Pirate, Young thought, though it didn't cheer him like it might normally have. Doc worked methodically, giving no outward merit to the size of the large splinter, or giving any outward sign that he'd just lost his last patient. That would come later, in the thought-provoking quiet of solitude or the long, lingering darkness of night.

Holden, true to character, dug out a cigarette from his pack. In the Korengal Valley even the nonsmokers took up smoking, whether it was to relieve overstressed nerves or fill in a few minutes of mind-numbing boredom. Over the course of a few weeks, "have a smoke" became Doc's first piece of advice. Homesick? Have a smoke. Experiencing uncontrollable shakes? Have a smoke. Can't sleep? Have a smoke.

Holden didn't have to be told. He lit up the moment Doc stopped messing with his face. He took a long drag, sucking in the coveted nicotine. Then, with a cigarette hanging out of his mouth, he took up his gun and started shooting again.

Sergeant Alvin Green, twenty-seven-year-old Bravo squad leader, assisted Young and Chibuzo with cover as they hustled Smith's body inside a tiny wooden shed with missing boards and goat shit everywhere. Green, just as fit as the rest of them, had the face of a pudgy-cheeked baby, and small beady blue eyes. The only things in the world that he cared about more than the flag of the United States of America were his beautiful blonde wife and tiny one-year-old son, Tate. During a long, boring stretch at Post Dallas, Young had once asked Green why he had re-upped in the military to be sent overseas rather than staying home to serve his family. Surely they needed him.

Green's response was, "Serving my country *is* serving my family. I can provide a roof over my wife's head whether I'm here or there. But if I'm not willing to defend the land that the roof sits on, it will never be their home."

"So, you're sleeping under a boulder with me freezing your ass off so that your family can have a home? What about you? Don't you want to be home too?" After all, unlike many of them, he *had* a family.

Green just smiled, pulled out a picture of his wife and son from his chest pocket and handed it to Young. "I *am* home. Anywhere I am, as long as I have them resting here against my heart, I'm home."

"You're a romantic," Young jested.

Green laughed. "Yes, I am." Then he leaned in close. "I'll remind my wife why she likes being married to a patriotic romantic when I get back," he said, then winked.

"Alvin Junior, the second?"

Another smile. "Hell yeah." And bit by bit, Green allowed himself to be drawn in to a moment, a place, far away from Afghanistan. The smile slowly disappearing from his face, he stuck a cigarette in his mouth.

Inside the goat shed, the sounds of gunfire and rockets shook the wooden walls. They couldn't stay here if they wanted to keep Smith's body from being blown to bits. They wanted to send him home in a flag-draped coffin, with a body inside, the way Kendrick had wanted. Kendrick was constantly worrying that if his grandparents, who had raised him, didn't have a body to see if he died, they wouldn't understand. They would forever wonder why he hadn't returned to them for "welcome home" festivities of iced tea and strawberry cobbler.

"Where's our air cover?" Green shouted at no one in particular.

"I don't know!" Young answered anyway. Touching the shoulder of the blank-faced kid with dried blood on his face who had followed him, yet again, he ordered him to "Stay here!"

Green grabbed the thin shirt on the kid's back as he tried to follow Young out the door. Green yelled, "Ouch, you son-of-a—" and the kid was out the door, tight on Young's heels.

"Keep up then!" Young yelled even though the kid didn't speak English. Something told him, the kid understood just fine, despite the language barrier.

Snap! A bullet nipped the air right next to Young's ear, distracting him from watching his feet. "Shit! Mother—"

Two small hands landed on his belt line and shoved. It wasn't much of a force, but it was enough. Young's boot just barely missed an improvised explosive device buried just beneath the disturbed soil. Young inhaled sharply, threw his rifle over his shoulder, and scooped the kid up under his arm. Less feet on the ground, less chance of blowing up from an IED. Dodging behind anything providing even partial cover, he headed towards where Bennett was shooting in damn near every direction, like a fireworks presentation gone wrong.

As Young swung in next to Bennett, he dropped the kid onto his feet and re-grabbed his rifle. Bennett smiled and gave the boy a quick thumbs-up. "Welcome home, Little Asshole. How was school?"

The boy grinned briefly then crouched against the wall, eyes darting in every direction.

"Good. Keep a look out," said Bennett.

"We're pinned down, and there's IED's out there," Young warned him.

Bennett had his eye focused down his sight and smoothly pulled the trigger. "I know, man," he said, his voice grave.

Young wanted to ask Bennett, "which part did you know?" when across the way, a sniper got an angle on Ramirez's position. A bullet meant for him sparked off the top of the wall just above his head. He immediately hit the dirt and started low crawling between chunks of stone, effectively cutting him off from Knight and Holden. Another round sparked off the stone, missing him by less than an inch. Young scanned the buildings and hills behind him, popping off rounds at anything that moved, but there were more of them then there was of him. They seemed to be getting closer. "Come on," Young hissed under his breath, "Move your ass, Ramirez."

All at once, about a dozen armed Taliban jumped out and rushed Ramirez, hollering and firing their AKs from waist level. Ramirez rolled onto his back, holding the trigger down on his SAW. Half the men were cut down, falling to their knees and faces. The other half ditched behind any structure large enough to conceal a man. Ramirez let off the trigger. If he fired without stopping for too long, he'd either run out of ammo—going through nine hundred rounds a minute—or the barrel would melt. He carried an extra barrel, but he wouldn't have time to switch it out if they rushed him again. And rush again they did.

Out they jumped, from separate directions this time. One fired down at Ramirez, hitting him in the leg. Ramirez grabbed a grenade, pulled the pin, and held it for what seemed an extremely long count as the resolute fighters quickly drew nearer like a pack of hungry wolves, keen on the first bite.

Young hit one man in the chest, Bennett hit another, and the two fell almost in unison. *Not enough, not enough,* Young's head chanted. He took off so suddenly, running as fast as he could across the street, the boy didn't have time to bolster himself and stayed behind. Bennett didn't though. Young heard his heavy footfalls behind him right before the blast of Ramirez's grenade as he threw it at the two closest fighters bearing down on him. His SAW started up again but not fast enough. Three fighters came up behind him, one aiming from the waist and another preparing to nail Ramirez in the head with the butt of his AK. Young lifted his own rifle, slowed his sprint, and shot at the one pointing his AK. Direct hit. Bennett barreled past, leaping the shortened stone wall like a musclebound bull just as the other fighter struck Ramirez in the head. Bennett repaid the favor by smacking into him, with the full speed of a linebacker. There was a short-lived scramble before Bennett wrapped his thick arms around the skinny man and slammed his body down over a stone that jutted out. The spine of the man produced multiple eerie cracking noises, like someone stepping on a pile of brittle branches. He went motionless, eyes wide.

The last two men weren't yet prepared to give up. This was their chance at grabbing a soldier or two to exploit. Whether dead or alive, it didn't matter. It was a means to boast, "We can take one of yours at any time and make an example of him. You're not safe here."

The tall, younger, bearded fighter fired madly at Bennett, while the shorter, grayer one, wearing a turban and a devilish grin, turned on Young, proudly revealing a live grenade in his hand. Bennett took half a dozen rounds through his groin area, doubling over, and yet somehow ferociously fired his rifle back at the same time. The young bearded man fell in a heap.

Bennett, holding his mid-section, glanced at the stalemate between Young and Gray Beard. By chance, Bennett was closer. Young shook his head, but it was too late. Bennett charged the man, lifting him off of his feet in a giant bear hug. At the same time, Young jumped on top of Ramirez, covering his body with his own as the blast wave penetrated through his soul.

For one ephemeral moment, he saw Bennett sitting on a broken crate back at camp, smiling broadly around a hand full of cards in a game he was winning. He rarely won at cards, but he wasn't one to go down without a fight. On the occasions that he did win, he looked as though he were on the top of the world.

Bennett was on the top of the world now.

When Young looked back, both men lay dead. Pieces of them scattered about like confetti. He'd never be able to look at colored paper confetti again and not see the pieces of his friend strewn all over the ground. His soul split down the center and a tormenting sorrow inside of him bled so profusely he could barely see through the blur. He couldn't even register a voice hollering his name, tugging his arm. His feet scarcely moved, as though he were in quicksand.

"Young! Bennett is gone," yelled Private Flores. "Help me get Ramirez out of here!"

Private First-Class David Flores, from Albuquerque, was born and raised with six younger siblings in New Mexico. Flores admitted to having joined the armed forces in order to escape gang rivalry he'd inexcusably brought on himself through a desperate string of bad decisions. His decision to enlist was to avoid dragging his family down the path he'd trampled out for himself. Despite his mother's begging, the decision was definitive. Therefore, Flores enlisted in a different war. The war on terrorism.

Flores was "adopted" into a much larger brotherhood after that. He'd acknowledged that it had been hard, but not as hard as fearing your mother would be beat over the head one night, your little sisters gang raped, and your little brothers following in your angry footsteps. No, this new brotherhood was defined by seven core values. Values that he'd been unknowingly craving all along. Here, he'd learned of a different kind of courage. The kind of courage a soldier faces in war. Courage that is born of love and devotion for your brothers, and they for you.

Flores was stationed at Ramirez's head, ready to lift. Ramirez was blinking slowly, blood trickling down his forehead and into his ear. Young grabbed Ramirez around the legs, nodding and lifting at the same time. Bullets buzzed overhead. They ignored them, depending heavily on the return fire of their brothers to provide what screen they could, with what little they had, while they made their way over the uneven rubble as hurriedly as possible. The three of them bore gear that sagged and rattled with every short choppy stride. Once behind a squatty wall, they set Ramirez down, grateful that Doc had arrived at almost the same time, gun up, guarding their backs. Doc and Young traded jobs without needing to say as much.

"What are you doing still carting around that kid?" Flores asked Young as he offered Ramirez water from his canteen.

Ramirez choked on the first sip, most of it dribbling down his neck, while at the same time, Doc examined the bullet entry and looked for an exit.

"What?" Young asked, confused. He'd almost forgotten about the kid, but now that it was mentioned, he recalled that the kid had, luckily, stayed behind.

Flores gestured with a nod to a short figure squatting behind Young, head hanging low.

Young breathed. It was good to see the boy was okay. He didn't know why it was good to see, but it was. "Can't shake him," he grumbled.

Flores looked at him. "Well, you better. He can't come back with us."

Young couldn't argue with sense, so, instead, he zeroed in on a man wearing loose-fitting shirt and pants. He was toting a Russian-made machine gun——a PK—and ammunition box. A killable offense for any fighting-age male. Young squeezed the trigger, steady and even, until the hammer fell, sending the bolt carrier flying forward. A bullet fired, causing the stock to nudge his shoulder. The shot hit the man center mass and he fell out of sight. A familiar humming hangover lingered in Young's ears, until it was drowned out by the roaring of another close-range struggle around the corner. It had to be Knight and Holden.

"Shit." Young scrambled for Sarge's position.

When he obtained a visual, he saw that the group of men tearing towards Knight and Holden were too close for him to use his M203. Out of his peripheral, he observed a second group of men clambering down the hill, who would be on them soon as well. Those he could blow up. He loaded his grenade and fired.

The explosion shook the ground, disassembling both earth and man; the eruption was enough to temporarily cause the remaining gunmen to hunker down. They began pelting Young with a torrent of bullets. Mostly, they missed. One round came so close, it ripped through the flesh of his left shoulder and continued on its way. Young paid it no heed, running again, and firing into the large group of men who were sweeping over the fierce, fighting Holden. Some Taliban fell. More didn't.

Where were they all coming from? It was like a steady flow of water from a spring of death.

Young's feet wouldn't move fast enough as his eyes helplessly latched onto Holden's. Did Holden just wink at him or was it just him blinking under the wrapped eye? In a breath, Holden's hands were emptied of his gun, and he was overtaken. Knight fired endlessly at the men bombarding him, creating quite a magnificent pile of wounded, or dead, bodies, until his rifle went silent. Fearlessly, Knight used his empty rifle to strike one man in the face, blood spraying from the man's mouth like a fine mist, before 39-millimeters filled his chest. Young roared in pure rage and desperation. He fired at the jumble of enemies that had come upon them, aiming to drive them off. Then his rifle went silent, the clip as empty as his chance of success.

Half a dozen muzzles swung in Young's direction causing him to hit the dirt. With shaking hands, he grasped for a new magazine. Bullets buzzed over his head, the higher pitched the closer they were. Just as he jammed the magazine into place an earsplitting blast detonated from inside the heap of fighters that had overtaken Holden. Young covered his ears too late and he was left with a sickening wave of nausea and unsteadiness. The enemy would have dragged them all off, but not now. Holden had told them countless times that he would die by grenade for his brothers in combat if it ever came down to it. Young had assumed he'd meant someone else's, not his own.

"Damn it, Holden!" Young screamed. He felt his mind began to sway. A healthy mind feels solid. When it begins to sway, a person begins to wonder what is left of it.

Young stared at the place where Holden had been when they'd made eye contact. Young knew for certain now that Holden had indeed winked at him. There would be no more surfing for the surfer. All that was left was a pile of twisted and mangled charred pieces—one indistinguishable from another. Young screamed again; his words indistinguishable even to him. His throat swelled with rawness.

A dark hand yanked him to his feet.

3

Specialist Young threw a blind fist, striking the hard left cheekbone of a man.

"Homie!" Private Flores yelled into his face, grabbing onto the front of his uniform, but otherwise not engaging him. "Same side—"

Before Young could process either visually or auditorily, he brought his right elbow up, hammering it into Flores's jaw, jolting his head back. Flores's helmet flew off. Young was about to follow through with his left arm when his amygdala finally caught up and he was able to stop himself.

"Shit. Sorry."

Flores mustered a half smile, releasing him. "Toes. It's all about the toes," he said, referring to his favorite mantra, "keeping ya on your toes." He used it anytime he wanted to be testy or unexpected, like a "get out of jail free" card.

"Screw the toes," Young snapped, swinging around to the sound of gunfire.

Flores swung the opposite direction, his back pressing up against Young's. "I like my toes, strong, homie. Screw *your* toes!"

"My toes *are* screwed!"

Young had been experiencing tunnel vision and loss of depth perception on and off, all signs that his heart was pumping at a rate of somewhere between a hundred and seventy and a hundred and eighty. He'd been trained to deal with and fight through such indicators, but now his thundering heart froze his feet to the ground, his thinking jumbled until there was no thinking at all.

Flores started pushing him, forcing him to move his feet. "Grab Knight!"

Young nodded. It felt like his neck was made of limp playdough. The longer you rolled playdough in your hands the thinner and weaker it became. Afraid of the possibility that his head could roll right off of his shoulders, he did the best thing he knew to do—ignore it—and went back to work.

Knight's body, thin and tall, torn by bullets and shrapnel, lay sprawled. His eyes stared at the sky above him without blinking. Young looked away, grabbing both of his arms and began pulling, making very little progress, until Flores joined him after he'd retrieved Holden's identification tags from the carnage. They made their way as quickly as possible towards Doc and Ramirez. Not that there was anything Doc could do to help Knight, but there may be something they could do to help Doc and Ramirez.

An itching doubt stabbed at his gut. Why didn't he hear Doc's rifle firing anymore?

When they got to Ramirez's and Doc's position, Ramirez lay dead, a bullet in his head. Doc was nowhere to be seen.

A grenade exploded about twenty feet away. Dropping Knight, they both hit the dirt. Two living soldiers lay next to the two lifeless soldiers, sharing what little cover was there to be had. Young was taken by surprise when Flores suddenly jumped straight up, screaming obscenities in his native tongue towards all of the surroundings.

"Shit! Get down, Flores!"

Flores didn't listen. He kept on screaming and hand-gesturing like a madman. He *was* a madman. In truth, they both were.

"Get down!" Young tackled Flores's knees, dropping him to the ground.

Scrambling, Flores screamed at him, "I can't! I can't watch them all die!" He grabbed at Young's weapon, pointing it at himself.

"F--king shoot me!" he demanded. He released Young's weapon, and grabbed his own, pointing the barrel at Young. "We can't be taken. They said we can't be taken. We can't let them take us—"

"No," Young growled, shoving Flores's muzzle out of his face. It came right back.

Flores's face flushed with anguish. "They're *dead*," he said, his voice straining. It wasn't fear in his eyes, but rage. Insensible rage. "They f--king took Doc! He – us – we're all f--king dead alive, homie!"

It sounded like gibberish, but Young understood exactly. Dead alive was how they referred to a person when they were precariously balancing on an ever-spinning wheel of torturous effects, whether real, or perceived. It could be PTSD, the constant companion of a suicidal storm, or in this case, more literally, it was being captured. It was the worst kind of dead really, because you were still alive.

"Not yet," said Young over the constant bombardment of rounds digging into the earth around them. "I'll shoot you later if I have to." He was lying of course. He hadn't come here to kill his own men. "Right now, we've got to find the others. Last time I saw Green and Chibuzo, they were near a shack." He left out the part about Ricky's body. "If they're still there, maybe Doc's with them."

Flores shook his head in disbelief. "Doc wouldn't have left him," he said, referring to Ramirez. The rage in his eyes was still there, but the desperation had dissipated with the small possibility of a plan. A familiar task.

"He might not have had the choice. We'll take him."

"Both of them?"

Young glanced quickly at both the bodies. "Yes." He could read Flores's face; it suggested what he was thinking himself. If they took them at the same time, neither he nor Flores would have free hands to defend themselves. However, whichever one they left behind would be stolen, stripped, and dishonored, before they could get back. "We're taking them both. Are you up for it?"

"Can a helicopter make it to that shack for the extraction? Can we get all the guys out of here?"

"Yes," Young answered. *Whether it be in boots or a casket.* "We'll get them out of here."

Flores fixed his eyes on Young, and Young knew what was going through his mind so he shook his head. Now was not the time to discuss it. Most every soldier under the stress of combat and seeing friends die has, or will have, experienced a sort of ego depletion—a depletion of self-control or willpower due to mental resources having been exhausted. Or, they'd experience war neurosis—a psychological trauma triggering self-defense mechanisms. Young had experienced such only a few strides back. He hadn't acted impulsively; he'd just stopped acting at all. His mind locked up, like a small child retreating into a vault. It was Flores who had saved his ass. In this rotation, he'd return the favor.

Young lent Flores a hand and yanked him to his feet. "Let's go."

They both grunted wearily and started gathering their friends, throwing them over their tired backs, for the long haul over a short distance of bullets and grenades. For a lifeless body being referred to as "empty," it sure felt heavy.

Over Young's back, Ramirez's clenched fist fell open. A handsome, black, leather bracelet fell to the ground, landing in the blood-soaked dirt. Had a forgotten little dirty hand not scooped up the dark bracelet, it would have laid unnoticed. Head hanging low, the young Afghan shadow wrapped the treasure in the tail of his shabby shirt, tucked it into his shorts, and followed behind the soldiers without a word.

Flores and Young carried the bodies, shrinking further and further back, allowing the enemy to close in over the now-lost ground. From carrying the weight of another man and all of his gear, Young's skin poured sweat from every surface, soaking through his uniform so it looked as though he'd taken a dip in the river. Droplets dripped onto the dry earth as he and Flores stumbled and groaned along. Wild bullets spat in their direction, skipping off stone and digging into the dirt at their feet. They would have flinched, if they'd had the energy to spare. They didn't. Young's eyes were blurry with perspiration and Flores's legs looked on the verge of buckling. They both kept trudging, the shack in view—across the stretch of a street with no cover.

Amazingly enough, Young hears the ferocious barking of a dog in the distance. How he managed to hear a dog over the constant barrage of gunfire raining around them and the drubbing of his heart, he'd never quite know. But within that low anxious woofing, a different sound emerged. A thick and noisy pulsing.

Whoomp! Whoomp! Whoomp!

Chapter Three

1

Chibuzo rushed into view, signaling to Young and Flores with a wave of his thick arm. A few bursts of fire from behind a low mound in the ground and he sprinted a peculiar pattern across the dirt street. The moment he reached them, Young saw him measuring up who was the most fatigued. Though it must have been a toss up between exhausted and spent, Chibuzo lifted Knight from Flores's shoulder, taking their long-limbed Sergeant onto his own back without asking questions.

"We don't know where Doc is!" Flores yelled. "Is he with you?"

Eyeing the short boy huddled around their legs, Chibuzo paused before responding, "Doc's with Green." He turned away, not caring to expound, and searched the sky with his eyes.

With Green? What did that mean? Was he dead or alive? If he wasn't dead, Flores might see to the deed himself if Doc had abandoned Ramirez. Young didn't think Doc capable of abandoning the men he took care of day in and day out, but hell, he'd been surprised before. One's own skin is very expensive.

They all watched with relief as two Kiowa Warriors came into view, one in the lead, the other as cover. They swooped in low and fast, providing more concealment than the guys had experienced all day. The friendly machines pointed their noses out and began laying tracers across enemy positions. The left-seat pilot stuck an M4 out his door and aimed at the closer threats hiding behind walls and windows.

The Taliban forces weren't hightailing back into the hills this time. Young assumed it was because they knew they had so many in numbers. Only time would reveal who would win the war, but the opposition was definitely winning this battle. It was the Americans' turn to retreat. A game that each side took turns at.

"I'll go first," Chibuzo said. "Step only where I step." And he began the trek across the street as quickly as he could while Flores provided cover, along with shots from behind a mound on the ground on opposite sides of the road—presumably Green.

After Chibuzo had made it across, Flores tapped his shoulder. It was Young's turn to cross. He was carrying Ramirez and wouldn't be able to cover Flores, so Flores would cover for him the same as he had Chibuzo. Young hated leaving his soldier behind and for a brief moment considered making Flores carry Ramirez. It may have only been a street in most men's eyes, but it felt like a continent in that moment.

"Go, homie!" Flores screamed at him, hitting Young on the shoulder, right above where a bullet had ripped through his uniform and flesh earlier. Now he wanted to deck him, but he'd done that earlier as well, plus his hands were full.

As exactly as possible, Young followed in Chibuzo's steps towards the mound on the ground where he had watched him pause then continue on toward the goat shack. Chibuzo had gone on to mark the shack for medical evacuation by deploying a smoke signal. Young's heart felt attacked at the sight. Ramirez, draped over Young's aching back wouldn't benefit from medical care. It was over for him. Part of Young needed to bawl, but most of him wanted to kick ass. His soul was stuck somewhere in the middle as he struggled to lift his heavy boots off the ground, again and again, as he crossed the great continent of an old Aliabad street on what had started as a beautiful morning.

At about halfway, as Young drew nearer to the other side of the road, he saw Doc, now lying awkwardly next to Green. A series of messy bandages were wrapped around his head, all blood-soaked, one of which dipped to cover his left ear. But he was alive. His concentration was on something having to do with Green's sleeve. After a moment, he squirmed around in the dirt appearing to be tending to another injury belonging to Green. Then another. And another. It dawned on Young's worn-out mind that Sergeant Green had been hit multiple times. From the looks of it, he must have been trickling blood into the ground like a kitchen strainer.

"Blood stays on the inside," they'd all been schooled by their instructor—what felt like a lifetime ago. "Pay attention. What may seem like a simple bullet wound in the arm or the leg can drip steadily, which may seem meager, but you better take the time to patch it. When your blood pressure drops you go into shock and..."

"You die," the class had finished for him, per the habit. They had all laughed.

No one was laughing now.

He felt the tiniest hand grab onto him. *His shadow*, he thought, and then felt the wave from a blast up the road. His eyes flitted in that direction, and he froze. A herd of goats were heading his way, straight down the road. Another IED was detonated by a poor unfortunate hooved creature. It and the buddy next to it were cut down into bloody sections of gore. The herd panicked and ran.

Boom!

A goat leg flew, landing at Young's feet, nearly detonating the IED next to him.

Boom! Another explosion, another mutilated goat.

"Shit!"

During a less combative moment, Young might have mused, "Why would they sacrifice the village's small supply of precious meat?." The answer was simple. The Taliban didn't give a shit, and the village leader would take the matter to the Americans and be reimbursed for the loss—likely compensated at a price high enough that they would then be capable of tripling the original size of the herd. There was really only one loser here, and that was the man—and the boy—that the goats were rushing toward.

Young and his shadow continued painstakingly toward the other side of the road, not taking short cuts, but following what Young hoped was the path Chibuzo had taken. From the corner of his eye, he saw that goats were beginning to fall, without having been exploded. Flores was shooting them.

Many of the goats were laying about, some whole, others not, when Flores's rifle went silent and didn't start up again. Nearly to the mound, Young had to assume the magazine was empty and Flores was out ammunition. He made the last few steps to join Green and Doc and was finally able to drop Knight's body off of his back. The kid squatted next to Doc, looking like a cornered, beaten dog—ready to bite, or run, or both. When Young looked across the street to Flores, he saw that Flores's nose was smashed against his rifle, but his head was resting cockeyed against his shoulder.

The pilots of the Kiowas must have exchanged dialogue about the smoke signal because one of the copters turned, and was now hovering, preparing to pick up what bodies it could. The soldiers on the ground breathed thankfully.

Chibuzo had returned from setting the smoke signal, threw moaning Sergeant Green over his shoulder, and was waiting for the helicopter to touch down. Doc was stationed as cover in Green's spot, signaling Flores to hustle.

Flores didn't hustle. Flores didn't move.

A tight knot formed in Young's gut. Flores wasn't going to move, for whatever reason. He had to go back for him.

While Chibuzo loaded Green and Ramirez into the waiting Kiowa and disappeared to the shack for Ricky, Young left the kid behind the mound of dirt and made his way back across the street, carefully avoiding even the slightest disruption in the soil. *It was a miracle they all had managed to miss the IEDs when walking in the first time,* Young thought. Surely the rivals had marveled at the same phenomenon.

Indisputably, the soldiers had lasted longer than the fighters had expected. Although they should have expected it. Like Bennett—they did not go down without a fight. The right to freedom is not easily attained. It has to be fought, and often died for. It's not something that should be simply handed over or tossed into a well for wishes like a cheap token.

When Young reached Flores, he held his rifle at the ready and stooped. A bullet had entered his neck at the back of his head. No exit that Young could make out. "Flores," Young addressed him, placing his fingers next to the jugular, searching for a pulse, "tell me you're not dead, homie."

"No, just keeping you on your toes," Flores mumbled. Still, he didn't so much as open an eye.

A small fleeting grin touched Young's lips. "Let's keep it that way, huh? Can you move?"

"No."

"Okay. That's okay. We'll get ya outta here, brother. You just relax, have a cigarette, and I'll do all the work. How about that?"

"Titties," Flores mumbled, his jargon for awesome. "I'm gonna nap."

"No, no napping, homie. Your mouth seems to be working fine, so maybe Doc will give you a lollipop."

"I've always wanted one of those."

"I bet you have."

Doc's lollipops weren't the kind you got at the doctor's office for good behavior. Doc carried an opioid lozenge on a stick. It was easy to administer and provided quick pain relief through the absorption of fentanyl. The fentanyl was combined with inactive ingredients such as berry flavoring and confectioner's sugar to create a palatable pop.

"Doc!" Young hollered loudly, hoping to get over the roar of the noise currently echoing through the valley. Best-case scenario, he would need an extra pair of hands, but he was firing on worst-case scenario: If they moved Flores wrong and the bullet changed position, he could be permanently paralyzed, but more than likely, it would be lights out in an instant. Flores wouldn't even know it happened.

By the time Doc made it safely across the road, Chibuzo covering him from the mound, the helicopter had lifted, taking with it two dead brothers, and Green, in severely critical condition (a lollipop tucked in the cheek of his mouth). Green needed to go, Young understood that. There was little chance that he'd make it as it was. Still, Young regretted not getting Flores on that chopper.

"Don't worry, homie," Flores said to him when the air was free of whoomphing and bursts of gunfire resumed, "sometimes it's the handsome guy that's the hero."

"What's that suppose to mean?" Young asked as he pointed his grenade launcher at a busy hill of assholes firing down at them. He pulled the trigger on the last grenade he had. The hill exploded. "Are you calling me handsome?"

"Nah, Doc's handsome, but not you. You're ugly."

"Screw your toes then."

"Consider them screwed."

Chibuzo had manufactured a way to move Flores by breaking off the door of some little house. They'd just have to be careful not to dump him off it when the chopper finally returned. They didn't have to wait long.

The second Kiowa flew over to where they were all hunkering down with as little as a couple dozen bullets left between the three of them. Apparently, the pilot decided to "screw the rules." There was a handful of living soldiers completely locked into a death zone, and they wouldn't remain living if not evacuated—now. The pilot, seeing everything clearly, must have come to this decision on her own, because she swooped in a like bat and settled before them.

The small group didn't wait for an invitation.

Chibuzo and Young grabbed each end of the door that Flores was situated on. Doc, with rifle up and scanning behind them, and shooting when only absolutely necessary, knelt with the kid, who was sticking to him very much like gum in a girl's hair. Young had to hand it to the kid. He was tough.

With Flores aboard, Chibuzo and Young turned away from the helicopter, rifles up and ready, which was Doc's signal to hustle in, which he did. Chibuzo followed Doc aboard, and Young froze, looking down at their little shadow. The kid, who probably was the spitting image of his father, made no move to climb in. Instead, he was unraveling something from his tattered shirttail.

"There's not enough room!" the pilot hollered, seeing the problem. "We're overweight as it is! We've got to go!"

Fighters were rushing in.

"Get in!" Chibuzo shouted at Young.

Young looked at the boy. "I'll stay with him. Come back for us." Then he felt sharp biting sensations in his leg and, again, in his gut. He doubled over in excruciating pain, his legs dropping him to the ground.

Chibuzo and Doc immediately leapt out, grabbing him in their arms.

Bullets rained in again.

"We've got to go! We've got to go!" The pilot warned. The co-pilot was firing into the crowd of fighters, but it wasn't nearly enough.

"Hold it for thirty seconds!" Chibuzo half-pleaded, half-ordered, though he didn't have the authority to do either.

The Kiowa remained under heavy fire for exactly thirty seconds as Chibuzo and Doc hefted Young onto the hard floor. The vibration felt like it was sucking out his life, but he continued to breath. He continued to hold on. Green had held on with a hell of a lot more holes than he, so he could too. Embrace the suck.

Suddenly, he could relate fiercely with Ricky. He didn't want to die alone. And he didn't have to because Docs appeared, inches from his face.

"I've got you, brother," Doc said, as he pressed hard over the section of Young's stomach where it felt like a small forest fire had started.

Had he verbally admitted that he didn't want to die alone, or did Doc just know these things?

The Kiowa begin to lift.

The kid!

"Don't leave him!" Young tried to scream. "Don't leave the…" Everything hurt. His face felt cold as ice. "…kid. He's…one of…"

Doc, looking him in the eye, nodded that he understood. "I won't leave him."

Quicker than Young could track with his bleary eyes, Doc was gone.

Young heard Chibuzo holler, "Doc! What the?! Put her down! Put the bird back down!" His voice grew fainter by the ticking of time that was kept by the steady dripping of Young's own blood onto the floor.

"He jumped!" The pilot hollered back. "I can't put it—. Shit! Hang on!"

All at once, the chopper floor felt like it jerked out from under Young. A quarter of a blood-drip later, the cabin was filled with a bright light, accompanied by the sound of thousand freight trains.

In that light, the roaring sound, flashed the faces of his men—his brothers—and then his mother, when she was young and running him through a field of wildflowers, laughing and chasing … something. Was it a butterfly?

Then, there was nothing. Nothing at all.

PART TWO

Chapter One

1

"Carston Thomas, ladies and gents! He's done it again! World famous mountain climber! How does he do it at only ten years of age, you ask? Where will his future take him? There's no telling, ladies and gents! There's just no telling!"

Carston's face was lit with exuberance as he lifted his dark scrawny arms, placing his palms down on the top of his short wavy dark hair. The perfect line-up across his forehead beheld not even a single bead of sweat from his exertion. After all, he'd climbed these metal stairs thousands of times. Twice every morning that he could, he hiked them to put muscles on his toothpick legs. But if he didn't climb down, right now, he'd be late.

Late was never good. Late meant the folks sleeping on the sidewalks would be ill-tempered with him. Not that he blamed them. But he preferred them not-fussy as opposed to fussy if he was going to work alongside of them. Mama, of course, preferred neither. His associating with anyone on the street scared her. "People out there are like bombs," she'd once explained. "It only takes is one wrong move. I don't want it to be you standing on the tripwire."

Sighing, he descended the narrow flight of metal stairs clinging to the side of a red-brick convenience store. The stairs creaked noisily, and the bolts that once secured the single flight of steps to the stone were now a little loose and wobbly.

Carston and his mama had been living in Seattle, Washington in a small apartment that sat upon the roof of the store like a circus hat for three years now. It wasn't much to look at from the outside, but they kept it spic and span on the inside. Mama said there wasn't enough room in the tiny abode to lodge clutter. Besides, they owed it to Mrs. Ellsberg to keep the place up the best they could.

Mrs. Ellsberg and her husband, Howard, owned the apartment and the store beneath it. They had lived between these same four walls, before Carston and Mama had come about, almost their entire marriage. That is, until the unhappy day when Howard failed to return to his little circus hat home. A policeman had come instead.

At sixty-six years old, Mr. Ellsberg had been shot, caught between the baker at the pastry shop and a young man yearning to earn his gang stripes. The all-too-eager murderer nailed him once in the chest and again in the back after he'd fallen, just because he was there.

Mr. Olson, Carston's fourth-grade schoolteacher, had once told the class that losing drive-thru theaters had been a tragedy. Carston thought that Mrs. Ellsberg losing her husband of forty-eight years because he walked to the bakery to grab a donut-breakfast for two was the real tragedy. But no one had asked his opinion so his classmates had gone about the rest of the school day writing letters to the mayor and city council about the loss of a great avenue for community connection. That's not the letter Carston had written. Though he had received a passing grade, and a complimentary pat on the back for deeming himself qualified to appeal for aid and objecting to criminality, he'd been docked for not staying on topic.

The first day Carston had met Mrs. Ellsberg, she had spied him peering in her store-front window. He had his filthy hands plastered to the spotless glass, coveting the boxes of Twinkies on the shelf and the bags of jerky hanging on the end of the aisle. Mama hadn't noticed either of them. She was sitting on the curb, sobbing. When Mrs. Ellsberg stepped out, her body almost as wide as the door itself from her shoulders to her hips, he'd felt frightened of her and had wanted to run. She could have hollered for him to get his grimy hands off her window, beaten him with a broomstick, or called the police. All of these ideas had made his tiny knees quake as he stood before her, unable to run because Mama was still crying, her ratty, tired shoes sitting atop the storm drain. However, instead of any of those scary things, the wide woman handed him a granola bar. Then she surprised Carston by passing by him and sitting her plump bottom on the curb, right next to Mama.

Carston had thought for a while that if he and Mama weren't hated, maybe they were invisible. But Mrs. Ellsberg had seen them. She'd seen them both. And now she and Mama were talking—for what had seemed like forever—while he nibbled at his granola bar, one flake of oatmeal at a time, trying to make it last. He'd pecked it down to a bite-sized nubbin, which he held, dutifully, in his grubby fist, saving it for Mama. It'd seemed like a week before she'd looked over her shoulder and called him over. When she did, he remembered he'd been clutching a granola nubbin and handed it to her.

After Mama had introduced him to the wide woman with a hard stare, Mrs. Ellsberg explained that she just couldn't climb them old stairs on the side of the building up to her apartment anymore. She said that they would be doing her a favor if they agreed to live up there. "Take care of the place," she'd said. Then, she'd surprised him again by saying in her raspy voice, "The rent will be mostly on you, young man."

His eyes had widened like two bubbles. Mama tried to butt in, but Mrs. Ellsberg held up a hand full of weirdly bent fingers, shushing her. "He's the man of the house, ain't he?" Mama nodded. "Then, this is his job. Let him do it." Turning her old, dry-skinned face to him, she said, "Young man, don't you agree?"

"Yes," he'd answered, squaring his tiny shoulders despite his heart drumming inside of his ears. Briefly, he'd wondered how his heart could have crawled so far up there.

"Good. Your part of the rent, and I should warn you, I am persnickety, is this: you will attend school, you will help your mother, and you will help me in the store, every day. This will remain the arrangement for as long as you and your mama hold to the agreements made. Or I croak. Whichever comes first."

Carston hadn't known then what *persnickety* or *croak* meant (like a frog?), but he'd agreed. In fact, he looked forward to it. Mama cried again, but not in the same way she'd been crying earlier. She was smile-crying, which he thought was good.

Mrs. Ellsberg showed them up the stairs that day, and that was the last time she'd climbed them stairs, just as she'd said. Carston went to work immediately helping Mrs. Ellsberg turn a back room on the store-level into the world's smallest studio apartment. The closet-like space they'd organized into a makeshift home, made Mama feel guilty. Mrs. Ellsberg said she was relieved. And Carston? He was ecstatic. For the first time, he was the man of the house—being that they had a house now. And Mrs. Ellsberg had put him in charge of paying the rent, all by himself. She had also helped Mama get a job at the hospital doing laundry. Shortly after, Mama began taking school classes at night so that one day she could move up to making beds instead of washing them.

Bettering herself, Mama called it. But Carston knew it was more than that. Mama never wanted to sleep under a parked bus to get out of the rain with her shivering son in her arms ever again. And as long as he was the man of the house, he would see to it that she didn't have to.

At the bottom of the old creaky stairs, Carston turned right, and there was Mrs. Ellsberg's storefront, tucked neatly beneath an awning that protected it from the weather. Also tucked beneath the awning was a crew of homeless individuals, just beginning to stir under their thin blankets and discolored raincoats that were either one size too small or two sizes too big.

A black gentleman with only a smidge of gray left on his head and a sparse gray beard nodded his head. "Quite a night's chill," he said holding his jacket tight around himself.

"Yes, sir," Carston answered. He knew the man's name was Oscar, but anyone as polite and soft-spoken as Oscar deserved to be called "sir."

Oscar made Carston think of what his grandfather on his father's side may have looked like. He hadn't met him, of course. His father left long before Carston could create a memory of him, let alone introduce him to a grandfather. He'd met his grandfather on Mama's side, however—once. He was tall and pale like Mama, only he wasn't nearly as nice. Where Mama would give her shirt to anyone in need of it more than she, Joe (that's what she called him) was more inclined to shake you from his sleeve. Which is exactly what he had done when they showed up on his broken front doorstep.

"Better than some though, I suppose," said Oscar.

"Yes sir, I suppose so," Carston replied, remembering the fierce winter they'd had.

"She ain't open yet, sproutling," said the lady that everyone referred to as Boop. She must have been attractive at one point, but it hadn't been for some time. Definitely not in Carston's time. Boop's unkept stringy dirt-brown hair enveloped a weather-worn face that seemed to sink into her bones. She struggled with pronunciation since she had no teeth, but that didn't stop her from talking.

"That's all right," Carston said, crossing his arms across his chest. Oscar was right, it was chilly. "I can wait."

"What are you doing up so early?" grumbled a perpetually grouchy man, named Suicide Sam. "I heard you hollering from around the corner."

Sam had the opposite problem as Oscar. He had so much hair growing from his head and face, he looked as though he should take up residence in a cave. Everyone calls him Suicide Sam because he constantly walked into traffic. Mrs. Ellsberg said, *he ain't gonna kill himself, he just wants to cause a fuss.*

"All your damn whooping woke me. I don't take kindly to being woken!" Suicide Sam complained loudly.

Boop spat in her toothless slur, "You don't take kindly to shit, Sam."

"No cussin' in front of the kid," reprimanded Gargantuan, a surprisingly large and surprisingly young man who never made eye contact with anyone. Everybody knew he had some kind of mental handicap, but most left him alone because of his size. "Mrs. Ellsberg says, no cussin'."

"I wasn't cussing," argued Boop.

Suicide Sam glared at her. "Like hell you weren't."

"Look who's talking. Your mouth is as filthy as your—"

The lock on the store door jiggled and Carston cleared his throat.

The group began rising to their feet, moaning and groaning about nothing in particular—just moving, Carston figured. He often felt tempted to moan and groan when Mama woke him for school. But he could never bring himself to do it. Mama was tired too. He could see it in her face.

Mrs. Ellsberg stepped out and propped open the glass door with a rubber stopper. "For those of you that want a warm bagel this morning, you know where the cleaning supplies are," Ellsberg said in her raspy, take-no-scuff tone. "Store opens in one hour." Which everyone knew was code for, *my storefront better not look like a homeless camp by then.*

"Yes Mrs. Ellsberg…" four out of the five recited in unison.

Carston went straight to work facing the shelves so that all the products were evenly lined on the front edges with their labels facing out. The others dusted away cobwebs that may have formed since yesterday, swiped the windows with the stinky blue spray, and swept cracker crumbs off of the sidewalk. That is, the others, excluding Suicide Sam. Sam folded his blanket begrudgingly, stowed it away in his pack, and left in a huff.

As soon as Suicide Sam was out of sight, Gargantuan started counting down. "Three, two, one…" Car horns started honking in the distance, and Gargantuan's face grew a grin that stayed plastered there for the remainder of the time he worked.

As promised, Mrs. Ellsberg presented a warm bagel, wrapped in a napkin, to each person the moment they finished their task. The bagels were accepted, and the recipients vamoosed, going upon their way to do whatever it is they did during the store's business hours—per Mrs. Ellsberg's rules.

When Carston finished facing the shelves Mrs. Ellsberg brought him his own warm bagel. "You better skedaddle," she said. "You're apt to be late for school."

Carston laughed around a bite of bagel, and Mrs. Ellsberg glared at him. "It's Saturday," he said and promptly shut his mouth tight, apart from chewing.

She glanced at a calendar hanging on the wall, still open to March though it was now two weeks into June. "So it is."

He grinned again, this time keeping his lips tightly closed. He swallowed before speaking. "It's also the first day of summer," he added cheerfully.

"What's summer got to do with the price of popsicles?"

"Everything, I suppose," he beamed. "There's no school in the summer."

"What a shame that is."

"Not for a popsicle factory."

"I'm guessing I'll be seeing less of you then?"

"Not at all. More I expect."

A small grin barely hinted at one corner of her wrinkly mouth. To keep it from expanding, she scolded, "You talk like an old woman."

"Well, I hang out with one." He smirked at her, and this time she *did* smile, dingy, crooked teeth and all.

With the help of a huff and a grunt, she removed the smile and headed back to her work. "Full of poppycock you are, talking about your mama like that."

"Wasn't my mama I was talking about."

2

Chloe Thomas dropped her ripped-denim, child-size backpack on the end table next to the front door with her keys. She'd learned long ago that a small scruffy-looking pack was far less of a tantalizing target than, say, a purse, or a large overstuffed backpack boasting *goodies here, everyone, come get your goodies*. Even so, she rarely put anything of much value in it, unless she thought she might need it that day.

"Car!" she called, looking around the empty living room and kicking off her shoes. "Carston, you here?"

Her Nikes flew under the end table. They might be comfortable walking shoes—she'd made sure of that—but her feet still grew tired of carting them around. By the end of shift, those comfy sneakers felt more like lava moccasins.

Today had been a longer than usual kind of day. Partly due to her coworker, Anita, having called in sick and partly because a mother's apprehension tends to rev up when she doesn't know exactly what her son has been up to all day. Not that she questioned his behavior. It's everyone else's she questioned.

Carston jumped out from the hall, an open book dangling from one hand and headphones hanging from his neck. Chloe jumped too.

"Cripes, Car. You scared me," she said, accepting a hug from her only son. All was forgiven. "What did you do today?"

"Helped Mrs. Ellsberg in the store, took the lollipops she gave me down to the park to share, played some, came back, cleaned my room, and started reading." He lifted the book as proof. As if she needed it. Car loved reading, especially anything containing mountain climbing.

Chloe cocked her head. "Wait, who did you share your lollipops with?"

"A homeless guy, and Jess, a girl I know from school. Her mom walked her to the park, so you'll be happy to know that we were being watched after."

Chloe worked to make her face appear happy, though in fact she wasn't happy at all. She should have walked her son to the park and watched after him herself. A ten-year-old boy was just as easy a target as a girl. What if Jess's mom hadn't been there? What if some creep, like the homeless guy, had been watching instead? What kind of mother was she?

The single and working kind.

"You know I don't like you mingling with the homeless. They can be dangerous."

"Not all of them."

Not this again. Why, out of all things Car could be argumentative about, did he choose to argue about the homeless. He didn't argue about cleaning the bathroom or walking instead of having a bike to ride. He didn't argue about wanting to move to the same neighborhood that most of the kids at school lived in or wanting to watch movies that were too gruesome. No … her son argued about the homeless.

Chloe took a deep breath. It was only because he and she used to be them, she reminded herself again. "Yes, and that's why I said *can* be dangerous. Some of them are extremely so. You know that. Car, please."

"Mama, I can't avoid them. I work with them for Mrs. Ellsberg."

Not that he intended to avoid any of them, she wanted to grumble, but didn't. She was supposed to be the parent after all, not the child.

"Sit," she said, and he followed her to the loveseat. "I know you work with a few of them in the morning, under Mrs. Ellsberg's supervision, but I want you to promise me that you won't converse, or share lollipops, with any of the others. None." She dug her nails into the soft, flower-patterned fabric of the seat. "Promise me, Car."

He looked at her sadly. "Mama, you're asking me to lie."

Chloe let out a moan of frustration. "Car, for cripe's sake, give me a break here, would you?"

He smiled.

"What? What are you smiling about?" It was infectious, his smile, and she felt one tugging from within her. Distracted, she tried to keep it swallowed. She had to show how serious she was on the matter.

Car dug into his loose pocket and pulled out a Kit Kat bar and handed it to her. "I bought this at the store for you with the change I collected last week." Mrs. Ellsberg encouraged Car to keep the floors clean, including carelessly clutched change fallen from people's pockets, landing soundlessly on the rug near the register.

A soft sigh escaped Chloe's nose and tears welled up in the bottom lids of her eyes as she took the candy that was advertised by a catchy slogan of, *Give me a break. Give me a break. Break me off a piece of that Kit Kat bar.* Here, her ten-year-old son was taking care of her, rather than she taking care of him. It made her feel crappy—and loved.

"This is my break?" she asked.

He seemed pleased with himself. "Yep."

She studied it in her palm, feeling very tired. "Is this the only break I'm getting?" His face suddenly looked tired too, making her feel terribly guilty.

Car touched her arm lightly. "They're just God-made people, Mama," he said, repeating the exact words that she'd once whispered into his ear.

When he was younger, and they were desperate, they'd shared a fire to bite off the chill of a night with a group of rather loud, and slightly frightening, people. She hadn't liked the situation any more than Car had—he trembling in her arms—but it was a matter of survival. So, she'd said the only thing she could think of in that moment to comfort him. *It's okay, Car. They're just God-made people.*

Those words had been biting her ever since.

All Chloe wanted was to be free of the kinds of people that represented her past and her failures, not only as a person, but as a mother. The homeless were a constant reminder of all of the above. Their presence was like the stench of a dead mouse, lingering long after the hammer had fallen. It wasn't the mouse's fault, other than having been alive, and bait-able. She couldn't help but despise them anyway. Her inability to deny that she'd been one them for a time, didn't stop her from heralding, *she wasn't one now.*

Carston frowned, as if reading her thoughts. She felt ashamed.

"You don't want it?" Car asked, his glance alternating between her face and the candy in her hand.

She forced a smile and pulled him into her embrace. "Of course, I want it. Thank you so much."

That's all it took to give her heart the break she was searching for, and all felt right in their little part of the world again.

Except that it wasn't.

There was still the matter of Car toying with the way of life that, by the miracle of Mrs. Ellsberg, they'd managed to escape. There were so many dangers outside the fragile bubble they were living within. She pretended that everything was great so Carston wouldn't have to live in fear, the way she did. But she *was* afraid. And for good reason.

She'd been overhearing whispering that someone was inquiring about two people matching her and Carston's description. Every time she felt like a person recognized her, she ignored them, strutting proudly on, hoping they would come to the conclusion that they'd been mistaken. What would happen when they realized it *was* her? What then?

There was only one thing she could do. She had to ride this train called life forward, and not allow for it to fall off the track, slow pace, or stop for anyone—God-made or not. There was only one person she trusted, and that was Carston. Unfortunately, there was this thing about train tracks. The rails lead forward, and backward, and anyone could pull the emergency brake.

Chapter Two

1

On a dry evening in Seattle, the city park turned into makeshift lodging for temporarily displaced persons. Temporarily displaced persons were considered a mite different from the larger homeless population, having fallen into homelessness, for whatever reason—usually without intent—and lacking the desire and commitment to join tent city. Tent city was not considered a displacement but a way of life. An often preferred one. Free from all sorts of civil responsibilities, teeming with challenges of its own. The smaller displaced population were more like drifters. Sometimes they moved on to civilian life, where they'd fallen from, and sometimes they just moved on. One such man was leaning against a park tree, away from the others.

Linus—Doc—Winehouse's legs were bent, his feet spread apart so that his knees leaned against each other, staying put with minimal effort. His normally handsome features were buried beneath a mop of long dark hair hanging limply from his skull and a dirty beard, which doubled not only as a brilliant insulator against sharp cold winds, but an ugly disguise. Not that he was hiding from anyone, just himself. The jeans he wore still had denim and his Army-green jacket still had padding, though both were grubby and wearing.

The June nights were chilly yet, but if there was no rain, there was really no need to take shelter on a hard concrete sidewalk or doorway when the park's grass was comfy, and overgrown bushes provided some level of concealment. The benches were taken, even the sandbox underneath the slide where everyone knew kids sneaked a pee, was taken. The group of tattered, down-on-their-luck folks taking shelter in the park never pissed under the slide cause it was where they sleep. But they did piss on the trees, where the mothers of rumbustious toddlers reclined in the shade to relax and read, much like Doc was now, nose tucked behind his turned-up collar.

A scrawny lady, appearing as though she may be in her mid-fifties, approached Doc. The fact that she was lingering in the park at this hour, scuffling in her worn tennis shoes, wearing a ratty purple turtleneck sweater over black leggings with a hole in the right knee, exposed her as a fellow drifter. Her hair was dyed a strawberry-red color and pulled up in, not so much a bun, but a ragged rat's nest.

"Ain't none of mine," the scrawny lady said, "but if I were you, I wouldn't be leaning against that tree."

Doc looked up from behind his mess of dark hair, revealing warm brown eyes. "No one's been here all day, I claimed it."

"It's not that —"

"You're right, it's none of yours," he snapped, cutting her off. He was tired. No matter where he went, someone was always trying to dominate him. He was in no mood for a pretend conversation or the competition for dominance that always follows.

Strawberry Hair shrugged her scrawny shoulders and smiled. At some point, probably not so long ago, she'd been pretty. "Not looking to make friends, are you?"

"What gave you that idea?" He rolled onto his right hip and laid his head against the bark. "I just want to be left alone."

She squatted now, resting her chin on her boney knees. Oh, joy, she was making herself comfortable.

"What's your name?" she asked.

He said nothing.

"You're shaking. Need a drink, don't you?"

Doc pulled his shaking hands out of sight.

"Me too, friend."

Something bumped against his arm and a temptation to chatter his dirty teeth in her face rocketed through him, until he saw that she had offered her flask. He took it from her hand and unscrewed the top. "I don't want a friend," he informed her coldly. It felt wrong to treat her callously, but he had to. "So, you're the round heels around here, huh?" he asked and lifted the canteen, looking forward to that first large swig hitting him.

"I am *not*," she snapped, ripping the flask from his lips before he caught so much as a drop.

Doc folded his arms, pretending that he hadn't needed that swig as badly as he truly did. It was no use. Any fool could read the resentment in his eyes. He'd meant to chase her off, but not before he'd had a complimentary drink. What was done was done.

"You play the role of Miss Round Heels, because you don't have anyone," he barked, hoping to insult her. It wasn't a very good one, he knew. By nature, he just wasn't all that insulting.

"I do," she spat. "We were curious about who you are, but now I'm just going to tell everyone that you're the son of a motherless goat. You can thank me too cause it's a lot nicer than an ass with a stretched-out hole."

He'd touched her nerve. Good.

"Makes sense," he said, going for the goal. "We can't both have the same name." He turned away, wrapping his arms around himself, shaking worse than ever. "Crawl back to your fleapit," he grumbled.

Strawberry Hair stood. "You're not better than me," she said sharply, then stomped away.

He watched her scrawny legs as she marched towards her friends. She was in desperate need of a meal. Almost worse than he needed a drink. He felt bad for her. Not bad enough to call her back. He had his own troubles. Laying his head against the bark of the tree, his nostrils began working. He began to wonder, if by chance, he'd pissed himself. The stench was unbearable.

Halfway through the night, Doc, son of a motherless goat, woke to a man's boot making firm contact with his shoulder. He toppled over, nose first, into the grass. His first instinct was to jump to his feet, but his hands were in his pockets. Besides, he rarely jumped for a fight anymore.

"What the heck, man," Doc growled. "If this is about—"

"You're sleeping on the piss tree," the tall man interrupted as he removed his dick from his pants and began relieving himself.

On hands and knees, Doc hustled out of the splash zone. "Shit."

The man yanked his head toward a cluster of bushes. "Over there. We have rules."

Rules? This coming from someone who'd just booted another man from his slumber and was now pissing on his tree? "Over there what?" he demanded.

"Shit," the man answered.

Without warning, there was a terrible pain in his stomach. Since he was more or less in position, he wretched. Nothing came out. There was nothing *to* come out.

"If you're sick, go somewhere else," the man ordered, putting away his gear and zipping. "We don't need the group coming down with whatever you've got, pal."

"I'm not sick, just hungry."

After the man quietly stalked away, Doc relocated to a new tree, which smelled a great deal better. Meaning, thankfully, he hadn't pissed himself after all. Small blessings. Sticking his hands back into his pockets, preparing to wait for dawn, or doom—whichever—he felt another small blessing. A hard, little lump connected to a paper stick deep inside the right pouch. A lollipop. He pulled it out and held it up to his face, squinting.

Doc had forgotten that a dark-skinned boy had given it to him yesterday. He'd been so angry at the gall of the boy, treating him like a stray mutt, Doc had smacked it from his hand, letting it fall to the ground. However, soon as the boy ran off to play with some curly-haired girl, he'd grabbed it up—fast—and tucked it away. He'd since forgotten about it. Now, here it was.

Back from the dead.

Doc's expression turned immediately sour. He glared at the candy as though it had made an ugly face. He pulled his arm back suddenly, preparing to throw it away. Far away. Nothing good ever came back from the dead. But he stopped.

Maybe it was never dead. Maybe it was okay. He made a deal with himself that he would investigate. If it turned out rotten, then he would throw it away. As he fumbled with the candy's crinkling covering, a few of the nearest drifters glanced over at him, but a new drifter wasn't all that interesting, except for whatever rumors Strawberry Hair might have already spread.

Strawberry Hair was tucked under the arm of an old man, fast asleep. The flask that she'd had felt mostly empty when Doc held it, and maybe it was now, but what if there were just a drip or two? What would they be worth to her? He stared, wondering if he could convince her to offer the flask again. He could even pay her back, he reasoned.

No, he couldn't. If he could pay her back, he would just go get his own drink. A full bottle in which to drown himself. The old man who held Strawberry Hair with an arm glared at him. That plan was busted before it began.

Since there were few other options, Doc grumpily stuck the lollipop in his mouth. His mouth began salivating so hurriedly it actually stung. The flavor was better than he remembered but not very filling. The more he sucked the angrier he became. A lollipop was not what he wanted. A lollipop was not what he *needed*.

2

"Hey, mister."

Doc opened one eye. It was morning. Damn, he'd made it, again. "Hey, mister."

Doc followed the sound of a child's voice with one eye. Standing over him was the same black boy from yesterday. Today he was holding a small brown paper bag.

What was with these people? He didn't want to be spoken to. Wasn't his foul odor and bad mood good enough reasons to turn a blind eye to his presence here? If there was a handbook it would read: To erase yourself from reality, provide a foul odor and a bad mood. What was he doing wrong? He sat up, staring at the bag in the kid's hand.

"Brought you something," said the boy. He held out the bag

It couldn't be booze. Could it? Doc snatched the bag away from the boy. The weight of it and the way the contents shifted inside told him immediately, it was not booze. He peered inside, dissatisfied, as he knew he would be. There was a slice of white bread, folded in half, with something red squishing out of it and a single-serving-size of a carton of milk.

"Go wear your goody-two-shoes somewhere else, short stack" he mumbled, shoving the bag back. "I'm not a stray dog."

"You're not hungry?" asked the boy. "You look hungry. It's not much, I know, but if I'd taken more Mama would have noticed. She doesn't want me talking to you or sharing with you. She thinks you could be dangerous. Well, not just you, that is. All of you."

He glanced around. The park was empty; all of the other hobos had vacated before the police came and kicked them out. "All of who?" he asked grouchily.

"The homeless," the boy answered, fidgeting. Good, short stack was feeling a little uncomfortable. A little out of his element.

"Fetch me booze and *maybe* I'll talk to you," he said, knowing full well a kid wasn't going to bring booze to the park, or to a hobo. "Bugger off. If you hadn't guessed yet, I hate kids."

A small grin played at the corners of the boy's lips. "If you don't like kids, then why do you hang out at the park? You're bound to run into one." Now the short stack was smiling, full out, not bothering to hide his amusement at all. It was a nice smile. Good teeth. Very annoying.

Feeling as though he'd been snared in a trap of his own making, he snapped, "So that I can hate at them." Well, heck, what else was he supposed to say? The kid had a darn good point.

"My name's Carston." The kid extended his hand.

That was a mistake. The boy should never offer his hand to a stranger in a park, or anywhere. Doc had to teach him. He grabbed onto Carston's hand, too firmly, and yanked the kid down to meet his hairy face. The kid's eyes bulged in alarm. Good.

"Your mama is right," he growled in the boy's face. "I am dangerous." The knowledge that his breath stunk made the moment even better. "You could disappear today and reappear again tomorrow, or next week, in a dumpster across town. You're a fool to trust me, or *anyone*. Listen to your mama and stay away from us."

The boy nodded, but his impulsive alarm was already fading, his confidence returning. Tough kid. Stupid kid.

Doc shoved the kid away from himself, surprised that the short stack didn't tumble very far. Either the kid was stronger than he appeared or Doc had grown weaker. So, what if he had gotten weaker? he reasoned. Except on the inside. He couldn't afford to be weak on the inside. "Scram!" he yelled at the kid. "Go back to your toad-eater mama!"

This got the kid's attention. Doc suspected that it wasn't so much that he'd risen his voice as it was that he'd insulted short stack's mama. The kid was right to be angry. *He should be angry—all the way back home, to where he belongs.*

"I said *scram*!" This time his voice came out scratchy and sadistic sounding. Though it hadn't been his intention, the affect worked. The boy dropped the brown paper bag and backed away. After a few paces, he turned and left the park.

When Doc was sure that the kid wasn't going to poke his head around some bush, with a smug smile on his face, he collapsed at the midsection and positioned himself onto his hands and knees. Struggling to move his stiff joints after having sat for so long, he crawled until he reached the paper bag. Grabbing the bag, he rolled the top down, and stuck it in his mouth – looking very much like the stray dog he claimed that he wasn't. He proceeded to scuffle with his own legs, straining his back slightly, until he came to a standing position and let out a long breath.

Geez. That was harder than it used to be. The day and excursion had warmed him slightly so he wiggled out of his jacket, one arm at a time, jostling the paper bag from hand to hand. Not taking care of himself took a hefty toll. That was okay. He had a long list of sins to pay for. Those sins were thirsty, and they cried every minute of the day that they wouldn't be satisfied until he'd paid for every one of them with his misery, possibly his soul. Correction, *absolutely* his soul. Absently, he brushed at the black leather bracelet bound around his wrist like a manacle, and thought, with great suffering, *possibly not even then.*

3

Mrs. Ellsberg was ringing up a carton of whole-fat milk and box of saltine crackers for a young lady in a threadbare pastel pink top with a milk stain on it and a fussy baby propped on her hip when Carston walked into the store. When she'd spied Carston leaving this morning, he'd had at least three small paper bags in his arms. His hands were empty now.

"Excuse me one moment," Mrs. Ellsberg told the young mother as she scooted out from behind the counter, receiving only a simple nod and eyes that remained down cast. "Where'd your lunches go, young man?" she asked Carston sternly as they met on the same aisle.

Carston stopped, his eyes bouncing around and his fingers disappearing into his pockets. She pulled a loaf of bread and a jar of almond butter down from the overstocked shelf. "I saw you take off with an armload. Headed to the park, no doubt."

He wasn't much for lying so he said, "Oh, that wasn't my lunch."

"No?" She gave a hard glance at his empty hands. "Well, your arms are empty now, so go grab two large cans of powdered formula." She swiveled on a flat-bottomed black shoe and clarified over her shoulder in a loud voice. "The one that's nearly expired. Finally, I have someone here that can make use of it." She returned to the young mother who was now swaying in an attempt to soothe her babe.

"It appears you didn't see the special," Mrs. Ellsberg told the young mother as she filled a bag with the groceries. "But I fixed it for you. I hope you like almond butter."

"Yes, I do. Thank you," the young lady barely whispered.

Carston joined them, two large cans of powdered baby formula in hand. He glanced at the baby knowingly and passed the formula to Mrs. Ellsberg, who then dropped them in the bag with everything else.

"About to expire," Mrs. Ellsberg explained.

The young lady's lips parted before she remembered her manners. "Thank you," she said bashfully.

Had the lady been given the opportunity to read the expiration date, she'd have known Mrs. Ellsberg was lying. But Mrs. Ellsberg didn't think of it as lying, per se. It was downplaying. That was all. She used to have to explain such things to her exasperated husband as he watched money go down the drain. Oh, how she wished he was still here to give her a hard time and then grin proudly when her back was turned.

The young lady didn't read the expiration date just now, and Mrs. Ellsberg hoped she wouldn't bother to check it later either. With a bit of luck, the girl would just remain pleased that she and her baby would eat this week despite that no-good boyfriend of hers. Rumor was, he claimed to have gone out of town on a job and hadn't returned in almost four weeks now. Mrs. Ellsberg suspected he wouldn't be returning at all. She'd seen the way he'd looked at the shy young lady and baby hunkering in his shadow. It was a look of bitter antipathy, like he blamed them for sucking up the last of dinner's broth. His broth.

Mrs. Ellsberg made conversation. "I heard that Mr. Peterson, down at the coffee shop, was looking for help. Would you happen to know of anyone? He's in an awful pinch."

The woman's fingers laced around the bag's handles and stopped. An idea registering. "I'll ask around." She pulled the bag and jug of milk off of the counter. Her eyes flickered and met Mrs. Ellsberg's for the first time and then quickly fell again. "Have you heard of any good babysitters?"

"I have, in fact." Mrs. Ellsberg grabbed a pen. "May I?" she asked, gesturing to the receipt in the woman's bag.

"Please."

Mrs. Ellsberg fetched the receipt out of the bag, jotted down a name, address, and number, and returned it. "She's an older woman. Very kind. She watched over a little boy I know." Both of them glanced at Carston. "But he's grown enough now to watch himself. Last I heard, she was feeling blue without a whippersnapper to look after."

The young mother thanked her. Despite the added groceries, when she walked out the door her shoulders seemed to bear a little less weight than she'd born when she first walked in. Even the baby on her hip was happier now that they were on the move again.

Mrs. Ellsberg rarely missed a beat, and she didn't now. She turned to Carston, who was climbing aboard the stool that she kept stowed behind the counter for when her feet started to ache. The stool legs squelched loudly.

"Not your lunch, you say," she said. Carston's face drooped a little, realizing he hadn't gotten by just yet. "What was it then?"

"It was just a small bite to eat for a few folks."

Mrs. Ellsberg braced her wide hips between both of her fists. "A small bite to eat for a few folks," she repeated, making it abundantly clear she was not impressed.

Carston grinned up at her that silly way that he did when he felt he didn't have to make a point because someone else had beaten him to the punch.

"I can *afford* to help a few folks," she said sternly. "Your mama can't, *and* she doesn't approve of you wandering around with strangers. As her son, you owe it to her to be more respectful."

"But what about my being the man of the house?" asked Carston. "Is it not my job to lead?"

"Just where exactly are you intending to lead the two of you? Into an empty cupboard?"

His head dropped, and his gaze found the floor. "No ma'am."

In a moment of weakness, she cupped his chin in her hardworking fingers and pulled it up. "You have a calling to help; I know this. But you're going to have to figure out how to fulfill that calling without disobeying your mama. No more lone ranger shenanigans."

"Are you saying I can't go see them? I can't help? I want to be like you. I want to help."

Regardless of the fact that his voice was a little on the whiney side, Mrs. Ellsberg felt a pinch in her chest. Indigestion, she decided and promptly dropped her hand to her side. "Your questions are arguing in disguise, young man. I believe your mama has been perfectly clear. Has she not?"

"Yes ma'am." Carston jumped down from the stool and started for the door. Mrs. Ellsberg hoped that maybe he was going home to go think up a plan of how he could help others without being disobedient. But who was she kidding? Kids sulk. Especially ten-year-old ones. Carston was no exception, even with his heart of gold.

"Carston!" Mrs. Ellsberg called. Though looking as dejected as a kitten sitting on the wrong side of the window glass during a rain, he turned. Calling him by name never failed to get his attention. "Have you finished that book you've been reading?"

"Nearly, I'll be done by the time Mama gets home today."

"Good." From under the counter, she pulled out a rectangular cardboard box, just the right size to contain a single book. She tossed it to him. "You're going to need this, I think.'

Carston's face lit up, and he began to rip into one end of the box as a young man in bright, baggy clothes and a backwards hat stepped through the door. The man began walking the narrow aisles without looking at anything in particular. It seemed he was gaging the space, calculating distance, appraising worth. Mrs. Ellsberg didn't like the way the young man's presence felt. Not to mention, when he turned his head to look around, she could easily make out the large red shape on the back of his hat that was made to look like an accidental splatter of paint, or blood. The words in the center of the splatter read, "I'd Kill for That." Carston hadn't paid the man any attention, his mind reeling with excitement as he peeked in the open end of the box, seeing the bound edge of a new book. Mrs. Ellsberg paid the man enough attention for both of them.

"I hope you'll find that helpful," she told Carston. "Now scat."

Carston, his nose unwittingly stuffed into a slender box, scatted. "Thank you!" he hollered and disappeared out the door and around the corner.

"What exactly is it that I can help you with?" Mrs. Ellsberg asked the young man with the backwards hat.

The man put on a smile that was more scheming than friendly, and approached the counter. "Maybe you should ask what I can do for you."

Mrs. Ellsberg's eyes narrowed into slits. "What's your meaning, child?"

His smile drooped slightly, and she could see an obvious displeasure in being referred to as a child—though compared to her, that's precisely what he was. With a little effort, he managed to smile again. He leaned over the counter, his arms slithering across the top like two snakes until his unkept finger nails just about touched the buttons on the front of Mrs. Ellsberg's oversized blouse. "Why don't you call me Mailman. I carry a very important message."

Mrs. Ellsberg leaned in, rather than out, and met his face with hers halfway across the tabletop. Mailman's eyes were hazel and almond-shaped. Her raspy voice took a challenging tone as she asked, "What's this codswallop that has you strutting into my place like a peacock?" When she swayed her weight, ever so slightly, a glare of light reflected into his eyes. His pupils contracted, and frown lines appeared between his brows. He blinked.

Mailman presented an undoubtedly rehearsed message. "There's been an increase in gang activity on the street. There are dangerous people doing dangerous things. My associates and I have been watching situations unfold, and we're concerned for your safety and your business." He shrugged as if what he was about to say was no big deal. Mrs. Ellsberg had a feeling it was a very big deal. "We can help. My boss is prepared to offer you protection, for a fee."

"A fee? I see."

"Its safety insurance," he clarified.

"Safety insurance," Ellsberg repeated. "As in, you want me to give you money in exchange for my safety?"

"That's right."

"What makes you and your boss qualified?"

"The boss and my associates and I are plenty qualified. Fortunately for you, we don't like seeing people being hurt and taken advantage of, and we're prepared to help. But you see, we can't do that for nothing."

Though there was nothing legitimate about the young man standing before her, other than legitimate coercion. "I see. This indubitably sounds like a job for the police," Mrs. Ellsberg said.

He shook his head as two men from the construction site down the way walked through the door. "You know as well as I do, those pork chops can only mop up messes *after* they happen. They ain't standing right here offering to protect you and yours right now, are they?"

"Out of curiosity, what's your fee?"

"A cash fee of three hundred dollars, upfront, to demonstrate your sincerity. Then we talk. It'll be two hundred dollars every month after. It's a small sum for peace of mind."

Mrs. Ellsberg doubted that this "mailman" knew the meaning of peace of mind. "Two hundred dollars and then you'd be my bodyguard?"

Mailman glanced over his shoulder at the two construction men as they loaded their sun-tanned, bulging arms with drinks and snacks, then back to her. "No, I won't be standing here all of the time. Two hundred dollars gets you put on a list."

"A list?" Mrs. Ellsberg asked doubtfully. Mrs. Ellsberg straightened her back and when she did, they stood very nearly at the same height.

"The boss is very influential." What he lacked in height he made up for in deviousness. "People are planning to torch these streets. They *will* torch," he added, making his point, and her imminent misfortune, clear. "If you decide to cooperate with our offer of protection, you'll be safe and sound, spared."

The two construction men, arms full of snacks, approached the counter and stood directly behind Mailman. They were scowling at the wording on his hat. The taller one with sand-colored hair asked Mrs. Ellsberg, "Do we have a problem here?"

Mailman turned and daringly cocked his head at them. "We're having a decent conversation here. Wait your f--cking turn." Turning back to Mrs. Ellsberg, he casually tapped the counter as though he were nothing more than a reputable claims adjuster, here to investigate a simple declaration. But he boogered up that image when he added, "I'll be by tomorrow to collect your answer for the boss."

Mailman spun to face the distrustful men standing in line behind him. He tucked his ring finger and pinky in on both of his hands and pointed two fingers at each of the large men, with his thumbs sticking up. Rather than pulling the trigger of his make-belief guns, he winked and started towards the door.

"Excuse me for one moment, gentlemen," Mrs. Ellsberg said to the skeptical-faced men and made her way around the counter. Hustling after the young man in the backwards hat, she called, "Mailman, one moment, young man."

Mailman turned. His face lit with expectation.

"I have an answer for you, right now," Mrs. Ellsberg told him and held out her fist.

Mailman smiled, extending his palm. Mrs. Ellsberg dropped the object. He immediately looked down at it, frown lines forming. In his palm sat a bright-yellow circular pin-on button covered with tiny smiley faces. Her late husband had given it to her on one of the anniversaries of having opened the store together. The button read:

Happy? Tell your friends.

Unhappy? Tell the boss.
Wait,

Mrs. Ellsberg read the last four words for Mailman, out loud, in case he couldn't quite decipher the point in print alone. "I have no boss."

4

Orson Finlay sat on one side of a large room made up of concrete walls, his "employees sprawled inelegantly around the room like the comfortable, handy nodes they'd become. The room was sparsely awarded a single black leather couch and four chairs, all of which were haphazardly gathered around a low wood table that looked like someone had just dragged in half a tree, dropped it there, and called it good. Orson's bottomless red-like eyes were surrounded, like pinwheels, with deeply etched lines, crafted, not from age, but from years of violence and sternness. They bore into the soul of the uneasy young man standing before him. The young man was dressed in baggy, bright-colored clothes and wore a hat, turned backwards. The hat that the boy before him wore boasted threateningly, "I'd Kill for That". This scrawny pipsqueak hadn't yet demonstrated enough restraint or obedience to be sporting such promises.

For now, Orson understood that pipsqueaks, such as this, had to embrace some sort of ridiculous makeshift marker—a fear tactic, some sort of display of dominance, usually in the form of petty bullying—until they established a real marker, a reputation. The hat, to some extent, held such a soft prediction as to his level of commitment, so Orson remained softly optimistic, for now.

Slowly, with great restraint, like removing a dirty Band-aid still stuck to open raw flesh, Orson tore his eyes off the boy and looked thoughtfully at the words he'd carved in perfect penmanship into the concrete wall. They were the very words his own father had said to him over a dead body once. He'd only been thirteen years old then, but the lesson had been an unforgettable one.

"There is but one lock and one key that releases the success within a man, Orson," his father had said. *"Purpose is the lock. Action is the key."*

Mailman's eyes nervously followed Orson's, landing upon the carved-out words. With a surprising brilliance that Orson in no way expected to last, the boy's mouth remained shut.

The dead man at Orson and his father's feet had "borrowed" an extremely large sum of money, without permission, to fund a personal whim. *"Mr. Corn has lost track of both of his lock and his key,"* his father had explained. Then he'd extended a long-fingered hand to Orson, requesting that he hand over the report card from school. Orson had rolled it up, like a scroll, and was holding it behind his back. It contained mostly F's. *"Hopefully, you haven't done likewise,"* his father had said.

Many such hardy lessons were instilled into him over the years. Although he was rarely of the same mind as his father, he could agree with this one basic abject lesson. In fact, it ended up being the sole abject lesson in which he'd based all of his decisions, including the one he'd made when he was eighteen that had ridded him of his brutal father, once and for all. In doing so, he'd gained both his independence and the opportunity to run the profitable family business. It had taken a little while for his mother to embrace the advantages of such a drastic modification, but she had come around, eventually. And for good reason. She was a tough woman, born for survival. Likely, she'd been the one he'd inherited the knack from, so she could hardly blame him for that, now could she?

Now, brawny as a bull, with brown hair and a graying red mustache and beard, Orson had released the success within himself. He owed his success to both his purpose and his action.

Rolling the yellow pin-on button with smiley faces on it in his palm, Orson turned his gaze back to Mailman. "What was the purpose of your visit to the little store, Maurice?"

Mailman almost managed to hide a flare of anger at being called by his name. Almost. Though, damn if he didn't have a valid complaint. It was a hideous name, and plainly, it reminded him of years of childhood torment. Big boo-hoo.

"To sell your protection insurance," Mailman replied, shrinking beneath Orson's scowl of disapproval.

Orson nodded, though his scowl remained. He'd been told that he scowled even when laughing heartily or sleeping, which was ludicrous. Everyone knew that the lines in his face were purely ornamental, and that if he were truly scowling someone would be the wiser, or dead. Which brought the focus back to Maurice the Mailman. Orson decided to delicately pass the time waiting for Mailman to come up with something better by continuing to display his formidable scowl.

Mailman's eyes darted to the button in Orson's hand, to the words on the concrete wall, and to the button again, like a ping-pong ball. Orson could tell that he knew the solution was in the message on the wall, but was he able to prove he knew how to come up with an answer as a result?

"I *will* sell your protection insurance," Mailman amended. He'd tried to say it with a good amount of mustered confidence, but his feet, inching backwards, gave him away.

"Should she not accept?" Orson asked. His fingers closed around the button with a snap.

Smiles emerged on some of the faces of Orson's "employees". Two of the more skeptical viewers, a white female with dangerous brown-yellow eyes, and a black gentleman, by the name of Terrace Paine, remained stone-faced. They were the type that chose to hold their applause until the enigmatic outcome had been made known.

Terrace Paine, Orson's right-hand man, sported a graying goatee, long dark dreads, and large silver-framed glasses. A cigarette hung from his lips. As the eldest member of the gang—the only member specially spared from Finlay Senior's original gang—Orson saw him as a man as unquestionable as birth, and as wise as a thousand deathbeds. This earned Paine the exclusive honor of serving as Orson's conscience, which, on its own, made infrequent stopovers, and never stayed. Orson's conscience was an unreliable friend, and an even worse guest. That's where Paine came in.

Paine had been the only man from his father's regime that Orson had admired and respected. Not feared. Fear and respect are not the same, though most people got the two confused. In the end, fear kills you. People kill things they are afraid of. Respect, as in Paine's case, will spare you. Both Paine and Orson had been born as only children and raised in a fearful environment. They carried their fathers' blood in their veins. But where Paine understood things of life other than anger and murder, Orson did not. Orson wanted a constant reminder, a check box, for his decisions to be filtered through. He didn't want to become what he hated. He didn't want to lose himself in the action and forget his purpose.

If Mailman sensed the room's changing energy, he didn't let on. His feet and little beady eyes were dancing to the same twitchy unease he'd been pirouetting to when he'd entered. Orson imagined that the skin along his spine and Mailman's ungodly colorful t-shirt were moist with sweat. The knowledge of such things added delight to Orson's natural instinct for predation.

"I warned her that there are dangerous people doing dangerous things. That we're concerned for her safety and her business."

"And yet she handed you *this*," Orson barked, his fingers splaying impatiently, revealing the hideous button.

Mailman dropped his head. He had no cards left to play. Or so Orson had thought until pipsqueak picked his head up again and boldly stated, "With your permission, I'd like to be the one to deliver your response." And there it was. Like an in-house bred lion just released into the wild. Sprung from beneath the surface, an innate desire to hunt. To act. "I can torch the place if she refuses to accept again. I can send *that* as an unspoken message."

Orson stole an inquisitive glance at Paine, then stood so suddenly that Mailman leapt backwards. Orson shook his head excitedly. "I admit, I had my doubts. I had my doubts!"

Mailman half crouched in defensive alarm while simultaneously checking over his shoulder to ensure that one of the others weren't about to drive a knife or a bullet into his skull. Maybe he wasn't as dumb as he'd initially projected with his terrible taste in attire. Orson stomped over and grabbed Mailman by the shoulder hard enough to send his own unspoken message, *you better not be screwing with me, Maurice.*

"Stand up boy!" Orson said. "What the f--k are you doing? No, no, we don't torch the place. Remember, it's not my goal to harm the citizens. We protect the citizens." He laughed and his voice boomed off of the walls, joined by the laughter of others. "Send this message instead," Orson said, draping a heavy arm over Mailman's slumped back, furnishing valuable instructions.

Orson's version of peace was not your typical armistice, freedom from strife, ceasefire kind of peace. His version of peace was more of an organized operation of cooperation. When citizens and businesses cooperate, there's peace in the community. Orson provided the community with protection from rival gang activity, and the community provided zipped lips and blind eyes as to Orson's drug trafficking. Though the phony idyllic idea of a crime-free world and peace for all of mankind compared to Orson's Protection Insurance was about as slick as chalk, one could roughly argue that Orson's influence was indeed a craggy form of peace. It was all a matter of perspective.

When Mailman left, Orson heard him mutter under his breath, "You'll regret this, old hag. Nobody puts my head on a chopping block."

Gaily, Orson thought, *there, there now, just one step closer to making good on the words ironed onto the back of your hat. Words are required to have meaning around here or else not displayed.* A smile stretched across his beard.

5

Carston plopped down in the middle of the living room floor with his new book, *No Summit out of Sight,* about Jordan Romero, the youngest person to climb the Seven Summits. As tempting as it was to start reading it right away, Carston ran his finger over the blue cover with Jordan standing atop a beautiful mountain. He fanned through the fresh pages until he came to the small section that he knew in his heart would be there—pictures. Every self-respecting true story included pictures, usually somewhere near the middle, which is where he found them glistening up at him in full color. His heart throbbed, a little in excitement, a little in jealousy.

How had Jordan done it? How had he accomplished such a goal? These questions cascaded through Carston's mind. The answers were on the other side of a mighty river, too big to cross. Was it even possible for someone like Carston? A kid from the city? A kid that only a few years ago had slept on the street? Carston closed the book, hoping to close out the questions.

"I can," he told himself, but on the inside, he felt like he couldn't. He felt stuck. The mountains were too far away, too far up. Just like the mountain of a problem he had right now, between his homeless friends and Mama.

It was purely undeniable that he felt called to help the homeless, he didn't know why. It was something that had come instilled in him. Maybe it was because they felt a little like family since he and Mama didn't have any. Maybe it was because they felt like the safer place to be after he and Mama had hidden among them to escape the scary place. It didn't matter why he felt connected to them, just that he did. If only Mama would try to climb up *that* mountain with him, the mountain right here in front of him that she feared so much, he would promise not to let go of her hand. Then, when she reached the top, she would see what he saw. People all over the world, needing help.

Dispiritedly, he set aside No Summit Out of Sight and crawled onto the loveseat with the book he'd already begun and intended to finish before Mama got home for work. Opening to the page he'd marked with a page holder, he picked up where he'd left off. If he allotted himself two hours to read, he'd still have time to start dinner before Mama returned. That way she could sit back and have a nice relaxing evening before he started talking about ascending mountains, and homeless, and such.

Chapter Three

1

Carston had four sausage links sliced and tossed into a pan with a dab of butter, chopped onion, and chunks of green pepper when he heard the metal stairs squeaking softly. Chloe opened the front door and stepped in.

"Does my nose deceive me?" Chloe's voice asked as she paused to remove her shoes, "Or do I smell sausage sizzling in a pan?"

"It's sizzling Mama," Carston answered, stirring. When her curious head peeked around the corner, he smiled at her. "It'll be ready in a minute."

She leaned against the door frame, smiling proudly. "As will I."

Carston added four eggs to the pan and stirred quickly. The runny eggs hissed as they cooked on the hot surface. "Sit down," he ordered, swishing his spatula through the air at her. "I'll bring it to you. Sit, sit, sit."

Chloe grinned girlishly, laughing so softly he wouldn't have known if he hadn't been looking right at her. He loved the sound of her laugher. It made him think of the time the two of them had dug their soft mittens into the snow that had piled up on the sidewalk after a hard storm while steamy hot cocoa waited on the stove top for their return. Sadly, she seldom laughed. After carefully carrying a plate of eggs and sausage to Chloe where she sat at the small table, he commented on just that.

"You should laugh more."

Taking the saucer, she said, "This looks delicious, Car. What makes you say that? I laugh all the time."

He shrugged, retrieved his own dinner saucer and plopped down. "It just makes your face prettier."

Chloe was looking at him from the corner of her eye. "Thank you, but I know you, Car Thomas. You never say anything without having something specific on your mind. What it is? Lay it on me."

Quickly he stuffed two bites into his mouth and began chewing, largely overexaggerating.

Poking him across the table, Chloe asked, "What? You don't agree that I laugh all the time?"

"Nah, you do" he said around the food in his mouth. Mrs. Ellsberg would have had a fit. "Sometimes. Just not enough. You just work really hard. You should play more."

She nodded. "I wish I could. I know I'm gone a lot or working on classes. But I'm here now."

That she was. And now that she was, how was he going to break the subject that was really on his mind? It wasn't the frequency of her laughter, though it could use a boost in its rate of occurrence, and it did make her face prettier.

"What'd you do today?"

He shoved another bite into his mouth, keeping it busy until he could think up a way to bring up what was on his mind. "Mm, same."

Chloe's eyes lit up with an idea. "How about a board game after dinner? In the mood to be whooped?"

Still chewing, he nodded. He loved playing games, whether or not he was whooped.

"Car? Do you have a tooth that needs pulling?"

His lips tightly clamped together so sausage wouldn't fall out, he looked at her, surprised. He knew she wasn't referring to a baby tooth in need of pulling. He had all his big boy teeth. She meant a thought, stuck in his mind, in need of tugging into the open.

She laughed—actually laughed—which made him laugh. This time chewed-up sausage *did* fall out onto his plate, and a few small pieces made it onto his lap.

"Car!" Chloe burst. It was her turn to be surprised. She wasn't mad. She was still happy, which he liked to see. She emptied her dish then said, "That's a yes."

After they were done, Chloe pulled the small assortment of their board games from the top of her closet. For the remainder of the evening, they played game after game, sprawled out on the floor, with a bag of raisins between them for snacking. Carston had won a few, Chloe winning the rest. He didn't mind her winning. In fact, he let her win a couple of those times cause when she won, she'd jump to her feet and dance happily, like she didn't have a worry in the world.

After Chloe had run out of ways to lounge comfortably on the floor, she said, "My back is starting to hurt, Car. I need a break. Would you like to take a walk with me to grab a soda?"

"Yeah!" Carston sprung to his feet and waited while Chloe did the same but more slowly. They hadn't talked about what he wanted to talk about yet. He just hadn't found a good way to bring it up. It was a contention between them, and he didn't want to ruin their fun.

As they stepped outside Chloe wrapped her coat tightly about herself. "Zip up your jacket, Car. It seems the sun has abandoned us. Feels awfully cold this evening."

Carston stopped in the middle of shutting the front door, his eyes widening. "Wait!" He dashed back into the house, grabbed the throw off the end of his bed, and met her outside, shutting the door behind him.

Chloe looked down disapprovingly. "Car, what are you doing? Put that back inside the house."

"It's extra. I don't need it."

Chloe stationed herself firmly at the top of the stairs, refusing to descend. "You're right, you don't need it out here, and you are *not* giving it away. I've bought a dozen new blankets and you've given eleven away. Put it back where you got it from."

Well, the tooth that had been lodged in his mind all evening had a firm string tied to it now. It wasn't the way he had hoped to present it, but Mama was determined to yank. Out it would surely fly, as unexpected as a hockey puck from a cuckoo clock, twenty minutes ahead of time.

Typically, jumping feet first into new territory, especially dangerous territory, is, at a minimum, a better thought than vaulting head first. Though sometimes jumping, no matter the fashion, is applicable. Especially if it meant ripping a tooth out from the roots as quickly as possible. Naturally, Carston took the leap, pavement pounders over noggin.

"Hear me out. You don't want me to visit homeless people alone," Carston explained "so, I have an idea." He didn't give her time to respond. He just rattled it out as quickly as possible. "You and I could go together. We could go on walks and take sandwiches and water in a backpack. Anytime we come across someone in need, we'll have things to share. I wouldn't be disobeying you by visiting them alone, and you can see that I'm fine and even meet some nice people."

Sounded brilliant to Carston.

"No," said Chloe, crossing her arms over her chest. "It doesn't matter if I am with you, holding your hand, gone to France, or dead. I don't want you visiting them *at all*."

"That's not possible, Mama. I *have* to."

"You don't *have* to, Carston." Chloe's face was flushed, and it wasn't from the chill of the evening. "In fact, I forbid it!"

Carston's mouth flopped open. That was the least fair thing she'd ever said. She knew how strongly he felt about helping people. They were God-made people. They needed his help. Someone had to step up. He was the perfect boy for the job because he truly cared. Mrs. Ellsberg had shown him that you could help people, one at a time, if you truly cared.

Carston's eyes watered. He swallowed, trying to blink them away. He was stronger than this.

Chloe squatted down in front of him. "Car, baby," she soothed, placing a hand on his shoulder. "Please don't cry. I just want what's best for you."

"I'm not crying," he lied, hugging the throw to his chest. "Why don't you support me?"

Chloe looked at the ground between them and then back at him. "I support you in every way that I can. It's not too much to ask my son not to pay social calls to strangers. It's really not. I'm not a bad parent. I'm not. No good parent would allow such a thing."

"I know you're not a bad parent, Mama." Carston sniffed. That's not how he wanted to make her feel, and he was sorry he had. But she had to see. "My heart tells me to help people. How did that get there if God hadn't put it there Himself?"

Chloe looked away to find the right words. "I know God has given you a heart for helping people, but sometimes we have to wait for the right time. A little boy should not be walking the streets alone, helping complete strangers with who knows what kinds of problems. Please put the blanket back inside."

He hugged it tighter. "I just want to carry it."

"All right," conceded Chloe, growing tired and cold. "You may carry it." She took a corner of it and began tugging it all the way around him. "In fact, you may wear it. All right?" She offered him a tiny warm squeeze, more for his spirit than his body. The wool woven into the throw blocked the chill nicely.

Carston nodded and followed her down the creaky stairs and around the corner. Mrs. Ellsberg was closing up the store, and her crew of homeless were elbowing for room under the awning. It wasn't supposed to rain but a wet, foggy mist was soundlessly covering the city. Soon, the slow steady drip of moisture having drawn together and twisted into tiny canals would tickle the drainpipes and the noses of those without cover.

"Evening, young sir," said Oscar from behind the open cover of a thin, tattered book. From the looks of it, he'd been settled in for a time, using the light from the store windows to illuminate his pages.

Chloe had stopped and was looking at the group with dismay, so Carston stepped forward. "What are you reading?" Carston asked.

The others were busy hustling around, tossing open blankets, deciding where each would sit, excluding the outside edge (which was dedicated to the newest member of the group—Gargantuan). In doing so, Boop accidentally bumped into Carston by backing into him as she spread out her sleeping bag.

"Sorry there, sproutling," said Boop. In her eyes, he was just one of them, so, she went about her business.

Carston could tell this bothered Mama very much.

Oscar tapped a finger on the relatively dry page he'd been reading. "Hemingway, *The Old Man and the Sea*. It's my favorite."

Carston noticed the shabbiness of the book's condition. "How many times have you read it?"

Oscar placed a finger on his spot, closed the covers together, and looked at it as though the book would provide the answer. "I don't rightly know. A hundred? It's the only one I've got." He looked up with his dark, kind eyes and held the book, torn in places, out to Carston. "You're welcome to borrow it, if you like."

Carston leaned closer, preparing to accept the book, just to hold it and look at it. He needn't borrow Oscar's treasured possession. Chloe pulled him back before he could.

"Thank you, but that won't be necessary," Chloe said and pushed Carston toward the store door. "Let's grab our sodas before Mrs. Ellsberg closes the till for the night."

"Soda…" Gargantuan repeated. He was towering over everyone, looking at the spot on the ground that he was preparing to situate himself on.

Chloe said nothing, sidestepping around him.

"Put a sock in it, Gargantuan," scolded Boop. "Sit down. You're not supposed to talk to customers."

He sat. "Mrs. Carston's not a customer," he complained.

Chloe shoved Carston through the door as Suicide Sam interjected his loud opinion. "That's not even her name! Like hell she ain't a customer!"

"No cussin'," Gargantuan reprimanded.

Suicide Sam paid him no mind. "Don't like us neither," he continued. "Too good for the likes of stinkers and boozers like us!"

Gargantuan leapt back to his feet. His enormous position and thunderous words, "I don't drink booze!" could be seen and heard from inside. Chloe casted a momentary look over her shoulder, hustling Carston toward the refrigerator section where the non-alcoholic drinks were kept.

"I thought they weren't supposed to be here until *after* closing," whispered Chloe.

"Technically, it *is* after hours," said Carston, opening the cold door and grabbing a root beer.

Chloe did the same. No caffeine for Mama before bed.

"He's right," Mrs. Ellsberg said from across the store. "I'm here, but I've been closed for thirty minutes."

"I'm sorry," Chloe apologized. "Should we go?"

Mrs. Ellsberg went to the big windows and began drawing down the shades. Other businesses left their stores lit so that if it were robbed, the intruders could be seen by a good citizen passing by, and exposed. Only, very few good citizens passed by after dark. Therefore, Mrs. Ellsberg didn't believe in showcasing her merchandise in the full enticing bloom of light. She said that keeping the place lit and in full view was a hope tactic. Sometimes it worked; sometimes it didn't. When it you put it like that, it sounded like gambling to Carston. Besides, since she lived there now, she liked her privacy.

"For Pete's sake, no," Mrs. Ellsberg answered and made her way back behind the counter and rang them up. She was putting change into Chloe's open palm when there was a ruckus outside among the group. She glanced, seeing nothing, of course, now that the shade was down. She grunted. "Give me one moment. I'm going to quiet them down a smidge before you go dawdling on out there."

She disappeared out the front door, floor broom in hand.

2

Chloe was content to wait by Mrs. Ellsberg's register counter. However, she was too slow at grabbing for Carston's arm when he darted for the window. Carston was pulling back a corner of the shade before she could holler "stop!"

"It's him!" he exclaimed feeling excitement turn in his stomach.

"Who's him?" asked Chloe, making her way to the window now. "Get out from there, Car." This time she successfully got hold of his arm and yanked him away of the window. "Who's him?" she demanded to know, glancing at the lock on the door. The look in her eye suggested she was tempted to turn the lock over, but she restrained herself. Mrs. Ellsberg was still out there. They could hear her giving stern orders to quiet down.

"Sit down, Sam," Mrs. Ellsberg's voice could be heard clearly. "I believe I will handle *my own* affairs, if that suits you just fine." From the sounds of a soft thud against the glass and squelching of a thick jacket sliding downwards, her orders were being heeded. No big shocker there. Mrs. Ellsberg had a way of putting her foot down on nonsense.

"Did you bring someone here?" Chloe's voice brought his attention back. She looked scared, but it'd been a long time since he'd seen her look *that* scared.

Carston hesitated, feeling kind of scared too. He wasn't supposed to be talking to strangers, but it wasn't Mama's overprotective tendencies he saw shadowing her hazel-green eyes. "I didn't bring anyone here," he answered. "It's just the guy from the park."

"The one you shared a lollipop with?"

It was noticeably quieting down outside.

She glanced toward the window. "Did this person ask any personal questions?"

"No. He told me to scram."

Mrs. Ellsberg opened the door. "We have a guest this evening," she said. "He's been given the rules, and the others, though unhappily, have agreed he may stay at the Under the Awning Motel." She said this with a bit of hilarity twinkling on her face. She'd made a joke. Not a very good one, but still. "We'll go from here as far as to any further arrangements." She looked directly at Mama now. "Your walk home will be perfectly peaceful, I guarantee it."

Carston beamed. This was a textbook answer to his dilemma. With his new friend (all right, a bit of an overstatement) here, possibly becoming part of the crew, he wouldn't be disobeying Mama by talking to him.

"And what about the morning?" Chloe asked, crossing her arms. She was not as easy a sell.

"He'll be a gentleman, I assure you." Mrs. Ellsberg opened the door wider and began motioning with her arms like two fans. "Out with you now. Go enjoy your evening. I'm going to retire to my bedroom. I'll keep an ear out."

Chloe cautiously agreed and stepped outside into the misty air, soda in hand. Carston followed.

The moment the cold air hit Carston's face he looked for the bearded man from the park, the one wearing an Army-green jacket. He was easy enough to spot, leaning against the store, like the others. Only, he was on the outside edge now. No one ever wanted that position because the person on the outside edge was the first to break the wind. The man had his arms wrapped around himself. He'd brought no sleeping bag, no backpack—nothing. All he had were the pockets of his jacket.

"Did you leave your stuff somewhere?" Carston asked before he thought better of it.

Chloe swung around like a dancer—an angry dancer—and glared at him. "Let the man be, Car." She tried to grab his arm again, only he'd tucked it under the throw this time. Grabbing the blanket instead, she was about to haul him physically around the corner and up the stairs when the man spoke, drawing their attention.

"Car? As in Carston, the short stack that…" The man faded off, seeing Chloe's agitated expectation. She was waiting to hear for herself what Carston had done. "…that gave me a lollipop, and went on his way."

Carston smiled.

"Uh-huh," Chloe grunted disbelievingly.

Carston kicked a foot out from under the blanket for the man to see. "You told me to wear my good-two-shoes somewhere else. Did you leave your stuff somewhere? The others bring their things here for the night. You can do that too."

"You speak out of turn, Car," Chloe wiggled her fist full of wool blanket. "Let's go."

"That is, if Mrs. Ellsberg lets you come back," Carston corrected. "But I'm sure she will."

Suicide Sam growled, "We're full."

"I don't have any stuff," the man said. "Suits me better that way."

Carson frowned. The man didn't have a blanket, a bed, nothing? That wasn't right.

Chloe frowned too, though Carson supposed for a different reason. Most likely it was because she disapproved of this conversation altogether.

The man might have noticed the contention, or simply despised sympathy, because he added, rather snappily, "I intend to keep it that way."

Still frowning, Chloe said "Let's go" and pulled hard enough that Carston was forced to move his feet in her direction, or fall on his rump. "It's bad enough that he already knows your name," she complained. "If I ever manage to keep you from talking to strangers, I'll probably be holding a winning lottery ticket."

Mama didn't play the lottery.

Carston swiveled around and began following her, though he dragged his feet like he was shuffling through atrociously deep snow—on a June evening. "He's going to know my name tomorrow anyway when I come down to help Mrs. Ellsberg."

Chloe let out a long, exasperated moan but didn't stop pulling him toward the staircase.

Oscar called from around the corner in his pleasantly soft voice, "Good night, young sir."

Carston took in a large breath and was about to holler "good night" at the top of his lungs to the entire group when Chloe gave him a good hard yank. "Don't you dare bellow into the night like a banshee and scare all the neighbors."

At the front of their apartment, Chloe opened the door and the warm air from inside met them. She stepped in, removing her jacket. "Feels good in here," she said gratefully. Halting, mid-step, she looked down at Carston guiltily.

Carston had removed the extra throw from around his shoulders and was now looking at her with, *duh,* written all over his face.

Chloe sighed. "Fine," she grumbled. "Run the blanket down to him." Carston didn't have to be told twice. He busted out the front door wearing a huge smile.

"But run right back up!" she called after him. "And be careful on the stairs!"

Chapter Four

1

This time, Mailman used the cover of darkness to make a return visit to the old hag's store. His hands were empty, buried deep inside his coat pockets. His pockets, however, were full. Tucked inside was a carefully folded newspaper, a tin of grease, and a lighter—supposedly Orson's message. To Mailman, it was his first step to full, authorized, revenge.

The directions awarded to him were to grease the newspaper, cram most of it under the glass door, except for a tail of paper on the outside, then light it on fire. The fire would skitter under the door, turn the greased paper into flames and smoke, and activate the smoke detector. Orson meant it to be a scare, and wanted it to be believed that a rival gang had done it.

Mailman saw it as something else. So, if the smoke detector was a dud and life or property was damaged, what was Mailman to do? Nothing, that's what. The hag had it coming.

Turning the corner, Mailman observed, with excitement in his belly, all of the lovely unmanned storefronts. Orson wanted to play make-believe business with them, manipulating their pathetic, security-hungry minds for a small monthly dose of cash. Mailman curled his lip. Petty. Mailman wanted to smash all the glass into piles of glittering shards and take everything he wanted, right now. Including the cash. *All* of it, not just a dose. The first time he'd made all his sales pitches and walked out empty-handed (like a little mailman should), it had depleted his entire bag of self-control. All those stores brimming tauntingly with goods and cash drawers. His bag of self-control was small. A tick could carry it.

Naturally, Mailman liked taking and having the things he wanted. Who didn't? But there was something more that put a hot excitement in his belly. Destruction. Oh, just thinking the word made him sweat droplets of would-be pleasure. Destruction was to Mailman as a snort of coke and warm lubrication was to a whore. It didn't much matter what it was, property or person, just so he was the one to raise the emblematic torch and watch it burn.

Orson likely assumed that Mailman was performing this stupid little "mailman" act to pad his hide, like the others. But if the truth were told (in good time, in good time), his aspiration was to become the most feared "messenger of destruction" in the city. Of all time! Orson was the fastest route to that destination, that was all.

Mailman tickled the lighter that was resting inside his pocket with his fingers. He'd once read that every man needs an aspiration. He had his. Oh yes, he had his.

The last storefront that his gaze landed upon happened to be the darkest, and the one he'd come to provoke. Stupid lady, how easy it would be for him to slip in, unseen, and rob her blind. Rumor was, she lived in the store somewhere. He wasn't an old lady–raping type, but a fiery figure appealed to him. The flesh of his left cheek twitched a tic as he smiled crookedly. His eyes sunk, like two glowing fangs of a poisonous snake, into the small dark abyss under the store's awning. The smile faded.

There, in the obscurity of the awning shadow, shapes began to take form in the configuration of sleeping bodies. Roughly, a half dozen. What in the hell? Anger slithered over his would-be pleasure, leaving a trail of irritating scratchy scales. What in the hell! In that hag's poorly lit murk, she'd concealed a militia.

They're only homeless twits, his coke-infested, whore-ego whispered.

One or two wouldn't be a problem. For some ridiculous reason, homeless were considerably weak individuals. However, a half dozen of them being woken and shooed would make a commotion. Commotion produced witnesses. Orson had two solid rules for this particular job.

1. No harm.
2. No witnesses.

Orson had been very clear, this job was meant, only, to tip the old lady a wink. If Mailman wanted to remain a living member, he'd succeed in just that. Shit. That didn't leave very many options. Mailman quickly scrolled like a computer log through his choices.

First on the list, he could take his chances and do it now, with the homeless population circling, watching. He could intimidate them. They were easily intimidated. Most of them wanted no trouble. But as a group (like any group) there was a possibility that they'd feel empowered enough to stand up to one little gang banger.

Second down the list, he could hunker down and wait. Instinctively, his shoulders convulsed against the cold. Nah.

Third, hold his fire—a sad thought—and postpone until circumstances suited Orson's criteria.

Technically, he'd not been given a time constraint. What he had been given were rules, and breaking them was an absolute no-go, for now. Mailman decided to select the third option. Postponing, though dicey, seemed the lesser chance of having his head on the chopping block again. Mailman slunk back into the shadows of the closest building. He sure hoped Orson would agree.

2

Early in the morning, over a small mug of hot chocolate, Carston was excited to begin his new book. Curiously, he opened the new cover to the first crisp page. He didn't have much time and only meant to read a few words, maybe a single page, just to see how it started, before heading downstairs to work. Ten minutes later, he'd read the Acknowledgements, studied the Seven Summits map, read the Prologue, *and* the first chapter. However, in his defense, the Prologue and first chapter had both been refreshingly short and chokingly chilling.

He was so excited to read more. But he had to wait. Right now, he had to go down to the store and help Mrs. Ellsberg with the opening. He was already later than usual. It was then that he'd remembered that the group had a new member this morning. He shot straight up, threw his cup in the sink, and raced outside, jacket in hand. Slamming the door shut behind him, he hurried down the stairs like a bolt of lightning, spun on his heel, and dashed back up, only to repeat the process again.

When he was done, his heart pumped healthily in his chest, but he wasn't winded. That was a sign that he was ready for more, and he smiled to himself, ready for the task—whatever it would be. He'd have to think on that some more. It's not like he lived near a mountain, or even a county mole hill. He lived in the city.

Headed to work now, his breath visible in the morning air, he heard the arguing before he saw it. He must have blocked the familiar voices out of his mind while he was still running the stairs, pretending to be a mountaineer in training. He turned the corner, and the scenario unfolded before him.

"He stole my job!" Suicide Sam complained loudly.

The newest guest was sweeping up wrappers into a dust pan that someone had evidently torn into tiny pieces during a moment of bone-cold boredom.

Boop was wiping the marks off the glass where they had leaned against the windows. "You've never once did a job for breakfast," she scolded Sam. "You always hightail it out of here first thing, even if it's your mess that's been left behind."

"I was going to sweep *today!*" yelled Sam.

"No yelling," Gargantuan recited, seemingly without a care in the world, as he laid a rug out in front of the door, smoothing down a corner that had been folded under.

Sam lunged at the newcomer who hadn't been paying him any mind until that moment. "Give me the broom! That's my job!"

For a brief moment, Carston saw a glint of fight in the brown eyes of the man wearing the green jacket. It, disappeared almost as quickly as it had come, and he released the broom without objection. Sam began viciously sweeping at the concrete in an enraged fashion, doing a terrible job. The newcomer stood there a moment, letting the bristles fly over the toes of his shoes, then he shuffled inside.

Carston followed him. "Mister. Hey mister."

The man turned and snapped, "Don't follow me that close. Don't follow me at *all*."

Mrs. Ellsberg had been restocking shelves—Carston's job—and turned around. "Might I ask, what is it you are looking for, Mr....?" Before the man could answer, she spoke sharply to Carston, barely glancing his way, "You're late."

"I'm sorry, Mrs. Ellsberg," Carston apologized. "May I?" he asked her, gesturing with a nod of his head to the shelf she'd been stocking.

Mrs. Ellsberg moved out of his way. "Certainly. Always better late than never. So they say, anyway. I have my doubts on that."

Carston went straight to work. It was his fault that Mrs. Ellsberg hadn't been able to prepare the group's earned breakfast yet, and he could see them outside, chores done, waiting.

"I was sweeping—" the man began to explain, and Mrs. Ellsberg cut him off.

"I have eyes in which to see with. There's been quite a ruckus since you've arrived."

"I'm not staying," he said emotionlessly.

"That's not the question at hand. The question is, what is your name?"

The man in the green jacket said nothing.

Mrs. Ellsberg continued. "If you'd rather not share that bit, that's perfectly fine, not that my telling you so is required. But I would like to know, what it is that people call you, what *I* should call you."

"Yesterday I was called son of a motherless goat." This made Mrs. Ellsberg pause. "I was also called something to the effect of having a stretched-out ass—"

Mrs. Ellsberg lifted a hand. "That'll do. I do not permit profanity in or outside the store. Shall we go with something new? Something that you'd *like* to be called?"

Carston muttered under his breath, "Go with something new."

"I came in to ask if there was anything else you needed done, to earn breakfast," the man said, ignoring Mrs. Ellsberg's question entirely. Then, without warning, his face contorted, appearing out of sorts with the words coming out of his own mouth. "Never mind. Forget it." He turned and started toward the door on legs that were too thin and too weak.

"You deserve breakfast," Mrs. Ellsberg spoke to the man's backside. "I know you don't think so, but you do."

The man paused, his weary head hanging from the top of his undernourished neck.

"Even the boy can see as much. Is that not why he took you his lunch yesterday?"

The man's spine stiffened. Not a lot, but enough that even Carston had seen it. Then he left, passing arm to arm with Suicide Sam, who turned and tailed him out of sight, waving his arms theatrically, yelling, "Go! Go! I eat your food, you lowly piece of—"

As soon as Suicide Sam felt he had conquered his foe, he celebrated by stepping triumphantly out into traffic. Car brakes squealed, and horns blasted as he weaved through them, headed upstream, yelling something about murderous drivers and ugly babies at the top of his lungs.

Mrs. Ellsberg wiped her hands on her apron. "Better be getting the others their breakfast. Remember this, young man," she said in a sad, scolding tone, "there be no rest for the wicked."

As she went about preparing hot oatmeal in small Styrofoam bowls, Carston stocked shelves and checked dates, wondering to himself what *no rest for the wicked* meant. He'd never heard Mrs. Ellsberg refer to herself as immorally disturbed before. He really didn't think she was now.

3

Chloe sent her distracted son silent daggers over the dinner table. He was devouring the new book Mrs. Ellsberg had given him rather than the macaroni and hot dog sitting on his plate. It had been steaming when he'd wiggled into the seat. He'd even managed to pick up his fork. But that's as far as he'd made it. At this instant, the fork dangled loosely from his fingers, its presence completely forgotten. His eyes flitted back and forth across the pages, igniting his imagination, and temporarily blinding him from both vision and time.

The boy could walk the apartment blind, and often did. His feet moved him around while his mind soaked in the wonderful bliss of another world, or of the same world but different shoes. However, the feet wearing the shoes that were currently suspended under the scratched-up table belonged to a boy named Carston. Carston needed to eat his dinner.

"Car, can you set your book aside long enough to eat your dinner, please?"

Carston looked up at her, wide-eyed. "Did you know that Jordan was only nine years old when he made his goal to climb all seven summits of the world?"

"I didn't know that. Car—"

"His dad taught him to live his life, not just watch it." His eyes glistened with bright notions. Notions that he wanted so badly, that she'd never be able to provide. "Isn't that great? I never thought of it that way. People watching their life go by instead of actually living it."

A sharp pain stabbed her heart causing her hand to instinctively cover her sternum. "That's not us, Car. We're living our lives."

He nodded eagerly. "I know, Mama, but I don't want to stop here. I want to set a goal, like Jordan did."

Oh no. Chloe felt her motherly spirit begin to weep. She wanted to be able to help her son reach his goals, she did, but she wasn't like whoever Jordan's parents were. She couldn't afford to take Car on tour of the world and buy him all the stuff he'd ever need to be an expert climber. A part of her, the selfish part, wished he'd just give up, move on, find a passion for…

For what? For coloring inside the lines?

Carston had never colored inside the lines. Chloe remembered well that when Car was a small boy he always colored the pictures inside the coloring books backwards. Rather than color the shape, he colored all of the area around the shape, vibrantly and with great enthusiasm. The effect was astounding. The shape itself was humbly plain, different, and therefore shone because of its pure uniqueness amongst the beautifully chaotic surroundings.

Carston was like one of those pictures.

"You look sad," Car noted, drawing back her attention.

He was also observant, always detecting her unsuccessfully hidden feelings, and calling her on them. She could venture to say he knew her better than she knew herself, only there were some things she'd never explained to him. It seemed he had lost most of those terrible moments to the hazy fog of being too young to remember. She hoped those moments stayed there, hidden, simply a faraway recollection of a dream that had never happened. She also hoped that the monster from the nightmare never paid a visit in person.

Chloe stood and picked up her son's dinner plate. "I'm going to rewarm this," she said, turning away and heading for the microwave. "What kind of goal?" she asked, her back turned to him. She didn't want him to see her reaction when he laid down his contemplations. More so, she didn't want her skepticism to blot any more of her gray dread onto his vibrant picture of life than it already had. Life had a way of manufacturing such dreary disappointments on its own.

"I want to be a mountain climber," he said excitedly.

Chloe knew this already. Still, the weight of that mountain pressed down on her. How she wished his dream would change to something simpler, like learning magic tricks, like the other kids. She'd even bought him a set of magic cards and a hat. Carston had given the hat to an old lady standing in the rain waiting for a cab. The cards he still had, though he was no better at presenting the card of her choice now than he'd been when he'd first received them.

"I've been running our metal stairs," Carston continued. "I can do it now with no problem. So, I want to set a new goal. A stronger goal. Only, I don't know what to do."

The numbers on the tiny microwave screen had counted down to zero and started beeping. She opened it, removing Car's plate. "A goal to get stronger," she said thoughtfully and gratefully. She'd been afraid he'd spring out with a much bigger goal, scaring the bejesus out of her. Like one of those trick-cans full of paper snakes. She wouldn't be buying *that* for him again.

"Yeah. Can you help me come up with an idea?"

The great mountain of Car's dream lifted, a little, and Chloe felt relief wash over her. She set his dinner plate back in front of him. "I'd love to," she answered. "Let's start by putting food inside of you. Its hard to get stronger on an empty stomach."

He smiled and stuffed one end of the hotdog into his mouth. He made a muffled noise that sort of resembled "see?"

Sliding into her chair, she set her elbows on the table. All the little goals she could ever possibly come up with still pointed to climbing that mountain for Car. He was smart and patient enough to recognize that a goal as big as his took time. But how much time were they talking about? Carston could see a majestic mountain calling out to him from on a map in his head that represented his future. But Chloe knew that, though this mountain was as real to him as she was sitting across from him, the possibility of such an aspiration simply wasn't on any map within their possession. No matter how many goals she could think of for the time being, she had no earthly idea how it ever would come to be.

A part of her wanted to say as much, to caution him not to dream too big, or too hard, but she couldn't do that. How could a mother tell her one and only child not to dream? She couldn't be the one to force him to color inside the lines. Life might do that to him on its own, but she'd be darned if she would be the one.

Carston was right: he needed a goal to keep him busy while she went to work, washing hospital linens, and taking online college classes well into the night. Maybe, just maybe, she would be accepted into nursing someday. She would be able to save enough money for them to leave. Then things could change. This was the only plan she could think of to try to make their lives better. Like a mountain, it was a slow climb trying to escape the gutter she was born into.

"Okay," Chloe said. "How about using the playground equipment? Climb the slide or the monkey bars."

"I can already do that."

"All right, but how well? Is there room for improvement maybe?"

He grinned at her pridefully. "Pretty well, Mama."

She took his scrawny arm in her hand, squeezing it teasingly. "With this?"

Carston laughed. "I'm training for endurance, like a runner, not a weightlifter."

Chloe's eyes lit with an idea. "Can you lift your *own* weight? Can you pull yourself up using only your arms? What are they called? Chin-ups?"

"Yeah!" he agreed excitedly. "I hadn't thought of that. I can work on chin-ups."

Chloe smiled. Sometimes happiness was such a simple thing. "Yes, work on touching your chin to the bar. And let's make a goal of reaching a certain number. What number should we make it?"

"I think we'll have to make the first number *one*," Carston said.

"It's good to make your goal attainable," Chloe said, "but let's not discount how strong you are and how strong you can be. Let's make the number something you can work towards. It's a goal, after all. I think you'll get to *one* faster than you think."

He looked at her doubtfully.

"Ten," she said flatly. "Ten chin-ups. And when you do it, I'll buy you a soda."

He smiled broadly and stuck out his hand. "Deal."

While Carston readied for bed and Mama yawned, opening her used laptop for a few hours of tedious studying, the guests of "Under the Awning Motel" were trickling in a hair faster than the evening drizzle. All except one.

Boop was meticulously spreading out her bag with her back turned to Gargantuan who was cooing quietly over something he held in the palm of his hand. Suicide Sam was griping, to no one in particular, certainly to no one who cared, that he'd lost his right shoe today. And Oscar, the quiet gentleman, whom no one understood what he was doing out here, was reading from his favorite tattered book. Not one of them paid any mind to the fact that a young Asian man, one of Orson Finlay's main ring members, was walking straight towards them.

4

The young Asian man they called Dagger stood directly behind Boop, as she adjusted her bedding, frowning down at her disapprovingly. Suicide Sam's mouth actually took a short breather from complaining long enough to gage the intentions of the bold-faced man standing before them. He didn't much like what he saw.

"What do you want?" Suicide Sam asked sharply, pulling out his grumpiest tone to match his grumpiest expression.

Dagger's eyes glanced at him dismissively, then they ran over the rest of the group. Cheekily, he lifted the front of his shirt, exposing a long, curved steed blade. "Looking for someone," he said.

Boop turned at the sound of his voice and quickly shied away. Both Oscar and Gargantuan looked up, stiffening.

"Yeah? Who?" Boop asked, attempting to smooth over her alarm.

Ignoring her, Dagger tilted his head at the men, like a crow on a highwire looking down at garbage on the ground. "A white female with blonde hair—"

"There's a lot of white females with blonde hair," interrupted Sam.

Dagger stepped forward, bellowing in Sam's face, "Shut da the fook up!"

Sam didn't recoil—but he did shut the fook up.

Dagger stood and stretched his shoulders so that his shirt stretched taut across his chest, and the handle of his dagger pushed against the fabric of his shirt. "Would anyone else like to interrupt me?" he asked snidely. Sam guessed that the man was looking for an excuse more than he was looking for a reply since his fingers were twitching at his shirt hem like a gunslinger in the old days when West meant wild.

No one spoke.

Dagger's fingers stilled, and his cold, dark eyes looked almost as hungry as they were disappointed. "She used to go by the name of Chloe Stone. Maybe no more. Has a black kid. Can't miss them."

Again, no one said anything.

"Don't everyone speak at once."

"Are you a policeman?" Gargantuan asked innocently. Dagger's hungry eyes turned toward Gargantuan as though a large T-bone steak had just been dangled in front of him

"He's stupid," Oscar quickly volunteered. "Has the brain of a child."

Dagger said, "Children shouldn't play on da streets at night. Very bad things happen."

"I'm not a child!" yelled Gargantuan, rising to his feet. Suddenly, he was towering over the small man, though he wasn't looking at him. His back was partially turned away and glaring down at Oscar.

Gargantuan's hands clenched tightly into two giant fist balls. Without warning, his eyes widened in horror. Slowly lifting his left fist, he opened his fingers. A few tiny gray and white feathers floated down from his fingers. Inside of his huge palm lay a small lifeless bird. Gargantuan, realizing his mistake too late, let out a wail, piercing the early evening and inciting all the local dogs to begin barking and howling in unison. The giant child fell to his knees, tucking his right hand gently under his left, and began sobbing over the little life that had been his joy and friend for a short while.

Boop's hand flew to her mouth, and Oscar stood, slowly and carefully. Everyone's eyes were on the grieving Gargantuan and his deceased friend, including Dagger, who had unsheathed his blade. He was pointing it at the giant child-like man. Now that the giant had been brought to his knees, Dagger returned the blade to its sheath, looking disappointed yet again.

Unable to stay upright in his state of terrible grief, Gargantuan fell over and curled up on the cold concrete. Cradling his dead bird, he sobbed. Dagger laughed. The others stared at him as he did. He laughed so heartedly that he nearly fell over backwards.

For a moment, Sam contemplated changing his name from Suicide Sam to Murderous Sam. Though, as soon as he leaned against his hands to stand, Dagger noticed. The laughing ceased. Dagger bore down on Sam, quick as a gush of wind, his fancy, double-sided blade pulled and tucked neatly below Sam's chin. The muscles connecting Sam's chin to his face betrayed him and quivered like the little wimps that they were.

Dagger tilted his head like that grotesque crow on the wire again and whispered giddily into Sam's face, "I don't need a reason." The sharp tip poked and drew a line so fine that Sam didn't know if he was dead, or merely scratched. Dagger shrugged as though it were no big deal one way or the other. "The insides fall onto da outside," he explained as Sam sat in an almost catatonic state. "Your spirit begins to leave. I take it in like air. You is not you anymore. You is me."

Dagger's lips stretched into a thin smile, and Sam realized that there may be worse fates than being a sorry pitiful grump living on the streets. He could be sucked in, like air.

Watching, also frozen, neither Oscar nor Boop seemed to know just what to do. Although Sam was fairly certain he wasn't dead yet, those two were proving to be decently useless in a pinch. They had to be afraid that if they spoke or flinched Dagger would execute the story he was telling on the entire group. Pussies.

Sam managed to swallow with what little saliva hadn't dried up in his mouth and found, with great relief, his throat was still intact. Without any sane reason, he began to feel his anger resurfacing. A small revival of rudimentary survival instincts, and he'd forgotten, he was *suicidal*. Sam narrowed his eyes. "F--ck you." His voice was hoarser than usual, but he was proud it found itself fit enough to show up.

Dagger's smile broadened, and he stood. "I like you, fooker."

Gargantuan's head lifted. "Cussin'. There's no cu—"

"Shut up," Boop ordered. "Cry over the bird."

Gargantuan's head dropped, and though he was quiet, he did cry.

"Never heard of anyone by that name," said Oscar, referring to the original inquiry. He was lying, of course. The old man had a soft spot for the boy and his snooty mama.

Sam, having worked on a farm as a young man, knew that when it came to things such as food and wood, soft spots signify rot. Sam had no need for rot or soft spots.

"Neither have I," Boop added, hooking onto the lie train.

Dagger pointed his blade at Suicide Sam. "And you? Ever seen da two I'm looking fo?"

"Who's asking?" He felt the eyes of the others land on him like little grubby black flies.

"That's none of your fooking business who's doing da asking."

"How 'bout a reward?"

"Maybe."

"Cash?"

"Maybe."

"Maybe," Sam rolled the word around in his mouth like a fine wine—as if he knew what it was like to roll fine wine around. "For a bottle of booze, I'll keep an ear out. Don't even have to be the good stuff." He could feel the hate rolling off of Oscar and Boop. Gargantuan was too simple and mopey to have any clue as to what was going on outside of a few scattered feathers. But as for the other two, they were plain jealous that they hadn't thought of this angle first.

Slipping his blade back into his specialty sheath, Dagger responded. "You keep both your ears out, if you don't want to learn what it's like to function without them." He leaned in close and used his thumb and index finger to gently stroke one of Sam's ears. "Are they working?"

Suicide Sam gave his best shit-faced salute. "Yes sir," he said mockingly. "They're working, sir. Both ears. Wide open. Hell yeah. Get some. Must be some *fooking* pretty girl…"

Dagger didn't pick up on the fact that Sam had made a dig on his accent and lost interest in what he likely thought of as the human version of bellybutton lint. He walked away, Sam still blabbering in relentless Suicide Sam style. If there'd been any mid-day traffic, he'd have gotten up and started dancing in it, anticipating that good hard smack he'd been waiting his whole life for.

5

Doc sat in the dark on a broken pallet, thinking about that short stack of a kid and his too-good-for-lowlife mama with the pretty face. He didn't want to run into them again, so he'd intentionally stayed away. It didn't keep him from thinking about them however. It was hard to not think of them when the blanket that Car had given him kept rubbing against his cheek causing the clean scent of flowers to float into his nostrils every time he inhaled.

Dutifully, Doc had grumpily declined the soft throw, but not surprisingly, the kid had left the throw with the black gentleman, who'd set it next to him, giving it a gentle pat. The boy had grinned knowingly, and Doc had woken the next morning with the detestable blanket wrapped around him. Who names their baby *Oscar,* anyway? What, like the furry green thing that lives in a garbage can on Sesame Street? To Doc's knowledge, the soft-spoken gentleman had never lived in an *actual* can, though at this point in his life, he was darn close.

There was a loud clash of noise just down the street, and Doc jerked upright. His eyes immediately started absorbing his surroundings with razor-sharp focus that only a moment ago he'd largely discounted as immaterial. The unexpected attack on his eardrums caused a severe vision of an exploding grenade flash before his eyes. Doc dove, with speed he wouldn't have guessed he still had, off of his pallet. Wrapping his arms around his head, he hit the hard concrete in brutal bellyflop form. When nothing exploded, he looked up.

Down the way an extremely intoxicated old man—oddly resembling Gandalf, from Lord of the Rings—was lying amongst a pile of garbage cans that had toppled over under his unsteady weight. The old man waved a glass liquor bottle above his head in triumph. It hadn't broken. Laughter at the Gandalf look-alike temporarily warmed the gloomy night air.

Nearest to Doc was a handful of mismatched folks huddled in a quiet circle. Only they had noticed Doc's strange behavior. Among them was a man twice Doc's age with a distorted face. Doc recognized the deformation as scar tissue from shrapnel having ripped through it. To the world, this unattractive man, who had clearly once stood bravely upon enemy soil to bear the consequences of freedom, was now a monster. The man's world-weary eyes met Doc's. The man simply nodded his head and went back to losing himself with a cold stare into the flicker of the group's dinky fire.

For a split second, Doc wondered why the man didn't march into the local VA and ask for his due assistance, but Doc already knew the answer. Some men couldn't. Not that they weren't permitted, they were. They just *couldn't*. The things they'd seen, the things they'd experienced, those events had warped their minds into an abnormally twisted mess of agony. These tortured souls could no sooner wrap their minds around the idea of being normal or around the idea of deserving assistance, than the man with the shrapnel deformities could have back his handsome appearance.

As a medic going into Afghanistan, Doc had been taught that every soldier's mind responds differently to combat, even within identical circumstances. He'd even learned how to recognize the early signs of such a budding plague. It was one thing to have the ability to identify the plague developing within one's self. It was entirely another thing being powerless to stop it.

"He's coming this way!" Doc yelled needlessly; they all saw the boy.
"Feck me," Bennett muttered down the stock of his rifle.
Bullet rounds embedded into the dirt all around Young, Bennett, and Doc as they watched the small boy flailing, quick as his scrawny legs could carry him, straight towards them. Young hadn't given any orders to shoot as he stood there, coiled to tackle the small boy, but Doc's finger was on the trigger, at the ready, all the same. They might be blown to Kingdom Come before he had a chance to squeeze it, but this was Young's call, and they trusted him. They had to. Three men working together was always better than three men working separately.

It was hard to calculate if it'd taken the boy a year to finally make it to them, or just a blink of an eye. Either way, the boy arrived and tried to dart past Young, who reached out and stopped him, yanking him right off his winged feet. A loud screech escaped the kid's mouth. Young quickly searched him, relieved that he'd found nothing. The boy's arm was released, and they all expected him to bolt, only he didn't. Instead, he stood before them, shaking and dirty.

"Get!" Young commanded, giving him a shove.
The kid remained and stared at Young with the tiniest grin on lips.
"Why the feck is he smiling at you?" asked Bennett.
"Because he's alive, I suspect," Doc answered.

The boy squatted and took turns staring at each of them.

"He's creepy," replied Bennett between shots. "Who does he think he is?"

Young smiled at the kid and shoved him up next to Bennett. "He's the son-of-a-bitch that gave away the enemy's position too early. Shake his hand."

Doc smiled.

Bennett glanced at the kid suspiciously over his rifle stock, then nodded his big head. "Okay, kid," he said, and stuck out a large, white hand. "Put her there, little asshole."

Little Asshole smiled, revealing a fallen out lateral incisor.

"Can't be much more than eight," Doc advised them.

Doc's gut twisted a little just then, and he felt an odd sensation of gratitude toward the boy who acted in the place of angels and doom. They owed him their lives. Without hesitation, Doc did what he was trained to do—he patched the boy up.

Not bothering to dust himself off, Doc picked himself off the ground and resituated himself on his broken pallet. He leaned against the side of the brick wall that someone had taken an awful lot of time to spray-paint. Wanting to close his eyes and shut out the chaotic world buzzing around him, he fought to keep them open. When he shut his eyes to this world, the other world came crashing back. It did so without the restraint of the brittle cracking reins of Doc's collapsing mind.

Little by little, as the night grew quieter, Doc's heavy eyelids closed. His hands twitched, and his face grimaced. Once again, he was right back where he didn't want to be.

6

After Carston had dressed and victoriously ran the staircase, he turned the corner and knew right away that something had happened. Boop and Suicide Sam weren't bickering and bossing at each other as they usually did. They seemed to not even be on speaking terms. Added to that, there was an edgy feeling to the air, as if breathing in pins and needles. Gargantuan was sitting, motionlessly, staring at a bunch of tiny grayish feathers, making no move to pick up anything, and Oscar was nowhere to be seen at all. Neither was Carston's new, not-so-friendly, friend in the green jacket.

Rather than ask questions, Carston jumped in and began helping with the chores. He didn't have a clue what had happened, but he knew that he wasn't about to wade into their rough waters without a raft. It wasn't until later, after they were gone, and he was munching on a breakfast bar, that Carston asked Mrs. Ellsberg.

"What's going on?"

"I'm a mite flummoxed about that myself. All I's know," she said, setting her till of cash inside the drawer and locking it, "is that Oscar requested a small box to bury a dead bird in. After I gave it to him, he thanked me and left. The others haven't said a word. I'm guessing that Gargantuan was upset enough over it that no one wanted to set him off. You know how he can be."

"How did the bird die?"

Mrs. Ellsberg shook her head. "I don't know. Probably just flew into the window."

Carston hoped it hadn't been some kind of shenanigan to get a rise out of Gargantuan. However it had started, it hadn't ended funny.

Once his job of helping Mrs. Ellsberg at the store was through, Carston walked to the park, heading straight towards the playground. He had chin-ups to work on. There was more than one reason to accomplish the amount of chin-ups Mama had set. His climbing goal and earning a soda, and one more reason. If Mama were to buy him that soda, she would first have come to the park and watch him do those chin-ups for herself. At last, she would be a part of what he was doing.

All morning, Carston rotated between struggling to pull himself up on the monkey bars, running laps, and playing with the kids he knew from school. His friends from school invited him to join them in going to a movie, but he declined, determined to train. His training thus far hadn't been exactly thrilling, however. Every time he attempted to pull himself up, he felt like a worm writhing heavily at the bottom of a hook. He was about to give up for the day when he decided to give it one last try before heading home.

Hanging, feet pumping, trying to climb the air if nothing else, Carston's face was beet-red with exertion and frustration. Mama wouldn't be coming to see him for some time, if ever. He dropped, defeated. Glancing around, he noticed a face camouflaged amongst the flowering bushes. A familiar face. Was it possible that it was more sunken today then yesterday? Carston started toward the man, kicking himself for not bringing a lunch to the park today. He'd promised Mrs. Ellsberg he wouldn't take food from their cupboard to feed the homeless anymore, but he would have gladly shared his own lunch.

"Are you hiding?" Carston asked the man with the green jacket draped over his knees.

The man looked up and answered grumpily, "No."

"You look like you're hiding."

The man responded with a slight irritation. "In case you haven't noticed, I'm not exactly the part of the *public* they were speaking of when they said, 'hey, let's build a *public* park,'"

"You're not leaning against your favorite tree," Carston noted.

The man looked in the direction of the tree that Carston had first found him resting under. "Yeah…learned something about that tree."

"What?"

"It's the piss tree."

"The…" Carston couldn't bring himself to repeat the word; it didn't quite feel comfortable coming from his own mouth. "Do you mean, where people—"

"Piss. Yeah."

"Oh. I use to climb that tree."

The man's mouth opened, nothing came out, so he shut it again. Carston plopped his rear down on the cool grass. As he did so, his mouth opened again. Just as before, nothing came out, so he shut it and looked away.

"What's your name?" Carston asked, earning himself an extremely annoyed stare. "Well, I have to call you *something*. I can't keep calling you, that guy I met behind the bushes in the park."

"Yeah, don't do that. Makes me sound like a pedophile."

"What's a—"

A crusty hand raised, stopping him from finishing. "Just don't call me anything, all right?"

"What do other people call you? And don't say son of a motherless goat. First of all, it's not even possible. Every goat has a mother, or they wouldn't have been born. Plus, I'm pretty sure that it sounds worse than a peddling crocodile anyway."

A thick, brown brow raised.

"Or whatever you said."

"Stop talking to me: I'm a stranger. Can't you get that through your head?"

"You're not a stranger anymore," Carston argued. "You're part of my morning work crew."

"I don't think your mama would agree with that logic, and I'm not part of any morning work crew. I'm not a part of any crew, especially one that you're a part of."

"You sound a little bit like the girl in class who's always whining that she doesn't want to play any of the games that the boys are playing."

The man glared at him through slitted eyes.

"You smell like alcohol."

More glares. "How would you know what alcohol smells like?" the man asked cantankerously. "Does your perfect mama drink in the closet?"

"No," Carston answered, confused. "She doesn't drink in any closets. I just know what it smells like."

"Fine, I smell like alcohol. What does it matter? It's none of your business."

"It doesn't matter, I guess. It's just that the smell makes my stomach sick. So, what do people call you? Other than Peddling Crocodile."

"No one calls me Peddling Crocodile."

"Sure, someone calls you Peddling Crocodile," Carston said, crossing his arms over his chest. "I do. And then probably everyone else after that. But I'll have to ask what it means—"

"Unless I give you something else."

Carston nodded.

"Fine," *not* Peddling Crocodile snapped. "Call me Doc. All right?"

Carston beamed.

"You're happy now," Doc remarked sullenly.

"Yep! So, is it Doc as in Bugs Bunny, or Doc as in doctor? Doctor Peddling Crocodile." Carston laughed at his own joke.

Doc didn't laugh with him, but neither did he look angry. "Go away, short stack."

Carston didn't budge. Instead, he sat there, staring and wondering at the possibility. "*Were* you a doctor?" he asked.

"No," Doc said crossly, scowling at the near mention of him being anything other than a homeless bum. Granted, the answer came fast enough to be indicative of the truth, also grumpily enough to be considered defensive. Carston knew these two indicators by heart because Mama was a human lie detector.

Due to his standoffish behavior and almost always grumpy dialogue, Doc could have easily been mistaken as a scrooge, but Carston didn't think so.

"Did you sleep at the store last night?"

The grumpy, "no, I didn't" ensued. Then Doc picked up the blanket folded neatly beside him and held it out to Carston. "This is yours. I don't want it."

"I gave it to you to keep," said Carston, waving the blanket away absently.

Doc looked incensed. "Why do you care?" He sounded incensed too.

"Because something happened last night that put everyone in a weird mood this morning, and Oscar was gone, burying a dead bird. I had hoped you knew what had happened."

Doc shook his head. "That's not what I…" He stopped, shaking his head. "No, I don't know anything about that." He held out the blanket once more. "I don't want this. It smells funny."

Carston grinned. "It's a gift, which means no returns. Besides, it's probably just the soap you're smelling."

Doc's brown eyes locked onto him. For a moment, Carston wondered if he was about to be thrown across the park. Then a miracle happened. Doc smiled. Blown back by disbelief, Carston stared a little, then noticed another small miracle. Something more surprising than Doc's smile were his teeth. They were straight and would be shiny white with a good brushing. If under that unkept mask of hair, Doc was no bum, then what was he?

"What have you been trying to do all morning?" Doc asked.

"What do you mean?"

"You keep going back to the monkey bars and just hanging there, kicking."

"Oh that," Carston said feeling a bit embarrassed. "I was trying to do a chin-up. I'm training to be a mountain climber. Someday."

"Looks like you're training today. A mountain climber, huh?"

"Yeah, that's what I want to be. I've been reading about it for years. I can sprint up our apartment's staircase without even breathing hard. Mama and I have decided that the next logical step would be to lift my own weight. Only…I'm can't do it yet. But I'm working on it."

"All morning. I saw."

"Well, what about you?"

"What about me?"

"Can you lift your own weight?"

"I used to, all the time. It's what we…" Doc trailed off, his eyes looking past Carston.

"We?" Carston asked.

Doc's eyes snapped back. "There's no we," he said crossly. He looked away—far away.

"Can you help me?" asked Carston.

Doc looked at him, his expression empty, as though he'd lost his place in the conversation. "Help you? With what?"

Carston nodded. "Chin-ups. Got any tips?"

"Turn your hands around."

Carston looked at his hands, flipped them over, and looked at them some more, confused.

"Put your hands up," Doc said, lifting his arms in demonstration. "Like you're holding the bar."

Carston did, and they sat across from one another, with their arms in the air, like two monkeys without a branch.

"See how you're looking at your knuckles?" Doc asked.

Carston looked at his knuckles. "Yeah."

"That's a pull-up. Now, rotate your wrists so that you're looking at your fingernails."

Carston did. "Was I doing it wrong?"

"No, it wasn't wrong. Pull-ups are what you'll eventually need to do for climbing. It's called grip strength. But pull-ups are a hard place to start. Try doing some chin-ups first, then you can transfer back later."

"Grip strength," Carston repeated thoughtfully.

"Yeah."

Carston's eyes lit up, and he jumped to his feet, excited to try. This was the stuff he needed to know. "Thanks, Doc!" he called over his shoulder as he sprinted off toward the monkey bars.

This time, Carston sprang up, grabbed the bar as he normally would, then turned his hands around so that he could see his nails.

He grunted and pulled, and grunted and pulled, his feet kicking with effort. He applied all of the might his little body could hold, plus a little hope. To his great elation, his body lifted. Not all the way. He couldn't get his chin to the bar. But he'd pulled himself halfway up. When he dropped down, his heart was pounding at the inside of his chest from the labor and the thrill of possibility.

Carston turned and hollered "Doc!," waving to the face in the bushes, "I...", only the face was already gone.

Chapter Five

1

"Uncooperative pricks," Orson growled to his head man, Paine, "the whole lot of them."

"Time is what they need," Paine recommended and took a long drag from his cigarette.

Coco was reclined on the sofa next to Dagger, who was perched on the arm of the chair. Coco's white arms and legs dangled from her brown sundress. Her face was soft, with naturally red lips and dark lashes, but her expression was cold and severe. She believed thoughts displayed outwardly were a sign of weakness, an inability to keep your cards turned inwards. Her golden-brown eyes watched the room like a patient, but deadly, hawk.

"How much time?" Orson asked with a notably impatient tang.

Time was something beyond Orson's command, and, therefore, he preferred not to lean upon such a fundamental quantity. Coco agreed with Orson's irritation. Too much time gave people the illusion of holding a degree of power, a measure of procrastination. There was patience: a carefully guided opportunity to passively assist a person into a self-discovering submission. And there was mismanagement of tolerance, which not only generated, but almost condoned, resistance. Walking the thin tightrope between the two was one of Paine's many skillful roles. Coco watched with assessing reverence.

"They're not accustomed to our way of stability," Paine explained. "They're still under the impression that law regulates them. Let us grant them our generous patience while we clear their old board." The "board" referred to the symbolic chessboard embodying the tug of war between oblivious civilian life and gang domination and rule.

Out of the corner of Coco's eye, she noticed Jax. Jax had been her tutor back when she'd first been recruited. He had done the recruiting after watching her in a brief, but brutal, struggle she'd had with two large men in the back alley of her old job. He hadn't helped her. She hadn't needed it. Instead, he'd watched as she defended herself perfectly from the men who'd attempted to ram her into a dark protected corner. He'd liked her ever since, and she was woman enough to admit she'd given in to his strong black frame. Reclined, as she was, the diamond earring he wore in his right ear twinkled in the light as he folded his hands—a habit of his when he was struggling with the waiting part of the game.

Jax preferred working all of the time. That's just who he was. Coco's cold talents were unleashed less often. Therefore, the two of them functioned separately more often than as a pair.

Most of the members were here for simplistic reasons. Jax was a born leader, the cold corporate world having no interest in an uneducated man. Seven, a black kid, not quite nineteen, itched to act out against all of society for the transgressions of a few. It made him extremely susceptible to following anti-law, anti-society-driven-power purviews. Delilah, she was the curly brown-haired girl, with dark brown eyes. She was as fun-loving as they came. Not the bully type at all, she had a lamely hidden basic desire to be noticed and appreciated. She was noticed here, and everyone appreciated the fun she inserted into their everyday, sometimes dry, sometimes bloody, circumstances. Dagger, on the other hand, he was there for different reasons, and it wasn't his charming personality. His reasons were scarily similar to Coco's, making him the person she—yes, sadly—understood best.

Neither Coco, nor Dagger, cared a speck about taking a wrecking ball to society, nor providing bought security, nor about being accepted into something other than themselves. They were both members and outsiders, at the same time. What they had in common, different from the others, was that they both were good at killing. Where the others *could* take a life, Coco and Dagger were at complete ease with it, sleeping especially better afterward even. This element, this flaw in their personalities, made them extremely useful to Orson. They were at odds in one area, however.

Coco required a minimally cold reason that aligned with her crooked moral compass to take a life. Dagger required none. It made her physically sick how he relished in the aftereffect, like a dog rolling in a carcass, mopping up every last molecule of stank.

Coco flicked one brown-yellow eye in Dagger's direction. He looked cool as a cucumber to everyone in the room, except Coco. Coco felt an energy—a negative energy—pulsating off of him. She recognized it because she experienced the same energy right before she took a life.

Orson's focus turned to Mailman, the newest member. "How's the board looking?"

"Messages have been sent," Mailman replied. "I set off fire alarms, smoke detectors, crushed the laundromat owner's side mirror 'cause he didn't have any of those, kidnapped a little dog—"

"Kidnapped a dog?" Delilah asked. "What'd you do with it? Can I have it?" she asked excitedly.

Mailman's response was a short "no." It meant the dog could be dead, or that Mailman was simply a jerk. He continued on with his list of duties like they were rap lyrics. It was at the end that he paused noticeably, as though deciding on something, before giving Orson a single nod, signifying that he was done.

Coco and Jax glanced at one another. Jax lifted one brow. He'd clearly caught the slight hiatus in Mailman's rehearsed rant and was pondering the same question that Coco was. What was is that he'd left out?

"Good, continue with those orders," Orson said to Mailman, who looked relieved. Then, Orson turned his focus to the rest of the group. "The same goes for the rest of you. Proceed with your orders," and if Coco wasn't mistaken (and she rarely was) Orson looked right at Dagger, "and your assigned areas, lest you be removed."

By removed, Orson meant dismissed. And by dismissed, he could mean discontinued from life as one knows it, or life all together, if it that's what set comfortably with him in that moment.

Coco didn't know what that was about. Had Dagger been straying from his assigned area? Did it have anything to do with the way negative energy was pouring off of him? If it was a matter of loyalty or obedience, there was a problem. Loyalty and obedience weren't big deals to Orson, they were The Deal.

Everyone in the room acknowledged their agreement with Orson's orders in one way or another. The room knew The Deal after all. If someone didn't like their orders, they could object, within certain limits—created mostly by Paine. They were even allowed to leave, in most cases. Though leaving only remained an option *before* one screwed the pooch. If the pooch was screwed already, well, so were you.

Coco had seen members' "dismissals" and had been the "dismiss-or" a time or two. There was no doubt that she'd see it again. People, in general, were lazy, self-motivated jerks. To tow a line that pulled another person's wagon usually only lasted so long. Once that line ceased to jingle one's own self-motivated bells, it grew heavier and heavier, until it broke. Or was cut—dismissed.

2

"I paid your half, in advance, to find her," Mitchell Mateo explained dryly to Dagger.

"I will," Dagger assured him.

Mateo was the tallest man Dagger had ever seen. His skin, a dark black, had a strange gold undertone, especially on his clean-shaven head. The loose, partially unbuttoned shirt he wore hinted subtly at the existence of a large tattoo that Dagger had never fully seen but had heard were giant claw scrapings. They were made to look as though he'd been attacked by the largest lioness ever to exist. The claw scrapings supposedly started at the back of his broad shoulders, trailed over the top, then down his pectoral muscles, stopping just beneath the nipples. Rumor had it, it was a favorite place for women to grab, digging their nails over the tattooed scratchings. Laying over the tat was Mateo's infamous silver necklace. It was half an inch in diameter and specially engraved with jagged lines and diamond patterns to replicate the appearance of a boa constrictor. Mateo was the "Boa" of his business, the fabled stealth hunter, more than capable of swallowing his prey whole. In this case, however, the great "Boa" needed Dagger. Imagine that.

Apparently, Mateo's long-lost girl and her son had run off a couple years ago. For some time, it was believed that they'd either managed to escape elsewhere or, preferably, were dead. The narrative had changed, however, and quite by accident.

Word of a young black crusader for the homeless—a kid—had managed to drift with the tides of the walking bum zombies. Now, word on the street was this black kid and his white mother were shacked up somewhere within Orson's expanding territory. Which, for a dope-addicted whore, was pretty smart. If it'd even been on purpose. Mateo could no sooner cross Orson's border than he could print an ad in the local paper. Provoking Orson was the last thing anyone with anything they didn't want to lose wanted to be accused of. The great and mighty "Boa" fed aggressively on vulnerable women and men with imprudent hard-ons. He didn't make his money by provoking confrontations with men like Orson. Mateo made his money off of his "properties" doing their job in his sporting-house.

Therefore, properties deciding for themselves to toddle off was a big no-no. What if all of Mateo's properties decided to act off of precedent and just toddle off whenever they saw fit? What if they all decided they could simply hole up anywhere within the province of

Orson—because Orson was so much more powerful, no one would dare cross him—and live out their days happily ever after?

Screw that. That's where Dagger came in.

"I expect my packages in a timely manner," Mateo spoke sharply now, requiring Dagger to drag his focus back. They were sitting across from one another at a card table, which today held no cards. Today it held tightly wrapped packages of dope. For Mateo, the dope held many purposes. Here, it was sold, given to Mateo's properties, given to Mateo's high-paying clients, and consumed for the simple joy of consuming.

Dagger liked dope. His blood liked dope. His soul liked dope. There was only one thing he liked more.

"I'm starting to wonder if I've hired the wrong man," Mateo said, observing him with those round golden eyes.

After years had gone by, Dagger wondered why in the hell it mattered, other than the principle of it. She'd ran off, without permission. Added to the poisonous venom of her desertion, she'd taken the boy with her. Dagger assumed that the girl probably lacked more value than she was worth, but the satisfaction of Mateo hearing her beg for her son's life before she died may be partial compensation. Dagger didn't care if she begged or not, just so her blood ran over his fingers while it was still warm. The boy, he'd be destroyed for certain.

Dagger hadn't seen the potential in Boa's circle in the past, but Boa was starting to turn up the heat. Greed had to be fed. Greed breeds sin. Sin breeds sex. Sex breeds money. Money breeds greed. And there was Mateo, at both the beginning and the end. Latching onto that circle was Dagger.

"I am da right man. I will find them," Dagger assured him. "I'm getting close. They've been seen."

"You'd better not be mistaken," Mateo said. "You don't want to owe me, rather than me owe you."

It was true. Dagger had already spent the money he'd been paid upfront with. He couldn't rely on Orson to back him. If Orson knew that he'd contracted out, he'd be screwed. He was on his own on this.

"It's them."

Fingering his necklace, Mateo said, "Let's raise the stakes. When you find them, you can have the first dib."

That got Dagger's attention. Raise the stakes? The stakes were already pretty high. But what the hell, he was confident. "Dibs on...?"

"From the way I see it," Mateo spoke with the smooth glide of a legless creature, "the way you're quivering, there are a few different angles that would be abundantly enjoyable to you. Am I a right?"

He was right.

Dagger had hoped that under Orson, he'd have been able to feast on his core delights more often. For example, when was the last time he'd slit open someone? Figuratively, he couldn't remember. He *could* remember, of course. It had been too long. Hopefully, with any amount of luck, this deal with Mateo would continue to offer an outlet, or two.

"Depends," Dagger answered.

Mateo smiled, shrugging his mighty shoulders. Dagger could see immediately why the girls would do anything he asked. "Take your pick."

Dagger smiled. Just what he wanted to hear.

Mateo was right, Dagger needed to find the packages. His veins were already vibrating with anticipation. Oh, so much more of a motivation than the money. Money bought dope, but it didn't buy death, or allow him to breathe in someone's spirit like air. Sitting here, doing nothing, Mateo's promise made Dagger feel as though he might suffocate.

That was about to change.

3

He hadn't noticed. Thank the gods of fire—all of them, it didn't matter which mythological world—Orson hadn't noticed.

Mailman had thought, for sure, that a man with Orson's supposed perceptual talent would have detected a straight-up omission. After all, it had flaunted emptily before him like a giant missing float in an otherwise crisp line of decorated parade displays.

Mailman breathed a sigh of relief as he climbed aboard the shitty ass bicycle that he'd lifted off some kid at the skate park. It'd been a shitty kid, and it was a shitty bike. Nonetheless, it got him around, and without the trouble of putting money into the pocket of some fat man sitting behind a desk, or being hassled by cops for sitting behind a wheel using city streets. Peddling along, he turned his bike toward his assigned area, jumping curbs and weaving around pedestrians.

"Hey, kid!" a man shouted after him.

Kid, Mailman thought comically. What was that man's issue? He'd missed stamping the shiny black toes of the man's shoes with his dusty tires. What did the man have to complain about? A gust of wind? Mailman waved at the man using only his middle finger.

"Watch where you're going!" the man yelled angrily.

Mailman slammed on the brakes, skidding and sweeping the bike sideways, and nearly collided into a woman. The woman squeaked and jumped out of the way. Mailman paid the startled woman no attention, glowering instead at the man in the suit walking much like he had irritable bowel syndrome.

The suit stopped walking, his offended face taking on a serious look of concern. Mailman slowly raised his hand, tucking his ring finger and pinky in, thumb sticking straight up, and pointed two fingers at the man. Curving his index finger, he pulled the imaginary trigger.

"Bang," Mailman said under his breath.

The man flinched, and Mailman imagined that the make-believe bullet wasn't one of lead but of fire. A lovely image of the man bursting into flames filled his heart with glee. Mailman threw his head back, laughing boisterously, severely satisfied. Then with just a touch of melancholy, he flipped his bike around to continue on his way. No more toying around. He had a missing parade float to see.

Chapter Six

1

Everyone who had slept out front of Mrs. Ellsberg's store the previous night had already left. The only person still hanging around, other than the occasional customer, was Carston. He was in the back room stacking cardboard into a giant pile taller than himself. When he was done, Mrs. Ellsberg would put the cardboard out on the curb. Some of it would disappear, to be turned into makeshift huts, beds, and pathways, and the rest would be picked up and recycled. Mrs. Ellsberg didn't care where it went, just so it wasn't in her back room taking up space.

While she finished up a transaction for a small group of middle school boys, she heard the front door open. As the boys snatched their plastic-covered sugar comatoses off of the counter, Mrs. Ellsberg thought she recognized the male figure who slipped in. He was now making his way up the hygiene aisle at the pace of an unhurried bride in the moment of her big debut during her long-awaited-for ceremony. One glance around the boys' heads as they turned to leave, and she knew two things for certain.

The first thing she knew was she'd been correct; it was the gangster child that referred to himself as Mailman. His return presence meant he either refused to comprehend the blatant response she'd handed him on his last visit, or he'd come to avenge whatever cold consequence her failure to comply had laden him with. Either way, the second thing she knew for certain was this sideways snot-eater meant her trouble.

2

Trying to stay away from park, where he knew he'd run into that kid, Doc strolled new streets. He even happened across a half-eaten breakfast sandwich, still in the paper bag. He didn't brood over where he was going. It didn't matter where he went or where he ended up. Every street left him in the same terrible place—still having lost every brother he'd ever had, still not deserving to be alive, and still having not punished himself enough for surviving.

From somewhere nearby, Doc heard kids laughing and playing. He glanced up, thinking the annoying kid couldn't have traveled this far from home. No way his mother would allow it. That's exactly why Doc had steered his weary feet this direction—so that he wouldn't run into the short stack. Yeah, if that were the case, then why did he keep finding himself lifting his eyes at the sound of every kid?

A pang in his stomach made him wince, and he wondered if it was a bug, or just slightly rancid cooking oil. With nothing better to do, he just kept walking, like one of those missions he'd gone on in Afghanistan. Missions had always meant a lot of walking. He didn't mind the walks then; he'd figured they made him stronger, and they had. He didn't mind them now either; he figured they made him weaker, which was the goal. It was against the rules to kill himself.

Putting a gun to his head was a thing of the past. He'd tried it and had failed. His dad had sabotaged his pistol, had stolen the ammo when Doc hadn't been looking. Anyway, it didn't matter now. The pistol was stowed away, at his parents' house, with his other things. He realized now that shooting himself would have been too easy. It wouldn't have provided him the opportunity to suffer—as he was meant to.

The best way of atoning for his sin of being alive was to suffer himself. His brothers on the other side would allow death to call upon him when he'd paid enough. He just hoped that at some point they'd be satisfied. The thought of never receiving their forgiveness was too much of a burden to carry. In truth, it was one of his worst fears. What if they didn't forgive him? What if they refused to accept him? What if he was doomed to an eternity of torment?

Doc's breath started rushing in and out at a pace that he couldn't control. There was a crushing sensation in his chest. It squeezed so tight that he was petrified that his heart would crush his soul before he'd had a chance to be forgiven. A panicky breathlessness grabbed hold of him. The world around him started to turn black and his pathetically weak legs gave out from beneath him. Not bothering to use his arms to catch himself, Doc fell flat on his face.

Whoomph.

There were two sharp pains as the concrete made impact. He felt his forehead bounce off the hard surface and the sting of his tender flesh peeling away from his kneecaps. Blood trickled over his eyebrow into his eye. Reflex had forced his eyes closed. Now that the event was over, he just laid there. The impact of the fall seemed to have knocked the breath right back *into* him.

He sighed.

To passersby, he must have looked completely beaten, ready to give up, ready to give in. But he felt in his soul, there was more to be had. More strength to give away. More agony to take in. His ugly damned heart just kept beating. It may be hidden deep within a crusted declining body, but it was still beating. He'd curse it later. Right now, he decided to just lay there and soak in the warmth of the sun.

"Oh my!" a woman's voice broadcasted. Doc heard her shoes scuffling across the pavement.

"Go away…" he moaned, but his voice was so muffled he doubted she could hear it.

A gentle hand touched his back, - and his eyes flew open. What sort of woman dared to touch a filthy bum? Another bum? His nostrils went to work. No, couldn't be a bum, there was a lack of stench. Then again, maybe he'd just grown accustomed to all the different stenches.

"Go away," Doc moaned into the pebbly ground. "You're interfering with my Bahama vacation."

A woman laughed and her hand attempted to turn him over, with no luck. "I've got bad news for you, Doc, you're not in the Bahamas. And from the looks of it, your vacation hasn't gotten off to too good of a start."

At the sound of his name Doc lifted his rather heavy head and looked up to see who this woman could be. Staring down at him was the woman that the kid, Carston, had come to the store with. His mama. Doc couldn't believe his own eyes, and not because she had a pretty face, though she did. The sweet scent of flowers circled around her like flies over a summer garbage can. It was nice.

"You…" He'd meant to present an offensive statement that would scare her away from him, since his stench wasn't doing the trick, but his voice betrayed him and croaked out like a sick frog. "You," he tried again. It sounded exactly the same as it did the first time.

She smiled. "Yes, me." He watched, surprised, as she sat on the concrete and crossed her legs like a pretzel. He'd never been able to do that. Not the sitting part, the pretzel part.

"How do you know my name?"

"Carston told me." Of course he had. "Are you able to sit up? I need to talk to you."

Doc struggled into a sitting position and started to stand, but her small hand touched his leg, freezing him in place. How was his filthiness not repelling her? Was this not the same woman?

"Your knees look as terrible as your face," she said.

"Thanks," he muttered.

She looked embarrassed. "That's not what I—"

"I know," he said, yanking his leg away from her unwanted physical contact. Blood from the cut in his forehead was beginning to glue his eyelid partially closed. "I'm fine. I've seen worse. You came all this way to talk to me?"

"No, I didn't. But now that I've found you," she said, composing herself. "It's about Carston."

"What about him?"

"I just...I just think its best that you stay away from him."

Doc had to swallow his hoot. "Are you kidding?" Doc burst. "Do you not know your own son?"

Her delicate shoulders rose and fell with her heavy huff. "Well, of course I know my son."

It took an awful lot of work to keep the amusement off his face, and even then, he wasn't sure he was having any success at it. "I've been *trying* to stay away from him. He won't leave me alone. I tried calling him names. I tried being mean. I tried to scare—"

Her small, but fierce, hand flew up, and her palm appeared in his face. "You tried to scare my son?"

Doc shrugged. "Not a serious scare. Besides, he doesn't scare."

Another heavy huff and she was caught momentarily speechless. Then she was on her feet so fast that, for a moment, she was only a blur. Maybe it was just the aching in his head smudging his vision. "Well, that's not the point. You...you just stay away from him. All right? Can you do that?"

Doc shrugged again. "Listen, I don't want your son talking to me any more than you do. That's why I'm over here."

"Over where?" she asked huffily. She looked around, and he expected that she'd answered her own question. "Oh. Well. Good."

Placing his hands on the ground, grunting, Doc worked to stand. Being weak in the presence of a pretty woman, especially this pretty woman, was not a highlight in his regime of self-punishment. It was downright embarrassing. More so, it was upsetting that he suddenly seemed to care.

"What are *you* doing here?" Doc asked, though it was absolutely none of his business.

The cynical expression on her face reflected her agreement on that point. "Walking home from the bus stop."

Doc resisted looking down at his wrist for a watch he no longer wore. "This early?"

Her head cocked. Cynical again. "Is it—"

"Nope," he interrupted, "it's not." With that, he turned away from her and started shuffling in the direction that he knew was opposite of her home.

He had liked the park. It had made slowly draining the life out of one's body more peaceful. Which was the exact reason why he needed to find another spot. That, and he agreed with…whatever her name was…on the need to stay away from her pestering kid. There was something about that boy that egged Doc. It wasn't the food. It wasn't the company. It was something else. There was something special about the kid. Doc didn't like it. It went against everything Doc battled with.

"Doc?"

Doc turned. He shouldn't have, but it was too late now. He had, and now he was looking at her again. Her blonde hair was pulled into a ponytail, and her casual working outfit was hard core failing to hide her smooth slender figure. It was her shoes he decided to admire. They were sensible. In a world full of dolled-up fake women, sensible was an admirable quality. It was also a safe place to stare at without taking a bag of bricks to the face.

Her fingers fidgeted with the hem at the bottom of her blouse. "I don't know what to say."

Doc looked up, then around, absolutely confused. "All right, don't then."

"You helped him."

Doc's eyebrows spiked upwards and he started to shake his head. In no way had he helped that kid. Doc wouldn't encourage the little dust mite to hang around any more than he already did.

"He told you about wanting to become a climber," she explained. "Other than helping…"

"Bums?" Doc offered.

"Yes. No! Helping homeless people is what I mean. Other than that, climbing is all Car thinks about. He told me that you helped him with that."

Doc started shaking his head and decided the ache wasn't worth it. "No, I didn't. I wouldn't have said a word to him if he hadn't come over and started bothering me again. I just told him to turn his hands around to make him go away."

"Doc, you *did* help him. You helped him to believe."

The worst thing about having a mind splintered by combat was the knowing that your mind was slowly coming apart, but he knew that he'd said nothing to make the dust mite believe anything. Was her mind splintering too? He shook his head. "I don't know what he told you, but—"

She was smiling again, and he suddenly wished he knew her name at least. He could ask Carston, next time he saw him. Oops. There wasn't supposed to be a next time.

"Listen, I believe that you probably didn't intend to help. The thing is, Carston doesn't have a father. He doesn't have anyone to show him simple things like that. It meant a lot to him. So, it meant a lot to me."

Doc took a step backwards. "I didn't help him. I wouldn't." She seemed to be studying him, deciding on her next move. Hopefully it wasn't a brick to the face. He took another step back, to be safe.

She put out a hand, like one would to a nervous dog. "I just wanted to say, thank you."

"Fine," he said. This time his sick frog voice didn't betray him, and the word came out as gruffly as he meant it to.

"My name is Chloe."

"Fine," he snapped again.

"And I'm sorry."

"It's nothing," he grumbled, though he had no idea what she was sorry for, and turned away.

"Doc?"

Another man might dip into the well of emotion and play her on it. He wasn't that kind of man. Damn his feet for slowing. Damn his feet for stopping. He'd have words with them about that.

"Would you…would you allow me to look after your wounds?"

With his back still turned, he snapped, "I know how to look after them myself."

"It doesn't appear you have the supplies," she said sensibly. Had he admired her for her sensibility earlier? He took it back.

Doc made the painful mistake of shaking his head from side to side. Added to the headache that had arrived, his thoughts were tangling and puzzling him. Getting patched up was accepting help to better his condition. Against the rules. Then again, he could go on suffering for longer if he didn't die from infection. Totally rule abiding. Which one was correct? Neither? Was it a trick? The splinters of his fractured mind were poking his already-hurting head. Which one was correct? Which one was correct?

"Doc?"

Her voice broke the spell, and he looked back at her. It was his turn to not know what to say. He needed help deciding which way was correct.

"Can I help you?" she asked gently.

He tried to think, nothing came about. No thoughts were connecting. "Can you help me?" he muttered the question back to her. It's the only words he could remember at the moment.

"Yes," she said without the hesitation. "I can."

He nodded, and she beckoned him to join her, so he did. As his feet shuffled forward, he was muddily aware that Chloe was having to lead the way. He was busy fighting a severe falling sensation. He felt completely lost in a daze of disconnected pathways. He was inside a confusing maze comprised of high-definition memories of chaos, stirred together with broken fragments from the world around him. They were all wavering unsteadily like a mirage. It was difficult to stand. It was difficult to walk. He followed, grasping on faith that

Chloe might be able to help him find a way out of this maze. Doc hated this feeling of disconnection more than anything in the world, almost as much as eternal damnation. It scared him. Nevertheless, even amidst the consuming anxiety and incapacitating fright, he grasped that this time was different. This time he wasn't alone.

3

Chloe and Doc had walked in silence most of the way. Chloe found herself surprised at how many people *didn't* pay them any mind. Apparently, homeless people, and those walking with them, were unnoticeable. With Carston around, she'd grown accustomed to regarding the homeless. She'd forgotten that, for others, that just wasn't the case. Homeless people made most working people uncomfortable, even if it was only a fear of being asked for a handout or to purchase a used newspaper that'd been in the trash an hour ago. If Chloe were being honest, she'd admit to having felt the same way a time or two.

Speaking of being honest, every time she turned to make sure Doc was managing alongside of her, she was beginning to take notice of other things as well. Things such as: behind Doc's scruffy beard hid a rather handsome face. His skin was smooth not pitted. His dark hair, though completely at odds with itself for which direction it wanted to point in, looked healthy and thick. Behind the cautionary bells clanging in her head, she thought she saw more to Doc than he wanted people to see. Someone who wasn't angry and struggling with how the world had turned out to be and how it had destroyed the hopeful young man he had once been. Then again, maybe she was just seeing things that Carston wanted her to see.

Still, to her amazement, even in Doc's vulnerable condition, she felt safer walking with him than she did walking alone. She reminded herself that was not why she invited him along. She was only helping him because he needed it and because he'd helped Car. This one event wasn't going to ruin her self-isolation policies.

They'd still be there waiting for her to return to her perceived title of "bitch." She wasn't a bitch at all, and she found herself at odds with whether she wanted people to know that or not. Chloe couldn't afford to be seen as weak or take unnecessary risks. She wanted to be seen as formidably strong, and somehow that equated to being misunderstood as utterly heartless.

By the time Chloe and Doc had reached her street, Doc's state of mind had improved greatly. Like a finger being snapped in front of his face, he straightened his back—making him taller than she'd judged initially. He'd even looked down and smoothed out his jacket. The most unexpected thing he did was gently move her aside, so that she was walking closest to the buildings and he was walking closest to the street. This gesture of chivalry was astonishing. She'd heard that chivalry was dead. At any rate, Chloe was glad he was making a recovery. She had been starting to wonder if she'd made a mistake, subsequently inviting him into their lives after having just banished him. Maybe the company that he thought he so detested was good for him.

By the time Chloe and Doc reached Mrs. Ellsberg's storefront, Doc had regained his cognitive functions so much so that he reached out and took hold of her wrist. Agitated, she swiveled to face him.

"Go home," he said calmly. "I don't need mending after all."

His pupils were noticeably larger than they had been before, but it wasn't her he was looking at. She turned to see what was in the direction that he was gazing. "I—"

"Just go," Doc snapped. She stared at him angrily. How dare he speak to her that way. "Right now," he growled, releasing her arm so she could do just that.

Chloe hesitated, trying to gage the meaning of this attitude. Maybe her silly imagination had gotten the best of her, trying to envisage a nicer version of him. What had she been thinking? Whatever had happened inside his wobbly mind on the walk over here was in a full-blown tantrum by the time they'd arrived. There was no way he was going to allow her to doctor his wounds now. He was behaving like a rabid dog, snapping and growling at her. Well, truth be told, she wasn't feeling all that warm and fuzzy towards him either.

At least she could say that she'd tried to help him. Surely Carston could approve of that much. Satisfied with her efforts, Chloe turned and walked briskly away. Stubborn agitation fed her quick pace, past the storefront and up the stairs leading to her apartment. She knew nothing about this man, other than that her son was trying to befriend him. Why had she trusted him? It must have been a lapse of judgment. She'd had those before, and they'd ended with her in terrible places.

The metal steps creaked beneath her feet. As she reached the top, her mind bombarded her with suspicion, of the frenetic variety. What was going on with him? Why the sudden change? Should she be calling the cops? Should she barge back down there and punch him in the nose? Should she pack her and Car's belongings make a run for it?

Chloe took a deep breath, attempting to calm her fears. Being constantly under a barrage of overthinking, paranoia, and nervous nightmares was exhausting. Once she got inside, Carston would help her see things straight—without her gray pessimism to cloud up reality. Carston always helped her see things straight. Chloe opened the apartment door.

"Car! I'm home! Are you here?"

There was no response.

Chloe slipped her small pack off of her back, dropping it on the end of the couch. "Car? Baby?"

Still nothing.

Dark, scary thoughts quickly gathered like storm clouds. Where was he?

4

Once Chloe had disappeared around the corner, Doc turned to Mrs. Ellsberg's storefront. From where he was standing, he could see straight up an aisle, like a runway. At the end of the runway, he could make out Mrs. Ellsberg positioned behind her counter. In front of the counter stood an overconfident young gangbanger wearing a backwards turned hat. Even at this distance, and the blurry effect of looking through glass, reading the young gangbanger's leaning, threatening posture was easy. More concerning, however, was the something in the kid's hand. Doc couldn't make it out, but he could guess, and he wasn't about to let this menacing play out to the punk's liking.

In a calm gliding motion, Doc strode over to the door, pushing it open just enough to slip silently in.

5

Even from the backroom where Carston was stacking cardboard into a tall, neat pile, he'd heard the tension in Mrs. Ellsberg's voice.

"You're back," she said. "I take it your boss didn't like my answer."

Carston stopped working to listen. It was wrong to eavesdrop, he knew. It was just so hard not to. It's not like it required a listening device to hear a conversation through a single wall and the open door.

"The boss is more patient than I. Too bad for you," a male voice replied.

Carston's mind was reeling with questions. Who was this man? Who was this boss they were referring to? And what was the question that they hadn't liked the answer to?

"I guess you've noticed an increase in crime lately?" asked the man. "Should have you a little worried."

"Heavens to Betsy, I hadn't noticed an increase until *after* I'd met you," Mrs. Ellsberg replied.

"They've been trickling in, trying to claim their territory. It's going to get worse for those of you who don't want someone like us on your side. These thugs, they don't have much regard for—"

"I pray, do tell," Mrs. Ellsberg cut in, "you never said who *us* were."

There was a short silence before the man snipped, "Trust me, you don't want to climb down that rabbit hole, lady." It was clear the man's phony patience had worn off. Even his arrogance couldn't quell his looming fury. The burning fire in the man's voice had Carston pressing his back against the wall, scared to move. "All you need to know is that this is the last chance I'm going to give you. I won't offer a business deal again. Pay the fee, or be burnt out."

Unrattled, Mrs. Ellsberg asked, "You're in charge then? Not a boss? Tell me, are you in this by yourself? What are you trying to earn money—"

The man vocalized a growl that seemed to thunder through the wall. "I'm not in this by myself!" he yelled. "And you should be grateful, or I'd have killed you already!"

Carston's body shook, and he couldn't make it stop. Kill Mrs. Ellsberg? What should he do? What *could* he do? He thought of the landline in Mrs. Ellsberg's room, but she kept that door locked during the day.

True to character, Mrs. Ellsberg sounded as calm and steady as the drip in his and Mama's leaky faucet. "Put that away," Mrs. Ellsberg said in the same motherly tone she used for scolding Carston when he left his things lying about. "Where's your paperwork?"

The angry man bellowed, "What paperwork?"

"You said it was a business, there should be paperwork. A contract to sign?"

"Listen, fat lady, you're on my last nerve. I—"

"Oh hogwash," interrupted Mrs. Ellsberg. "Based on the valiant bravado that you've demonstrated here today, I do believe you have a lot of nerve. But, before you go and do anything stupid," cautioned Mrs. Ellsberg, "you should know I've installed one of those fancy pancy doohickeys since our last visit. Right there, over the front door. Go on, take a look. I ain't got a gun pointed at your head."

Something spicy was rising from Carston's stomach into his chest, burning the back of his throat. Just as he forced himself to swallow there was a strange sound; the breaking of glass, but not as sharp as it sounds when it falls on the hard floor from the top shelf. He felt himself flinch and take one rushed step towards the door before his mind stopped him. If Carston let the man take the money and leave, he could call for help sooner than if he exposed himself, and the man stayed, and…

"Carston," Mrs. Ellsberg's called softly. This time her voice noticeably shaking. "You may come out now, young man."

Arms and legs shaking worse than Mrs. Ellsberg's voice, Carston did as he was told, stepping tentatively around the corner. "Mrs. Ellsberg?"

She turned to him, looking just as healthy as she had before. She was still standing behind the counter, and to Carston's surprise, Doc was standing opposite of her.

"Doc?" Carston asked, confused.

Doc looked equally surprised to see Carston.

"Carston, get the police on the line. Quickly," Mrs. Ellsberg ordered. "And, Doc, is it? Thank you."

Carston jumped to the phone as Doc answered Mrs. Ellsberg with a nod.

"Come over here and let me take a look at that hand. And what happened to your head?"

Doc lifted his hand to inspect it himself, and Carson saw a trickle of fresh blood was flowing from between his index finger and thumb. His forehead was gummy with dried blood as well. It appeared he'd been collecting wounds all day.

Dispatch spoke into Carston's ear, "What is your emergency?".

Doc stepped over something on the floor so Carston raised onto his tippy toes to see what was there. Carston told the dispatcher what he saw. "Um, there's a man, with a gun, lying on the floor." The puzzle of what had happened started to take form in his mind. "He was threatening to kill Mrs. Ellsberg."

Doc kicked the gun away from the man's loose grip. It slid behind the counter, out of sight. No one touched it.

"He's on the floor?" the dispatcher asked.

Mrs. Ellsberg grabbed Doc's hand, examining it, saying, "This isn't too bad. I can clean this up in a jiffy."

Carston nodded before he found his voice again. "Yep, he's on the floor. My friend saved us."

The man on the floor moaned.

"Could you please hurry?" Carston asked. "I'm afraid he's going to wake up."

While speaking to the dispatcher, Carston noticed Doc look at Mrs. Ellsberg alarmingly. It wasn't her he saw. It was something else, but no one but him could see it. Abruptly recoiling, he yanked his hand away from Mrs. Ellsberg and staggered backward a few steps.

"The man with the gun on the floor is hurt?" the dispatcher asked.

"Passed out I think."

"Give me your name and address."

Carston did. He heard the dispatcher call him by name but didn't hear anything else. The man on the floor was beginning to stir. Carston's belly leapt into his throat and began performing jumping jacks. The man came to, startlingly quickly and fussing angrily with his tangled limbs. He was searching chaotically for his missing weapon. It was good that Doc was already on top of the situation because Carston nearly choked on his tongue in effort to speak.

Doc jumped on the man's back, one leg straddling each side. Carston saw Doc heroically capture the man's flailing right arm and bend it backwards. The man fussed all the harder, cussing and screaming. Carston watched, motionless, as the dispatcher spoke firmly into his ear,

"Carston, talk to me. What's going on? Tell me what you see? Can you get to somewhere safe?" Carston didn't answer. He didn't know why he his lips wouldn't transfer his thoughts into the phone. They just wouldn't.

Mrs. Ellsberg turned to him then in her calm, poetic style. Simultaneously prying the receiver from Carston's seizing fingers, and retrieving her bedroom key from her apron. She tucked the hard, cool key in his palm.

"Go. Lock yourself in. Quick now."

Carston felt like his feet were strapped into cinder blocks as he struggled to lift each foot and head toward the door to the back room. Time seemed to have slowed the muscle twitches responsible for moving him forward. Using a great amount of strenuous effort, Carston heard Mrs. Ellsberg say, "This is Lois Ellsberg, the suspect is fighting," as he finally turned the corner.

The loud rustling continued as he fumbled with the key and the tiny slit of a keyhole in the doorknob. The language spewing from the man wrestling on the floor with Doc in the other room made it very difficult to concentrate on this intricate task. His fingers trembled so badly the key kept dinging against the metal all around the keyhole, like a drunk trying to throw darts. Struggling, he heard the familiar whoosh of air from the store's door opening. Someone was making a run for it.

Then all was quiet.

All except for the soft shuffling of shoes on the hard floor.

Carston froze. Who had bolted out the front door, and who was he alone in the store with? He was soon to find out. Someone turned the corner into the back room. At the same time, the key finally slipped into the lock. He could have tried to turn the key, could have tried to open the door and bolt inside, but he didn't. Instead, Carston gulped and turned around, prepared to face whatever was coming his way.

Doc stood in the doorway. He looked rougher than usual, but to Carston, he looked like a hero.

"Doc…" Carston whispered in relief.

Hot tears began pouring down Carston's cheeks without him giving leave for them to do so. Unable to stop them, he rushed at Doc and threw his thin, quivering arms around Doc's waist. He didn't even mind the smell. No doubt, he'd call for Mama later (like tonight when the nightmares started), but for now, he felt safer than he had in his entire life.

As fate would have it, he didn't have to wait until tonight's nightmare to call for Mama. The front door of the store opened, and he heard Mama's voice.

"Car?"

Chapter Seven

1

Chloe gasped when she saw Carston zing around the corner from the back room as fast as his tennis shoes could carry him on the slick floor, tears rolling down his cheeks. His body hit her like a ton of bricks, and she wrapped him in her arms.

"Baby, what's wrong?"

"A man came in the store and was threatening Mrs. Ellsberg with a gun," he answered wildly. His already small voice was made even smaller by the muffling her shirt provided. But he'd crammed his face into it, and she didn't dare pull him away.

"What?" she gasped. "Where's—"

"He's all right," Mrs. Ellsberg offered, obviously a bit shaken up herself. "He stayed in the back room almost the entire time."

"Almost?" Chloe croaked. What did *almost* mean? Had her baby been in danger? "Where is he now?" Chloe asked.

Her neck took to swivel mode, but it needn't have, she knew the answer the moment she'd asked. A frantic young man had slammed into her on the sidewalk as she stepped off the staircase. He hadn't said anything, no apologies, no "get out of the way, lady," nothing. She'd stared after him for a moment and continued to the store door.

"Ran out the front door," answered Mrs. Ellsberg. "Carston called the police. They're on the way now."

Chloe knew her eyes were bugging out of her face, but she couldn't seem to draw them back in. Not with what she was hearing. "Baby, you called the police?"

"Yes," another muffled response from her son, "but it was Doc that saved us."

"Doc? The Doc from outside? That Doc?" Chloe tried to wrap her mind around the man that, only a short time ago, had to be led here, injured, from falling on his own face. How had he been capable of saving anyone. "*Doc* saved you?" she asked again, still stunned, and still sounding to herself like a broken record "Where is Doc now?"

Carston lifted an arm, and a finger pointed to the back room. Chloe looked up. There, Doc stood in the doorway. No extra injuries that she could tell. He didn't look as weak as she'd remembered him. Exhausted, but not weak. No man, no matter how dirty and malnourished, looked weak to a woman who'd just had the life of her son saved.

Warm tears poured from her eyes. She should thank him, she knew, but she felt traumatized and speechless. There was something potent in his focused expression. It could be the strength that she was recognizing. It'd been there before, only he'd had it successfully hidden under layers and layers of distrust and detachment. A steel door as delicate as a moth's wing opened inside of her heart. She knew she'd never be able to see Doc in the same way as she had before. Reality taught her that she ought to continue viewing him as the unpredictable dangerous creature that he was. He was a severely isolated homeless man with battles that she would never fully understand waging wars inside of him. She ought to stay as far away from him as she could.

Chloe buried her face in her Car's short hair and hid. A cowardly move, she knew, but she did it all the same. It wasn't a proud moment for her, but she couldn't continue to look at Doc when all she saw was a handsome, brave face under that guise of homelessness. Maybe this was the way Car looked at people—seeing them for who they were, on the inside—and maybe this was the way that all people should look at each other. Well, that was fine and dandy for them. She, on the other hand, couldn't afford to take those sorts of risks.

Doc stuck around to speak to the police. Yet another surprise Chloe would have to add to the long lists of surprises she'd encountered regarding that man today. She'd assumed Doc would scat. Most bums have their reasons for not wanting anything to do with law enforcement. However, while the dust settled inside the store, and the police did what police do, Doc remained. Chloe imagined that he likely felt uncomfortable being grilled with questions, but it didn't show. He only stepped away once and that was when Carston was being addressed. Chloe assumed he was only doing the manly thing, allowing her and Mrs. Ellsberg to perform the female coddling rituals. Which they did, unnecessarily. With each passing moment, Car seemed to need less and less affirmation as he watched and mimicked Doc's sound composure.

Sound? Had she really just used *sound* as a descriptive word for Doc? Hadn't she defined him as *unpredictable and dangerous* a short bit ago? Sound and unpredictable were about as contradicting as sugar and vinegar.

When the police had all the information they needed and the store had been tidied up, Chloe asked Carston to run up to the apartment and fetch her first aid kit. Doc heard that and started toward the door.

"Wait," Chloe said to him. "I told you I'd help you."

Doc's eyes darted this way and that as though a short debate with himself had arisen.

"Please," she added quickly, afraid he'd fall into the same abyss that he had earlier in the day. "It won't take but a moment. I promise you can scowl in silence the whole time. Car has a zipper on his lips, when necessary. I had it installed about a year ago."

This produced the smallest of lift in one corner of Doc's mouth.

Mrs. Ellsberg busied herself with putting the shop back together, closing up early, and pretending that she didn't have the excellent hearing of a bat. A bat's hearing helps it navigate without sight by emitting squeaks and listening for the echo to bounce back to them off of surrounding surfaces. In the same way, Chloe knew that Mrs. Ellsberg would be listening to the echo of their voices as they bounced off the store walls. In which case, Chloe hoped Doc took her up on the promise of silence.

First aid kit tucked under his arm like a football, Carston busted back in through the glass door. All of the adults jumped simultaneously. Surrendering the kit into Chloe's hands, Carston nodded proudly. Doc took one look at Carston and hesitantly nodded too.

Doc reluctantly sat down in the chair that Mrs. Ellsberg had brought him, and Chloe sat her kit on a stool, opening it. Car seemed to have forgotten all about the day's troubles and was googling over the situation at hand. Mrs. Ellsberg huffed, grabbing Carston by the collar of his shirt and dragging him backwards behind her. No vocal objections were made, but both Chloe and Doc saw the wide grin on Car's enthralled face as he was lugged out of sight.

"I'm sorry about him," Chloe said. Doc was staring at the kit now. She couldn't tell if he was gawking emptily at it or if he was afraid of it. "It doesn't bite," she told him, "And I'll be as gentle as possible."

Doc pried his eyes away from the first aid kit, choosing to look out the window instead. "It's not that."

She wanted to ask "what then?" as she used alcohol wipes to clean the dried blood from around the gash in his head. Her gut told her not to meddle. He was sitting compliantly, and she hoped he could manage to stay that way until she'd finished cleaning him up. Anyone could get an infection if a wound is not cleaned thoroughly enough, but homeless people were at a much greater risk of infection due to their living conditions and lack of provisions. She wondered if he was up-to-date on vaccinations and briefly thought about offering to accompany him to the nearest clinic. Again, her gut stopped her from meddling. As a substitute, she bit her tongue. It hurt badly enough that it made her think twice about meddling a third time.

After she'd cleaned the gash, she stroked an antibiotic cream over the wound and covered it with gauze. "Leave this in place so no contaminates get in, okay? If you're willing, you can come back in a few days and let me check the wound and change the bandage."

He leaned forward to stand, and she gently pushed his shoulder so his back remained against the chair. He smelled like he hadn't had a bath in far too long. "I'm not done. I haven't cleaned your knees."

"They're fine."

"Let me be the judge of that," she said, kneeling in front of him. "Your jeans have torn, but not enough that I can see." She looked up at him. "I have an idea that I think you're going to hate."

He stared down at her, listening, but she couldn't get a good read on what he was thinking. He could be just as overly calm as he'd been since the incident, or he could be about to bolt. There was no telling. She remained knelt down in front of him in hopes her presence there would keep him from jumping up and toppling her over. Probably a bad assumption on her part.

"No," he said firmly.

"No? You haven't even heard my idea."

"I'm not removing my pants."

"That's not exactly my idea." She glanced toward the back room where she knew Carston and Mrs. Ellsberg had their ears stationed as close to the open doorway as they dared. She lowered her voice. "I was thinking, you could borrow the bathroom upstairs, clean out your knees good, and I'll patch the pants while you do. Just this once. It will not be an ongoing habit." There had to be boundaries. And with homeless people, those boundaries had to be firm.

He seemed to be warily considering her idea.

"If you agree to the last part, I'll agree to the first," she added, very much wary herself.

Doc shook his head. "I don't think so," he answered. "You shouldn't have a man in your apartment."

Chloe stood, placing her fists firmly on her hips. "I shouldn't have a man in my apartment? And what business is it of yours?"

Doc looked left, then right. "Let me think." He looked right at her, and she felt those dark eyes reach inside of her. "If the man in question is me, I suppose it's just about as much my business as it is yours."

"Look here, mister! I'm not offering—"

"Mama," Carston's voice, and body, popped up from out of nowhere.

Doc and Chloe jumped.

"Can Doc stay for dinner? While you're patching up the knees of his pants, I can make macaroni and cheese." Carston winked at Doc. "The *good* kind."

Chloe turned to Carston. "What do you mean the *good* kind? You don't like my macaroni and cheese?"

"I like it," he said. "It's just not the *good* kind."

Chloe rolled her eyes.

"I'll pass," Doc said, standing. This was all just a bit much for him. He pressed a finger to the bandage on his head. "This will do. Thanks." Then he tromped past them, grabbed a bottle of wine from the top shelf, and vanished out the door.

Chloe felt her jaw drop. "He…he just…"

"Stole." Carston finished for her, also stunned.

"Well, good thing he didn't go in our apartment."

"He's not a thief," Carston defended.

Chloe turned to him. "Car, I think his actions just proved otherwise. This is exactly why we don't trust all people. You just never know what someone is capable of, until its already done."

Carston's head was hanging low as a work horse at the end of the day. "Maybe Mrs. Ellsberg gave him permission?"

Chloe put her arm around him. "Come on, baby. Let's go make sure Mrs. Ellsberg is all right, then we're going tuck in for the night."

Carston nodded and Chloe felt her heart sink with every step. She too wished that she could hear that Mrs. Ellsberg had given Doc permission to take the wine, but she wasn't holding her breath.

Sure enough, when Carston had asked Mrs. Ellsberg if she'd allowed Doc to take the bottle, she seemed regretful and that she had not. It made all three of them sadder than Chloe could have predicted. It would have been better not to have known.

Despite Chloe's concern for Mrs. Ellsberg's welfare, and numerous protests about her staying alone downstairs, Mrs. Ellsberg swore, repeatedly, that, "good grief," she was fine and didn't need any blasted supervision. Though she'd admitted that she'd been shaken at the time, she'd delt with worse. Chloe understood. Mrs. Ellsberg had lost a very good man and a faithful husband. Chloe couldn't argue with that the woman had dealt with worse.

2

After Doc had attacked the gang banger and Mrs. Ellsberg had grabbed his hand up, he'd seen flashes of disturbing images and sounds. Images of dozens of guns pointing at his face, and loosely garbed men yelling at him. He wished he could delete them, but even medication didn't do that. Sometimes those images snuck up on him with the silence of a cat; other times they roared in like a lion. All day his demons had been nipping at his banged-up heels. Today's incident brought them to a head. Then, the boy's presence at the scene had made it worse. He didn't even want to think about the hug.

The unforeseen, unwelcome hug that Carston had poured out all of his fear and overwhelming gratitude into was more than Doc could take. He knew the unwanted hug would exasperate his reoccurring trauma to unbearable levels. It had started almost immediately, and he knew it wouldn't let up. It would only get worse. It had been all he could do to keep it in and keep it together throughout the investigation and then the patch-up by Chloe. His losing control was not something he wanted them so see. And yet, he'd failed.

At the very end, when he'd almost made it, Doc had pilfered a bottle of wine. Right in front of them. He so desperately needed something to dull the roaring demons within him. Something to ease the pain of what was to come. He'd tucked that bottle in the flap of his jacket, and walked out. The moment he'd done it, he was sorry. It wasn't him to take what wasn't his. But once he felt the weight of it in his pocket, there was no turning back.

Perhaps, if the old gal understood that it was a matter of drowning the evil that had surfaced resulting from the incident, she might have handed it to him herself. Try as he may to convince himself that the bottle was merely a well-earned reward for his heroics, he couldn't escape the truth. She hadn't handed him the bottle herself. He hadn't even given her a chance to. He'd taken it, right in front of the one person that believed he was wholly good—the boy.

Back on the broken pallet, leaning against the cold spray-painted wall, he tried again to reassure himself. *I'll pay for the bottle. First thing in the morning.* He wouldn't, of course. He had no way of paying for the bottle. The terrible hole in his chest grew deeper and wider each time he attempted to recite the promise to himself.

Over the course of the night, while the other bums moseyed around aimlessly and licked at the spoiled contents of dirty cans they'd found in the dumpsters, Doc poured the bottle of wine into that deepening hole. The sweet liquid was neither satisfying nor fruitful. It was doomed from the beginning. Everything his hand touched always turned to dust. He was no healer, as he used to dream of becoming. He was no hero.

Doc held on to consciousness, cowering from his nightmares, and the truth of his failures, for as long as he could. He thought, *I can hold on a little bit longer*, as he faded away.

Sweat poured down Doc's face. It should have stung his eyes. They were blurry for sure. Still, he kept running, kept firing, kept trying to get to them. He knew he'd reach them. He always did. Not that it did much good in the end. Maybe this time he could change that. If he tried hard enough, he could change that.

Ahead, he saw Young and Flores carrying Ramirez to a place of cover behind a short, crumbling wall. It wasn't much of a cover; cover was a scarce commodity since the Taliban had occupied the buildings and the hills. The Taliban had a clear shot at almost every angle. It was the worst trap Doc had ever been caught in. Even so, he ran through the hailstorm of bullets. It was his job, his calling, to help people.

Doc arrived behind the crumbling wall at the same time as Young and Flores did, Ramirez strung between them like a roasting pig. Doc kept his gun up, guarding their backs, their fronts, their sides. The moment they laid Ramirez in the dirt, Doc and Young seamlessly preformed half of a do-si-do—without the flamboyant, hooped skirts—consequently trading places.

Ramirez was choking on the water Flores had offered him. Most of it was dribbling down, combining with the dirt on his neck, and the blood from the gash in his forehead.

Expertly, Doc sheared open Ramirez's blood-soaked pant leg, locating where the bullet had entered. Quickly, he turned the leg as much as he dared, looking for an exit wound. There was none. That wasn't good. It was better to go clean through. Doc went to work on wrapping it with a bandage. Getting the bullet out would require surgery. Later.

Doc was wrapping up Ramirez's pressure bandage as the sound of a close-range firefight erupted. The noise struck Doc's ears like a thousand bees. He knew every sting by heart. He'd heard them replayed, over and over, a thousand times.

Young bolted off toward the roar.

"Shit!" Flores yelled, clearly torn.

"Go!" Doc yelled. "I've got Ramirez!"

Flores didn't have to be told twice. He was gone in less than a tick.

Goosebumps swept over Doc. He knew what happened next.

No matter how vigorously he swept the unending deadly landscape with his rifle, trying to pop a bullet into every approaching shadowy figure, nothing ever changed. The bearded men just kept coming. They were no longer shadowy figures but giants. Giant men with guns. Giant men yelling angry words that didn't sound like words at all. Gibberish.

Ramirez, even in his dazed state, picked up his rifle and began firing what was left of his ammo. Between the two of them, men did fall, but it felt as though they just stood right back up and keep rushing. Ramirez stopped shooting.

"Fire, Ramirez!" Doc screamed. He needed Ramirez's help. They weren't making it without him. "Fire!"

Ramirez did nothing.

Doc glanced over his shoulder, wondering if Ramirez had run out of ammo. But what he saw was what he had already known. Of course, he knew. It went this way every time. Still, every time, Doc willed it to change.

Sometimes Ramirez, with a bullet hole through his head, would speak to Doc, tell Doc it would be all right, for both of them. Those times, Doc would rush to him and wrap him up in his arms. "I'm sorry," Doc would cry. "I'm sorry!"

Other times, Ramirez, with a bullet hole through his head, would just stare off past Doc, seeing nothing. Saying nothing. He couldn't, because the back of his head been blown open, his brains spewed on the ground in tiny chunks. With no other choice, Doc turned back to the fight. But he'd already lost.

A dozen rifle muzzles stared down on him. The bearded men were ecstatic, screaming even louder now. Their voices thundered like a stampede of elephants in his pounding head. Doc lifted the muzzle of his own rifle, ready to take one last man down with him, but his rifle was ripped from his hands. Closing his eyes, he waited for the sensation of a bullet to drill a hole through his skull at a velocity twice the speed of sound. In these nightmares, Ramirez sometimes seemed to think everything could end up okay. So, longingly, Doc looked forward to that one-time Ramirez would be right.

What seemed like a hundred hands reached down and plucked him off the ground as easily as he'd once plucked a flower for a pretty *neighbor girl. However, this flower was kicking and screaming, putting up a mighty fuss as they dragged him across the deity-forsaken land. He refused to go easily, and he sure as hell refused to be captured alive. He'd rather be shot for making trouble than stripped and burned for all of the villagers to marvel at.*

Squirming like a toddler in a uniform and boots, he screamed at them, "Shoot me, you Mother—"

They paid him no heed and continued dragging him over the uneven ground. A sharp rock jutting out from the crusted dirt, coarsely rasped over Doc's spine, splitting the flesh open to bone. Hollering at the first of many approaching agonies, he bucked his body so hard that he came down on that very same sharp rock with the back of his skull.

In a world that seemed so very far away to everyone except Doc, everything would have gone dark at that point. In the nightmare version, however, he would have been unluckily transported to the exact moment he'd regained consciousness. However, in this episode of Doc and the worst day ever, the vivid memory of the blow of the rock woke him from his unpleasant slumber with a jolt.

It took Doc's eyes a few full rotations of observing his surroundings to feed his mind with enough information to convince his hammering heart that he was no longer in the grip of the Taliban, fearing both life and death. Now that he was awake, and somewhat aware, he'd narrowed it down to fearing only life.

Here in this unwitting world where people think the act of being *free* is the equivalent of being *idle* and that maintaining that freedom—which was paid for with blood—are simple acts of being amenable, Doc was a prisoner. People stared with their critical, disapproving eyes. They, the very ones he'd volunteered to lay himself down for so that they could live free without any true understanding of the evils of the world, judged him without facts, without a jury, and without grace. He was a prisoner of war, right here in America.

When he'd first been discharged, the Army counselor had said, "Time will heal your emotional wounds, as well as your physical ones." She'd been wrong. He took all those lacerations everywhere he went. He'd have to take them, oozing, to his grave. The same counselor had also encouraged him to "Go home to your parents. They've reached out to me and they want to help you." Well, his parents may have started out wanting to help, but it didn't take long for them to start discussing having him admitted to a mental hospital so that they didn't have to be woken in the dead of the night by his terrifying screaming. They had shoved so many pills down his throat he'd turned into a drooling zombie. Finally, he managed to walk (stumble) away, with nothing but the clothes on his back. He hadn't contacted them since.

All of his old high school buddies had cautiously treated him like a ticking bomb. Understandably, they didn't want anything to do with him past muttering, "Hey, nice to see you," through their lying teeth. After all, they had families now. Some of them had kids to protect from the likes of people like him.

But it was his Army brothers who wore him down to a lifeless nub on the inside. They were all dead, of course. So the only voices they had were the cruel ones that Doc assigned to them. They were always cutting him down, telling him he'd not saved any one of them, that he should have died, that he hadn't suffered, as they had. There was no point in arguing; they were right. He agreed unequivocally.

But some days, it hurt a little more. A little differently maybe. Today, he needed to feel something other than what he deserved. Today, he needed to feel something he *didn't* deserve. Just once. He wasn't asking for a pool of compassion. Just a granule. No. Scratch that. Smaller than a granule. He'd take smaller than a granule. A super tiny speck. Just a speck of mercy could maybe save his soul.

"Please?" Doc begged the early dawn, absently rubbing the always-present black leather bracelet on his arm. His voice echoed off the long, spray-painted wall. "Please?"

All the other homeless folk were still wrapped tightly in their tarps and bags, either paying him no mind, or simply unable to hear him over the howling of their own demons.

Doc's demons dug in their talons, and he screamed angrily. "I'm *not* all right, Ramirez! I'm not all right!" Something in him broke, and his demons stepped back just enough to let Doc's grief overtake him. He began to sob. "Why can't I just be with you?" he pleaded.

Of course, the early dawn had no words of wisdom it was willing to share.

"I'm already dead on the inside. Why? Why am I still alive?"

It's your fault.

"*How's* it my fault?" he bellowed daringly. Once, just once, he wanted to know what he could have done differently to change the outcome. If he could go back, he would do anything to change it. Anything.

You could have been a better soldier, a better medic. That would have done the trick.

Doc's heart sunk to depth unmeasurable. That would have done the trick. He knew that. He covered his shameful face with his equally shameful hands and sobbed.

Chapter Eight

1

The next morning, Mailman woke to the obnoxious sound of a barking dog and the same thought that had been running circles in his head all night. *Who the f--k had that been? No regular bum off the streets, that's who.* Mailman had spun on that question since he'd arrived back at his apartment He sat up from his restless slumber, feeling no more revived than the filthy mattress he'd given a brief pat before declaring safe enough to sleep on.

The pay he'd received from Orson had made it possible to put a roof over his head. He hadn't been able to afford to turn on the heat or air-conditioning yet, but there was a roof over his head and a lock on the door. If only Orson trusted him to pick up all of the monthly fees rather than just deliver messages (like a good little mailman) to his section, he would be able to pocket enough extra cash for things like heat, and maybe even a mattress that didn't smell like puke and piss. Hell, he could steal a mattress, but he couldn't steal heat or air-conditioning.

Yesterday, when he'd gotten home, he'd slammed the door so hard a picture had fallen off the wall and crashed to the floor. That's when the neighbor's dog had begun its barking. The picture and the glass were still on the floor in shards, and the neighbor's dog was still barking. He groped at the back of his head, not surprised at all to find a sore lump there and a mess of hair that was pasted together where the blood had dried. On the floor was his favorite hat. Only by the grace of the fire gods had he managed to pick it up off the store floor before he'd run. The nasty couch that the last tenant had left behind, he'd scooted it across the hard floor last night with an angry kick. It had let out a loud wooden squawk then, and now it glared at him from its awkward angle across the small room.

"Don't look at me that way, or I'll throw your out and burn you into a pile of ashes. Actually, that sounds pretty good, useless piece of garbage."

There was another useless piece of garbage that he wanted to burn. That scrawny bum who had hit him over the head. He'd gotten the surprise on him, that's all, he was only street scrap—meant to be fed on by the dogs. Even then, Mailman had easily gotten away from him, unscathed. That guy had no real stake in the game. Still, that scrap had cost him his pistol. He should have known the old bat's homeless squad would be stationed close by, even during the day. Using street scrap like junk yard dogs was almost laughable. Bums don't feel concern. Most of them are too high to feel anything. The old bat was a fool. However, despite her stupidity, Mailman was convinced she was good for the money.

Customers strolled in and out of that joint like it read "Saloon" on the sign and had music and drinks overflowing into the street. She was a greedy woman. And arrogant. So arrogant. Had she just handed over the money he'd politely requested, he wouldn't be seething in his boring apartment with a pounding head. Instead, he would be standing in front of Orson with the money (most of it anyway) saying, "The old bat's deposit on her insurance policy, your Highness." Then Orson would have wiped that stupid scowl off his stupid face and seen that Mailman was someone with purpose and action. Just like Orson's stupid wall slogan peddled.

Mailman had found himself using hours upon hours of the night doing some hate-thinking. Aside from fire, it was one of his favorite things to do. It had an oddly centering effect on him that had earned him all sorts of names growing up. He'd learned to cork it, when necessary, but he much preferred it uncorked. He enjoyed the high of hate, and it helped him deliberate and prioritize important matters.

Considering the day's event, Mailman found himself hate-thinking about the "missing float." During his report to Orson, news about the old bat store owner (or the lack of news thereof) had glided right by Orson's unsuspecting nose. The "all-knowing" ringleader hadn't even noticed that he'd left her out completely. At the time, Mailman had been afraid that his lack of progress with her would have made him look less-than to the others or, worse, been grounds for demotion—or dismissal. But now…now that he'd done his hate-thinking, he could see the picture much more clearly.

Orson Finlay wasn't as worthy of all this highly regarded hype he'd been receiving as everyone seemed to think he was. Maybe his name had been time honored but likely not merited. Mailman had heard that Orson had stolen the gig from his old man. Offed him, right in front of his mother. But what if that's all he'd really done to deserve the title of Big Bad Orson Finlay? Shoot, Mailman had offed a couple of someones too and had rather liked it. It was said, Orson could be *gracious*. What did that mean? Mailman thought it meant the Big Bad Orson wasn't so big and so bad. He'd venture to say that the man was weak.

Mailman smiled. *There seems to be a giant unadvertised opening in Finlay's hierarchy. Orson ought to be careful, or else someone could take it.*

Still, first thing was first. Mailman needed to prove that he was worthy, where Orson Finlay was not. Which included stepping up his game. No more costly mistakes.

2

"You made a mistake today, friend," Orson growled into the face of an individual easily identified by the small tattoo on his neck of a silvery colored spider with a prominent air bubble attached to its abdomen. "What's a Water Spider doing crawling here? You must be lost."

The young Water Spider member announced, "I wasn't aware these were your parts."

Although, the trespasser was only a block into Orson's territory, he appeared neither surprised nor intimidated. The two pals standing just behind him also appeared unsurprised. The one with a hook-shaped scar above his lip looked a mite edgy, and Orson knew why. It was almost rib-tickling.

"Here I am taking a stroll down the lane, enjoying the morning air, and you three dupes show up to piss on my picnic."

"I don't see any picnics," said the Water Spider, an overconfident grin drawing a thin line between his button nose and hairless chin. "Picnics require friends, and you like to eat breakfast alone."

Orson looked at him skeptically. "Am I on my way to breakfast, or have I already eaten?"

The grin stretched a little wider. "You've already eaten."

"I'm impressed, you've done your research. I must admit, I'm behind the curve on you boys cause, well, I simply don't give a shit about you. But let me see if I can play a quick game of catch-up." He stroked his beard. "It seems that one of you here hasn't earned his tattoo yet. How miserable for him. So, what's it to be? A group patty cake match? Last one clapping gets an entertaining spider tattoo? That's one tatt I don't want skittering about on my skin. Have you ever considered changing it to something more…threatening?"

The Water Spider gang was made up of primarily Asian members, indicated by their name, from where the actual tiny underwater spiders are found. Despite the spider's size, their venomous fangs deliver a mighty punch that would leave a person seeking medical services. Being referred to as a spider usually implies that the person spins complex and involved webs to tangle and trap victims. However, it was usually the female water spiders that spent the most time on their underwater web-making. Not the males. Orson wondered if he should tell the men standing in front of him, or just keep it to himself.

He decided to keep it to himself. Water Spiders was, after all, an accurate description of the gang. They spun their plans into complex little webs, and, in turn, their robberies, invasions, identity thefts, and murders, were usually successful. Besides, tattoos are sort of permanent. Like the Finlays, the Water Spiders had started out as a family. Unlike the Finlays, not much had changed over the years.

The original Finlay family business was comprised of drug trafficking, human trafficking, and the big one, murder. Finlay Senior's biggest fear tactic was his notoriously quick and bloodthirsty draw. Crossing him was not on the menu. You either made a point to not cross paths with him, pledged absolute allegiance to him, or had your rotting flesh assist in fertilizing Seattle's most unsuspecting soils. It was a tidy—brutal—process, with no room for bend. Living under the roof with such a man had been the worst kind of hell.

There'd been many times that Orson had felt he was breathing his last breath over something as small as grades or rebellious teenage attitude. His mother, Victoria, on many occasions, had been the only thin thread standing between he and his father. Although the fabric of her power was thin as silk, she was as adored by Orson's father as she herself loved silk. Being that Victoria was the single human born on this earth that Finlay Senior vowed never to touch when angry, her words, "If Orson's blood soaks into this earth, it's as good as mine," always caused him to pause long enough for Orson to live another day. However, there'd finally occurred an instance that forced Orson to change the family dynamic forever.

Once again, Orson was being beaten within an inch of his life. This time it was for having accidently stumbled upon one of the human shipments' verifying photographs lying openly on the table. It being a half-day at school, he'd returned home early. He'd simply walked by the table when a photograph amongst a few papers had caught his eye. It was at least twenty Latino women, all lying huddled together in almost complete darkness. This was the first time Orson had learned of this venue of his father's business, and it would certainly be the first time his mother would have heard of it.

Father's rage had been quick and pitiless. All Orson could hear was the grunting of Father as he pounded his giant boot into Orson's gut and head, again and again.

Victoria entered the room in her soft slippers, a loaded revolver in her hand.

Victoria wasn't one for guns or killing, though she was well aware that her husband was. She'd only killed a man once, and although she hadn't liked it, she didn't regret it. The man had busted into her room, hell bent on defiling the great Finlay's oh-so-treasured wife as relished retribution. She'd shot him in self-defense with the revolver she kept in her nightstand, but he hadn't died. He'd collapsed on the floor, moaning for mercy. So, before her husband's goons could reach the bedroom and deliver him to undergo an unending amount of torture, she'd shot him again, killing him. For the sake of mercy.

When her maid had hastily run to her declaring that Orson was being killed at the hand of her husband, Victoria retrieved that same revolver from inside her nightstand. She'd found her eighteen-year-old son smashed against the floor, no longer even able to protectively cradle himself in a fetal position. His blood was running about the granite flooring. She'd pulled back the hammer of her revolver, pointed it at the man she'd vowed to love and protect – which she had up until that point.

Decisively, Victoria announced, "If Orson's blood soaks into this earth on this day, or ever again, it's as good as *yours*."

The thick tension that had filled the room on that somber day, and the uncertain stillness in his father, whispered that Victoria's finger was lightly feathering the touchy trigger. Finlay's recently born hate for his traitorous wife was rolling off of him in waves that Orson could feel even in his unsteady state. It was in that critical moment Orson decided his father's reign had to be done away with.

Orson had beckoned his mother to his side, begging for her to be sensible and not shoot dear daddy. Not wanting to truly kill her husband—she loved him after all—she went to Orson's side. She crouched down next to him, her robed knees soaking up the slick blood.

"I'm sorry," Orson whispered, then ripped the revolver from her hands, and pushed her away.

Orson shot his father. Shot him, not once, but with all six bullets in the cylinder. Unsurprisingly, it took all six bullets to bring down such a callous, cold-blooded man. Once the old man had fallen, *his* blood flowing all over the floor, and Victoria screaming uncontrollably, Orson crawled over to his father. Using the butt end of the revolver, he pounded his father's thick skull until it caved in. Orson remembered, vividly, that glimpse of exposed, pink-colored brain tissue. At the time, he'd thought it curious—he'd thought it'd be black.

Once Finlay Senior was fertilizing a section of Seattle's most unsuspecting soil, Orson claimed the family business and all of its assets. Naturally, he'd kept the familiar drug trafficking, in addition to calculated brutality in order to secure his place, but he'd moved away from human trafficking. It was neither his nor Victoria's style to steal people. Some may say that the Finlay's stole lives through the consumption of and addictions to drugs, but it was strictly a voluntary program. It didn't take long to secure the majority of his father's known territories. Then, slowly he began adopting a new angle that would serve to protect him, and his prospering business. Community insurance.

Citizens and businesses needed protection from rising violent gang activity. The cops could no longer provide adequate protection because the powers that be had replaced their officers' cuffs with wooden-handled mops. It was hysterically comical. All their ridiculous red tape gave Orson's men ample time to sit, have a picnic, and duck (as if that were necessary) while they batted blindly about trying to catch fruit flies with fishing nets. All of this, of course, gave Orson free power. With that power, Orson decided he could do a hair better. With a word, Orson decided what happened, and didn't happen, inside of his territory. With such power he created a protection plan far above what any police agency could do. All that was required of a citizen were two very simple and easy fees.

1) Silence in regard to any of Orson's activity.
2) A small monthly cash installment. It wasn't excessive. Orson didn't need their money. He had money. He required only enough that confidently spoke on the citizen's behalf that they were unequivocally "in."

Orson felt that having the community "in," rather than "out" was a game changer. It was an idea that the other gangs had yet to pick up on. A gang's worst enemy wasn't the police, or even rivals. It was society. Society was holding all the cards. Admitted, or not, society was the field in which crime was sowed. A gang couldn't simply wipe out the community surrounding it, or it'd be wiping out itself. One would be a fool to wipe out your own fields of prosperity, recruits, and honest, hardworking veils in which to conceal your illegal money-making goings-on. Such was Orson's experimental angle, and it was making him near bullet-proof. He was actually gaining society's support. Much more powerful than their fear. Yes, a lot had changed since his father had become fertilizer. All for the better.

Hook Lip stepped forward. "You're right, I must earn my tattoo. I mean you no harm."

Orson nearly choked on his own laughter. "Well, bust my fiddle. I find myself so relieved. I hadn't realized my life was hanging so precariously before your merciful threads."

Hook Lip seemed unfazed by Orson's sarcastic declaration. "My initiation is not to harm you. That would be unwise."

Oh, so right you are.

"I must show my ability to negotiate. All I need is a strand of hair cut from your beard."

Orson looked at Hook Lip as though the small man was entirely insane. He added a scowl for good measure and growled, "Grow one."

Hook Lip actually chuckled, and even his "friends" were looking at him like he was insane. "Not mine. Yours. May I?" he asked, taking a step forward and holding out a hand as though he were making friends with a shy kitten.

It was Orson's turn to chuckle. "You're straight up asking me for a piece of my beard? You've got some grapefruit-sized gonads."

"It's said, if you want something, you must ask."

"Who said that?" Orson asked.

Hook Lip looked around bashfully and quietly answered, "My mother."

Orson chuckled again, as did his "friends" that were looking more and more like cold-footed brides, slowly backing away from a huge mistake. But Orson was starting to have fun. He stroked his beard. "And if I say no? Then what?"

"We negotiate."

"All right then. No. Now what?" Orson asked, curiously. Hook Lip looked slightly taken off-guard. Had he truly expected his charm to work so easily? "Do you even know who I am?" Orson asked. It wasn't rhetorical.

"Your name is Orson."

"Yes. Anything else?" Orson raised his eyebrows expectantly.

Hook Lip shoved out his hand, and Orson grabbed it, ready to break the arm into two separate pieces. "My name is Tom," Hook Lip declared.

"Don't tell him your name, you—" the two cold-footed brides began lecturing angrily. It looked like the initiation wasn't going so well for poor Tom.

"Tom?" Orson asked, quite entertained. "You're shitting me!"

"No," Hook Lip said, "I wouldn't shit on you, sir."

Orson laughed. "You can't possibly be a *Tom*."

"Tom," Hook Lip confirmed. "Let's speak of how I can convince you for a piece of beard."

"No. Instead, you tell me why you're hanging with these arthropods?"

"Money for my family."

"Well, are you good at thieving?"

Hook Lip glanced behind him. His "friends" were growing progressively more and more angry and unsatisfied with his performance.

"Don't look at them. Look at me. Have you ever stolen anything?"

Hook Lip lifted his chin proudly. "No, I negotiate."

"How's that going for you, so far?"

"Well, with the time limit I've been given, a little bad."

Orson felt his scowl deepen as he switched his focus to the leader. "How much time does he have left?"

The leader's thin grin returned. "He's out."

Just then a young lady with flowing red hair and a white apron tied about her waist began sprinting down the sidewalk toward them all. "Mr. Finlay! Mr. Finlay!" she was shouting. A white takeout box was swinging to the rhythm of her pumping arms. "You forgot your extras!" she called.

Orson held up a hand to her, stopping her in her tracks. "Go back, Cynthia. I'll retrieve my extras when my business here is concluded." Cynthia didn't wait for an explanation, but spun on her heel and returned the way, and at the same speed, in which she had come.

Orson turned back to Hook Lip. "These dupes set you up for failure, Tom. You were never going to succeed, and they knew as much from the beginning." Orson turned to the dupes. "So, the question remaining is, what happens upon failure, boys?" No one answered because everyone, but Hook Lip, knew the answer. Orson asked another question. "Why don't you give Tom a head start, since you conned him into my territory to be gunned down?"

Hook Lip's face drained of color. Could have been having just learned that he'd been talking to the boss all along? Could have been hearing that his "friends" had been planning his convenient death in order to be rid of him. Could have been his breakfast wasn't sitting too well. Or maybe all of the above. Who knew?

Dupe One and Dupe Two pulled pistols from their oversized pants. Orson mirrored them in an improved version of their own reflection—faster and more precise—and ended with a pistol in both of his hands. The dupes had their muzzles pointed at the back of Hook Lip's head.

"This ain't about you, Orson," Dupe Two clarified.

Orson marveled at their level of overconfidence. Chances were, Dupe Two was right and felt his statement was a relevant clarification since Orson was the backdrop and it would be unwise to start a war. In which case, all Orson had to do was take a step sideways and leave them to it. Then again, there was another chance. The entire situation could be one big grand scheme, in which Hook Lip wasn't the target at all.

Hook Lip had yet to reach for a weapon. Likely he didn't have one, making him a definite target. Perhaps not the *sole* target, however.

A partial Dr. Seuss poem materialized in Orson's mind. He hadn't even thought of Dr. Seuss since he was five.

One fish. Two fish.

Little fish. Huge fish.

Orson was not a fan of chances. Especially when it came to his life. He was an enthusiast of certainty. The one thing he was certain of right now was, he had extras waiting for him down the walk that he'd planned to eat for lunch. Yes, he could afford fresh, but he liked the marinated flavor of extras after having been reheated. That's why he always ordered extra. Call him bizarre.

The ear-ringing thunder of gunfire split the air on either side of Hook Lip, who'd closed his eyes as tight as a fish's ass. Both Dupe's bodies jolted before they fell. Neither had the time to squeeze their triggers. Orson was his father's son after all. For better or worse.

Hook Lip's eyes flew open when he'd received no holes and flinched as Orson stomped past him. Orson put a shot in each Dupe's head. Brain matter splattered behind them. Hook Lip's hand flew to his mouth, and his eyes looked just like the eyes of the fish with the tight ass.

Orson looked at Hook Lip's surprised eyes ogling the tiny chunks of pink brain matter. "Thought it would be black, didn't you?" he asked.

"Huh? No," Hook Lip answered, sounding and looking a little green around the gills.

Orson shrugged. "Guess that was just me."

Hook Lip shifted his weight over both feet, though neither were steady. "I told you the truth when I said I mean you no harm, sir."

"You said that." Orson pulled his phone from his pocket and sent a quick text in code. "Walk with me, Hook Lip."

"Hook what?" Hook Lip asked, but Orson was pulling ahead. "Okay," he said, jogging to catch up. "Yes, sir." He glanced over his shoulder at the bodies lying on the ground. "What about—"

Orson slapped him on the back, aiding in pushing him along. "Don't worry about them. Are you as good with numbers as you are negotiating?"

"Sir?"

"I may be in need of someone with negotiating skills like yours. For now, though, I've lost an accountant. I need a replacement."

"Lost?"

"He died."

Hook Lip looked over his shoulder again. A car pulled up and was "taking care of" the scene. Orson turned toward the cafe where Cynthia would be waiting with his extras. But Hook Lip paused. He looked a little queasy yet.

"Are you coming in?"

"Orson…Mr. Finlay, sir. How did the accountant die?"

"I didn't kill him, if that's what you're asking. He was seventy-three and had been eating cheeseburgers for every f--king meal since he left the nipple.

"The only things that I ask is that anything you may see or hear, never was seen or heard, and your work shall never be mentioned. Note to the wise, its best if you think only in terms of numbers, nothing more. Keep it simple, and it'll provide for your family until you die of heart disease, or whatever other disease you decide to subject yourself to."

"One condition, sir."

Orson gave Hook Lip an expression of impatience.

"Piece of beard?"

Orson laughed. "Grow one." Then he turned and went inside, leaving Hook Lip in the doorway, grinning the proud grin of a man who had been better at negotiating than he had thought.

Chapter Nine

1

A hundred hands were ripping him apart.

All Doc could see were faces and turban-covered heads. They bobbed within inches of his face, obscuring the sight of anything beyond. Hands were crawling over him like an angry mound of red fire ants. Instead of biting, they tore away fabric, pocket contents, his belt, his weapons. They disarmed him of every last possession they stumbled across. The joke was on them. He didn't have much left. But they couldn't steal his fight. He would fight until his last breath. He'd be damned if he'd roll over and let the Taliban use him against his fellow soldiers and civilians.

"Get off me! Get off—" Doc yelled, kicking and punching.

He'd taken one of the men by surprise. The sole of Doc's boot came into contact with the sensitive area of one of the men's groins. In return, the butt end of a rifle connected with Doc's cheek bone, sending his head spinning around until the side of his face was halted abruptly by the hard ground. Wildly aware that the back of his head felt like someone had taken a chain mace to it, he recalled it having been struck it against a protruding rock before losing consciousness. Remarkably, even that agonizing pain wasn't his number-one pressing concern at the moment. He had to keep fighting. No matter what they did to him later, he had to make them pay now.

Doc kicked again, with all of his might, and caught another Taliban member (or maybe the same one, it was hard to tell) under the chin. The man's teeth clacked loudly at the force of his jaw being driven into his skull. Stumbling backwards, the man disappeared, but three more men took his place, dogpiling on Doc's legs. Seemingly unaware of all of the commotion of their compadres, the others groped endlessly at every fold of Doc's uniform as if it were their last chance at immortality.

Although Doc tried repeatedly to buck off the weight of the men, the effort was futile and exhausting. Each new labor was less persuasive then the last. Still, he kept at it the best he could, not ready to die just yet. He wondered why they didn't simply kill him. It would make their pilfering job a whole lot easier. If they were keeping his life intact to make some sort of public display, they could think again. As long as his heart was beating, he'd continue to fight. As surely as the wind met their dry, cursing lips. If it was torture that they wanted, they could come and get it. But it wouldn't be free.

Two disgruntled Taliban began arguing bitterly over Doc's backup pistol that had been jammed beneath his uniform. Consumed by their desire for ownership, simultaneously, they released both of Doc's arms. Perhaps they merely presumed their domination over him had been made clear enough that holding him down was no longer necessary. Wrong.

Doc lashed out, grabbed both of their heads and smashed them together with a blunt thunk. "Screw you!" he shouted and then sunk his teeth into the dust-covered forearm of someone who attempted to regain control of him.

The taste of earth and salt and blood rushed through Doc's senses before the arm was yanked away. He was grabbed up by the hair on his head. All of the once-intact hair follicles screamed silently as they were ripped from his scalp. Doc's head fell back to the ground with a sickening thud. When he blinked his heavy eyes open, the hand that had picked him up was still clutching a fistful of hair, tauntingly, as if daring him to reach up and take it back.

Doc had lost track of who had hold of what or where the pistol had disappeared to. Before he could muster the strength to continue his fight, a hot, searing sensation slashed through the upper cartilage of his ear. He heard himself holler as the faces around him laughed and chattered. A *warm liquid dripped into his ear canal, and he knew. They'd cut off a piece of his ear, like that of an earmarked stock animal. The man who'd done the cutting flung the piece of ear behind him like a superstitious person would throw salt over the shoulder for luck. Glaring down at Doc, the man seized him by the jugular and jaw in one fell swoop. There was no time for objections. Grimy fingers snaffled Doc's mouth open with a piece of rolled up fabric that tasted like a goat's back end. Then the man presented a knife, holding it closely for Doc to study. From the fresh smeared blood shining brightly over numerous layers of caked and dried-on blood from unknown sources, Doc figured it was the same knife that had been used to slice off his ear. The man smiled, then stuck the tip of the knife in Doc's mouth, digging into the gum beneath his lower incisor. Horror rushed through Doc's veins as he realized that he was about to have all of his teeth extracted.*

The loud familiar sound of rounds being fired from an American weapon filled Doc's ears. The echoes coincided with the strange jolting motion of the men hovering around him. Some crumbled slowly like cake being dunked in coffee. Others fell as quickly as mosquitos that had drawn too close to a patio bug zapper. The asshole preparing to try his hand at dental school 101 turned, crouching and alarmed. Reflexively ripping the knife out of Doc's mouth, he readied himself to use it in battle. The blade, probably decades old, sliced a thin slit in Doc's lip as it exited. A tic of blood seeped out. No attention was paid to such an insignificant wound. An altruistic soul, whether he was an enslaved farmer or an infidel-hater weighted to the old Islamic law—differing severely when put side by side to such things as democracy, human rights, freedom of thought, and women's rights—lifted the pistol that Doc recognized as his own. The affronted man pointed it at Doc's head.

For a soldier about to undergo execution, Doc felt moderately calm. Did he want to survive? Yes, very much. But the important thing in his current circumstance was that someone from his side was here and shooting up a hailstorm. Whoever it was would be able to retrieve his body. In the end—the very end—all he wanted was to be taken home. It was an odd comfort amidst the chaos, knowing he would be laid to rest on home soil, not left here to have his bones spat on and feasted upon by wild dogs.

Preparing what could very well be his last effort, to assist whoever had come to aid him, Doc primed himself to lunge at the man pointing the pistol at his head. Right before Doc sprang, the man's body lurched abnormally. For a brief moment, the man with Doc's pistol resembled nothing more than a terribly dressed mannequin, with eyes wide and frozen. Then, his pistol arm slowly dropped as his brain began conveying that a round had punctured his heart. The man sank to his knees, as though to pray, only he didn't. Instead, he toppled over. Without request or consent, the ground of all ages commenced to soaking up his blood, the same as it had done for countless others.

Doc pried the pistol from the man's hand and checked it. Empty. It hadn't been loaded. Quickly as possible, he was stuffing it back into his uniform when a pair of hands grabbed him. He jerked, prepared once more to get back into the fight. Knowing a friendly, with ammunition, was nearby, gave him hope.

Doc buried his elbow into the face that presented itself an instant before it came into focus. Unfortunately, it was the face of Sergeant Green that came into focus. Doc was relieved to see it and felt himself breathe, which is something he hadn't recalled doing, until just now. After having just taken an elbow, with blood spurting from his nose, Green didn't appear nearly as pleased.

"If you'd been anyone else, Doc," Green growled, moping his nose with his sleeve, "I would have decked you back. No matter how shitty you look."

Doc allowed himself to be hefted into a sitting position. "You still can. I'm glad to see you either way."

"Can you walk?" Green asked.

"Yeah," Doc answered and began positioning his partially numb legs under himself.

Green hoisted Doc to his feet, stationing himself in Doc's armpit and grabbing his waist. Doc, with his arm over Green's shoulder, began running. The two of them looked like best buddies running excitedly *through a county fair to the next carnival ride. Only there was no county fair, and there were no carnival rides. There was only the constant pounding of pain in Doc's head and a throbbing ear. The occasional burst from Green's rifle kept his mind alive enough to keep his feet moving. He didn't know where they were headed, or to what end. But anything was better than where he'd just come.*

Minds were designed to be changed.

2

Despite an elephant-like build with arms like tusks, Billy had always had a master. He stood behind his most recent boss, Rawson. Rawson had on him two pounds of meth and a Glock.

The pusher approaching them, wearing a grungy outfit and beanie cap that should have been plugging a toilet somewhere was one of Rawson's long-time buyers. More likely than a preacher clutching a bible, the pusher was concealing a Sig Sauer, the civilian version of the Army's M18, and inspiration to its human namesake. Sig had probably tucked the pistol close to the ten thousand dollars he was about to surrender. All in exchange for a supply of crystalized candy. Interactions with this particular pusher were usually quick and to the point, but it was imprudent to assume that past remained present. You never know where a man's head was, or what kind of corner he'd backed himself into since the last time you'd met with him. There was always risk involved during the transfer of money and candy.

Thus, the employment of "Backup Billy." That's how Rawson referred to Billy.

Billy had learned in grade school, quite by accident, that when he wanted something, all he needed to do was step into a person's space. That person almost always cowered. He could see it in their eyes as they peered upwards at him. His size alone intimidated them. It was a good thing too, because truly, Billy didn't want to hurt anyone. And *being* hurt in return, which almost always seemed the case when two kids got into it, was not on his list of top ten. However, over the years, he'd discovered, even when he had to step into brutal mode, he was rarely badly hurt. Muscle building helped. Then there were a few tricks up his sleeve and, of course, his size. More so, when paired with a boss who was known for being both commanding and dangerous, Billy rarely had to do anything but stand at the stern and hover menacingly.

Sig reached them, stepping into the shadows of the bridge they met beneath.

"You brought my smiles?" Rawson asked expectantly.

Sig patted the left chest of his thick jacket. "Two pounds worth."

Sig was waiting for permission to reach into his pocket. Anyone who dealt with Rawson knew not to reach for anything until approval had been bestowed. Rawson may have lost a client or two with such policies as "shoot first, ask later," but he'd never been relieved of his supply without a proper amount of respect and cashola.

"Good. Let's see it."

Just as Sig was reaching into his jacket, a ghastly-looking creature caught Billy's eye. The creature was grubby with long, dark hair and an Army-green jacket. He was walking—no, stumbling—toward them. He looked like a drunk bum, but he could also be a rat or a cop in disguise.

"Wait," said Billy. Sig stopped reaching for his paper dough. "On your right, boss," he alerted Rawson. "Bones outside the graveyard."

Rawson turned his head, also observing the staggering fool drawing nearer by the second. It was unclear what the fool's objective was, or if he was even conscious to the world around him, let alone what he was about to walk into—a stream of trouble. If cops presented themselves, Billy would take the man hostage while he let Rawson slip safely away. If no cops presented themselves, the man was certain to catch a bullet rather than the butterflies he seemed to be chasing.

Hunkered in a dark slot beneath the bridge, on the outer edge of what was transpiring, a woman was watching all of this take place. She was the type of person no one paid any attention to. It was no secret that people like her neither had anything to lose, nor gain, by becoming involved in illegal street affairs. In fact, she occasionally benefited from such illegal substances when she had the means. Now, with her partner gone, she had no one to care about, nor anyone to care about her. There was no reason to keep her head above water anymore.

This forty-three-year-old woman with fading, red-dyed hair was about to roll over and pretend to be dead herself until she noticed something familiar about the man lurching and floundering along. She squinted at the light beyond her little camp spot. The daylight was bright compared to the hole she was hiding in. Yes, she recognized him. She was sure of it. This was the man from the park who had a tendency to scream, and sometimes walk, as he slept. She'd pitied him once—he being all alone. Then she'd called him son of a motherless goat, which he full well deserved after what he'd said to her that day. She'd vowed not to allow herself to pity him again.

Now, she watched as he unknowingly lurched and swayed dangerously towards the middle of a deal. She wondered to herself, would he wake just before they killed him, or would a bullet zing through his head as he slept? Either way, son of a motherless goat was about to be stuck in a hell to which there is no way out.

3

Green and Doc were only thirty yards away from the main road they'd walked right down the middle of this morning. Doc could just make out Chibuzo holding down a position alongside a long deteriorating shack. It was clear that he had been on the only mission there was left to do – hold that point. Behind the shack was an open field where a bird could set down. Their only way out of this mess.

To reach Chibuzo, he and Green need only to cross the exposed street. Once they did, they could help fortify the location, and hope to hell that a bird would arrive before their "if you're reading this, I won't be making it back" letters arrived home. Crouching best they could as they edged closer, Green laid out the plan.

"Doc, you cross first. Pilot us through those mines. I'll follow behind you and cover our six."

Doc nodded and immediately began his attempt at reading the ground to the best of his ability. Whoever had laid the mines had a done one heck of a job. Luck had been on their side walking in, so Doc hoped luck would assist them in walking back out so that they wouldn't be blown sky high. Skipping the "Go Team on three", they started to cross.

Numerous shots shouted out all at once. There must have been a hundred shots to Green's one. The peckers had been hiding behind rocks, picking the dirt from beneath their nails and buying their time for a moment such as this.

When Doc turned, he observed at least a dozen places where bullets had penetrated through different places on Green's body. It was Doc's turn to quickly dip beneath Green's pit and drag him across the road toward a small depression in the ground. They had to outrun lead, while leaving a trail of crimson blood crumbs. The shack was too far. The depression would serve as cover that was just about as inadequate as any other.

Chibuzo joined in on the gunfight with Green, who was managing to shoot over his shoulder, despite his new lead-made holes. Doc made it to the depression, and Green dropped, rolling over onto his belly. All the while, he never ceased returning fire on the peckers surrounding them. Doc went straight to work as well. Starting with the worst, he began plugging the holes that Green had procured. Some could be corked, while others had to have makeshift tourniquets applied in order to cut off the blood supply pouring from an artery.

This was the dreadful day that Doc had fully grasped the enormity of war and the impact it had on the human soul. In the abysmal moments that had formed this day, he'd managed to push away the fragments of his collapsed naivety again and again so that the decay did not deter him from his duty. The distress signal pulsing from within his soul portended that the likelihood of him making it out of this day, as low as it was, was far greater than the likelihood of him making it out of this day with his mental health intact. Still, he was hellbent on seeing to it that these men did—who was left of them. At the end of the day, Doc would hand them whatever he had left of his own life to keep theirs intact.

Shuffling in with strained effort, Young and Flores approached the far side of the road, with Knight draped over Young's back. This time, Chibuzo and Green were ready for the attack that would come at the time of their compadre's crossing. At the earliest sign of pecker movement, they began the assault first. Young made it but had to return for Flores when Flores failed to follow after taking a bullet through the neck. Despite the circumstances, air support finally arrived, and they piled PFC Smith, Sergeant Knight, and Sergeant Green onto the first bird. The second bird, while heroically taking on fire, dipped to rescue the last four men: PFC Flores, SPC Chibuzo, Linus—Doc—Winehouse, and SPC Young.

One second, Young was declaring that he was staying behind with the kid. The next, Young was doubled over in pain, his legs dropping him to the ground in heap. Chibuzo and Doc immediately leapt out, grabbing Young in their arms while bullets rained.

"We've got to go!" The pilot warned.

"Hold it for thirty seconds!" Chibuzo yelled.

The Kiowa remained, under heavy fire for exactly thirty seconds as Chibuzo and Doc hefted Young in. Doc leapt immediately in and pressed his hands over the gushing hole in Young's abdomen.

"I've got you, Brother," Doc comforted.

Young's abdomen gushed blood in spurts between Doc's fingers. His legs needed tending, but it was the abdomen that would kill him. In recent times, bulletproof chest plates were commonly worn—something the military hadn't always provided. The plates deterred a lot of fatal chest injuries. That was an improvement on the number of military deaths. That was good. But in Smith's case, in Holden's case, in Ramirez's case, in Bennett's case, in Knight's case, and the case of many others, chest plates weren't good enough. Not enough for the soldiers who got their legs blown off. Not enough for head injuries. Not enough for the families who waited, endlessly, for husbands and sons and brothers to return home that never did. No, for them, it was not nearly enough.

Doc would have given his own chest plate, if the Taliban hadn't looted it, to have saved any one of his brothers in combat. But it wouldn't have helped them. And it wouldn't have helped even now as Young's blood welled up over his fingers. In fact, Young's chest plate was securely fastened as he yelled up at Doc, trying to get his pained voice over the roar of Kiowa blades.

"Don't leave him…Doc. Don't leave the…kid. He's one of…us."

Doc turned back to Young. "I won't leave him," he said and lifted his hands from Young's gut, quickly seizing Chibuzo's arm. "Take over for me. And send a bird back, will you?" Then, Doc jumped.

It would later be rumored that the echo of the blast from the RPG exploding on board the Kiowa as it was flying away could be heard throughout the valley. The valley so appropriately termed, "Valley of Death."

4

The woman in her mid-fifties hanging in the shadows of the bridge, watched Son of a Motherless Goat as he wobbled zigzag-like nearer and nearer to the three guarded men. Their trigger fingers had surpassed itchy and were now seemingly enflamed and aggravated. She could tell by the cagey way they moved and how they pulled their hands in close and tight. She assumed their hands where lingering over the very locations in which their weapons were lying in wait.

Turn back, she silently willed. *Turn back!*

It was no use. Son of a Motherless Goat was on track to walk straight up to the agitated group. He'd never know what hit him. Those men would never ask. They'd just complete their deal over his dead body and go about their day as though nothing had happened.

The cops wouldn't care either. Another dead bum. No big deal. Happened all the time. Moving along.

The shouting and commotion rose. Her hands started quivering and her gut twisted around and around like barbed wire. A person might suspect that she was afraid the men would notice her and destroy any evidence her mouth could otherwise provide. That's not why her insides felt as though they were ripping apart and her hands trembled. She trembled because she knew she ought to do something. Somehow, she should stop the trajectory of this altercation before it became a homicide. But if she interfered, it could become a *double* homicide.

The choice to interfere or not interfere was absolutely her own. There was no one to make her. Even God didn't force His will upon a person. When an option came down the pipe, it came down as a choice. It was the results that weren't free.

The fuss over the small group's uninvited guest was growing. This was her chance. She hoped the men's heightened nerves would mask the dashing of her movement and the slapping of the loose sole of her right shoe against the pavement. Her success depended upon not being noticed. Leaving her things behind, the woman first slunk in reverse, trying to become one with the shadow of the bridge. Then she hurried, in the opposite direction, as quickly as she could, hoping to remain undetected.

5

Young never was the kind to send a man into a fight if he, himself, wasn't willing to lead the way. That's why all the men respected him. That's why Doc respected him. That's why Doc did what he did. That's why he jumped. That's why he risked his life for the kid.

At the sound of a hair-raising explosion and the feeling of having one's gut spun like the top of a bread bag, Doc and the kid dropped to their bellies. Scrambling through the tingling sensation of not knowing if you still had, or would continue to still have, appendages, they clambered for the nearest structure. When Doc looked up, he saw pieces of the

Kiowa that had been carrying Young, Flores, and Chibuzo speedily dropping from the sky, in pieces. His heart plummeted even faster than the metal beast, utterly devastated.

Something grabbed hold of Doc's arm, tight enough to break it.

Doc's eyes flew open. Afghanistan and his burning brothers were gone. There was no kid. Instead, there was an enormously angry man in a solid black blazer looming before him, Doc's arm caught in the man's rigid clutches. A small man in a sleek silk shirt stood aside of the larger, a fierceness simmering directly below the calm exterior. The third man, in brown trousers and a brown-dyed jacket and brown beanie, lingered just feet behind the first two. He wore an aggravated expression and seemed unable to stop his hand from twitching over the opening of his jacket.

"What's your business here?" The voice of the larger man boomed down at Doc.

"Hey!" Beanie man hollered, his hand slipping halfway inside of his denim jacket now. "We're talking to you, shit for brains!"

Silk Shirt slid up and squinted. "He's not brainless," he informed the group. He sang into Doc's face, "I *see* you. You're not too smart, are you?"

Doc didn't answer, but under the present circumstance, it looked to be absolutely true.

Silk Shirt continued. "Here I am, hanging with my business associates, and then you come tromping up without so much as a lick of sense." He cocked his head tauntingly. "What was it you thought you would do?"

Doc shook his head. Nothing. The movement made him queasy. His consciousness was struggling to navigate the slippery gap separating sleep from awake.

"Are you a cop?" Beanie demanded.

With one hand, the big guy tightened his grip on Doc's arm, with the other, he snatched up Doc's throat. It was impossible to put up a struggle in his current condition.

Doc tried to croak "not a cop," but no sound came out. His mouth simply flopped soundlessly.

Silk Shirt shook his head. "Nah, he ain't no cop. A cop would have plenty to say right about now. He's a nobody. Don't make any difference anyhow. He done crossed the wrong street."

Silk Shirt's head barely nodded, and Doc felt the vice grip on his arm free, right before something as hard as a rock impacted his temple and split open his eyebrow. It had been too sudden to wince, and he sure as hell wasn't going to cry out. Any sign of discomfort only pumped a euphoria-like high into guys like this. As it was, Beanie was already all but dancing around them, like a hungry wolf waiting for his turn at a tasty bite.

Doc could make out a pearl pistol handgrip poking out of Beanie's jacket. He could tell that the man was just aching to use it. Silk Shirt, on the other hand, wore a poker-faced expression that spoke nothing of his specific intentions. Doc didn't have to deliberate the dangerousness of this unrevealing silent utterance very long. Without so much as a blink of an eye, the hard muzzle of Silk Shirt's Glock materialized, digging firmly into Doc's thin empty gut. That small act, yet largely chilling sensation, spoke volumes.

"Son!" the shrill voice of a frantic woman screamed. "Son! Where are you? Lordy, please guard the steps of my handicapped boy." The woman's commotion was enough to cause Doc's captors to pause. The distraught woman looked across the street, right at Doc, and her face lit up with relief. "Son!" she declared, pressing the palms of her hands together as though in prayerful celebration. "Son! Thank God!"

The men looked from her to Doc with the question "son?" marked all over their faces.

Doc continued staring at the woman. There was something familiar about this disheveled woman, but he was fairly certain he was no son of hers. Still, he must have looked as handicapped as she'd been announcing. The muzzle digging into his gut disappeared, and Beanie's pearl handgrip slid seamlessly back into his jacket. The big guy released Doc's throat, and at the nod of Silk Shirt, Doc was given a hard shove. His body stumbled into the street a mite faster than his feet. To his surprise, he managed to stay upright.

Fairly certain this woman, who was likely more handicapped than he, was not his mother, Doc headed straight for her all the same. Having narrowly escaped a bullet to the abdomen kind of warmed him up to her. Hopefully, as he grew nearer, if it dawned on her that she'd not given birth to this man, she could, for both their sakes, continue pretending. Hands clasped at her bosom and all.

The closer he got the more bow-legged the woman turned out to be and the more familiar her scrawniness became. Her stringy hair had been died strawberry-red some time ago and was slowly working on growing out.

"Strawberry Hair?" Doc asked.

Her hairy chin wobbled as she grabbed him up and began shuffling him along. Continuing her act of frantic mother, she chattered like a high-speed electric train. "You mustn't wander off like that," she scolded. "How many times have I told you not to open the door? You could have been hit by a car or fallen and scraped your knees. Just look at your pants! You did fall! Your pants are torn. I've been looking for you for over an hour. What if I hadn't found you? What if it had gotten dark? What if the Lord hadn't saw fit to look after you? You best thank Him in your prayers."

"Son?" Doc whispered under his breath after they were a far enough away.

"Yes, Son of a Motherless Goat. Don't you remember that's what I'd called you. What's this *Strawberry Hair* deal?"

"That's what I called *you*."

"Huh. Is that so? How you spoke to me the first time we'd met; I would have thought you'd have made up an uglier name to call me. Does round heels sound familiar to you?"

"I only meant to chase you off."

"And without a drink," she smirked.

"Yeah, without a drink. That stung a bit."

"Your wee little brain hadn't thought that one all the way through, had it?"

Doc chuckled. "No, it hadn't."

"What brought you to this part of town?"

Doc didn't want to get into the details of what he was hiding from. "I could ask the same of you."

"Lost my partner. He was sick."

Doc's chin dropped. "Sorry. I didn't realize."

"Wouldn't have changed anything if you had. He had no one except me and now I have no one at all. That's the thing, you know."

"What's the thing?"

"Exactly. Most folks don't have a clue what it is. They go through life raising and nurturing banking accounts, chasing images of perfect bodies, perfect faces, hoarding possessions. As if all, or any, of that could possibly add up to something, let alone *the thing*."

"Let me guess, you know what *the thing* is.'

Strawberry Hair puffed out her small, tired bosom. "As a matter of fact, I do. I know the one thing that puts *life* in *living*."

"No offense, but you and I aren't exactly prime examples of what folks call *living*."

"That's cause most folks are too busy chasing something that ain't even real. Something that they think will change other folks' opinions of them. Ever notice, the more a person has the less cheerful they are?"

"I guess." That wasn't exactly his problem though. He'd been pretty happy finding his place amongst a crew of military family. He'd become cheerless after having lost everything he had.

"That's cause all that stuff, it ain't real. It's fun to chase, but once you have it, once you feel it in your hands, you finally see it for what it is. Nothing. It's not totally pointless, mind you. It's an attractive web. You want it. You want to have it, to show it off, to lie in it. Then the spider comes along and traps you in all of that soft glittery thread. And sucks the life out of you."

Doc paused, suddenly curious, and looked at her. "What happened to you?"

"You won't believe me, but once, I had it all."

Doc nodded—he believed her—and they continued walking.

"I was a singer," she said, a smile stretching across her face.

It stuck him, as it had that night in the park, that, at some point, she must have been very pretty. "Really? What'd you sing?"

"Everything. But my favorite has always been bluegrass. Yes, in my time I've had lots, and I've had nothing. There was only one time I've had *the thing*."

Doc realized, that given a few moments in the past, or a few moments into the future, he wouldn't believe the things she was saying, or even listen. In this moment though, he was paying attention.

"What'd you do with it?"

"Like a fool tends to do, I lost it. I'd do anything to have it back," she said. "A version of it anyway. I wouldn't let it go to waste this time—I can tell you that much. I bet you've had it one time too."

They had reached a corner, so Doc stopped and turned to Strawberry Hair. "We've made it far enough from the bridge. I think it's safe to split ways now."

Strawberry Hair looked up at him. Her expression conveyed disappointment, but she nodded agreeably.

"It's best that neither of us go back there. If they show up and recognize you or I—"

"I know," she said. Then, she stuck out her hand. "My name is Natalia. You can call me Nat."

Doc accepted her hand. "Natalia, that's a beautiful name." And vaguely familiar. Had she told him her name before? "I guess I can tell you. My name is Doc."

Nat's nose wrinkled. "You don't look like a Doc. That's the best you could come up with?"

"Actually, there's this lady, gave me the name Son of a Motherless Goat once."

"Ha! Well, she sounds like a crazy old goat herself. I suppose you may as well stick with Doc."

"That's where you'd be wrong," Doc corrected, garnering her full attention. "She saved my life. Turns out she is a bit of an angel."

Nat's face flushed and Doc turned away, pretending to check for traffic.

"Doc?"

"Yeah."

"You best get that eyebrow looked after. It's terribly deep."

Doc said nothing.

"Doc?" Nat persisted.

Keeping his back to her, still pretending to check traffic, he grumbled, "Yeah".

"The thing that puts *life* in *living*. It's love."

Doc closed his eyes against the sound of that word entering his ears. He'd seen love in his day. He'd seen one person lay down their life for another. He'd also seen hate. He'd seen so much death that to see life felt like smokey figures in discolored mirrors.

"I've seen you with that boy who brings us snacks and blankets. He wants to be your friend, you know?"

Doc couldn't hear anymore. He started walking away.

"Don't make the same mistake I made, Doc. Don't walk away from everyone thinking they'll be there when you get back. You have to *be* someone to *have* someone!" Nat called after him.

"Too late for that," Doc muttered to himself.

What she was saying didn't even make sense. You have to be someone to have someone, what did that even mean? Maybe Nat was just a crazy old goat, and he'd been temporarily entranced by her bleating.

Chapter Ten

1

    The armed man that had visited Mrs. Ellsberg's store had only been the beginning. Over the course of the following week, petty crime in their neighborhood seemed to explode from that single incident like a seahorse giving birth—a thousand babies bursting from a single pocket all at one time. In the same way, lots of small partially coincidental occurrences exploded into their neighborhood. An increased number of missing pets, smashed flower pots, small fires that went nowhere and destroyed nearly nothing (though always exceedingly close), and an increase in graffiti painting. Small, but numerous.

    One such painting was found on the exposed wall of Mrs. Ellsberg's store, indicating that such a person had utilized Chloe and Carston's staircase in the night. The artist had terrible penmanship (who could expect more). It read, "To whom it may concern…" with the letter "M" sprayed beneath. Mama and Mrs. Ellsberg were both disturbed by the act, Carston knew. Though both attempted to act as though they weren't.

    In addition to these new activities, Mrs. Ellsberg and Mama also seemed to think that Carston hadn't noticed the murmurings of the adults that visited the store. For the benefit of their silly notions that Carston may be blind and deaf, not simply young, he played along. He didn't bring up their concerns or ask any questions. Still, he knew, and he knew it had something to do with the man with the gun, and the fact that he was still out there. He also couldn't help but notice that Mrs. Ellsberg was more diligent about closing and opening on time. Mama was more nervous than ever about him walking to the park while she was gone. But, so long as he pretended that he knew nothing, and Mama continued to refuse to acknowledge that he possibly could, he'd continue to be allowed to go on his walks and use the park playground as training obstacles. It was a dirty game he and his mama were playing.

Carston was no fool. He fully understood that the adult world was brewing some sort of dark sludge. He needed to be careful so he was mindful of his surroundings and didn't talk to strangers. It was risky, but he also quizzed Mama every evening that she was doing the same thing. He was the only man in her life; it was his job to make sure she was being careful. She always gave him a funny look, as though wondering if a mere child could possibly have surmised the situation. Carston simply ignored her funny face and kept on talking, smoothly changing the subject to what he'd read that day, or climbing, or both. She almost always followed along, appearing incredibly relieved that she was mistaken.

How she managed to convince herself day after day that he was utterly clueless, was beyond him. Despite the fact that he clearly was, and always had been, the man of the house, Mama so desperately wanted him to be "just a kid." She didn't want to involve him in "grown-up stuff." Still, her fantasies didn't stop him from doing his job. Every night he checked that the lock on the front door was secure, then tip-toed into Mama's room to remove her open laptop from the bed, cover her with a throw, and turn out her light. He'd been taking care of her for as long as he could remember, but neither of them ever mentioned it. He was supposed to be "just a kid." The game of pretend is a powerful game, so Mama pretended that she wasn't terrified, and Carston pretended that he didn't know that she was, and why.

If all that hadn't been enough, Doc hadn't come around since the store incident. Even though he'd stolen a bottle of alcohol from Mrs. Ellsberg, Carston still worried about him. He could have moved on, but he also could have fallen sick. There was no way of knowing. Carston couldn't help being concerned. There was something about the man that Carston had liked from the beginning. The theft had severely let him down, still, it couldn't be discounted that Doc had stepped in to save Mrs. Ellsberg when he had no reason to. It was a bit confusing actually. Nevertheless, Carston had come to understand one thing about the homeless; they played by an entirely different set of rules in order to survive. They were more resourceful with what was available, more tough-skinned when it came to outside opinions, and each had at least one serious flaw that compromised normal decision making.

Mama was right to be concerned about the dangers associated with the various reasons that people are driven into homelessness. Carston knew those dangers were real, and many times were dominant traits of the person he came into contact with. The fact still remained, God needed someone to be His hands, and Carston had been born with two.

Carston had a Bible to read, and it sat first in the line of books he'd collected upon the top shelf. It had been his first book, fittingly given to him by one of his first friends. She was older than him, beautiful and sweet. They'd spent a lot of time together, she reading and he listening. Inside the Bible, she'd pointed out many times that it said "fear not." Sometimes Carston was afraid, so he pretended that he wasn't and wore a brave face. Afterall, the game of pretend was a powerful thing.

After helping Mrs. Ellsberg with opening the store and munching down granola bars with Oscar and Boop, Carston headed to the park. He still ran the staircase first thing every morning, but he'd added laps around the park to increase his stamina. As a kid, he'd always climbed the long metal slide, imagining it was some great mountain somewhere, but now he climbed it with a little more sense of purpose. Now he climbed both the slide side and the ladder side, taking turns using mostly his legs or mostly his hands, over and over again until his muscles burned.

Every time he approached the monkey bars to practice his chin-ups, he couldn't help but glance at the bushes where Doc had been sitting before, hoping to see him. Today, like the others, he didn't see Doc. Carston jumped, grabbing the cool bar in his hands, and pulled. He'd managed, with regularity now, to pull himself halfway up. He'd yet to pull himself all the way to his chin. His biceps would burn and simply refuse to take him any further. He was beginning to wonder if he'd ever be able to pull himself up when he noticed a kid, smaller than himself, lying on his back under the swing throwing a full-out tantrum that his mother had said it was time to go. The kid was clinging to the swing's seat, and every time his mother tried to pull him away, he clung to the seat all the more, pulling himself upward.

Huh.

After the mother had successfully detached the kid from the swing and dragged him away, Carston went to the swings. He lay under the seat of the same swing the kid had been clinging to only moments before and stared up at it. It was still swinging ever so slightly from the tantrum display. Carston felt enormously foolish lying there staring up at it. Commitment and determination outweighed the feelings of foolishness. Grabbing the seat with his hands the same way the tantrum kid had, he began to pull his weight up. Over and over again. In time his biceps began to burn. Not so much that he couldn't continue, so he continued. He continued until a little girl appeared and asked if she and her sisters could use the swing.

"Sure," he said, smiling widely when he had a difficult time pulling himself up the last time so he could stand.

"What were you doing?" the little girl with blonde pigtails asked.

"Getting stronger," Carston replied.

"Why?"

"Because I'm going to be a mountain climber."

"Why?"

Carston thought about it, then shrugged. "Just want to, I guess."

The girl seemed content with the answer and went on swinging. Carston picked up his backpack, having completely forgotten to eat his lunch, and headed for home. On the way home he thought more on how to put into words *why* he wanted to be a mountain climber. There seemed to be no excellent answer; other than the same he had for wanting to help the homeless. He just did. Truth was, his heart called for it in a way that couldn't be explained—or ignored.

That afternoon, he sprawled out on his bed with the book Mrs. Ellsberg had given to him. Reading and munching on his lunch, he turned page after page. By page 227, Carston had reached the conclusion of Jordan's climb of Australia's Carstensz Pyramid. At the end of a blog written by Jordan's liaison, Patrick, who had served as Jordan's guide, Carston stopped. Rather than progressing through the story, he read Patrick's, the liaison's, words over and over again. There was something there that he wanted to experience over and over. A lesson he didn't want to forget. The sensation in his gut that pulled him to join the pursuit of mountains—all sorts of mountains really—was right there, in words. Patrick had managed to put the *why* onto a page. Patrick's advice to Jordan, and now to Carston, was:

"Keep on searching for another summit, and tell the world that there is always a mountain to climb, a great destination to go in life, never waste life for doing nothing."

Carston couldn't have put it so eloquently, but he recognized the fervor in those simple words and the inescapability of the quest. Carston had no choice but to climb towards his destination. Deep down, he'd always understood that the destination wasn't just about a place; it was about the people you met along the way. Family, friends, unlikely friends, teachers, strangers. They were all a part of the journey. They were all a part of the final destination. Birthed from such insight, one thing from Patrick's blog grabbed hold of him tighter than the rest. He never wanted to waste life for doing nothing. Not when he knew there was something he could do.

2

Chloe climbed the short steps onto the bus, skimming the numerous seats. When just one silently called out to her, she plopped down wearily. As the engine rumbled and the floor vibrated anxiously beneath her feet, Chloe sighed and began her ritual of staring out the window.

Watching the buildings and shrubbery and people slowly slide by was one of Chloe's few indulgences. Whenever she'd had a long day at work, she literally basked in the obligation-less bus ride home. As temporary as it was, being in a place where she had absolutely no responsibilities whatsoever and could watch in leisure as the busy world glided by was a perfect diversion from her own woes and worries. From the outside looking in, it would appear that she had very few woes or worries. She had a rent-free apartment. A job. A wonderful son. What more could she want? However, from the inside looking out, her worry basket overflowed. In addition to worrying that their apartment could vanish from beneath their feet, or that she could be laid off from her job, or if, heaven forbid, Carston ever got seriously hurt or kidnapped from the sidewalk he walked alone every day, there was one additional all-consuming woe.

Boa.

Of course, she hadn't known him as Boa when she'd first met him. She'd known him as Mitch. Mitchell Mateo. A dark handsome man, so tall, and eyes so gold, she'd fallen under his spell almost instantly. She'd heard the tales of girls being wooed into the clutches of a bad boy, but she hadn't seen it happening to herself. She'd wanted to be free from her drunkard father's depressed and futureless shack so badly that falling head over senses with the handsome Mitch had been easier than the persuasive pulls of a river to the ocean. He'd made her feel as free and high as the rain in the sky—before it falls.

Against her father's pathetic attempt at convincing her she was running into a train wreck—drunkenly cussing from his recliner that she could never come back home if she ran off with him—Chloe followed Mitch right out the front door. She'd rebelliously climbed into his waiting car with her single, small bag perched on her knees. It hadn't mattered what anyone would have said; she'd have followed Mitch anywhere. All she'd wanted was to be free of the life she'd been born to. Then, she'd been romantically convinced that even the trenches would be better. There was no way for her to know that those trenches weren't in the too distant future, and they weren't romantic at all. For the time though, the path to those shady and daunting ditches were cleverly disguised as a constant party.

Mitch's parties contained droves of men and girls, music, private rooms, and drugs. The people that came paid thousands, just to get in the door. Mitch was obviously the head honcho, so Chloe had tried to be his best, and most obedient, girl. Being Mitch's best girl won her top honch-a, which made her feel important, for the first time in her life. No one pestered her about drinking or taking hits. No one dared ask Mitch's favorite girl to a private room. Her game was simple. It was to please Boa, be Boa's number one, and entertain guests. She could do that. That was until Boa brought in a new girl. The moment that younger flirty blonde stepped through the door Boa started to change Chloe's game.

Little by little, Boa coaxed Chloe into group make-outs, all sharing and intermingling. She tried to stay close to Boa, but Boa encouraged the other men to fondle her. It seemed to please him, so she'd allowed it, always careful to not cross any boundaries that would have Boa throw her away. It grew apparent that the boundaries that once protected her were vanishing. Men started touching her, everywhere. Boa didn't step in. Sometimes he even stimulated the situation, getting the action started himself then passing her off. That, or he ignored her entirely. Boa had always petted other girls and allowed them to pet him, but once she'd seen him drop the thin panties of the new girl and insert himself, Chloe knew. The invisible switch had been flipped. Chloe no longer belonged to Boa. He'd discarded her. Any authority she'd had over others, or herself, was over. Nothing stopped the drunk and high men from dropping her panties. It took a few men ripping through a couple pairs of her favorite baby-pink silk panties to get that through her thick skull. When she'd begged Boa for assistance, he'd simply glanced over, grinning, and kept doing whatever it was—or whoever it was—he was doing.

There came a point that Chloe's back ended up against the wall and she'd had no choice but to go see Mitch, privately. She'd knocked timidly on the open door of Boa's office as he was counting money. He didn't answer so she stepped quietly in.

"Mitch, I need to talk to you."

He kept counting.

"I...I'm a little scared. I'm your girl. I want to keep being your girl. *Only* your girl. Even if that means sharing you, I can. I..."

"Humph."

She felt the desperation creeping up. Her heart was pounding. "You don't want me. What did I do? What did I do wrong? I don't understand."

Silence.

"Mitch?"

His back stiffened, and he immediately stopped counting. Looking up with those gold eyes, he said, "Don't call me by that name. You and I are no longer that familiar."

She opened her mouth, more confused than ever. They weren't that familiar? How could that be? He had her whenever he wanted. "What do you mean?" she asked despairingly. She rushed over to him, kneeled on the floor next to his chair, and clung to his beautiful arm. "Please tell me what I did. Please, I'm scared. I feel lost—"

"It's not what you did," Boa interrupted, a cold expression upon his face. "It's what you *will* do."

"What will I do?" Chloe asked, her voice cracking. She was desperate. She'd do it. Anything to be safe from her condition.

"What I tell you." He went back to counting without explanation.

"Okay," she mumbled obediently. What choice did she have? She was stuck. "What would you have me do? I can serve beverages? I can help prepare the private rooms?" He hadn't confirmed, so she kept on. "Aid in the nurse room?" She'd done all of these things before, when the circumstances had called for it. She could certainly do them again. Anything to be shielded from the constant expectations and provided with provisions.

Otter, a large man with a belly the size of kettle large enough to feed an army, entered. His arms were so hairy Chloe had never been able to make out the tattoos underneath. Of course, she hadn't gotten close enough to inspect them. She didn't want him getting the idea that she was interested in him. "Boa, our guest in room twenty-one is complaining that his entertainer is bleeding."

"So?"

"She's bleeding profusely. He claims she's damaged and that's not what he'd paid for. He demands a new entertainer."

Boa paused, his fists balling around the cash. No one demanded anything of Boa. Chloe knew that. Otter knew that. Everyone knew that.

Boa growled, "She wouldn't *be* bleeding, if it weren't for his ways." Boa was a violent man, but not with the girls. Unless the sin was egregious.

It wasn't a good time to speak up, and to this day Chloe couldn't say just what had possessed her to do so. Simple desperation she supposed. "Mitch, I'm pregnant."

Boa gave her a single enraged glance that hissed, *how dare you.* He needn't say anything. The wrath of that glance singed a piece of her so severely that that spot wouldn't cease its painful oozing, even years later. It was that dreadful moment that she'd finally realized her father had been right. He may have been a drunkard, but he'd been right. Mitch hadn't been her prince, saving her from a futureless life. He'd been a snake. He'd never loved her. He'd never cared for her. She'd never been his number-one girl. She'd been his number-one slave. His number-one fool. Unlike the girls who served as entertainers, Chloe hadn't even required drugs to do the things she'd done. She'd been a fool. There was no one to blame but herself, and there was no one to rescue her.

Boa addressed Otter, ignoring Chloe, adding even more sting to her confession. "Take the girl to our nurse. Bring our guest to me."

Chloe, seeing that her issue of being with child was not of any meaningful importance, and wouldn't be addressed, turned to leave the office. Nothing good was about to happen for the guest, and she didn't want to be present to see it.

Boa caught her arm. "Chloe, go stand in that corner," he said and pointed at the corner of the office directly across from where he was sitting at his table. "You can be a part of this."

"Okay," Chloe said tentatively. Perhaps he intended to look after her after all. Perhaps he intended to have her learn the ins and outs of management so she could assist him on running the floor rather than the parties.

She stayed, of course, because she was a fool. And because if Boa hadn't specifically told you to leave, you stayed. The head of a boa constrictor tattooed on the tender flesh of all the girls that worked there verified whose property to which they belonged. She just hadn't seen it for what it was at the time. She'd seen the marks on their flesh like the secret handshake she'd shared with her childhood friends. Who wouldn't want a secret handshake? Anyone wanting out of Boa's constricting hold, that's who. Another thing Chloe hadn't realized before, no one really ever left. No one giggled about plans for the future or walked excitedly through the halls with sticker-covered luggage. From time to time someone would up and disappear though. One moment, a girl was there. The next, she's not. Everyone had assumed those girls had had enough and left. Looking back, that's not what had happened at all, and Chloe's heart broke for them.

When Boa's guest entered the office, Chloe leaned against the wall to be further away from him. The man's hands were covered in blood. He hadn't even bothered to wipe them off. Chloe shivered. What had he done? His clothes were disheveled having thrown them on in haste. Otter was nowhere to be seen. Chloe shivered again.

Boa didn't even glance up. Instead, he calmly counted hundred-dollar bills into a thin pile. When he was done, he slid the pile across the table, closest to the man with bloody hands and a narrow smile.

"Let's be clear," Boa said, "I don't provide damaged girls, and I don't take kindly to when a guest damages my property."

The man, looking at the thin pile of cash, lifted his chin in the air and grumbled, "The girl must have started her monthly. I didn't damage any property of yours."

"In that case," Boa said calmly. "Choose."

"Choose what?"

Boa nodded at the pile of cash and then at Chloe.

Chloe nearly choked on her own throat. She would have puked it out if she hadn't swallowed it back down. What? She was being offered as an entertainer? She wasn't an entertainer. She was Boa's girl. Was, but still. Sure, theoretically, she'd entertained, but only in the great party room, never in the private rooms. She wasn't one of *those* girls. Most of the time they were high. They barely knew what they were doing.

The man looked at Chloe. Every bone in her body begged not to be left to him, unsupervised. It'd be her blood staining his hands next.

"Isn't that your—"

"*Was*," Boa said matter of fact, cutting the man off. "In fact, you would be her first official guest."

The man grinned the devil's grin.

Chloe's legs buckled and she nearly fell. She'd rather be dead as opposed to what was about to happen. She looked around with wide eyes for a way out. There was no way out and no one to help her. The man and Boa were between her and the open door. Entertaining had always been her choice, or so she had thought, but this wasn't a choice. This was rape. How could Boa let this happen to her?

"One condition," Boa said and pointed a finger at Chloe where she stood. "She doesn't leave that corner."

It could have been Boa's way of protecting her, not allowing this obviously violent man to take her to a private room, but Chloe had ceased thinking Boa had ever been about protecting her. No, the more likely answer was, this situation was intended as a test and a punishment. In Boa's mind, he would be punishing the man for damaging his property (causing Boa to lose money) and punishing Chloe for becoming impregnated (causing Boa to lose money). Then there was this matter of would she do what she was told to do? For Boa, she always had.

Chloe drew away the first time the man's sticky hands tried to touch her. The man was wicked fast and grabbed her pitilessly. After that she shrunk within herself, squeezing her eyes closed as tightly as possible, trying to keep the man, and the pain, and the humiliation, as far from her mind as possible. She didn't have the stomach to allow her eyes to see what her body was going through. As long as she didn't see it, she wouldn't cry. Then, someday, when it was over, maybe, she could forget it had ever happened. Maybe she could move on. For the child already growing inside of her, surely, she could withstand anything.

She'd been wrong on all accounts. Time would reveal, the punishment was never to end for Chloe. She wouldn't be able to withstand anything, and she'd never forget the man with the bloody hands as he took and took…and Mitch counted his money.

Chapter Eleven

1

Careful is what he'd been. Oh, so careful.

Mailman sat in a chair at a cozy two-person table by himself looking out the window of a hole-in-the-wall coffee shop. Not surprisingly, the barista with two braided pigtails brought him a free short black coffee, now that he and her boss were pals. He held a hand up to her, denying her peace offering. Mailman didn't need pals. He never had pals before and got along just fine. What he wanted now was unquestionable submission.

"Bring me a tall coffee," he said, "with a double shot." He had no idea what he was saying, but he figured she did.

The barista stopped short of handing him the cup and glared. Then she spun around and took the cup and herself right back where she had come from, none too happy. Well, at least she had more balls than her boss. Her timid boss had signed on the bottom line of Mailman's offer to protect the shop from rising crime. And by "signed," he meant the timid coffee shop owner handed over Orson's required fee, plus a tad more that Mailman had tapped on for shipping and handling. It was fair, considering the amount of work he'd been putting in lately. Also, it was necessary if he wanted to move up in the world. Move up, right into Orson's place.

How to move into Orson's place was the thought he'd been chipping away at. First on the list was to gain control of his assigned domain. It would appear as though he were being a loyal, hard-working little ant, when in fact, he was picking up the first block of his own future empire. Unlike Orson, Mailman wouldn't coddle these pompous people into some sort of ridiculous cocoon of confidence. Orson had it wrong. These people would never have respect for so-called security if they didn't know what they needed security from. Half the time, these puny pathetic people just needed security from themselves. What they needed was to experience, and drink, the fear of the man in charge—the Messenger of Destruction—lest they be destructed.

Mailman's stomach twisted excitedly. What a great plan. A strong plan—unlike Orson Finlay. Orson had gained an empire because his old man was weak enough to have allowed it taken from him. Mailman would gain an empire because Orson was just as weak and overconfident. The stupid Finlay family duo only had one thing correct. Their stupid Finlay family moto:

Purpose is the lock. Action is the key.

Mailman had purpose, and he would act…and act…and act, until all the scared little people bowed down to their master. His belly was so hot with excitement he could barely contain himself. The flesh of his left cheek twitched as his crooked smile grew. The undercover Mailman had grown tired of patiently waiting, tired of patiently playing Orson's game. The Messenger of Destruction wanted to act. He wanted to burn something down!

Outside the squeaky clean window of the hole-in-the-wall coffee shop, and across the street, the Messenger of Destruction scraped his hazel-eyed gaze over the brick surface of a hand-me-down clothing dive. It wasn't much to speak of, with its small display window and single potted plant holding open the wooden door that had been painted and repainted too many times to count. The young lady inside had pretty much ignored Mailman when he'd gone in, bidding her to join Orson's ridiculous insurance plan. In a way, he couldn't blame her. But then she'd gone and practically laughed in his face with her small, demeaning smile and condescending polite wishes that he "have a good day." If he'd wanted to have a good day, he'd had lit a match to her new-to-her flower printed dress and watched her flail around on the floor.

The young clothing lady was just like the old bat from the grocery store, and nothing like her, all at once. The grocery store was profitable. There was no money to be made from petering around racks of used clothes. The little imp barely brought in enough dough to keep the lights on. In fact, she *saved* people dough. She was a bad businesswoman, and a menace to his future empire. Her failing venture would be the perfect sacrifice to be made an example of.

Yes! His ego praised. *Burn her pocket-sized business to the ground!*

2

From behind an open newspaper—the oldest trick in the book—Dagger watched Mailman practically prance out of the coffee shop. What a dope. Dagger wasn't sure why Orson had signed on the baggy-clothed moron. Sure, he'd brought in a few businesses and a couple wads of cash, but jeez, he was a dope. Now that he was gone and couldn't tattle that Dagger was out of his assigned area, Dagger could finally do what he'd come for. He signaled the barista.

When the cute gal, braided pigtails on both sides of her head, came up with a smile, Dagger handed her the newspaper. "Not what they used to be," he said. "Can I get another coffee? Supposed to be meeting a friend, but she hasn't come in yet."

She gave him a fleeting look of compassion as though he'd been stood up. "Of course. I'll be right back with that."

While she was gone, he kept a keen eye on the people passing by. He'd come up with answers more than once by just being diligent. No such luck today. When the barista returned, she traded a hot full mug for his empty cold mug. Before she walked away, he touched her arm.

"Maybe you could help."

She stood there, empty mug in hand, looking at him doubtfully.

"I was thinking, what if she'd come on da wrong day, you know? Mistaken da date?"

Her compassionate look returned. "Maybe," she agreed.

"If I told you what I know, would you tell me if you've seen someone like her recently?"

She shifted her weight. "You should probably give her a call or text her or something."

Dagger looked down at his coffee. "If she's stood me up, I'm afraid to call. I'm just going out on a limb that she could have possibly made a mistake. I don't think I can take the same rejection twice."

"All right," the gal with braided pigtails said. "Tell me what you know."

"Her name is Chloe, but that could just be a user name. She's blonde, green eyes, and very pretty. Got a son too. Dark skin. Ten years old. They're supposed to live near here. That's why we chose this coffee shop."

The gal's expression changed slightly. It went from a dull listening face to a perky registration of familiarity.

"You've seen them?" he asked hopefully, playing the interested role he'd conceived. "Was it recent? Last week at this same time maybe?"

Her expression changed again. "No, it wasn't recent. It's been some time ago now. I only remember them because of the boy. It was an obvious date—just the two of them. He was so cute, pulling out her chair, hanging on every word. Wish my dates were like that. Just so cute."

In Dagger's eyes, there was nothing cute about either one of them. There never would be. They were a job. A big paying one. A loss he couldn't afford. In reality, they were so un-cute, he'd enthusiastically introduce both of them to the edge of his steel dagger. He'd die to see their blood turn to scarlet and feel it run over his fingers.

"You wouldn't happen to know where they live, do you? If I knew that, I could drop flowers on her doorstep, with a note." He didn't want to come off like a creep, so he added, "Da rest will be up to her. Not much more than I can do than that, is there?"

The barista began shaking her head before he'd even finished. What was the meaning of that? Did she not believe him? Did she think she shouldn't share information about a woman she didn't know to a man that she didn't know? Did she simply not know where they lived? If they'd been in a back alley rather than he sitting here in her place of work, he'd be able to get the answers he wanted a lot faster.

"I understand. Could you at least point me in the correct direction? Maybe luck would have me bump into her on my way to my bus stop." He had no intentions of getting on a bus. He'd go to the next place, play the next role, and find this bitch, and her kid.

"The bus stop!" The barista's face lit up. "I've seen her waiting at a bus stop."

Dagger tried to match the gal's optimistic animation. "Really? Which one?"

She pointed.

Dagger jumped to his feet, not caring at all about the strange coffee concoction she'd talked him into ordering when he'd first arrived. His veins were vibrating with anticipation. He grabbed her empty hand, pumping it up and down, and kissed it. "Thank you," he said.

He left money on the table and walked briskly out the coffee shop door. The moment he rounded the corner, out of view, he began wiping at his mouth. Despite the revolting awareness that he'd touched that gal's hand to his lips, and the burning sensation of having tried to remove the top layers of his own flesh to rid himself of her, he smiled.

Chapter Twelve

1

Chloe's bus was running on time. Not per the usual five minutes late "on time." Actually, on time. It's a long list, what a woman can do with an extra five minutes added to her life. She could stop in one of the many shops between where the bus let her off and her apartment to: smell a flower, actually touch the sleeve of blouse she'd been eyeing, purchase a small trinket for Carston. If she waited to spend her five extra minutes at home, she could: sit on the stairs a moment and breathe in the fresh air, surprise Carston by jumping onto his bed while his nose was in a book and his headphones were in his ears, take the time to actually file and paint her nails rather than quickly whacking them all off. She had stopped painting her nails after she'd gone into hiding. Carston had changed all that though. He had melted her heart buying a tiny bottle of Lilac Purple polish for Mother's Day and voluntarily taking the time to lavishly apply it for her, all by himself.

As she stepped from the bus, a small crowd of individuals waited to get on and take her place. She would have thought it strange, but really, when it comes down to it, is anything in Seattle strange? Plus, it was a Friday. People would be headed out to party away their memories of the work week or go to a game to offer assistance by screaming out their voice box and popping in a couple of hot dogs. Chloe wasn't into any of that. Nowadays, she related deeply to the small, shelled creature, the hermit crab. Work and home were all that she needed anymore. It was Carston who forced her to stay connected with the outside world.

To Chloe, the outside world was a dangerous place. She'd seen what it was capable of, and she wanted no part of it. At one point, she'd been desperate enough to run to it, cling to it even. Anything to combat her fear of being swallowed up and left behind, like her father had been. Now here she was, hiding from it rather than running to it, still afraid of being swallowed up. Carston, bless his innocent heart, didn't see the world the way she saw it, the way she'd experienced it.

Carston saw sad souls rather than snapping teeth. He saw the raging beast—the world—as a lost sheep in need of a shepherd. Somehow, he saw beauty in all of the ugly. He would drag her on walks, insisting on stopping to speak to strangers, insisting on finding good in the darkest of places. Maybe it was his way of combatting the anxiety she projected onto him day after day. Maybe he was trying to help her find an antidote to her past. Or maybe he had something she didn't—strength.

As if all that weren't enough, Carston had a big piping dream to climb. Climb what? Climb where? Why climb at all? She didn't know the answers to any of these questions. She'd asked him once, and he'd said, "I don't know. There's a climber inside of me waiting to come out." Chloe was a little afraid of that climber inside of Carston waiting to come out. That climber would take him far away … or get him hurt. Probably both. Almost daily, her son begged to go hiking. Any of Seattle's urban trail systems would be fine—her choice. Chloe couldn't bring herself to take him. She was too scared to be seen, to be found out. After all, she'd been climbing too—out of the dark valley she'd once been buried in—and she was scared of falling. Carston didn't understand all of that, and he wouldn't have to if she could just keep protecting him. Undeniably, she knew that she couldn't protect him forever, and that scared her too.

The small crowd waiting to get on the bus pressed into her, barely waiting for her to clear the steps before they rushed in. Her heart beat a little faster being in such close proximity to all of them. She didn't like being touched, which made it a darn miracle that she was working to be a nurse someday. She'd be touching countless strangers. Then again, she didn't mind touching others, by her own choice, like she had with Doc when she'd bandaged him up. She just didn't want to *be* touched. Doc had been her first patient, besides Carston, and helping him had felt natural. In fact, helping him had felt good. Plus, working at the hospital made her feel safe, like she was being watched over. Laundry was good and all, but it wasn't quite the same as she imagined nursing would be.

After the rush for the bus had subsided, Chloe noticed one Asian male had remained. He was sitting on the bench, the ankle of one leg resting on the knee of the other. He glanced up at her, staring a moment too long, then bent over and untied his shoe and started re-tying it. Chloe had an uneasy feeling about him. Then again, she had an uneasy feeling about most men. Still, she couldn't help but wonder why he hadn't boarded the bus. Why had he untied his shoes only to retie them?

Chloe set off, taking a right rather than crossing the street straight across. When she reached the next intersection, she peeked over her shoulder. The man had his back to her with a slightly slumped posture like he might be reading. Maybe he was waiting for someone. Chloe crossed the street and started in the direction of home, only an additional block down, just in case. At every intersection, she used checking for traffic as an excuse to confirm that the man had not followed her, just as Mrs. Ellsberg had schooled her to do. Each time, he was nowhere to be seen. Of course. She was overly paranoid. Living in a constant state of being on guard was no picnic. Still, it beat being sorry for not having been wary at all.

Walking down a different street from usual, Chloe came upon a small store that looked packed to the ceiling with trinkets. Remembering that she was ahead of schedule, Chloe ducked in, bells jingling loudly against the door as she did.

"Welcome," said a bright-faced lady dressed in a tie-die dress and thin leather sandals.

"Thank you," Chloe answered, looking around. Sure enough, there was so many things packed between these four walls, they had taken to hanging items from the ceiling. It seemed there was something for every kind of interest. Toys, costumes, books, magic, you name it. Then she saw it. A basket of snakes.

They were fake snakes, of course, but snakes all the same. Suddenly, she hated this store. It felt as though Boa was there, watching her with his golden eyes, waiting for her to slip. Waiting for her to misstep so that he could wrap his great muscle around her, holding her closer and closer, until all of her breath was gone and she was no more.

"Can I help you find something?" the lady asked.

Chloe paused. What she really wanted was to leave. "I'm looking for something for my son. Something small." She added, "I don't have much time," hoping it would rush the lady along so Chloe didn't have to spend an extra moment here.

The lady smiled. "Something that says you were thinking about him."

"Yes, exactly."

The lady led her to a shelf of puzzles. "How about something to occupy his time?"

Although there were many sorts of puzzles, from a thousand pieces and up, down to something chunky that even a baby could figure out, none of them quite did the trick. It needed to be something special. Something Carston would cherish more than anything else.

"I don't—" Chloe stopped mid-sentence. There was a beautiful puzzle of the Seattle area. Only, Chloe knew that on the inside of that box the beautiful picture had been cut into pieces, very much like the actual geography of Seattle was cut down into territorial sections by varying gangs. She'd heard of such things growing up. Her father had warned her to stay clear of certain places, certain hand signs, certain colors even. It wasn't until she'd overheard a certain conversation between Boa and a man that she couldn't place by voice alone, that she'd come to realize, those sections could be utilized as more than just places to stay clear of.

After having lost the positional status of being Boa's number-one girl, Chloe's privileges dropped to the same level as the entertaining girls. They could have hated her out of jealousy, but they didn't. They had all been there at one point. Instead, they took Chloe's broken heart under their also-broken, wings. A line of young women mothering and coaching the newest young woman. It was those lost and stolen girls who had made Chloe's transfer, the expecting of a baby, and her mere existence, possible.

Despite the terrible odds of Boa's constant fury, Chloe had brought a baby boy into this underground world of greed and sin. All the girls, and even Boa's employees, fell instantly in love with the hazel-eyed, dark-skinned lump of joy. Boa could have found a way to be rid of the two, but everyone bestowed mercy upon Chloe and helped to keep her greatest treasure out of sight, and out of mind. There was one particular girl, named Tasha, who stuck her neck out the furthest. Her room butted up to an old, forgotten space full of cobwebs and books that she'd stashed. When it was no longer possible for Chloe to hide her condition, Tasha had cleaned the space and had quietly invited Chloe to move into the tiny space. After the birth, all of the girls took turns watching the lovable lap of giggles and dirty diapers on their breaks. They'd even conned Otter into holding the baby for ten minutes during inspection. He had done so and was caught cooing and laughing at the boy with bubbles popping out of his tiny nostrils. Otter had never mentioned that incident. Maybe it had been to save his own skin, but Chloe appreciated him, just a little, after that.

On the rare occasion that Boa set out to find Chloe—or fault in her—all he ever found was her working twice as hard as anyone. They had all worked together, providing Boa again and again, with every reason to turn a blind eye to Chloe's damning situation, and he did. For a long time.

Time eventually caught up with Chloe. Carston grew more every day. First, he crawled, then he walked, then he began talking up a storm. It became harder and harder to keep the energetic little boy out of sight and out of mind. Chloe and the girls would sneak him up and down unused hallways to run and play. It was never long enough or fun enough for a boy who ought to be outside playing in mud puddles and catching frogs. Carston, as good-natured as no little boy before, seemed unendingly content to play hide—never seek—with Boa's employees and use Tasha's books as building blocks. For hours Carston would color in the coloring books that had been snuck into him and listen to his revolving sitters read from the fantastic stories found inside of Tasha's books. Thankfully, most of them zoomed thirty thousand feet over his head, along with the eerie sounds of men visiting the rooms surrounding them.

The older Carston got, the more he'd begin to understand about the world they lived in. Eventually, Carston would need to be enrolled in school. Then what? "Hi! My name is Car. I live in a broom closest with twenty women."? Yes, they'd managed to survive here, and Chloe had not a penny to her name, but, God willing, they could find a way.

One dark night, with the thunder clapping somewhere over the roof that they never stepped out from beneath, Carston had come down with a stomach bug. She and he were up most of the night attempting to keep a small plastic flower vase hovering below Carston's trembling chin. Since the flowers hadn't been real, they ended up tossed in a corner, an arm's length away. When the early morning had finally arrived, Chloe felt eternally exhausted. Carston, of course, felt starved. Together, they tiptoed down the hall, headed toward the resident cafeteria. It was really only an old kitchen, sparsely stocked, with a roughly built wooden bar that food was set upon, potluck style. There was no dining area. The girls were required to dish a small helping, leaving enough for the others, and take it back to their rooms. Visiting the cafeteria outside of meal hours wasn't forbidden but was highly frowned upon. Eating was not an attraction Boa made money off of.

Chloe touched a finger to her lips when Carston skipped a few paces and looked up at her with those big, happy hazel eyes. They were coming up on Boa's office. There was no telling if he'd be in there this early or if he would still be tucked under a pair of legs. It hadn't been her legs for some time now. That was perfectly fine by her. His venom had worn off long ago.

The sound of voices drifted down the hall, and Chloe froze. Was someone coming? She signaled for Carston to jump into her arms, which he did gladly. She glanced over her shoulder. If she booked it back to their room, would she make it, undetected? It was a long way back to Tasha's room. It was doubtful they'd make it. The cafeteria was closer, but that meant running past Boa's office. What if he was in there? Giving a glance both directions again, and listening, Chloe decided that the voices were coming from Boa's office. The bad news was, he was in there. The good news was, she didn't have to run. She could probably sneak quietly past. It was risky, but Carston's tummy growled, so she steeled herself. She wouldn't allow him to go hungry. Anyway, this would probably be her best chance at sneaking an extra meal. Later, the kitchen and the hall would grow exponentially busier. It had to be now.

With Carston wrapped around her neck like a necklace, Chloe inched forward. In the short distance between her and the dreaded office door, Boa's voice was unmistakable.

"I'm a busy man, and the pickings in my area have been scarce. I have to have fresh material, you know. My business will die without fresh courses for the hungry."

Chloe knew what Boa meant by "hungry." It had nothing to do with feeding anyone. There had been a time that she'd thought that Boa's "parties" were fun and exciting. Now, she saw them for what they were. A business of exploiting young, lost girls for money. Once the girls were "caught" they were trapped within these walls, often drugged into submission, and given no means in which to survive—without Boa's generosity, that is.

"What are you implying, Mr. Mateo? You want permission to cross into Finlay's territory? I cannot grant you such a thing."

"No," Boa laughed with that rumbling affect that Chloe recognized as absolutely fake. "I wouldn't dare cross into Finlay Orson's territory."

"What then is it you ask of me?"

"Orson's territory grows every day."

"Yes," the voice confirmed.

"What if someone from inside of Orson's posse did the searching for my fresh material? What if that person brought the top-quality pickings me? I would never so much as set foot on Orson's ground, even accidently. I wouldn't want to accidently break any rules. In a way, that person would be protecting and preserving Orson's law. Wouldn't they?"

"No."

There was a fluttering sound like that of cards being shuffled. When the shuffling stopped, Boa said, "I heard about you. You have the tendency to be your own man, despite whose puppy you are."

"I am no man's puppy."

"Well, of course not. Puppies get kicked around, squeal a bit, then lie down at their master's feet. A lot like women." Boa laughed at his own ridiculous joke.

Neither the unrecognizable voice nor Chloe laughed with him.

"I'll get right down to it. I need help with my work. Are you interested in taking a side job, outside of Orson's orders?"

"Your work is not my work."

"One thousand per girl."

There was as short silence.

"I'm a busy man," Boa said impatiently. His downfall in bargaining was that he was used to having the upper hand—and his way. Whoever the man with him was, he was no stranger to the game and responded with equal indifference.

"I'll remind you, per Orson's orders, your presence is forbidden."

Chloe didn't have to be in the room to feel the hostility that Boa was broadcasting through the open air. Quickly, she scurried past the open door, not even bothering to steal a glance. Her peripheral alone suggested that both men's backs were turned. Small miracles. What were the chances? She didn't stop to celebrate but continued on to the cafeteria where she hurriedly collected what she could carry from the refrigerator *and returned back to her room, the long way. She'd rather run into anyone other than Boa, especially right now.*

Safely back in their room, young Carston started chowing down on a dab of cottage cheese they'd scavenged, and Chloe watched him, thinking. A plan was brewing, though she admitted it was more like a sentence scratched out on a paper napkin compared to an actual diagrammed map with a charted-out path. In fact, it was less of a plan and more of a cracked-out idea with lots of dangerous holes and unforeseeable twists and turns. Still, she couldn't unhear what she had heard. Couldn't unlearn what she had learned.

Today she'd learned that Boa couldn't step foot on the territory of Orson Finlay – whoever that was. Not without serious consequence. Clearly, he was vividly aware of this situation because he'd attempted to bribe one of Orson's men into doing his dirty work for him. But it hadn't worked. Orson's man hadn't been baited. That impressed Chloe. As a matter of fact, when it came to this Orson guy, Boa's powers were completely ineffective, if not utterly pathetic. This realization made Chloe feel surprisingly and delightfully giddy. Any enemy of Boa's was a friend of Chloe's.

Even so, the timing—the point of absolute abhorrence—had yet to come to pass. It would take Chloe fearing for something much dearer to her than merely her own skin for her to gain the courage to do something she'd never done before.

2

"Ma'am, are you all right?" the lady dressed in a tie-die dress and sandals asked Chloe.

"Yes, sorry," Chloe responded, slightly shaken.

"No puzzles then," the lady said perceptively, guiding Chloe to a shelf busting with figurines of dragons and fairies and all sorts of mystical creatures.

One dragon was clinging to triumphantly to the top of rock twice the size of him. His mouth was open in an eternal roar. Chloe knew without asking that his roar was one of pride and victory for having conquered the feat. She understood the desire to reach that pinnacle of success. She'd been working on it herself with her evening collage classes for some time now. Chloe sighed.

"Anything here that might interest your son?" the lady asked.

"Yes, I believe so."

3

The extra five minutes of time had been all used up, and then some. It was worth it though, Chloe told herself, the paper string handles of a stamped paper bag dangling from her fingers. She would have to hustle to get home close to on time. She'd forgotten that she'd also cautiously walked off course because of the bad feeling she'd had from the man sitting on the bus stop bench. Suddenly, she had the same bad feeling as she'd had upon seeing the basket of snakes inside of the store. The excitement of her purchase sank away as feelings of dread crept back up as she walked down the decently noneventful street. Self-consciously, Chloe peeked over her shoulder and checked the sidewalks on both sides of the street.

Nothing out of the ordinary.

No one that resembled the man at the bus stop.

She reminded herself that, according to that conversation she'd overheard long ago, she shouldn't have to worry about running into Mitchell the Boa. After she'd learned of Orson Finlay's existence, she'd begun to discreetly ask people in Boa's house about him. Fearing it would it get back to Boa, she had to slip it casually into conversation, which had been a challenge, but it'd paid off. She'd collected tidbits here and there. Enough to have a vague idea where Finlay's borders lay. One, very drunk, very helpful, dark-skinned young man with a chip on his shoulder against the world, claimed to have an inside. He'd bragged about a neighborhood still occupied by small businesses and old school civility. Finlay was looking to expand his domain there to be ahead of the future. For the time, no one held claim to it, but because of Finlay's expressed plans, no one dared. It was neutral ground yet protected at the same time. That's where Chloe had decided to run to when the opportunity presented itself. Those are the streets she now walked, headed toward her apartment over Mrs. Ellsberg's store.

4

With freshly tied shoes so he had nothing holding him back, Dagger strolled, well behind his target. Boa's Chloe was a clever, intuitive woman. She kept a keen eye on the streets, ahead of and behind her. He could normally respect such awareness, had it not been for the fact that it was he who was attempting to narrow in on her.

Gaining on the woman was increasingly difficult because of her anxious ways. He was having to constantly pop into doorframes and duck into alleyways to avoid her seeing him. He knew, without a doubt, she'd recognize him from the bus stop. They'd made direct eye contact, and she'd held his gaze far too long. No wonder she'd managed to escape and evade Boa. Neither of them had given her enough credit. However, despite the constant annoyance of her paranoid ways, she really wasn't that good. He was better. She was wearing scrubs after all. Even if he lost her, all he had to do was ride her bus to see where she worked. Some sort of care facility or a hospital. It'd be a dead giveaway.

There was a brief hesitation in her step, and then she moved, unexpectedly, into a store. Stupid. Her little shopping spree gave him ample amount of time to stroll easily along, straight up to the window, behind which she was shopping.

He watched her. She moved gracefully. The store clerk never left her side. That was fine by Dagger, it kept his target's mind elsewhere. Never once did she think to take a glance at the window. Like he said, she wasn't that good. Internally, he laughed at her, and his veins began to vibrate with anticipation. He could almost feel her warm blood pumping weakly over his knife hand already.

At the conclusion of the shopping spree, Boa's Chloe marched out of the store, back into the light of the summer's early evening, and Dagger stepped noiselessly back into the shadows of the next-door store's doorway. She was less than an arm's length away. He could smell her even. She smelled clean, like laundry soap. The good kind. Not the kind that the laundromat sold by the packet.

As she turned the corner, he counted off twenty seconds, giving her time to obsessively check her surroundings. It hurt to wait that long, as close as he was. But he had to wait until the garbage alleyway—roughly forty paces ahead—before he could make his presence known. He could do that. Even if he jogged the last couple steps. He'd be on her before she could see him, let alone do any obnoxious screaming. He really hated when women screamed. It was blood-curdling, bothersome, and pointless. If Dagger made up his mind to get you, you were going to get got.

Dagger started to smirk, then chided himself instead. He was too close to having what he wanted to blow it by getting overexcited. He'd save that for later.

At the end of twenty seconds and ten quick paces of his own, Boa's Chloe was almost to the alleyway, and he was catching up. Another ten paces and she'd be at the alleyway, and he'd be on her. Figuratively. As attractive as she was, she wasn't his type. No, his plan was to pull her swiftly aside and have his cloth over her nose and mouth before she could even say "Aaa!" Then, she'd disappear into some file of unsolved mysteries.

Five paces. To Dagger's great elation, his target had done him the favor of losing her regular focus and was looking down at the walk. Stupid. He was readying his rag when he caught a glimpse of a bum, straight ahead, walking opposing directions as he and his target. That was fine. Dagger would wait a couple extra paces, the bum would pass, his target would be only slightly past the alleyway, and he'd still pull her in with no problem. It was better even. The bum would serve as a distraction when she looked up rather than her going checking her surroundings again. Should the bum happen to turn around and see, well… Dagger would get to unsheathe his knife. It was perfect. He couldn't have planned it better. This was turning out to be a great day.

Not yet, Dagger recited silently. Two paces. Reaching out, like she was just an old friend, he was within reach of taking a feel of the fabric at the back of her shirt scrub. One more step…

5

"Chloe," said a man's voice that Chloe instantly recognized.

Glancing up immediately, Chloe saw Doc standing directly in front of her. He'd been looking right at her as he spoke, but his eyes were quickly drawn away, seeming distracted and confused.

"Doc, are you all right? What are you doing here?" Noticing a huge ugly gash in his forehead, she reached up instinctively, but froze when he dodged her touch. He was still staring into the distance.

"Did you know that guy?" asked Doc.

"What? What guy?"

Doc looked at her sharply. "That guy," he said, pointing toward the alleyway.

Chloe looked where Doc was pointing, seeing no one. "There's no one there, Doc. Are you—"

"There *was* someone. He took off the moment I addressed you. He was literally right behind you. You could have felt him, he was so close."

Chloe reached behind her, touching her fingers to the small of her back. Doc was right. She'd almost not even realized it, but yes, something had brushed her. She could still feel it in a way. "Oh, cripes, Doc! What did he look like?" Her legs started to shake.

Doc noticing her alarm, said, "You're all right, he's gone."

"Thanks to *you*," Chloe spurted, her voice coming more forcefully than she'd intended. She couldn't help it; her nerves were all but hightailing for the hills. "What should I do? Should I call the police?"

"I'll give a description if you do, but I don't think there's anything they can do since he didn't do anything, and he's gone now."

"But he could have! He was *going* to, I know it. I had the terrible sick feeling ever since—"

"Ever since what?" Doc asked.

She looked at him straight on. "What did he look like?"

"Short and Asian."

"Cripes, Doc. That's the man I saw at the bus stop."

"Did he speak to you?"

"No, but we both had a real good look at each other."

"Maybe it was nothing. Maybe he only meant to catch up to you to get your number."

Chloe shook her head. She didn't believe in "maybes." "I don't think so. If it hadn't been for you…" She trailed off, thinking. "What *are* you doing here?"

"Long story, but it turns out my head could use some attention, if I don't want to die of infection. I was headed to the bus stop to ask if you'd be willing to help me with it. I was going to meet you right where you found me lying on my face. Remember?"

"Yes, I remember."

"When the bus arrived, I hadn't quite gotten there yet, but I saw you get off. Then you turned away from the route you took when we walked together. I thought at first, maybe you saw me and didn't want to talk to me. Then I caught a glimpse of that guy, and he seemed to be following you."

"So, you followed me to," she accused. She regretted it immediately.

"Yeah." His voice was low, like maybe he'd done something wrong but wasn't sure.

Chloe reached out to touch his arm, then stopped. Her hand was shaking so bad that she couldn't make it settle. She didn't want him to know how scared she was, so she let her hand fall back to her side. "I'm glad you did. I don't want to imagine what might have happened if you hadn't been here."

"Probably nothing. I may have overreacted."

Chloe could still feel the chill from a touch where the man had reached out for her. "It wasn't nothing," was all she said. Her problems were none of Doc's business. He had enough problems of his own.

Glancing around, Chloe wondered, what had shifted in the time since she'd run off and had taken to hiding in this area to now? Had Mr. Finlay not taken control of this area? Had he changed his mind? Was it no longer safe? Where would she go? What should she do?

"Chloe," Doc said gently.

When she looked up at him, she realized that the tides had changed. It was *her* in need of help, rather than the other way around. "Would you walk me home?" she asked.

"Yes," Doc said without hesitation.

They started on their way, and Chloe no longer felt like she was being followed. In fact, just as she had the first time she'd walked with Doc, she felt safe. The only eyes she felt on her now were Doc's. He kept glancing over, checking on her. Credit to him though, he didn't ask if she was all right. She wasn't. He must have gathered as much. Bum or not, he was intuitive.

This new side that Doc was allowing her to see, it was different. It wasn't bum-like at all. Maybe it's how Carston saw all bums. Or maybe it was how a rescued victim sees their rescuer. Or, maybe, it's just how Chloe was beginning to see Doc—for the kind person he was, not for scary person he was trying to be.

6

Everything had been on pace for Dagger to have his reward by sundown. As it was now, Dagger watched his target walk away, with a bum of all people. Then he remembered. Her son, the black crusader for the homeless. Of course, she knew him through the kid. Dagger spat on the ground.

The bum was scrawny and weak, Dagger could have taken him. The only reason he hadn't was because the target would have gotten away, but worse, she'd been made aware. She was paranoid enough as it is. Watching them walk away, without so much as a care in the world, was better. He knew her bus, her neighborhood, and tomorrow, he would know her place of work. That way, he'd have a place to follow her from, in case she changed things up. It wasn't rocket science, although Dagger was pretty crafty. He'd gotten this far using nothing but his own wily wits and slack rumors.

As his target disappeared around the corner, Dagger unsheathed his knife and began polishing the shiny blade in habit and preparation. As much as he wanted to follow the homely duo all the way home and be done with it, his trusty wits told him to wait. It had been too close just moments ago, and although there was no way the target could be certain she'd been in danger, her guard would most definitely be up. Soon, he promised himself. Soon.

Chapter Thirteen

1

Carston was lying on his back in the middle of the apartment living room floor, his right calf resting on his left knee. Draped over his face was his book, open to where he'd last left off, but his eyes were shut. He was dreaming. Dreaming about training. Dreaming about climbing that first mountain. Then the next. Then the next. How far would he go? What places would he see? What people would he meet? Would he fall? Of course. Would he get back up? Yes. Would he climb if he lost a leg? Absolutely. What did he need to do to get there?

That was where he felt stuck. What linked the *now* to the *future*?

The metal stairway leading to the apartment door began rattling. Footsteps were approaching? Footsteps, plural?

Carston leapt into action, his book flying off his face and tumbling to the floor. As Carston landed on his feet, the book landed on its spine, fell over, and closed. Carston paid it no attention. He rushed to the window then slowed down. He had to peek out very carefully, as to not cause any noticeable movement that would catch an eye. At the same time, he placed his fingers on the deadbolt, turning it so very quietly. It clicked into place at precisely the same moment Carston recognized Mama in the lead, a small bag hanging from her hand. Behind her was Doc.

Carston threw the lock back open and pushed the door open for them to enter. "Doc!" he exclaimed. "What ya doing here?"

"Hi to you to," said Chloe.

"That's the second time someone's asked me that today," Doc replied dryly.

Carston threw his arms around Mama's neck. "Hi! What's in the bag?"

She laughed, and it sounded good, but reserved. "Its nothing... but a surprise! My bus actually ran on time for like the first time ever, so I stopped in at a little place." Something concerning crossed her face, and he wondered what it was, but she quickly erased it. She held out the bag. "It's a 'thinking of you' present."

Carston smiled, secretly hoping it wasn't another magic trick. Although entertaining, they weren't really his thing. Reaching for the bag, all sorts of ideas of what it could be entered his mind. None of them would be what he was really hoping for, but he loved Mama so much he wore his brightest expression of anticipation. He wondered if she could read him as easily as he could read her. He hoped not. He'd love anything as long as it let Mama know how very much that he loved her.

A quick glance at Doc was no help. His face was as readable as a page without words.

Carston reached into the bag and felt right away that it was a book. The brightest expression he'd put on started to become real. Mama could rarely afford to buy books. They were too expensive. Yet here one was. He pulled it out, and for a brief moment, his heart stopped—in a good way. In that way it tends to do when you get so excited that the heart forgets to pump.

The cover of book he held in his hand was a light bluish-green, similar to that of condensed ice that has had all the air squeezed out from it. The art was simple, but it didn't matter: it was a snowy mountain. The title read *The Ascent of Everest* by John Hunt. All at once, his heart began beating again, only much faster than previously.

Forgetting momentarily that he was the man of the house, Carston leapt with such enthusiasm, he nearly barreled his mama over with his explosive hug. She *had* been thinking of him. Really thinking of him. He knew the thought of climbing scared her. Somehow, she'd managed to put her own fears aside and think of only him. Carston loved the gift, and the thoughtfulness of the gift, beyond measure. Still, he loved her more.

"You're welcome," she said, her chest bouncing as though she were laughing, though no sound of laughter arrived.

Before Carston released his mama, he caught a glimpse of Doc's hand moving out to support Chloe from toppling over backward before thinking better of it and quickly pulling it back to himself. Carston smiled, then let Mama go.

"Thank you. I love it," Carston said politely.

Chloe looked at him curiously. "So, I gathered. Anyway, in case you haven't noticed, our mutual friend here, needs my superior nursing skills again. I'll just go fetch my kit." She turned to Doc. "After I get my stuff from the bathroom, why don't you use the shower and get cleaned up? It'll give you a chance to check for any other wounds that need a thorough cleaning. When you're through, I'll take care of that gash."

Doc didn't argue. Chloe hadn't given him any options but to go along this time.

After she'd dismissed herself, Carston stood before Doc, smiling. It had not escaped his attention that Chloe had referred to Doc as a "mutual friend." In addition to that, the man was standing inside of their apartment. What could have happened to have brought about this dramatic change?

"Your head looks awful. What happened?"

"Your head doesn't look that great either."

Carston laughed. There was nothing wrong with his head. Doc was joshing. "Do your ears hurt too?" Carston asked.

Doc looked confused. "No. Why would they?"

"Your wheels are working so hard, smoke it pouring out of them."

Chloe stepped back into the living room, kit in hand. Nearly stepping on the book Carston had left on the floor where he'd been daydreaming, she said irritably, "Car, pick up your things.

Why must I constantly remind you?" To Doc she directed, "The bathroom is all yours. I left a large white t-shirt and a pair of shorts in there. They should fit. Throw your dirty clothes into the hall and I'll start them on washing. I left out a razor also, in case you'd like a shave."

Doc appeared suddenly shy, looking down at his filthy shoes. Carston expected him to argue, but instead, he grumbled faintly, "Thank you." He disappeared down the hall, the bathroom door clicking shut as weightlessly as a hummingbird feeding on a bloom.

By the time Doc, clean and shaved, returned, Chloe and Carston had a stack of pancakes prepared and waiting on the table with a dish of butter. Carston had dragged over the small side table from next to the couch and had stacked a few of his largest books on it as a makeshift third seat. Doc's dirty clothes, including his shoes, were nearly done agitating in their small washing machine, with a dab of color-safe Clorox and an extra scoop of soap. The moment he laid his eyes on the pancakes, it appeared they were stuck there.

"You may as well stay for dinner. Your clothes won't be done for another forty minutes," Chloe said matter-of-factly. Her gaze at Doc had lingered a little longer than necessary, before she turned away and pretended to tidy up the kitchen. The kitchen was already clean.

"Sit by me!" Carston invited as he carefully climbed aboard his mound of books.

"Car, did you heat the syrup?" Chloe asked. The microwave gave a three-beep reminder that something was still in there.

"Yes," Carston replied, jumping down again. "I'll get it."

No matter what chair Doc chose, he'd be sitting next to both Chloe and Carston. He sat down the same time as Chloe and mumbled again, "Thank you. It's been a long time since I've sat at a table or had a hot cooked meal."

"It's not a big deal. I hope you like pancakes," replied Chloe.

Carston skipped back to his makeshift seat, warm syrup slopping in its tiny pitcher. "Do I! I've never seen such a tall tower of pancakes before! This is a *huge* deal! This is like the best day ever."

Doc nodded. "Pancakes are good."

Carston noticed that Doc's hands shook slightly when he lifted the platter of pancakes, declining to serve himself first. Only after Carston and Chloe had helped themselves to buttermilk cakes, did he delicately sink a fork into the top cake and transfer it to his plate. Again, he waited until they'd finished with the butter and syrup, then politely skipped the butter, and used only a dab of syrup. Carston, shoving bite after bit of delicious cake into his mouth, watched Doc earnestly as he took his first bite. Doc chewed, for what seemed like forever. Carston opened his mouth to ask why, when Mama interrupted.

"Car, do *not* speak with your mouth full."

Doc gave them both sideways glances. Carston hadn't been able to get a single word out before she'd shut him down. Carston gave Doc a guilty, but knowing, smirk. Chloe obviously intended to keep him from asking pestering questions, but how could he not? He chewed as fast as he could, then swallowed.

"What's your favorite thing to do?" Carston asked Doc.

"Walk."

"Why do you like walking? Where do you go?"

Doc was quiet for a moment as he chewed and swallowed. "I don't go anywhere particularly."

"What do you do when you're not walking?"

"Sit."

Carson giggled. "Have you ever had a job?"

Chloe glared at him. "Car," she scolded.

"Yes."

"What was it?"

Doc didn't answer for the longest time, making Carston wonder if it's because he'd never really had a job. Then he said, "I was in the Army."

Chloe's eyes widened in surprise, and Carston's widened in excitement.

"Really? What'd you do?"

"I walked a lot and did a lot of PT."

"What's PT?"

Although Doc hadn't eaten that much, he was noticeably slowing down. "Physical training."

Carston sat taller on his mound of books, and they swayed slightly. "That's how you know about chin-ups and pull-ups," he declared enthusiastically.

"I suppose so." Doc made eye contact with Carston for the first time since they'd sat at the table. "And how are your chin-ups progressing?"

This time it was Carston's turn to give a one-word answer. "Slow."

"That's good," Doc said. Going back to his cake, he only nibbled at the corners, not taking full bites.

"It is?"

"Yeah, you don't want to overtrain at your age. It could cause more damage than good."

"What should I be doing then?"

"You're doing all the right things already. Walking and building strength slowly will go a long way.

Carston's heart lifted. All this time he'd felt like he was behind in his training. To hear now that he was on the right track was exhilarating. "What about climbing? Did you ever do any climbing?"

"Sure."

"Really? Where?" Carston could barely contain himself.

"Afghanistan. It wasn't a mountain I set out to climb, like you're thinking. It was a way of life. A way of travel. The only thing we set out to do was complete our mission."

"Wow." Carston sat in awe, speechless for an entire twenty seconds. He'd never thought about that before. To him, to climb had always meant reaching the top. He hadn't realized that people around the world climbed out of necessity, not joy. "Could you teach me?"

Doc slid his plate away and folded his arms on the table. "You're overthinking it, Short Stack. There's nothing that needs being taught yet. Say you're traveling, on your feet, not in a car. What would you need?"

"A backpack."

"All right, yes. What do you need for yourself though? Don't think of stuff. Think of you. Just you."

Carston felt momentarily stumped. He felt Mama's eyes studying him, waiting for his answer, same as Doc. Carston thought of Jordan in the book he'd been reading. "The strength to keep going?"

"Yes, stamina."

"How can I do that? I'm not allowed to walk past the park."

Doc glanced at Chloe, then back. "I agree, you shouldn't walk the city streets. What you could do is go hiking. Outside the city."

"That's what Jordan does with his parents," Carston said excitedly.

"If its all right with your mom, maybe you could tag along with them," Doc suggested.

"No," Carston said. "Jordan is the boy in my book. He's working on climbing all seven summits."

Doc nodded his understanding, then peeked at Chloe, raising an eyebrow and giving her an "are you game" questioning look. Finally, someone on his side, Carston thought.

Chloe shook her head. "I don't even own a car."

It was quiet for a moment while Carston worked up courage. "Doc?" he finally asked, "Would *you* go with me?"

The word "no" was forming on Doc's lips. Carston felt the disappointment sinking in. Would he always suffer being trapped at the ready and willing, but never arrive at able? When would it change? What would it take?

Chloe said, "I don't know how I would feel about that."

Doc and Carston both looked at her. Neither saying anything.

It was that moment that it dawned on Carston, the one disheartening word that Carston was terrified to hear hadn't made it past Doc's lips. Even now, as they looked at Chloe it still remained caught up. Perhaps it was snagged somewhere between Doc's usual dialog of "bug off, short stack" and "actually, I'd love to." Or maybe it only got stuck on piece of pancake gummed up in the back of Doc's throat. Whatever had happened to it, "no" never made it out. This was the moment Carston felt his life might truly begin.

2

The discussion of whether Carston would be allowed to go out of town to hike with Doc had been put on hold. Chloe just didn't have the strength after such a trying afternoon; what with being followed and now Doc's presence in her apartment. It was a lot to emotionally sort through, and she hadn't even had a moment of free time to try. She couldn't complain; she was grateful that Doc had come looking for her. If he hadn't been on the sidewalk, right in front of her, saying her name, there was no telling what could have happened.

After the dinner dishes were stacked in the sink, Chloe directed Doc to sit on the couch. On the cushion next to him, she lined out her medical supplies. He sat there, watching her, taking turns looking at her and watching her hands lay out the things she needed. His relaxed manner spoke volumes at how much more at ease he was this time, as opposed to the last time she'd seen to his wounds. Then again, last time, it was him, not her, who'd been part of a trying experience.

Chloe began carefully examining Doc's forehead. "It looks better than it did before you cleaned it in the shower, but you were right. This gash would have gotten infected in a hurry. It's very deep. There's no way you would have been able to keep it clean enough."

"Yeah."

"You know," she said thoughtfully. "This would be a lot easier if you allowed me to cut your hair back a bit. It's long enough it gets in the way. It's going to be in the way later when you're trying to keep it clean."

Doc reluctantly agreed that she could trim it back, so she did, trimming it back evenly over his entire head. The towel she'd wrapped around him caught most of the hair she was removing. As it floated down through her fingers, she couldn't help but notice that it was as soft as she'd thought it would be.

Making small conversation, Chloe started to ask if he'd like sideburns, when she stopped abruptly. She'd reached his left ear. When she'd lifted the hair away from the ear, much of the ear was missing. Based on the straight-across way the top of the ear was shaped—or not shaped, as it was—the ear did not seem to have been born that way. Chloe was shocked at the sight of it and shaken by what could have caused it. She was unsure how to continue. She worried that touching it would cause him pain. Then again, she also worried that not touching it would offend him, like she thought he was diseased or something. She jumped slightly when he spoke.

"It was cut off."

Still pausing, her fingers hovering above the ear, she said, "I see."

"It won't hurt if you touch it, but you don't have to if it makes you feel uncomfortable. What you've done already is fine."

Carston had been lying on his belly on the floor, watching the entire time. Now he jumped up to take a look at this strange phenomenon. "How'd it get cut off?" he asked excitedly.

Kids always got excited over the strangest things. "Car," Chloe scolded, catching him by the wrist, before his fingers touched it, "don't you dare."

Doc chuckled lightly. "It's all right, I guess," he said, turning slightly to look at them both.

Carston touched the ear with a giant smile on his face. "Cool!"

Chloe smacked his hand away. "All right, that's enough." She went straight to work trimming the hair from around the area, hoping the action would lessen Carston's distasteful exhilaration over Doc's ear amputation. Secretly, however, she took a certain amount of reassurance from the fact that Car had touched the ear and it hadn't seemed to bother Doc at all. Still, Carston's curiosity didn't peter out.

"Who cut it off?" Carston asked.

"A man."

"Why did he do it?"

Chloe couldn't see Doc's face, but his pause gave her the impression that he was attempting to choose the correct words. "An ear-piercing gone wrong."

Carston's eyes bulged. "I'd say!"

Chloe didn't know if Carston believed Doc's story or not. She certainly didn't, but he lied back down on the floor, seeming satisfied. For now, anyway. She knew her son, his mind would dwell on it, and likely, more questions would surface later.

After Chloe had finished trimming Doc's hair and the towel and hair had been removed, she reached for her alcohol wipes. Remarkably, Doc didn't flinch the entire time she disinfected the area.

"How did it happen?" Chloe asked. She felt his eyes on her, but she kept working as though she didn't.

"The ear or the gash?" Doc asked.

There'd been more to the ear story, she knew, but she also knew better than to pry. He'd already given the only answer he was willing to supply about that. "The gash."

"Walked into a drug deal." He sounded so calm, as if it were no big deal.

She met his eyes this time. "Didn't you know?" she asked, not intending to show her concern. It was showing, nonetheless.

The corners of his lips turned up making him look even more handsome than he already was. "I would have known if I hadn't been asleep."

"Asleep? What?" she asked, astonished. How could he have been asleep?

"I sleepwalk," he answered. "I hadn't always, but I do now. Apparently, I slept walked right into the middle of it. Woke up when they grabbed me."

"Cripes, Doc. You could have been killed!"

"I wasn't," he said, sounding absolutely indifferent one way or the other.

"But you *could* have been," she insisted irritably. She forcibly reminded herself that she had no cause to care on a personal level. Nevertheless, she couldn't push away a certain question. She had to ask. For educational purposes. In case she ever found herself in the same circumstance. "How did you manage to get away?"

Doc's brown eyes locked on hers, making something inside of her, that she'd long since killed, stir again. The sensation both surprised and scared her. Chloe broke the eye contact, returning her focus to the gash in his head.

It was a terrible gash, but she could fix it up. No problem. She'd fixed equally terribly gashes during her time at Boa Mateo's. Some worse even. In those stenchy rooms is where she'd started to realize that she was good at nursing, and she liked helping the girls, even if only in a small way. In return, they'd helped her, in a very big way.

Doc's voice spoke, drawing her out of the dark tunnel she would have otherwise traveled down. "A…" he paused, apparently trying to drudge up the correct word again, "…friend…helped me. Without her, I'd be dead right now, for sure."

"Oh," Chloe said. A friend. A *female* friend. "Well, it's going to need stitches," Chloe informed Doc in the most professional, nonpersonal, voice she could muster.

"I trust you," he said, his face only inches from hers.

Although—or maybe especially since—the small space between them felt warm and relaxed, Chloe pulled back. She didn't pull back so much as to make it look like she couldn't handle the job, or herself. She pulled back just enough to regain a more professional, and a less intimate, distance. Suddenly, she wondered if she could do this at all. Be this close to him, and not be this close to him. "I can't—"

Doc looked down at her stitching materials. She knew he recognized them for what they were, and that she'd initially laid them out so she could use them. If she refused now, he'd wonder why. Then she'd be left to wonder what conclusion he'd come to—no matter what excuses she gave.

"I can't give you any local anesthetic."

"That's all right," he said, and she knew it was true.

She'd thought she'd recognized a special sort of strength in Doc before, right after that man had threatened Mrs. Ellsberg with a gun. Now she knew she'd been right. In all of her years, she would never forget how a bum, the man sitting before her now, had saved everything she'd ever loved. What kind of strength that must have taken. Even Boa didn't possess that kind of strength. Once, she's had to put stitches in Boa's leg after he'd stupidly kicked a brick wall in anger. That man had recoiled and cried like a baby.

"I'm sorry to be such an intrusion this evening," Doc apologized as she sewed his gash together.

Keeping her eyes on the task, Chloe replied, "It's not an intrusion. I'm glad to be able to pay back the favor."

"I did nothing. I was only—"

Carston, still watching everything with great interest, shifted on the floor. The movement caught Choe's attention. Carston was far more perceptive than anyone could guess. This evening, he was not only watching certain things with his eyes, he'd been picking up on things unseen as well. Chloe guessed that she failed to recognize at least half of what Carston caught onto. He kept such things held very close to his chest. So close, in fact, sometimes she wasn't even sure if she hadn't been making up the fact that he knew more than he appeared to know. Maybe she only fabricated that he understood certain things so she wouldn't feel so alone. This time, however, Carston's curiosity and enthusiasm got the best of him, and gave him away.

Carston sat up and asked excitedly, "What favor?"

Chapter Fourteen

1

How much fun was he about to have? There was nothing like what he was about to watch. Better than any movie.

Mailman popped a piece of popcorn in his mouth. It was too buttery and too salty, but he chewed it nonetheless. A good show was always better with popcorn. Mailman had been craving this for too long. He wanted a good show. In fact, he wanted the best show, followed by the best snack (debatable), and the best seat.

He had the best seat for sure.

Mailman kicked his feet gaily, and the heels of his shoes bumped soundlessly against the wall. He was sitting on the roof of the business situated straight across from the thrift shop. Taking a sip from his soda can, he looked down expectantly, studying everything about the building that housed all those ridiculously reasonably priced secondhand clothes. Someone really ought to put that poor owner girl out of her misery. What, with her barely scraping by in this thankless cold world. It was a sin.

There was a puff of movement behind the thrift shop. Then another. The puff became a never-ending thin stream of gray smoke. Smoke was so lovely the way it rose in the air like one single uninterrupted thought. Heavier and heavier the smoke grew, right before Mailman's gleeful eyes. It was becoming a flow of boundless beauty. Not as beautiful as what was to come, but a mighty and promising precursor. Foreplay really. His feet bounced against the wall as he tossed in another piece of popcorn.

Is it heating up your cold world? Mailman asked the girl—inside of his head only, of course. He'd really like to be there to ask her in person, to share this experience with her, but he couldn't afford to be seen. Orson had strict rules about "his" community members not being harmed. What a psychopath. Despite the fact that the store owner surely would have appreciated Mailman's personal attentiveness to her situation, sometimes sacrifices had to be made. For the better good. Maybe she would realize that later.

Hot fiery flames shot up into the air, sending delightful sensations pulsing into Mailman's crotch area. The flesh of his left cheek ticked. Then again, maybe she wouldn't.

2

Chloe had diligently made sure her and Carston's dinner guest and patient had been excused from the apartment before Carston had been sent to bed. The last thing Chloe needed was for Carston to get it in his mind that there were any juvenile crushes going on between her and Doc. Carston looked up to the man enough as it was. Why Carston chose him was beyond her. All the man had, he wore on his back, he slept on the streets, he stole, he tried to scare kids (unsuccessfully), he stank (well, not currently). And, she reminded herself…he was respectful, he saved little old store owners from robbery, he saved her from the grasp of a stranger's hand, he gave her son training tips, he'd once been in the military.…

Chloe paused on the thought that Doc had once been in the military and had served in Afghanistan as she pulled her feet into bed and snuggled into her sheets. She wondered what had happened there. What had caused him to return home and take to the streets? Or had it been something else that had driven him to the streets? Drugs? No, she knew a druggie when she saw one. Alcohol? Maybe, but wasn't alcohol abuse usually driven by something more? Trauma?

Stress? Mental instability? Yes, she's seen that in him firsthand, but again, she guessed that his current mental struggle stemmed from something that had happened in the military. Afghanistan specifically. It was all too common in soldiers returning from war. Although Veteran's Assistance was making leaps and bounds in providing better care for the soldiers who had been honorably discharged, there was still a great deal of room for improvement. Mental devastation and ruin just seemed too high of a price to ask of brave men and women like Doc. He'd put his life and future aside for everyone in the country but himself. Now he was outside, sleeping who knew where, while she, who had never set aside her life for any honorable purpose, was safe in her bed. It wasn't fair, but she supposed that's why men like Doc rose up in this world. To save those who didn't even know what they needed saving from.

A tear slid down her cheek as her mind grew heavier and heavier with each passing second, pulling her into awaiting dreams. Despite a strenuous attempt at coming up with a good reason why Doc had risen to a call that was now slowly destroying him, everything in the world began to disappear. What if she and Carston could help him escape his inevitable dead end, as Mrs. Ellsberg had helped her and Carston to escape theirs? But not tonight; she was so tired. She was always so tired. Intuitively, rather than consciously, her mind registered one last thing before it slid completely away, giving into her deep exhausting weariness. Carston.

Carston's gentle presence slipped silently into the room. She heard the faint click of the lamp next to her bed, soft sound of fabric as a lightweight throw was pulled over her legs, and then he was gone again. She would have vowed to remember to turn off the lamp herself tomorrow, only her fatigue seized her first, and she slept.

Chloe woke suddenly, bolting straight up in bed. With a near-useless groggy mind, she listened. What had she heard? What had woken her? The darkness of her bedroom led her to the conclusion that it was yet night and that the neighborhood would likely be mostly stagnant, with the exception of a barking dog or siren now and then. Still, *something* had woken her. She was not a light sleeper. Typically, she felt better knowing Mrs. Ellsberg slept directly beneath her. But not tonight. Something felt off. Something felt wrong.

Maybe it was the heat of the day, stuck in their upper apartment. Chloe flipped her feet out of the covers and slipped the tiny window up, just a hair. Maybe Carston needed her. He rarely did, but still. She tiptoed across the hall and peeked into his room. She saw him easily, with the moon shining through his window. His body was curled up like a cat, one toe sticking out from beneath the corner of his throw. He always looked so much tinier, and more vulnerable, when he slept. Chloe stood there, watching over him, as she listened again. What had woken her?

She was thinking that maybe it had only been the way Doc's brown eyes had returned to her in her dream, when she heard a strange noise. It wasn't loud. It was faint. So faint, in fact, she wasn't certain she'd heard it at all. Then she heard it again. Or maybe she sensed it again would be a better description of something so unclear, so unfamiliar. It wasn't logical in the slightest, but she felt tremendously threatened. What, after the day she'd had, being followed, then almost grabbed, it wasn't too farfetched to feel a little edgy, was it? Of course, her pounding heart was reacting a bit more than edgy. Chloe made her way to living area, then climbed onto the couch one knee at a time. With a nervous hand, she reached for the blinds, slowly bringing her nose closer to the window to peer out.

A loud ringing, filled the small apartment. Chloe pushed away from the window with both feet and landed on her rump with a heavy thud. Shocked and sitting on the floor, Chloe attempted to regather herself. It was only her phone ringing from her bedroom. In the small apartment, in the middle of the night, it sounded like a tsunami warning.

"Cripes," Chloe moaned, both disappointed and mad at herself for being so jumpy.

It continued ringing shrilly, keeping her heart rate elevated. For the love of not having a heart attack in the middle of the night, she needed to turn it down. The noise continued, reminding her that the ringing meant someone was on the other end, waiting.

"Who's calling me in the middle of the night?" she whined, lifting herself from the floor and rubbing her rump.

"Mama? Are you all right?" Carston asked, making his way up the short hallway.

Chloe met him and touched her fingers to the top of his tight dark hair. "Yes, baby, I'm fine. Go back to bed. It's just my phone." It felt like forever, reaching her phone, to shut it up. "Hello?" she answered.

Mrs. Ellsberg's raspy voice came over the miniature speaker installed in Chloe's small cell phone. "Sorry to wake you."

"I'm already awake."

"Oh? You already know?"

"Know what?" asked Chloe.

"Spiff it Up Clothing is on fire. From the looks of it, it's going to burn to the ground."

Chloe sat on the edge of her bed. "What? What about the neighboring buildings?"

"The Fire Department is all over it. I think they'll be able to save the other businesses, but there's sure to be a lot of damage."

"You don't think it'll crawl down the street, do you?"

"No, no, of course not," Mrs. Ellsberg soothed. "I only called you so you wouldn't be caught off-guard."

"What about the owner? Doesn't she live there? Did she make it out?"

Mrs. Ellsberg paused in responding. "Abby? I don't know. I'm going to skedaddle over there and take a look."

"No! Please don't go over there," Chloe begged.

"Shizzle, I'm not going in. I just want to see if she's all right. If she needs anything."

Chloe had a terrible feeling. The same terrible feeling since she'd woke up. Something was definitely wrong. Suddenly, Chloe wished she'd known, before this moment, that the young lady's name had been Abby. They could have been friends if Chloe would have been more of a friendly-type of person, like she used to be. These days, she just hid at work or hid at home, but she was always hiding. If not physically, then, without a doubt, socially. Too afraid of getting to know anyone. Too afraid of being "found out."

"If you see her," Chloe blurted suddenly, "give her my number. Tell her I want to help too."

Mrs. Ellsberg made a sniffling noise, said, "I will," then disconnected the call.

In the silence, Chloe looked up and saw Carston standing in the doorway.

"What happened?" asked Carston, his pajamas making him look seven again, rather than ten.

"Nothing, baby. Everything is fine."

He shook his head, always the perceptive one. "That's not true. Who's in trouble?"

"No one's in trouble. There's a fire, up the street."

"What caused it?"

Chloe paused, thinking of the man who had nearly grabbed her. Attempted kidnapping and arson—neither of which had yet to be proven—weren't relatable at all. The only similarity she was drawing was the general rise in crime. Shaking her head slowly, she answered, "I don't know. It was probably an accident, like leaving on a burner, or an electrical outlet. That kind of thing."

Carston's expression didn't change. It looked neither worried nor relieved. It dawned on Chloe that she wasn't trying to convince him, she was trying to convince herself. Carston then turned and headed in the direction of the living room rather than his bedroom.

"Where are you going?" Chloe asked, following hastily after him.

His back was to her, and he was headed toward the front door. "Checking on things."

"You most certainly are not!" Chloe hollered, slamming her fists into her hips.

When he turned around, she saw the young likeness of his father, Mitch Mateo. She nearly gasped and wondered if he would simply storm out the door, cold as ice. Then, just as swiftly as the nightmare had appeared, the horrendousness washed away. She wasn't looking at Mitch Mateo, she was looking at someone a million times better. In the young man before her, she saw the strength to rise to an occasion, like Doc, and the heart to make it count, like Tasha and Mrs. Ellsberg. She was looking at her son, Carston

"Mama—" Carston started to argue. Chloe held up a hand, stopping him.

Quickly, Chloe grabbed their coats from the closet, came back, and handed him his. Like the lyrics from the old song "Young Love," by The Judds, he didn't have to say what he was feeling inside, she could see the answer shining his eyes.

"I'm ready now, Car," Chloe said, and she opened the door for him.

3

Downstairs, the first thing Chloe noticed was the three glaringly obvious duos: firetrucks and firefighters, hoses and water, and smoke and fire. Even though the commotion was far enough up the street to lessen much of the clatter and hollering of voices, it wasn't far enough to lessen the unease.

Sitting in front of Mrs. Ellsberg's store were the guests of "Under the Awning." All, except Suicide Sam and Doc, who were missing. The others were still tucked inside of their bags and blankets. They were awake, of course, and watching with wide eyes. Tempted to ask them if they knew what had happened, Chloe opened her mouth. Seeing that they had barely so much as budged in their bags, she closed it again. The victory over temptation was all for naught, however, Carston asked them anyway.

"Did you see what happened?" Carston asked the group.

Barely able to pry her eyes away from the spectacle, Boop replied with a simple, "No."

"Good evening, young sir and Miss Chloe," Oscar said, addressing them both. "I don't recall seeing anything out of the ordinary."

"Did there happen to be anyone walking about before the fire started?" Chloe asked.

Carston glanced up at her, and she realized that she shouldn't have asked. He must be wondering why she would ask such a thing after she had said it was likely a burner or electrical outlet. It didn't escape her attention that he hadn't questioned her, although she wasn't sure what to make of that observation.

"There was a man, Mrs. Carston," said Gargantuan.

Everyone looked at him.

"Where was he?" Chloe asked, not caring now if Carston was onto her or not. "What did he look like?"

Gargantuan didn't answer and just looked back at the fire.

"There is always someone walking the street," Oscar advised, "anytime of the day or night. I wouldn't think too much about what he says."

"'Sides," Boop chimed in, "we are out here. Don't the sproutling, nor his mama, have to worry 'bout no person walking the streets."

Chloe gave the lady with unkept hair and no teeth a small glimpse of appreciation, though she didn't feel better in the slightest. Just then, Doc walked around the corner. It shouldn't have surprised her that tonight he looked like any other man who could have been walking back from having watched the fire. His clothes were clean, his hair was trimmed, and his face was shaved. Another thing that shouldn't have surprised her was that, suddenly and without warning, she felt entirely safe. The unease completely vanished in the matter of seconds.

Not wanting to believe that she had come to trust a homeless thief as much as she apparently did, Chloe yanked her gaze away from Doc's direction, setting her eyes on the only real alternative, the fire. As Mrs. Ellsberg had said, the fire was being well contained.

"Doc!" Carston hollered out. "You're still here!"

Doc didn't holler back and wake what few neighbors might still be sleeping, but if Chloe guessed correctly—and she wasn't about to look to see—she could feel his gaze on her still. "Car, stop your hollering," Chloe lectured.

"There's that handsome devil," Boop cooed upon noticing Doc's approach. "He sure cleans up nice." When Doc was closer, she patted the space between her and Gargantuan. "Settle down right in here, son, and watch the fire with me."

"I think I've seen enough of the fire," Doc replied, walking straight up to Chloe. "Mrs. Ellsberg is over there. I need you to come with me to bring her back."

Chloe looked into his brown eyes. "Abby, is she…"

Doc shook his head.

Chloe's hand flew to her mouth to cover the sound of her own upset. "Car," she said, "stay here, with…" She looked at the three of Carston's homeless friends and picked the one she hoped she could trust the most. "Oscar."

"Yes Ma'am," Oscar said, clearly grasping the gravity of the situation and what she was asking of him without so many words. "Carston, young sir, why don't you sit here with me, and I'll tell you a story about two brothers. It's a story that you'll never find in a book."

Chloe could tell that Carston wanted to go too, that he wanted to be there for Mrs. Ellsberg. But he had always been an obedient child, and the draw of Oscar's promised story was enough to entice Car to sit amidst uncertainty. After all, losing oneself in story as a poultice against reality was unwittingly one of Car's learned survival tactics. It was so deeply embedded within him, starting at such an early age, he'd probably never noticed the correlation.

Chloe followed Doc to where Mrs. Ellsberg was hanging her weight against a fireman, still begging for an answer to her friend's whereabouts. None were being provided. Suicide Sam was dancing amongst the chaos, to everyone's aggravation, wasting everyone's valuable time and attention in trying to have him removed. Before long, they started to ignore him, like a dog, and went back to work, paying no heed to the lunatic running in and out of the water and joining in on important conversations, nodding and listening intently, propping his elbow on the shoulders of the fireman next to him.

4

After Suicide Sam had gotten what he'd come for, he sat on the ledge of a firetruck. Chloe and the new asshole were leading the distraught Mrs. Ellsberg home. The new asshole appeared almost human this evening. One would speculate that he had the hots for Chloe. The fool, he didn't stand a chance. That girl despised speaking to anyone, especially street urchins. To each their own though. It was none of Sam's.

Spiff It Up's putrid fire was mostly under control now, though not before the building had been destroyed beyond repair. Earlier in the evening, Sam had seen the owner of Spiff It Up walking with a take-out bag from Oyster Dive. He'd been bored, and hungry, so he'd watched her walk all the way back, and lock up the outside door. Moments later, all the lights were turned off, and no one came back out.

Sam had become a bother to the work crew so that he could invisibly join in on the fireman's huddle. He thought he might overhear that the owner had, in fact, gone out for the evening. That she'd been at a someone else's house for a party or something. Sam's eyes were old, and his stomach was empty. He could have easily missed her leaving. But that's not what he'd overheard.

The talk that Sam kept picking up was that the entire structure had gone up into flames so quickly there was no way that an occupant could have made it out. No one was seen jumping from or appearing inside of any windows. If the occupant was home, she was believed to be deceased. They would only know for sure once the structure had cooled, and they could do a full investigation. Until then, she couldn't be accounted for, and it didn't look good.

Sam hung his old deteriorating hands limply between his aching deformed knees. She'd been in there all right. Mrs. Ellsberg would be devastated.

Chapter Fifteen

1

Carston had been so absorbed in Oscar's story about the two brothers that he'd ceased thinking about the terrible fire and the foul-smelling odor that had been discharging into the night air. As a matter of fact, the clamor and stench more added to the allure of Oscar's story than it took away. Carston sat, captivated, by the sound of Oscar's voice, as he was guided from stage to stage, witnessing the furrowing and unfurling of two unfamiliar, out of the ordinary, lives. Carston's head knew it was only a story, but the intensity in which Oscar told it made his heart feel as though it were as real as the cool concrete beneath his britches.

When Chloe had walked by, with Mrs. Ellsberg on her arm, Carston had glanced up. A part of him had wanted to go in, to help Mama calm and soothe Mrs. Ellsberg, but a part of him didn't want to budge. He could always ask Oscar to finish telling him the story another time. Would it be the same? Tonight, it felt as though the account was life and death. Tomorrow, under the glaring brightness of reality, it might feel like a story for babies. He didn't want it to end that way.

"Car, you can go upstairs to bed," Chloe said as she helped Mrs. Ellsberg to the door. Doc held the door open for them. "There's so much activity going on in the street tonight, I don't think you have anything to worry about. I'll be up later."

"We'll be here all night," said Boop.

Chloe looked at the toothless woman much like she had before—kind of surprised—only her expression seemed softer. "Thank you," she said.

"Mama," said Carston, "Oscar's story isn't done. May I please hear the end?" Her expression looked doubtful. "It's summer, I can take a nap after helping Mrs. Ellsberg in the morning. I promise not to be testy tomorrow."

"I'll be happy to keep an eye on him, ma'am," offered Oscar.

"As will I," Boop added.

Carston wondered if Boop was enjoying the story as well as he. Gargantuan had already fallen fast asleep, despite the commotion. He could sleep through anything since he simply wasn't affected by life outside of himself like most folks were. Carston had a tiny unsubstantiated hope that Mama would allow this one-time event of him staying out with his homeless friends. Knowing that the chances were closer to nil than they were slim, Carston was surprised to see her head nod.

"Fine, this one time. I'll just be inside, if you need anything. I'll be out to get you." Then she disappeared into the store.

Carston's face lit up, and he looked at Oscar, whose face was unchanged.

"All right, settle in, young sir," was all Oscar said. As Carston settled back against the window, like the others, Oscar picked up where he had left off. "It's the sort of choice one never expects to face. There has always been good. There has always been bad. But this... this had never been tried before, nor, I suspect, it shall be ever again."

Doc sat down in his usual spot. He would hear the words being spoken, but if he'd been listening, Carston couldn't know. It didn't matter. What mattered was, Doc was here too. That was enough.

2

Chloe stepped out into the night air, weary and burdened.

Being there for Mrs. Ellsberg during her time of need wasn't the reason for her weariness. It wasn't often the woman needed the support rather than was the support. Being able to do for Mrs. Ellsberg was a rare privilege. An honor. However, it was very late—early into the new day actually—and Chloe was fatigued. It'd been a hard day. Heck, it'd been a hard life.

So what? she thought.

She could give in. Give up. She could lie down and feel sorrowful about her past, and the weight she carried every single day because of it. She could yield to the never-ending terror that there was always something lurking around the corner waiting to grab her and Car and drag them back. She could stop running in her mind. She could stop hiding her heart. She could give in and let it finally, and completely, consume her. Although it seemed to, a little more every day.

Someone might advise her that she should just buck up. Stop being afraid. To stop fearing altogether, wouldn't that be the same as stopping the fight? She would place her foot down on that one. She had to fight, no matter how weary or burdened she was. She had to keep fighting, for Carston. She had to keep saving him from what seemed like the inevitable reunion of their past. If she fought hard enough, long enough, hid them well enough, his past could be substituted by his future. Right?

Carston was still propped up against the store window, with the others, only he had moved to be next to Doc. His head was now resting upon Doc's shoulder, and he was sound asleep. It was unnerving how comfortable Carston looked sleeping outside with a crew of homeless people. She couldn't blame him. If she blamed him, she'd first have to blame herself. It was she who had exposed him to it. And it was she who, without saying as much, had, in a roundabout way, suggested that amongst those unpleasant people had been their place of safety. Of course, she hadn't meant their safe place forever, as she now feared he felt.

"It's not so bad," Doc's voice interrupted her thoughts.

Her fretful gaze moved from her son's face to Doc's. "What's not?"

"His life."

Chloe sighed heavily, trying to purge at least some of her feelings of disagreement. She was trying to save her son, while simultaneously ruining him. The battle she was fighting was a losing one. Chloe kneeled next to Doc, momentarily defeated, willing to hear wisdom, from any source.

Lowering her voice, not wanting to wake the sleeping love of her life, she admitted, "I don't know what to do."

"Don't ask me. Look where I've ended myself up."

She looked at him sharply, needing advice, knowing there was a lot more to his story than he was letting on. "You're not like the rest. You're not fooling me, or my son. Why are you out here?" she demanded. Her tiredness was making her extra snippy.

Doc rubbed his lips together. "I'm exactly like the rest. I'm a failure. I am weak."

Chloe shook her head. "I don't believe you."

"Believe what you like," Doc said, looking away.

"Look at me," Chloe demanded, both too loudly and too angrily. Carston and Gargantuan stirred, neither waking. Doc's eyes snapped back to her, also angry.

"I won't have you gallivanting around with my son unless I know your story."

"I'm not doing any gallivanting," Doc hissed. "I've been trying to stay away from him!" He started to collect his legs beneath himself so he could get up and leave. "I never should have come to you for help in the first place. That was a mistake. Just add it to my long list."

"Shut up, Doc. If there's no pity parties for me, then there's no pity parties for you either."

That surprised him, she could tell. He froze, Carston's head barely perched on his shoulder. Another half an inch, and Carston's head would fall, waking him with a jolt. "You don't understand," Doc growled.

"You're right," Chloe said, "but I'm asking to."

"Why in the hell do you care?" The way Doc spoke, the word *care* could have just as easily been replaced with the sound of gagging.

"My son loves you!" Chloe confessed, raising her voice. If Doc hadn't been shocked by her telling him to shut up, he was shocked now. She added more calmly, "Whether you, or I, like it, we're in this together. And just so you know, so you're not overly concerned, he loves all people. But I'm looking at him now… and he loves you most."

Doc slumped back against the wall. Apparently, it was his turn to feel defeated. Either that or he was stunned into immobility. Chloe wasn't sure if she'd get another word out of him, or if he'd rusted himself into silence, like the Tin Man of the Wizard of Oz. After what seemed minutes upon minutes, she conceded that she'd unintentionally chased Doc from their lives and reached for son's arm.

"All right," Doc said finally.

Chloe paused, only inches from Doc's face again. "What does that mean?"

"It means all right," Doc said gruffly, adding a nod, as if it made the point clearer.

Their closeness was too much, so Chloe pulled Carston's arm, transferring him from Doc's shoulder to her own and lifting him with an enduring effort that told her that was likely the very last time she'd be able to lift her son into her arms, ever again. Carston was outgrowing her, and the thought made her heart break.

Carston's thin arms wrapped around her neck.

"You're wrong, by the way," said Doc.

She looked down at him over her son's shoulder. "About what?"

"He loves *you* most. He always will."

Tears welled up in Chloe's eyes as she breathed. "Doc, can I ask you a question?"

He nodded tentatively.

"I don't know how to save him in a way that won't also ruin him."

"That's not a question."

Chloe hefted Carston a little higher. He was getting heavier, if that were even possible. "What should I do?"

Doc looked at her long and hard. It was crazy, her standing there waiting for any kind of magical response to such an obscure question. How could he possibly even know what she was talking about? She hadn't let him in on her story any more than he'd let her in on his. He didn't know them, and they didn't know him. Not truly. How could he know what she should do when he didn't know the *what* in which she had to do something about. And yet...he told her exactly what she needed to hear. Exactly what she needed to do.

"Let him climb, Chloe."

Chloe wasn't entirely certain that letting Car climb would save him, physically, as was her most innermost fear. It was such a dangerous activity. What she did need to own up to was, letting Car climb would keep her from ruining him in every other way. Cripes, she hated having to admit that some homeless guy that Carston had shared a lollipop with at the park held the key to knowing how she could stop ruining her son. But he was right.

"Are we in this together then?" Doc asked her.

"Cripes," Chloe moaned. "I guess we are."

3

Carston dragged himself out of bed the next morning after his alarm clock had gone off, just as he promised Mama he would. He also dragged himself to the dresser, dragged on clean clothes, dragged himself to the bathroom, dragged a toothbrush over his teeth, then dragged himself out the front door and down the creaky stairs. The rusting stairs sounded extra loud in his tired ears after having gotten less than a few hours of sleep. He couldn't wait to get his job done so that he could drag himself back up those grating stairs and into his awaiting bed.

Under the awning, Mrs. Ellsberg's sleepy helpers were stirring just as slowly as Carston had. It had been a long night. Despite that, no one argued or tussled over whose blanket was touching whose or about what job each would do. There was a bog in the air, figuratively since they were all dragging through a swamp of fatigue, and literally, because last night's pile of rubble was still oozing an unpleasant stink. No one had the mind to bicker. Last night's loss was too fresh.

A community is comprised of peoples, not only near and dear, but also of peoples from down the street and those considered valueless. In Carston's short life, he had seen how loss had a way of bringing peoples together, mending what was wrong, reviving what was dead. For nothing is lost forever that God does not command to be. Therefore, it wasn't a time for Carston to grumble, it was a time for working alongside of his neighbors.

Carston went inside the store and found Mrs. Ellsberg sweeping the floor. "I can do that," he volunteered.

"I've got it, young man. It's a mite dustier today than usual, so if you could be sure the shelves are wiped as you go?"

"Yes, ma'am." Carston retrieved his stepstool and a rag and began facing the products on their shelves. "Everyone is getting along today," he told her.

"Yes. I see that Doc has rejoined us as well. How did you sleep?"

"Fast," Carston answered. It seemed like he'd just closed his eyes on Doc's shoulder when the alarm in his bedroom stared blaring.

Mrs. Ellsberg laughed, but it was short-lived. "Took the words right out of my mouth," she said. "What are your plans for today?"

Carston wiped down cans of assorted vegetables before pulling them forward and spinning them so that the labels faced out. "I was looking forward to a nap when I'm done. Now that I'm waking up, that doesn't sound quite as fun. Maybe I'll go to the park."

"They both sound like lovely ideas."

Carston stopped and looked at her sweeping this way, then that, little dust particles taking flight. "Have you ever thought about having someone babysit the store so that you could go to the park?"

Mrs. Ellsberg looked at him, a smirk playing on her lips, revealing her crooked teeth. "I haven't much use for a park," she advised him.

"You could swing."

Her eyes looked past him then and watched a memory play in her mind. "My husband used to push me on them." She looked back at him. "I know that sounds silly, but I was once younger than I am now. And lighter."

"Don't sound silly to me."

"It doesn't sound silly to you," Mrs. Ellsberg corrected and went back to swaying with her broom. "Besides, you ought to invite your mama."

"Mama is at work."

"Is she now?" asked Mrs. Ellsberg in that sing-song manner that suggested that she knew something that he didn't.

"She's not?" Carston asked. It was true, he hadn't checked. He'd had no reason to. He'd simply assumed she'd left to work, as she always did.

"Told me last night that she was taking today off from work. I think she's feeling a bit discombobulated."

"Because of the fire, or something else?"

"Something like that."

Everyone had finished their chores, eaten their bowl of oatmeal, and had vamoosed, before Carston was done with his work. Everyone, that is, except Doc. Doc nibbled at his oatmeal slowly and when he was done with that, he stuck around, against Mrs. Ellsberg's rules. It was strange that Mrs. Ellsberg didn't correct him. She went about her own chores as if nothing was out of the ordinary. Only, something was definitely out of the ordinary. Doc almost wore a grin. Not quite, but almost, which was close enough to cause Carston some serious curiosity issues.

"What's going on?" Carston asked Doc.

"I don't know what you're talking about."

"Yes, you do. Tell me."

"You sound an awful lot like your mama."

Carston cocked his head. "And you know that because you've been spending time with her."

Doc shook his head. "That's not a secret. You were there as well."

Carston shook his head too. Two could play that game. "No, I wasn't. What favor was Mama returning last night when she stitched up your forehead?"

Doc pursed his lips.

Carston puffed out his chest. He had Doc now. "Did that gash have anything to do with Mama?"

Doc looked almost relieved. "No, it did not. Have you seen her today?"

"No, I haven't." Carston left it simple as that, testing how much Doc knew.

"Car," Chloe's voice came up from behind him, "are you done with your work?"

Carston turned toward her, and his face felt warm with happiness. "You *did* take the day off! How come?"

"There's something that I need to do."

"What is it?" Carston asked.

"I would like to see how your chin-ups are coming along. Accompany me to the park?"

"Yes!" Carston declared excitedly, his stomach bubbling with joy. He started to dart off, ahead of her, then stopped. "But…I can't do ten yet."

"That's all right. I'd like to see what you *can* do. Then, I'll buy you a soda pop when we get back, as promised."

"Even if I don't get to ten?"

"Even, and especially. You need the energy to get stronger."

"Okay!" Carston said, delightedly. "Only…"

"What? What is it?" Chloe asked.

"Can Doc come?"

"Actually," Chloe said slowly, "he has to come. He's part of this now."

"Part of what?" asked Carston.

This time Doc answered. "Your training. After you show us your chin-ups, and get your soda pop, we're going hiking."

Carston looked at him, eyes wide with disbelief. "Training for *climbing*?" he asked, his heart so full of hope he could have flown like a bird, right then and there. When he heard the word "yes" he about did, he jumped so high.

"You need to understand, training is not a one and done," said Doc. "It's going to take a lot of effort on your part. It will be hard, the training *and* the waiting. This kind of commitment has no finish line."

"In addition," added Chloe, "working at the store for Mrs. Ellsberg and schoolwork come first and foremost. Always. There will be no exceptions. Is that understood?"

"They will!" Carston cheered. "I understand!"

"One more thing," said Doc. "I've agreed to get you started. Point you in the right direction. That's all. I'm not staying. That's my condition."

"Will you be around for my first climb?"

Chloe laid a hand on his shoulder. "Nothing lasts forever, Car. Let's not worry about that. Let's be grateful for what Doc is willing to show us today. Okay?"

"Okay," Carston agreed, not letting Doc's condition get him down. Carston knew enough to know that the commitment thing that Doc had mentioned was his problem, not Carston's. Carston just didn't know why.

Chapter Sixteen

1

Mount Si was the first trail that Doc decided to introduce Carston to. He could have chosen something easier, like Rattlesnake Ledge or Little Si, both of which he'd heard named more than a few times. Doc felt that Carston could handle more and needed more. Doc knew that there needed to be an element of challenge. He'd seen that familiar fire in Carston's eyes that he'd once had in his own. Should Mount Si happen to be too hard, then so be it, and good. Carston wasn't going to break. At first, if a challenge is lost, it does not break the contestant. It empowers them. It emboldens them to try all the harder, fight all the longer. A small loss gives authorization for great gains.

To Doc's knowledge, Carston wanted great gains. He wanted to develop skills and increase his training. Launching a challenge was the best way Doc knew how to do that. It's a thorny trick attempting to measure improvement if not given something to measure it against. So, Doc bought an ugly inexpensive van. Buses don't drop at trailheads and taking a taxi would be astronomically pricey, especially if done repeatedly. Chloe had gaped when he had pointed out the grey, exceedingly used silver van. It certainly wasn't much to look at, but apparently, she'd assumed he had no funds since he had chosen to suffer in the streets. He had money put away, he just had no intentions of touching it. He felt he didn't deserve it. His fallen brothers hadn't been afforded such indulgences. Purchasing a junk car, that would surely not be functioning by this time next year, wasn't something he considered to be a lavish contribution. It was a necessity. Nothing more. Doc had kept his driver's license as a form of ID, but he hoped Chloe would take over that role as soon as possible. Carston had to have the means to reach training locations once Doc had gotten them on their way with a good start.

The first section of the Mount Si's trail took Doc and Chloe and Carston up 900 feet of elevation gain, through a forest, that still showed signs of fire from the year 1910. After a mile, for a total of 1,600 feet, they reached a rocky area with stunning valley views. They were all breathing with moderate difficulty. None of them were used to this sort of activity. They had a lot of work to do getting their lungs into shape and inhaling and exhaling in an easy rhythm. Carston was the best off, having the energy of youth, and he played every day. Chloe was next, walking every day to and from the bus, and she was well nourished. Doc was the weakest link in this squad, which bruised his fragile, but relentless, ego. Up until now, he'd forgotten he had one.

"Let's take a short break here," Doc said. He needed the breather the most. No one pointed that out. In fact, they seemed happy to oblige in its benefits.

Chloe pulled her tiny backpack off and unzipped it. "I knew we'd be gone for lunch, so I packed us each a peanut butter sandwich." She passed them out.

Doc sat on the ground with his sandwich and leaned against a rock. From there he could look out over the lovely valley to the south. Carston copied him, sitting so close to Doc that he could feel the boy's heat pressing against him, reminding him of another, not so peaceful, time.

Doc and the Afghani kid clambered for cover on their bellies, hoping and praying that the tumbling pieces of the Kiowa didn't land on them. When none did, it was only by a miracle, though that's not the way Doc saw it. From Doc's perspective, this whole mess that he'd found himself in was an utter nightmare. This wasn't the way it was supposed to go. Both squads should have made it out of this day alive. They were a strong unstoppable force. Soldiers who came here to bridge the gap between insecurity and safety. Not now. They were gone.

Something grabbed hold of Doc's arm, and he flinched. The kid was lying so close to him that their sides were pressed together like bread and peanut butter. Once they believed they were generally whole, not having to pick pieces of themselves from out of the dirt, they got to their feet again. They had to move fast. It was unknown if the Taliban were aware of their existence on the ground, but they couldn't take the chance at waiting around to see. They had to remove themselves from the immediate area. It was soon to be overrun with men scavenging for things that might have survived the crash. Doc knew of only one item that he could successfully carry away from the heap that would be of use in this moment. He hoped it was still operational.

"Doc, are you all right?" Chloe asked.

Plucked from his past and dropped back into the present, Doc focused on Chloe's face. "Yeah. Yeah, I'm fine."

Chloe looked relieved. It dawned on Doc that she must be worried he could have a breakdown out here, and she'd be responsible for getting them all back. He couldn't let that happen to her, so to keep that from happening he said, "How about we get going again?"

"Sure," Chloe agreed, clambering to her feet.

Carston sprung to his feet, like a fawn disturbed from a nap, clearly excited for the next leg of the hike.

Another mile in and 500 feet up, they reached "Snag Flats," a section fitting for its name. It was flat, for which Doc was thankful.

"How you doing there, Short Stack?" Doc asked.

"Good," he wheezed.

"Maybe we should stop again," Chloe suggested, taking notice of the informational boardwalk depicting the area's past.

"Training isn't about stopping when it gets hard. It's about becoming stronger. It's about realizing an inconvenience is nothing more than that," Doc offered.

"An inconvenience," Carston imitated on cue.

"You sound tired too," Chloe accused. "You and I aren't necessarily the ones in training here, Doc."

"I am tired, but I agreed to be here." He looked at her. She'd agreed to be here…but it hadn't been her first choice. "Okay," he conceded, "thirty-second break." Doc straightened up and began unscrewing the lid to his water. "Hydration time."

"I took a drink while I was walking," said Carston.

"Good. So did I. Lesson one, we're a team. If any one of gets dehydrated, we're all dehydrated. It is each of our responsibility to hold ourselves accountable so as to not damage the team."

Chloe and Carston nodded, unscrewed the lids from their water, and started chugging.

Man, Doc's legs ached. He sprinted toward the down Kiowa as fast as his wobbly limbs could carry him. Jumping from so far up hadn't been the best idea. At the time, he'd been in a hurry and was betting on using the cover of the dust swirling about to scoop up the kid and disappear. Once the kid was safe, he could wait for the bird to return. Now though, there would be no return. It would be a while before anyone even figured out that Doc hadn't been on that flight out, that he hadn't burned up with the others, that he wasn't dead.

When Doc reached the wreckage, he knew exactly what he was looking for. The left-seat pilot would have had an M4 for defending the left side of the craft since it could only deliver tracers from the front. Doc hoped the M4 would not only be operational but also that it would not be out of ammunition or lost. When he spotted it wedged against the side panel and someone's unattached marred leg, he snatched it. He hesitated only long enough to inspect the interior for survivors. There were none, and their deaths had not been pleasant.

Rifle in hand, Doc turned away before his soul could evaporate at the sickly sight. Now was not a good time to give into the knocking of his mind as it struggled against the reality of his situation. If he stopped moving and planning forward, he would give into the pain and depletion, and the kid would surely die. Quickly, he sprinted towards where he'd stashed the short stack that he'd promised Young he'd take care of. On the way, he saw exactly what he needed to do that.

In the road lay, in Doc's direct path of travel, a dented canteen. What were the chances? Measly, but he took it as a sign that he was doing exactly what he needed to do in this moment. He grabbed the canteen, pushing on. If he kept lifting and pressing his boots into the ground—lift, press, lift, press—he'd make it. They'd make it.

When he reached the kid, the kid's face was dirty, and his body was shaking. But he was still here. He was still alive and holding on. Holding on to what? A hope that someone would care for him from this point forward? A dream to make it to America, out of the line of fire and bombs and Taliban that would cut off his fingers one by one for helping an American? Wanting nothing more than to sit down and let this hopeless world swallow him up, Doc opened the canteen. Water slipped out when he tipped it, so he handed it to the boy and watched him drink.

What lay in store for this young boy who'd watched his parents be decapitated this morning? Was there ever to be a secure future for him? A place to grow up without panic of the next violent attack? A place to go to school for writing and arithmetic with other boys and girls his age rather than enrolling for lessons in martyrdom? Doc was not convinced that one little boy encased within a country of bloodshed and slaughter could ever be safe. He wasn't certain he would ever be convinced. But to hell he would go if he didn't try.

"Doc," Carston's voice broke in, "I'm not afraid of it being hard."
Doc nodded.
"How hard do you think it will be?"
"Depends on how far you plan to go."

"To the top," Carston said assuredly.

"Then it will be very hard."

The next leg of the hike was strenuous. No one talked for a time. They each sunk into themselves, locating the necessary grit to continue while enjoying the feeling of nature and the simplicity of one another's quiet company. They were met by other hikers. Some were climbing at a decent pace going on ahead. Others were coming down and wished them a good day. With each step, Carston grew brighter. With each step Carston was more in his element. Inarguably, this was the direction his life had been pointing all along. The eighteen hundred feet between Snag Flats and Haystack Basin didn't diminish Carston's energy in the slightest. In fact, Carston seemed to be feeding on the influence that the close proximity to the summit provided. The trek was turning the eager boy into something of a warrior right before their eyes.

And for a moment, Doc saw someone else.

"We have to find somewhere to rest where we can't be found," Doc said, looking around at the options. He knew full well the boy didn't understand a word. Still, it felt better having someone to talk to, someone to share the decision with. "We won't make it out in the open."

The boy, whether he understood or not, was looking up at him, listening.

"Do you understand?"

The boy nodded, taking off at a run.

Unable to yell at the kid and alert the Taliban as to their whereabouts, Doc did the only thing he could do. He took off after the boy, following as best he could. Now and again, the kid would pause, look over his shoulder, checking to see if Doc was keeping up. Sometimes he would wait, other times, he darted forward again. Doc had to give the small human credit. In the timeframe of a shorter life than most, this trying land had transformed a mere child into an accomplished navigator. He was wicked fast and knew all the tiny crevices in which to hunker in.

In America, where the threat of dismemberment or servitude was not a common occurrence, he would have made a phenomenal football receiver or excelled in any intricate soldiering game like paintball or airsoft. Only this short stack wasn't play-acting: he was competing against real men who were out to harm him, and his people, if they didn't behave accordingly. He was enduring unquestionable and rattling suffering. Exhibiting at a very young age what most people don't even know how to recognize, let alone become: the kid was a warrior.

Behind an empty goat yard, they came across a large hole in the ground. The kid pointed at it expectedly. It was clear, this is where they'd be hiding. Getting on all fours, Doc followed the kid in, pulling his rifle between his legs. It was a tight squeeze and smelled horrendously of dirt, dog, and urine. The earth roof scraped firmly against Doc's back. On the ground beneath the palms of Doc's hands, he could feel the crunching of tiny bone fragments. Who knew what creatures they might have been before becoming the uncomfortable carpeting of a dog-dug dwelling.

"*This is nice,*" *Doc whispered.*

Apparently, the kid reached the back of the hole because he turned around, still on his hands and knees and looked Doc right in the face.

"*I'm going to call the front desk and complain about the bed bugs.*"

Despite the terrible day, despite he'd lost his parents, despite he was hiding in a hole that dogs slept in, a tiny smile appeared on the kid's face. Doc wondered if, among all of this chaos, if hiding in the hole had simply been a joke. Then the kid scrunched his legs and sat. Nope, not a joke. The kid was proud of himself. As he should be.

Not wanting to be faced the wrong direction if the Taliban came poking their heads in, Doc struggled against the small, compacted space. The walls and roof held him tight against his sides and his back, pressing in on him from all sides. There was absolutely no room to turn around. The dark space was entirely too small. Backing out was not an option. There was no way to peek out to make sure the coast was clear. If he backed out blindly, it was possible he would back right into the boots of a group of surprised Taliban. Great. Doc was stuck right where he was.

Doc called the hike at the base of Haystack. The last section of three hundred to five hundred feet up Haystack was rumored to be dangerous, particularly for beginners. It was easy to see that was true. It could be ascended, without gear even, but a fall would have serious consequences. If he wanted Carston to learn anything it was that training isn't about cutting corners, it's about preparation. None of them were prepared for the fitness level or climbing competencies that unaided scrambling up a rock mountaintop required. Many have and do chance it. Thankfully, it usually worked out for them. That's not how he wanted Carston to think. Carston needed to think about the bigger picture. It was not so much that *doing* less *created* more, as it was *having* less (ego) *produced* more preparation.

Chloe openly expressed her relief about being done for the day. Carston said he understood, though Doc suspected that he might only be in agreement for Chloe's sake. Before they left, Carston looked up. Doc imagined that he was attempting to see the route and visualize his inevitable success. It was then, observing Carston's anticipation, that Doc understood Chloe's anxiety. The rock before them was real enough, as was Carston's chances at being hurt. Doc's coaching would have to be unshakable. Doubts about his ability to keep the kid safe started tumbling in, one by one, like grenades.

What had he been thinking? He was in no kind of shape for the responsibility of keeping someone safe. He couldn't even keep himself safe. Just yesterday he'd walked right into a drug deal and had almost been shot. He would've been, if it hadn't been for Nat. Sure, he'd scaled some pretty serious areas during his missions in Afghanistan, but he certainly was no professional climber. He'd been a soldier and a medic. A horrendous one at that.

Halfway down Mount Si's picturesque trail, the team of three stopped once more for a quick water break. One of the last before reaching the bottom. Going down was always easier than going up. The day had been enjoyably warm, even in the coolness closer to the top, and nearer the bottom the trees provided spotty shade. As Doc was slipping his water bottle back into the pack that he'd borrowed from Carston, something touched the back of his leg.

Doc jerked and turned. It was a dog. A well-kept golden retriever with slick shiny hair.

"I'm sorry," the lady holding the end of the dog's leash apologized. "He thinks everyone is a friend.

Doc said nothing, staring at the dog long after the lady had given up on a response and continued on. The dog's freshly brushed fluffy tail waved a happy farewell. Doc didn't notice, his mind too busy playing out a different moment, from a different day.

Every sound above ground and outside the entrance he and the kid were crammed into made him edgy and anxious. Each time, Doc regripped his rifle. Thankfully, he'd crawled in with it between his legs, the muzzle pointed back toward the opening. If nothing else, he could fire blindly at an intruder and hope he got them before they put a bullet up his rear. It wasn't much of a defense. It was pretty much the equivalent of being caught with your pants down. There was little other option with the Taliban commandeering every house and crawling over every hill. Contorted, irritable, and battling claustrophobia, they waited.

Doc's weary body must have surrendered to sleep as a means of endurance because he woke with a start when something touched the calf of his leg. Recklessly, he yanked it forward. He must have stretched his leg out beyond the hole while he was dozing. A sick realization hit him. He was like the creature lurking secretly beneath an unsuspecting bed, and he'd just been discovered.

Panic set in. He rustled around a bit trying to make sure the muzzle of his rifle was well past himself so he didn't shoot off his own leg before he pulled the trigger. He felt more than he knew that the kid was awake now too, not that there was anywhere he could go or anything he could do. As long as the kid stayed put, the Taliban might never suspect he was in there. Doc's finger rested lightly on the small trigger, listening and waiting. He didn't want to fire a deafening blast, or waste a bullet, if it was only one man. If it were one man, he could allow himself to be dragged out then take on the enemy with his hands.

Nothing happened. No one yanked him out by the boots. He wondered if the sensation had been a dream, or perhaps someone had tripped over his leg, not realizing it, and continued on. While he was wondering, something touched the back of his leg again. It was more of a brushing sensation this time. At once, he the thought of a camel spider, or a scorpion, or a tarantula. The images in his imagination caused him to stop breathing. Then, it happened once more. Only this time, it was accompanied by a sound. Sniffing.

The kid whispered something that Doc couldn't make out. Then he whispered, "ruff, ruff."

A dog!

Doc released a long breath. Dogs in this country were notoriously unfriendly, and this one had cause to feel decently offended. Even so, at least it wasn't a poisonous spider or a bearded man pointing a gun at his rear. If the dog had come back around, it was possible the area was clear, and they might be able to crawl out of the hole. Hopefully the dog was shyer of Taliban humans than American humans and kids. They didn't need it to take to barking and give them away. A low growl reverberated through the dirt walls. What was going to be was already in the making. They may as well move.

Doc gave the kid's sleeve a tug then started inching backward. All of his muscles and joints ached. He hoped they wouldn't freeze up on him once he got them straightened out. He might still need them. The moment he and the kid were clear of the hole, the dog dove in, ignoring them completely. Luckily, the flea-infested mutt hadn't been in the mood for tussling. All it had wanted was to check on its stash of bones. Those tiny pieces were probably all the mutt had to put his teeth on in days.

"They're still there," Doc reassured the dog. "I'd give you another if I had one that I wasn't using myself."

Doc's driving had started out a little rusty that morning, but he'd gotten better by the minute, and it was pretty much like he'd never stopped by the time Carston and Chloe were deposited safely back home. The sight of them standing on the sidewalk, staring after him, after he'd declined their dinner invitation left him feeling haunted. What they didn't understand was that he could no more be a part of their lives than he could turn his life around and become a doctor. Certain things just weren't in the cards for him. There wasn't enough pluck left in his heart to beat the demons that tormented him. They were cruel and merciless voices that he believed to be the ghosts of his military brothers. A very small piece of him knew that they weren't, that they couldn't be. But that piece was very small and had a difficult time reaching through the mess that Doc had become.

After Doc was certain that Chloe and Carston had tucked in for the night, he took his place next to Gargantuan under the awning. Wrapping his arms around his midsection, he laid his head back, tired. His stomach moaned and complained of being empty, but today had been good, and he didn't deserve good.

"Saw your wheels," Sam growled almost as loudly as Doc's stomach.

Doc said nothing.

"What's a man like you doing with wheels? Did you steal them?"

Boop chimed in, "I saw that you'd given Chloe and Carston a ride. Would you give me a ride?"

"I think he's asleep," Gargantuan whispered, fiddling noisily with a couple of marbles in his hand.

"He's not asleep," growled Sam.

"Everyone pipe down," ordered Oscar. "Let the man, and I, sleep."

The group heeded Oscar's advice. Oscar sat at the top of the sleeping order after all. Doc exhaled quietly and tried to sleep.

The more Doc tried to sleep the further away sleep wafted. When all grew quiet, Doc opened his eyes, taking a quick peek at the group to make sure it was safe to do so. Then he gazed off at all the buildings and all the windows across the street, letting his thoughts drift hither and thither. Some of the windows still had a faint glow of light filtering through the blinds. He stared at one in particular that had an empty flowerpot in the sill. It reminded him of the window in Afghanistan.

The homes in Afghanistan were a fraction of the size of the homes here, the windows smaller still. However, the lightly glowing window and silhouetted pot, stroked a chord that was very much the same.

The Taliban fighters had subsided like a tide, and villagers were returning. The kid had led Doc to a door and tapped lightly. An elderly couple appeared. Their worn expressions and raised foreheads conveyed their unease. At first Doc thought he and the kid would be turned away, but the man motioned with his fingers for them to hurry inside as he anxiously watched behind them. The door was shut and bolted on Doc's heels.

The couple exchanged conversation with the kid. Doc wished Holden was there to translate. The old man nodded solemnly. After all, he was putting he and his wife at risk having a soldier in their home. He blew out the single candle in the room and gave the signal for everyone to sit down and hush up. Each of them took up a place on the floor, sharing the sleeping rugs. Except the woman. The woman moved about, collecting small portions of foods she had stored. She brought Doc and the kid each a pocket-sized saucer. On each was a modest chunk of goat cheese and a couple dried bites of what Doc assumed was goat meat.

Doc nodded his head as thanks. It was the best thing he'd had all day.

The man and woman laid their heads down and appeared fast asleep before Doc could finish both his bites. Doc marveled at them. In a world as unforeseeably dangerous as theirs, how did they sleep like that? He supposed they were tired from being driven fearfully from their home, but darkness hadn't fallen completely even. Doc reckoned he understood. Soldiers were much the same way. They had to eat and sleep, no matter what was going on. Doc laid down on the rug. It felt good to be able to stretch out. His head was resting against the wall, providing him a visual out the small window.

Out the small window, he had a perfect view of the neighbor's window. A small rectangle with one pot sitting in it. Anything could be in that pot: flour, water, hopes… but Doc imagined that since the Taliban had just swept through, it was likely empty. He stared at it, deliberating when and how he was going to get out of here. Come morning, he wouldn't be able to simply walk out as he had come in. There was bound to be lingering Taliban, or a civilian spy. He didn't want to put this home at risk any more than he already had. He would have to try to sneak out during the dark.

Something lightly touched Doc's shoulder, right above where the butt of his rifle rested. He turned his head, looking down. The kid's small hand had reached out and was now resting there. Just like the old folks, the kid was fast asleep, his eyes closed and lips parted slightly. What was Doc to do with him? A kid wasn't a dog. They couldn't adopt him like a stray.

A faint drumming caught Doc's attention. He listened. No, it wasn't drumming. It was a beating of the air. A familiar whoomp, whoomp, whoomp. He sat up. They'd come for the wreckage. How much time had passed? It had seemed like a lifetime, but it couldn't have been. Still, when you're the one on the ground, a couple of minutes could seem too long. It took less than a minute to be located and less than a second to be killed.

Doc moved to wake the kid with a poke, and stopped, his finger hovering just above the kid's shoulder. He couldn't take him to Outpost Dallas. He couldn't take him at all. He had to leave him here. With these people. His own people. Doc had done what he told Young he would. The kid was as safe as Doc could make him. Now it was time to go. Quietly, Doc worked himself to his feet, trying desperately not to be a disruption. At the door, he moved the bolt, then paused and looked back. As much as it hurt, the only thing he could do for the kid now was to spare him the goodbye.

Chapter Seventeen

1

That week, Doc and Chloe continued the process of taking Carston up to Mount Si for training. Each day they got a little stronger and little surer-footed. Carston loved riding in the old van. It felt like he was riding in miniature school bus. The entire second seat was his own. Most of all, he loved that Mama had taken time off time from work to join them. The only time Carston could recall Mama staying home from work was the time he had a really bad flu. It was only a matter of time now that she'd have to go back to work. He wondered whether—or not—he'd be allowed to continue training outside the city with Doc when she did. Or if Doc would be done too.

Carston tried to not worry too much about that right now. Mrs. Ellsberg told him, in order to enjoy life, you must focus on the joy. That's what he intended to do, for as long as this lasted.

The first to bust out of the van was Carston. The first to strap into his backpack, and the first to hit the trail was Carston. Taking the lead was fun. He had so much energy flowing out of him, he simply couldn't be still. He ran ahead of Doc and Chloe and back again, just to do it all again. Over and over. He jumped bushes and logs and circled trees. His legs itched with the excitement of going up and up and up.

"Car, please settle down and be careful," Chloe cautioned.

"I am—" Carston started to defend as his toe caught on a root and he tripped.

"She's right," Doc said. "You need to work on staying in the moment."

"Stay in the moment?" Carston asked, stopping to breathe. "What does that mean?"

"It means," Doc explained as he passed, taking the lead, "focus on what you're doing. It's one thing to have a plan, but that plan may go to shit."

Chloe cleared her throat.

"Things happen," Doc amended. "You may have to change the plan, and you may not be given any warning. If it's life or death, you can't afford to be caught daydreaming."

Just then a man in shorts and a t-shirt came running down the hill. The three of them were just able to move to the side as the man whooshed by them without a word.

Carston stared after him. "That wasn't very nice."

Doc continued on. "There will be a lot of nice people out there and a few that seem not so nice. If you remember that every one of them has their own challenges, and that those challenges have nothing to do with you, you'll be a happier person."

Carston stared after Doc this time, his mouth gaping. He turned toward Chloe and she wore a similar expression. They both laughed.

2

The next day, Doc took Carston to the park and barked orders at him from the sidelines. Run laps. Do chin-ups. Do pushups. Do sit-ups. Only after Carston was panting and grabbing at his ribs did Doc allow him in the van. Mama handed him a water, smiling.

"What was that about?" asked Carston.

"That was so you don't circle us like a vulture today," Chloe said proudly.

When they arrived at the base of the hiking trail Doc handed him his backpack. Carston flung it over his shoulders and buckled it on. It felt a lot heavier than usual. He jumped, bouncing it upon his back.

"What's in here?"

"You *and* your Mama's stuff," Doc answered. "She doesn't need the weight, you do." Doc took lead position and started walking. "That load is nothing compared to what you'll have to carry later."

Carston took up the rear. Doc hadn't volunteered how much weight it would be that he'd have to carry later. Carston had a feeling the number would sound impossible at this stage, so he didn't ask.

As they hiked, Carston realized that their little team of three was beginning to look more and more like the veteran hikers that came here to train. The veterans seemed to be almost pulled to the top by some sort of magnetic force. Although they hadn't reached that level yet, Carston felt his legs strong underneath him, lifting him higher and higher. Mama's breathing sounded effortless, and Doc appeared to be eating more.

When they reached the base of Haystack, Doc turned to Carston. "You're climbing to the top today."

Carston felt his face light up. "Really?"

Chloe had found an out-of-the-way place to sit. "Not before you eat," she said firmly. "Carston bring over your bag. You've got the sandwiches and extra water."

"Are you going Mama?" Carston asked.

"I'm waiting here," she answered.

Upon Chloe's insistence, Carson choked down his dry peanut butter sandwich. It went down about as easily as a mass of cotton balls. Doc's expression revealed he felt about the same. They were both excited. After they'd washed down the obstruction in their throats, they took their place at the base, looking up.

Chloe waved. If she was nervous, she didn't show it. Carston was glad. He wanted her to believe in him. She knew how badly he wanted this. In a way that he couldn't explain, he needed this. From the look on her proud face, maybe she'd needed it too.

"All right," Doc said, "let's go."

Doc sent Carston first, staying right behind him the entire time. Other than a "move your foot up more" or "there's a good handhold a little more to your right," Doc remained relatively quiet. Though scrambling up the boulders and rocky sides was tough and unlike anything else he'd ever done, Carston felt his heart being pulled forward. This is what he'd been waiting for. This was his destiny. He could feel it. Even as his legs burned and his heart pumped, not once was it too much, even with the added weight to his pack. Car supposed that's exactly why Doc had added it. He was ready.

When they reached the top, they both looked out over the beautiful view of the valley and surrounding mountains. They weren't so far away that they couldn't see the city. It was there, reminding them that the world awaited their return. Carston was in none too much of a hurry to get back to it. When he inhaled, the air was clean and crisp. It felt like, until now, a part of him had been missing. Carston smiled. One stealthy peek in Doc's direction revealed that Doc was experiencing something similar. On Doc's face was an expression that Carston had never seen before.

"What are you thinking about?" Carston asked.

Doc took a deep refreshing breath. "It's quiet up here."

"Sorry," Carston apologized, realizing that he'd disturbed Doc's quiet.

Doc stared into the distance as if he was listening to the quiet, waiting for it to be interrupted. "Not you," he said. "Other things. I think I could find peace on a mountaintop like this."

Carston turned and looked out, listening for Doc's peace. "Yeah," he agreed.

Doc broke the spell by removing his pack and digging through it. He pulled out a small disposable camera and pointed it at Carston. "Give me your best summit pose, of many to come."

Carston smiled brighter than he'd ever smiled before. His first summit! And more in the future. He threw his arms into the air. Using his index finger, pinky finger, and thumb, he signed, "I love you" to the world, and gave a loud "Whoo-hoo!"

There was a lackluster click, and Doc tucked the camera away. "Time to go down," he said as he swung his pack onto his back.

"Already? Can't we stay a little longer?"

"No, your mama would worry. A summit moment is just that, a moment. The only way to have it again is for you to climb the next mountain."

Once more, they were on their way. This time, headed down, leaving the summit for the next person to enjoy. The climb down was harder than the climb up. Where adrenaline and excitement had fueled the climb, sadness and fatigue mollified the descent. The moment he set his eyes on Chloe at the base of Haystack, and saw her smile, his heart rejoiced all over again. He threw himself into her arms.

"I did it! I climbed to the very top! I stood on the summit!"

"I know, Car! I'm so happy for you." And she was, he could tell.

In the van, Carston sunk into the seat and leaned his head against the window. "Mama? When you go back to work, will you let me keep climbing?"

"We'll have to see," Chloe answered. "One day at a time, Car."

"Doc can take me."

"I'm sure that Doc has other things he'd like to do."

"Like what? He's—"

"Carston Thomas!" Chloe's raised voice was loud in the confines of the van.

"A bum?" Doc asked. "I am that, and I am not offended."

"Well," Chloe huffed, "you may not be, but I am. That's about all I will take of this conversation, Car."

"Yes, Mama."

Carston looked out his window, growing sleepy. He couldn't stop thinking about what Doc had said about climbing the next mountain. "What will it take, Doc?" he finally asked. "To climb the next mountain?"

"Four things really," Doc replied. "Strength, stamina, and training."

"That's only three, Doc."

"In life, whether you follow your dream of climbing, or do something else entirely, there will come a time that your strength and stamina and training will run out. That's when you'll have to depend on your willpower, your inability to quit on yourself. It will be your most powerful tool in your most desperate moment."

Carson watched Mama fold her hands in her lap. She was listening, the same as him. He didn't have to guess that she'd experienced such a moment in her life.

3

Driving back to the city, the seat behind Doc fell eerily quiet. "Is he still alive?" Doc asked of Chloe.

She turned in her seat. "Yes, he's alive. Just sleeping."

"I didn't know he slept."

Chloe chuckled. "On occasion, though I admit, the boy's got no sit. The older he gets, the worse it gets."

"Must be exhausting."

"For me, yes."

Doc drove in silence for a minute before mustering up the courage to ask, "You mentioned before, Carston's father isn't in the picture?"

"No, he's not."

"Thomas, is that his father's name or yours?"

"Neither." She turned to him and asked pointedly, "Why are you asking me these questions?"

He shrugged. "Just making conversation." At one point in his life, he'd been rather good at making conversation. It'd been a while though. Apparently, it was a perishable skill.

"Well, stop. That's something I don't want to talk about it."

"How come? You don't trust me?"

"Incorrect. I don't trust anyone."

"To the contrary, you're riding in a car with me and going hiking in the middle of the woods."

She was quiet for a second then let out huge huff. "Ugh, I'm such a fool. Why do I keep making the *worst* possible decisions?"

"I don't know if I classify myself as the *worst* possible decision," Doc defended.

Chloe slumped in her seat and Doc stared out the windshield at the road, assuming that they'd ride the rest of the way in silence.

"Carston believes there's a God. Do you think that could be true?" Chloe asked.

"Unfortunately for me, yes."

"Unfortunately?" Chloe questioned.

"That's something I don't want to talk about."

"Fine. But you sound so certain. How can you be sure?"

"I've seen too much evil to believe there is no God."

"That doesn't even make sense," Chloe argued. "Why would evil make you believe there's a God? The lack of good and abundance of evil should mean there is no God, right?"

"The presence of evil fighting for power indicates that there is most definitely a God. It's inarguable. Think about it Chloe. If there is no God, then who is evil attempting to fight for the power from?"

"What about wars, like the one you fought in? What about crime? How can God allow such things to happen?"

"I'm not claiming to be an expert here. People do what they want. Making a choice is that, a choice. I can tell you this though, the price of those choices are not free."

Chloe nodded once. "Agreed."

"As for war, I don't remember the entire context, but I was once told, blood is the currency in which sin is fought. That much I saw with my own eyes. The generals of those wars had better be sure they're sending lives to fight against sin, and not for it. That's a lot of lives to have to answer to God for." Doc exhaled.

Chloe looked at him. "You feel you have lives to answer to God for, don't you?"

In lieu of answering, Doc swallowed.

"Mitchell Mateo," Chloe volunteered, surprising him. "Do you know that name?"

"No," Doc answered, glancing at her only briefly before returning his eyes to the road.

"That's Carston's father. We weren't married or anything. I was one of his entertainers. It hadn't been my intention to be recruited, but I had been young and foolish, and easily tricked. I was pregnant when I realized that I wanted out. Then I realized that there was no such thing as getting out. I'm not proud of the life I lived, Doc, it was a bad choice. I've been answering for it ever since, as you said. One good thing came of it though. One that I'll never regret. He's sleeping in the back seat."

"When did you get out?"

"That was my greatest mistake," she said, looking down at her lap.

"Getting out?"

"No," she answered. "Not getting out sooner. What finally drove me into leaving should never have happened. It was my fault. I should have left sooner. I should have been stronger, braver. I wasn't. I was weak."

"You were scared."

Chloe nodded. "Yes, though not as scared as I should have been."

She glanced at him and continued. "I don't remember where I was headed that day. If I'd been looking for someone or something. But I'd walked into a room that I wasn't supposed to walk into. The room was small and dark. Three men were in there, huddling hungrily around something, like dogs. I assumed it was one of the girls, but it wasn't. From the doorway, I could just make out an arm, too tiny to be one of the girls.

"To this day, I can't tell you what made me walk in there. I could have been throttled, or killed, for disturbing Mitch's clients, their flies open and pants hanging at their ankles. I wasn't surprised at seeing them, but they were very surprised to see me. They certainly were not expecting a woman. Never in my life have I ever been more thankful that I did something so stupid. I shoved past them as they hastily put themselves away. Standing in the middle of that circle was a child.

"The shock curbed my nausea, but it didn't curb my disgust and rage. I bent down to grab that child into my arms, screaming wildly at them. I didn't know who the poor thing belonged to, but I knew that it belonged to some distraught woman somewhere. It didn't belong there and didn't deserve what was happening. I had to find a way to get it out of there. Then, the face looked up at me."

Silently, tears slipped down Chloe's cheeks.

"It wasn't *someone's* child, Doc. It was *my child*. It was my *baby*, standing before those men like a lamb, Doc. My *son*." Tears streamed freely, and her breathing suffered. "That snake," she hissed, "he found my greatest treasure and stole him. He locked my baby in a room full of devils…because of *me*. He hurt the only thing I'd ever loved to punish me. It was my fault. I can't—" Her breath was coming and going raggedly. "I just can't… I can't forgive myself…"

Doc said nothing. There was nothing he could say that could help her, that much he understood.

Carston stirred in the back seat.

Chloe glanced at him and started wiping at her face, trying to compose herself. "Anyway, we ran. It wasn't safe. If it hadn't been for a friend, we never would have made it out." Chloe sniffed and added quietly, "I don't know if she made it."

"Your friend, she tried to leave too?"

Chloe looked away, facing out the window. "She didn't leave."

Again, Doc said nothing. They had more in common than he could have ever thought, and he was sorry that they did.

Quietly enough that Doc had to strain to hear her words, Chloe said, "How can my greatest treasure come from my greatest mistake?"

Still, there was nothing Doc could tell her. He didn't have an answer. There had been no treasure at the end of his mistakes.

Chapter Eighteen

1

As the bus rumbled down the street, Dagger sat on one of its filthy seats, again. He practically knew the route by heart now. This was Chloe's regular bus route he had no doubt. The box car on wheels stopped at the hospital, not once, but twice, easily explaining the target's scrubs. The first time he'd ridden the bus and seen the hospital in the window, he'd been so excited. What had the whore attempted to make herself into? A nurse? An assistant? A janitor? He couldn't wait to see Boa's face when she pleaded for herself. Then, the second time, and the third time he glided by on the bus, he wasn't so excited. Chloe still hadn't turned up. Where was she? Today was no different.

Dagger punched the seat in front of him.

A huge man with muscles in his jaw turned and glared down at Dagger. "You dare hit my chair?"

Dagger lifted a palm in peace. "Didn't know you were sitting there."

The man's large head cocked. "I've got friends on this bus." He poked a finger at Dagger. "You won't hit any blasted chair. Even if its blasted empty. Got it?"

"Got it," Dagger lied.

It wasn't prudent to make a scene. He needed to blend in so he wasn't made, and if or when his target showed up, he wouldn't be regarded as a threat. Which brought him back to, where was she?

It was possible that she was on days off. It was possible she was on vacation. It was possible that her new hideous scrubs hadn't arrived because the shipment had sunk in the sea, and therefore she couldn't go to work because hideous scrubs were a direct requirement. More likely, it was none of these. More than likely, Dagger knew exactly where she was. She was *hiding* because he'd *spooked* her.

Anger shot through his veins, and he had no one to blame but himself. Resisting the urge to slam his fist into the back of the seat in front of him again, calmly he folded his hands in his lap. Dagger continued to sit there behind some muscle man, as he came to the acidic conclusion that he'd blown his angle.

Still, he knew the target's neighborhood, her bus route, and where she worked. All of these things were staples that she'd have to come back to, like a water hole in the middle of the desert. It was only a matter of time. And when she did, he would be there, waiting for her. There was no escaping Dagger. She, and her son, were tiptoeing around his snare as it was. One wrong move and SNAP! Dinner time.

2

Hook Lip had been staring at screen for the last nine hours, he finally pushed back into his chair. He'd been going over the numbers of his new job and going over them again, attempting to gain an understanding of what had been, what was, and what was to be expected. Should Mr. Finlay call upon him, he wanted to be able to advise swiftly and accurately. He didn't want to be the kid in the advanced class that, when called on, didn't have the answer. In Mr. Finlay's line of business, that was inadvisable, if not deadly. So, he'd decided to study. In doing so, however, he'd found something.

Hour after hour, he'd poured over the numbers, the lines, and the columns, acquiring a base knowledge of how the last accountant had done things. He crammed like a college student desperate to pass, absorbing the numeral rhythm of the books, the rises and falls, the tides, the course. Hour after hour, he'd end up running into the same inconsistencies that had begun to take form in the most recent days. He'd stop and look at them, bewildered. Petrified to start this job off by presenting a flaw that ended up not being a flaw, ultimately revealing his stupidity, or worse, stumbling upon a secret that he never should have stumbled upon, he'd begin again. Despite his best efforts, time and time again, the inconsistencies did not pull up straight, but remained.

The final dilemma was, what should he do about it? Did he report his findings, or did he feign ignorance and pick up the books in good faith from this day forward? Could he be justified either way? Mr. Finlay's advice had not escaped his memory, *it's best if you think only in terms of numbers, nothing more.* What if he'd stumbled upon a secret that they hadn't wanted him to stumble upon? It could mean a not-so-pleasant dismissal. In which case, he should stick to inputting the numbers, letting well enough alone. On the other hand, they were still just numbers. He didn't have an understanding of their full meanings. If Mr. Finlay found out that Hook Lip had found something, and didn't report it, it could mean a not-so-pleasant dismissal. There didn't seem to be a winning option.

The doorknob to the room he was in rattled, and Hook Lip jumped in his chair and turned. No one, other than himself, Mr. Finlay, and Paine was supposed to have access to this room. What if someone was coming to destroy the files? What if the last accountant had been murdered to keep the evidence hidden?

Paine opened the door and walked in. Hook Lip sighed.

Glancing around the room, Paine noted, "Very few changes have been made."

Hook Lip followed his gaze. He'd taken down the last accountant's few personal belongings and dropped them in the open box that now sat on the floor waiting to be delivered to the family, or whatever. "Yeah, I'm not one for decorating."

Paine pressed the heel of his palm into Hook Lip's shoulder, impelling him to stand. Hook Lip did, and Paine dropped into the seat. "You've been in this room for some time," he said. "Care to tell me why that is?"

"Studying."

Paine relaxed his head into the back of the chair. "Are numbers so complex, or did you toil at locating the number pad?"

Hook Lip chuckled at Paine's joke at his own expense. "I found the number pad, sir."

"Is it experience you lack?"

"Yes, but I'm pretty good with numbers and patterns."

"If this is true, why then has it taken you nine hours to study them? Could it have something to do with why you haven't moved any personal belongings in?"

"Nothing like that," Hook Lip assured. "Permission to speak freely, sir?"

"It's not the military, Tom," Paine said.

Hook Lip tilted his head. "You know my name."

Paine nodded. "It's my job to know all of Orson's matters."

Hook Lip swallowed. They were getting awfully close to touching on his dilemma. "Okay," he said. "Honestly, I'm a little scared to be working here. I don't want to bring my family into it in any way. That's why there's no pictures."

Paine nodded again, apparently acknowledging the truth in his admission. "And of my question?"

"I want to know the numbers so if you or Mr. Finlay require information, I can provide it to you."

"And can you?" Paine asked.

Hook Lip hesitated. This felt like a test. What was the passing answer? What did Paine want to hear? Was he supposed to prove capable of providing discretion, or was he supposed to bring inconsistencies to attention? This wasn't exactly your average everyday accounting position. He didn't know the rules, or what to do.

"Tell me," Paine said, without a doubt picking up on the hesitancy, "you haven't spent nine hours studying, and have garnered no intelligence."

"In truth, I'm not sure. I mean...I did. I just don't know if it is something I was supposed to find."

Paine stuck a long cigarette into his mouth and carefully lit it, filling the small room with smoke. He leaned back and said, "Expound."

"Mr. Finlay's advice was to work the numbers and not think about what they could represent. I'm fuzzy on whether he would like me to notice inconsistencies in the number sequences, or notice nothing at all? I'm willing to do either, sir. Whatever is asked of me."

Smoke blew gently from Paine's lips before he replied, "So, you've found something."

"I don't know," Hook Lip admitted. Gesturing to the computer with his open hand, he asked, "May I show you?" Paine swiveled the chair to face the computer, and Hook Lip pointed at the screen. "Pay attention to these two columns."

Line by line and column by column, Hook Lip walked Paine through the same process that he had been going over all day. By now, he knew it by heart. When he was done, he stood back and waited, his stomach twisting nervously. Would he live to send a paycheck to his family, or would his memory be added to the last accountant's box?

Still staring at the two columns he'd been instructed to watch, Paine put his cigarette out on the top of the desk. When he stood, he did so slowly and deliberately. Swiveling on his heel, Paine stepped around Hook Lip, as Hook Lip dodged out of the way. Paine reached for the doorknob.

"Sir?" Hook Lip asked.

"You found something," Paine said, then he disappeared out the door, slamming it behind him.

Hook Lip dropped into the chair, exhausted, and still very much uncertain. It was clear that he'd just stirred up a terrible storm and someone was in big trouble. Very much afraid that it was himself, he glanced down at the box sitting on the floor. The unfamiliar face of the last accountant with his wife gawked back up at him.

"Have you ever made a mistake like this?" Hook Lip asked him.

The lips in the picture didn't move, but Hook Lip could have sworn it implied, *I'm dead.*

Hook Lip took a deep calming breath. "Yes, but I heard you ate nothing but cheeseburgers."

Chapter Nineteen

1

Carston looked up into his mama's face as she tucked the blankets around him. "It's okay if you like Doc," he told her.

"What?" Chloe asked, her cheeks flushing. "I don't like Doc."

"I'm just saying, it's okay if you do."

Chloe smoothed the blanket top. "Well, I don't. Not like that."

"You can find someone to love, Mama, it's okay."

"Oh, those stories you read, they put such ideas in your head."

"It's not stories. People have such things. Mrs. Ellsberg told me so."

Chloe looked at him, placing her hand upon his chest. "I already found someone to love, Car. You. It's always been you." Chloe placed a soft kiss upon his cheek and started to leave.

"Mama?"

"Yes, Car?"

"I remember."

She turned back to him, her expression battling between concern and pretending there was none. "What do remember, Car?"

"Tasha."

She tried to keep her voice even. "Do you?"

"Tasha was my best friend. After you, of course."

Chloe's chest rose and fell before she said, "She was my best friend too."

Carston threw back his cover and jumped out of bed. From his bookshelf, he grabbed his Bible and brought it back to Chloe. "She read to me out of this all of the time."

Chloe nodded, saying nothing.

Climbing back into bed, he said, "Did you know that when people do wrong in the eyes of God, He is forced to turn away?"

"No, I didn't."

"Yeah. When we do wrong, it's called sin. God can't accept sin any more than water can accept oil."

"That seems very deep for a boy," Chloe noted.

"Did you know that oil is 'water fearing'?" Carston asked, still himself amazed at the discovery.

"You read that in the Bible, Car?" Chloe asked.

"No, a science book. The word for it is hydrophobic. It means that oil is actually chased away by water."

Chloe's lips parted slightly. "I see. If this is true, if a person is sinful, then what hope do they have?"

"People used to kill animals," Carston answered, "because blood pays for sin."

Chloe's eyes were examining his face. "I've heard something similar to that. I was told, blood is the currency in which sin is fought." Chloe smiled and ruffled his hair. "When did you get so smart?"

Carston shrugged. "Certain things just interest me. God is fascinating, isn't He?"

"I suppose. Why did people stop killing animals? Not that I want that to start back up. I could never."

Carston brightened. "That's the best part! Did you know that God had a son? Just one. Just like you have me."

"Yes, my son reminds me every Christmas and Easter."

"His name was Jesus—"

"He was born on Christmas."

Carston smiled. "He wasn't born on Christmas, Mama. He IS Christmas."

"And Easter, He died."

"No," Carston laughed, "He LIVED."

"How can that be? You've told me before that He had died on a cross."

"He did, but that was three days before Easter. He died, giving His blood, for all people, so anyone that wished to have their sins paid for could. Then on Easter, He rose from the dead because hell could not hold the Son of God."

"Like the water and oil thing," Chloe noted.

Carston nodded emphatically. "Jesus is the only one that could have done it because he is the only one that has never sinned."

Chloe sat very still, processing.

"Did you know that He volunteered for that job?"

Very quietly, Chloe replied, "I suppose I hadn't thought about it before."

"Isn't that incredible?" Carston asked excitedly.

Chloe's expression softened. "Yes, it is."

"Mama, I want to show you something."

"What is it, baby?"

Carston opened the back cover of his Bible. On the inside cover was a dark stain. Carston gently pressed a finger to it. "This is Tasha's blood. It's from the night we left the scary place."

Chloe gasped and both of her hands flew to her mouth. "You don't remember…"

"She hid us in a small, dark place."

"A vent," Chloe confirmed, tentatively lowering her hands.

"The bad man was very angry. He yelled and hit her."

"He wanted her to tell him where we were."

"She didn't tell him."

"No, baby, she didn't."

"We were right behind her, in the vent, the whole time."

Chloe's chin wobbled. "She was very brave. The bravest I've ever known."

Carston chin started wobbling too. "I thought she was dead."

Chloe quickly wrapped him in her arms. He could feel her tears falling in his hair. "I know, baby. Me too."

"She wasn't."

"No, baby, she wasn't."

"When she woke up, she helped us out of that vent and led us a long way, to a door. You and Tasha were banging on it and screaming."

"I'm sorry you remember this," Chloe said between sniffles. "I'm so sorry."

"Why were you screaming?"

"It could only be opened from the outside."

Carston looked up at her. "Then, who opened it?"

Chloe met his gaze. "I don't know. The impossible happened. The door just opened."

"That's when he grabbed her," Carston said, his heart beating at the memory of Tasha's scream. "That's when she shoved her Bible at me. Why didn't she come?" Carston cried. "Why couldn't we save her?"

"Baby," Chloe murmured, "I'm so sorry."

"Why did she slam the door with her still on the other side? Why didn't we open it back up for her?"

Chloe grabbed his hands. "You already know."

Carston sniffed and nodded. He did know, he'd just had the hardest time accepting it. "She kept the bad man from us."

Chloe nodded, squeezing his hands in hers. "What she did was just like what you said Jesus did. I've blamed myself for years, Car, feeling the same way as you. But after what you told me, I realize no one on earth could have stopped her, and she wouldn't have wanted them to. She shut the door herself because she loved us."

Tears slipped down Carston's face, so he buried it in Chloe's chest. "I loved her too."

Chloe rocked him gently. "She knows."

After a few minutes, feeling a little better, Carston sat back a bit. "Mama, I know why you're sad about me. You don't have to be."

Chloe turned in place, seemingly frozen. "What? I'm not sad about you, Car."

"The reason we hid, Mama, was because of me.

Chloe shook her head. "No, baby, it's not—"

"It is," he insisted. "And why Tasha got us out."

When she looked at him, he could tell she was hiding it, still. Only, he knew what it was.

"It started with the men in the dark room."

Chloe inhaled sharply. It hurt her to speak of the event, he knew, but it had to be spoken of. She had to know the truth.

"I'm okay, Mama. Nothing happened."

Chloe bent over, placing her head on his shoulder, and started bawling. "How can that be?" she sobbed. "There were three full grown men in that room, Car. Three! I saw them—"

"No," Carston corrected, bewildered. "There were four."

She looked at him, tears clouding her eyes. "Baby, I saw them with my own eyes. I'm certain there were—"

"Four, Mama. The fourth man had his palm out, like this," he said, demonstrating, "And there was a hole in it. Didn't you see him? He was standing right between me and the other three."

Chapter Twenty

1

Mrs. Ellsberg was sleeping solidly under her thick comfy blanket on a twin-sized bed that barely fit in the room. Her slumbering face glowed of peace and tranquility, if such things existed.

Mailman stood over her, glowering, fairly certain such frilly conceptions were completely made-up. A fictional concoction of nonsense intended to pacify humanity's natural knack for hostility. Peace and tranquility had never existed, nor would they ever. Not in this world. Not as long as Mailman could help it. This woman especially didn't deserve to swim about merrily in such notions.

"Wakey wakey," Mailman sung into the pathetic face.

Mrs. Ellsberg's startled eyes opened, and with some effort, finally focused on him.

"It's not morning, but I just couldn't wait. I had to see you."

"Mailman?" she croaked. "What are you doing here?"

Her hideous voice grated on his nerves. Despite the tinge of hate bubbling inside of him, he smiled. "I came to give you one last chance to take me up on my offer. I've really been quite patient and generous. But…" he said shrugging his shoulder, 'I'm tired of playing games. Time to make your choice. Take my offer."

"Or what?"

"Burn."

"It was you," she hissed. "You burned down my friend."

Mailman ran a hand through his hair. "Oh, that. Yeah," he said, smiling. "But don't worry, I didn't enjoy it as much as I'll enjoy you when your time comes. Speaking of which, when would you like that to be? Now? Or—" He stopped short when he saw her eyes flutter toward her door.

"Your bodyguards aren't coming to save you," Mailman informed her.

"Bodyguards?"

"The homeless you have stationed outside the front door," he said, his voice dripping in mockery.

She snapped at him, "They aren't my bodyguards, and you better not have hurt them!"

Caught by surprise, Mailman hesitated. Not her bodyguards? Well, snuff out his flame. Still, she showed concern there. That could be used against her. "We'll see about that. As it is, they don't know anything. I came in the back way. They don't have to know anything about this, if you cooperate."

She squinted.

"Did you forget?" he asked. "The nailed-up back exit? All I had to do was remove a couple of boards. It really wasn't that hard. You see, you're not as clever as you think you are. But I am."

"What do you want?" Mrs. Ellsberg demanded.

Mailman bent down close. "I want my money," he growled. "All of it. Right now. And any time I say after that."

"Why haven't you just gone and gotten it yourself?"

He blinked slowly. He really hated her voice. "This is not about stealing, my darling hag. Its about you giving it to me by your own choice."

"This isn't choice," she argued. "This is intimidation."

"Choice, intimidation, isn't it all the same? What matters is that you pay what you owe me, until I tell you that you can stop."

"I don't owe you—"

"You *do* owe me!" he bellowed into her face. She grimaced as his spit hit her eye. "You owe me everything!" His fist slammed into the bed next to her. "Get that through your thick skull, you fat hag!"

She looked him straight in the eye, even lying prone in her bed, and asked, "And if I don't?"

He shrugged, unmoved by her stupidity. What she didn't realize was, he won either way. "I roast you like a marshmallow." He licked his finger, imagining sticky marshmallow there. "I like my marshmallows burnt, how about you?"

Mrs. Ellsberg nodded. "All right."

2

During the night, Doc woke to the smell of smoke. His eyes fluttered open; his arms wrapped around his middle section underneath the throw. Amazingly, it still smelled of flowers. But even the refreshing smell of laundry detergent could be easily shrouded by the stench of smoke. Looking right then left, a sliver of movement at the base of Mrs. Ellsberg's store door caught his eye, and he knew.

"Wake up!" he hollered, throwing his blanket off. "Everyone wake up! There's a fire!"

The others stirred, confused.

Doc was on his feet, pounding on the door. "Hello? Mrs. Ellsberg! Open up!"

Recovering quickly, the others threw off their covers and wrestled to be free from their bags. Boop looked at the steady stream of smoke slithering out from beneath the door with horrified eyes.

"Oh my—"

Oscar and Suicide Sam began pounding on the window. "Mrs. Ellsberg!" Oscar called through the glass. "Mrs. Ellsberg, wake up! Fire!"

Gargantuan began spinning in small, panicked circles. "Fire," he recited, wringing his hands. "Fire. Oh no, fire."

Mrs. Ellsberg wasn't dashing to the door. Doc swiveled on his heel, looking across the street. It was there, just as before. The pot. He hurried across the road to retrieve it as the others continued banging their futile fists against the thick glass. When he returned, he yelled at everyone to "Move!"

One glance at him, and they moved just in time for him to chuck the pot at the large storefront window. Boop covered her ears and screamed. The pot shattered into a dozen pieces. Gargantuan stopped spinning circles long enough to stare, shocked, just to resume spinning and wringing his hands again. Suicide Sam shook his head, possibly in disbelief that Doc would have intentionally destroyed the window. Currently, Doc didn't care what Suicide Sam thought. Nonetheless, the glass remained intact, barely scratched.

Boop and Sam restarted their pounding. "Mrs. Ellsberg! Wake up! Mrs. Ellsberg!"

Doc and Oscar's eyes met. They both knew: it was no use. They couldn't get in, and Mrs. Ellsberg, for some reason, couldn't get out. They hadn't been looking at each other more than a second or two when Oscar's eyes suddenly widened and gazed past Doc, and upwards. Doc turned. Nothing was there. Then it hit him. Chloe and Carston! They lived directly above the store which was billowing out more and more smoke by the moment.

"Call the fire department and get help!" Doc yelled at Oscar. "We've got to rip that door down!"

Oscar nodded diligently. "I will. Go get them. Please."

Doc didn't have to inquire as to whom Oscar referred to, and he didn't have to be told twice. He took off running for the old stairway that led to the apartment on the roof as fast as he could. Racing up the creaky metal stairs, two at a time, his heart pounded. At the top he slammed his fist against the door.

"Chloe! Carston! Wake up!"

Not a moment went by, and it was already open, Chloe standing on the other side. "What's going on?" she asked, her hair disheveled and her voice weak.

"There's a fire inside the store. You've got to leave the apartment, right now. Get Carston."

Carston appeared in the hall behind her. Arms hanging at his sides and standing in his pajamas, he looked at least two years younger. "Mrs. Ellsberg?" he asked, his voice unsteady.

Doc reached into the room, past Chloe, gesturing for Carston to join them. "We can't get the door open, but the fire department in on the way. Come on, Carston. You can't stay here."

"Baby," Chloe said, reaching out her hand to. "Let's go."

Carston did. He tore toward them, then bolted past. He was out the door and scurrying down the stairway faster than a cockroach darted for darkness.

"Carston!" Chloe called after him. "Wait!"

Unsuccessfully, Doc and Chloe rushed after him. He was too fast. At the bottom of the staircase, Carston surprised them both. Rather than taking a right, toward the store's front, he took a left and dashed into the darkness.

"Carston!" Chloe hollered over the stair rail. "Where are you going? Wait! Come back!"

Skipping the last few steps, Doc jumped the railing, and headed into the darkness in pursuit. Panic can cause any normally rational person to do strange things without thinking, let alone a scared kid. Who knows where the kid would end up? He could be lost or hurt. Doc wasn't about to let that happen. As the kid disappeared around the corner, into the alley, Doc pumped his arms and legs harder, not wanting to lose sight of him.

When Doc turned the corner, no one was there. It was completely empty. Doc slammed on the breaks, listening. If he could stop breathing so loudly, he could hear the kid's feet slapping against the ground and decipher which direction he'd gone in. He held his breath. Nothing. How had the kid run so fast in pajamas and bare feet? That's when he noticed the boards lying on the ground.

That wasn't right. He'd never seen boards lying on the ground before, and he'd certainly never seen an exposed opening to the back of the store. He stepped closer. It was definitely gaping, straight into the store. Someone had broken in and *set* the fire. Mrs. Ellsberg hadn't emerged, so she was either trapped, or hurt, or… Doc shook his head, erasing the final thought—for now. Since he knew things could always get worse, Doc assumed that they probably had. And he was positive he knew where Carston had disappeared to.

About to duck through the door, Chloe's voice screamed like she was being murdered, right in his ear. He spun around; half tempted to lecture her about calming down. Hysteria never made any situation better. Doc noticed immediately that lecturing would have been entirely pointless.

Chloe stood, terrified and tangled in the arms of the very man that had been just short of a breath away from grabbing her the other day. The man had a long-curved dagger held to her throat.

"Saw the smoke from your fire," the Asian man said. "Thought I'd stop in, and look what I found."

Chloe whimpered, struggling against him.

"I wouldn't do that, if I were you. You're bound to cut yourself before it's time." The blade made a deep dent her neck and Chloe stopped resisting.

Doc asked, "What do you want?"

The man looked at him scrutinizingly. "Be a hero, and I slit her throat." He leaned his lips into Chloe's ears. "Where's your boy?"

"I don't know," she whimpered.

"I think you do," he hissed. "Toying with me is a bad idea."

Doc knew in order to help Chloe, he had to get the circumstances to change, just a little. He couldn't risk Chloe's throat being slit by charging the man from directly in front. If Carston stepped out with Mrs. Ellsberg, surprising the man, a distraction could work. But Carston hadn't, and that made Doc worry too.

Chloe's eyes kept returning to the opening in the back of the store. She had to be beside herself not knowing if her son was all right. Doc wanted to go get him, but he couldn't leave her out here with a knife to her throat. It was obvious now that she wasn't a random target. Likely, no one would ever see her again. If only he hadn't let the guy get away the first time. He knew better than that. What had he been thinking? Nothing, that's what. He'd been so entrenched in his own misery he hadn't thought at all. He shouldn't have brushed the incident aside. He should have seen this coming. It's not like he wasn't trained to spot threats.

"We're looking for the boy too," Doc volunteered. "He may be hurt inside with the fire. Let's all go check."

"No," the man said firmly. "You go check."

Doc shook his head. "I'm not leaving her. If you want the boy, she has to go too."

"You're not calling da shots, bum! Move it!" He whispered to Chloe again. "Have any reason to think he'll be back, or is he running out on you?"

Doc took a deep breath. "Chloe, I'll be back."

A tear slipped down her soft frightened cheek. "I would rather you ran away then bring my son—"

The blade dug into her throat again and thin red line appeared. Doc tucked his chin and nearly charged the man right then, but Chloe's legs didn't buckle, and the man rushed to yell.

"She's fine, bum! It's a scratch. Move it, or she won't be!"

Chloe closed her eyes, rested them, and opened them again. "Find Carston," she croaked. "Please make sure he's okay."

"All right," Doc agreed. He'd received his orders. Find Carston—alive.

3

Stepping carefully through the opening, Doc listened for any evidence that the man was dragging Chloe away. There was no movement of the shadows behind him and no sounds of scuffling feet or fabric. It seemed the man really did want both mother and son. Who was he? What did he want with them? The man's fingers itched to kill; Doc could sense the hankering flooding off of him.

It was as plain as the sweet stench of alcohol when Doc needed to drown a memory, and there was none about. Just like that possessing need tends to do, the man's head wasn't thinking clearly. He'd already made a mistake. Doc would go find Carston all right, because Chloe was worried the boy was hurt, but he had no intentions of handing him over.

Though smoke was in the air, the storage room was not the source of the fire. Doc continued his way through the space, stopping briefly at the small room that served as Mrs. Ellsberg's living space. The bed was empty. It may have been a relief that Mrs. Ellsberg was not there, but neither was the bedding. That didn't seem right. He knew she slept here, every night. Stepping through the doorway that Carston had once rushed into his arms from, he knew he'd located the fire. But where was Carston?

The store was thick with smoke billowing off of the shelving that was on fire at the front. Doc looked around for something to try and put it out with, at the same time, wondering how it had been caught, when he saw her. Mrs. Ellsberg sitting on the floor. Her wrists and ankles were bound with rope. She saw him too, and her mouth opened to say something. Everything went black.

When Doc came to, he was laying in the chokingly smoky room across from Mrs. Ellsberg. She was nearest to the blazing fire, sweating profusely. Doc tried to sit up and found that his wrists and ankles were bound as well.

Struggling against the rope, he asked, "Where's Carston?"

She shook her head. What did that mean? He was about to yell the question again when a man spoke.

"Welcome to our bonfire." It was the man that had threatened Mrs. Ellsberg with a gun in broad daylight. Mailman, he called himself. "Always trying to save the day. Always the one to get in the way." Mailman strut over towards him, staying just out of reach. "Not today though. I'm ecstatic that you came. We're going to do some roasting." He laughed and rubbed at an itch in his crotch.

Doc looked back at Mrs. Ellsberg the moment Mailman turned away. He lipped "Where's Carston?" Again, she shook her head. If they didn't burn to death, he was likely to strangle her. Didn't she get it? Didn't she understand that Carston was missing? He would have sworn that Carston had come in here. It was exactly him to try and save Mrs. Ellsberg from the fire. If he had, what had happened to him?

"Hey!" Doc yelled at Mailman. "What'd you do with him?"

Mailman turned around from the corner of the room where he'd picked up a blanket and was now taking it to the fire to stoke the flames with it. The dry flammable material would be enough to shoot the flames up to the ceiling. When the ceiling caught, it would be over for them.

"Do with whom?" Mailman asked.

Doc thought about Chloe, with a dagger to her throat. Twisting his wrists this way and that, he tried to loosen the rope restraint. He couldn't sit here and burn to death while Chloe was out there. What if the man lost patience and left with her or just gave up on whatever sick plan he had and killed her right there? Doc struggled against the rope, receiving red irritations all the way around his both wrists. It was already beginning to feel like searing hot lava, and moist, meaning it had begun to bleed. He continued to fight the rope.

"I was only a Boy Scout for a month," Mailman said, "but it was long enough to learn how to tie really good knots. That rope will only give way after you've caught fire. By then, of course, it will be too late for you." He shrugged. "But not for me. I promise, I'll enjoy every moment. Your suffering won't go to waste." He nodded towards Mrs. Ellsberg. "Nor will the selfish hag's."

"Why are you doing this?" Doc asked. "Why don't you just take what you want? Why burn everything?"

Mailman stood outside the fire's reach, internal glee pouring from every pore. He smiled. "I *am* taking what I want."

Smiling, Mailman lifted the last blanket to chuck it in as added fuel to a fire that needed none. Mrs. Ellsberg squeezed her eyes shut and leaned away. Her skin was already red and beginning to blister where it was closest to the heat. She was coughing and trying to cover her nose and mouth with her shoulder. This was not what she deserved. This was not how she should go out, being scorched alive and reduced to ashes along with everything she'd ever built.

Struggling all the harder, Doc yanked and pulled against the ropes. His wrists and ankles burned, but not as badly as they were about to when this room became completely engulfed. Mrs. Ellsberg was doing the same, with no luck. And Mailman, with sweat pouring down his temples, stood there, blanket hoisted in the air like a trophy, smiling.

"A little hot in here, isn't it?" Mailman asked them. He bent toward Mrs. Ellsberg slightly to inspect the blisters forming upon her arm. "Aw... beautiful. Been awhile since you've been this sexy, hasn't it?"

Neither Doc nor Mrs. Ellsberg bothered to supply a reply, and he laughed at their pitiful desperation.

"I bet your friend, the clothing shop girl, was super-hot! Gave me a hard on from across the street!" Mailman threw his head back laughing. "Get it? Super-hot?"

Doc hoped Mailman would dehydrate like a raisin with all of his flouting about.

Mrs. Ellsberg screamed at him, her voice throaty and hoarse. Doc wanted to tell her not to waste her energy, but what was the point?

Mailman glanced at her, not at all concerned, and pulled the arm that was holding the blanket back. "It's warm enough in here, I don't need this. Let's burn it."

As Mailman prepared to toss the blanket forward, there was a loud explosive sound. The store front window shattered, sending the window covering flying inward like a gust of wind had caught it. The fire breathed, its width expanding like a chest. Mailman tumbled backwards, landing on his rear. Mrs. Ellsberg screamed, trying to cover her face the best she could, and trying to gain just an inch's worth of distance from the breathing inferno. As Doc continued his struggle, never just willing to give up, he saw something hunkered inside the bottom shelving in the far corner.

Carston's face.

Amidst the chaos, Carston popped from his hiding place. This must've been the moment he'd been waiting for. A pause in time. A chance. Doc wanted more than anything to yell at him to stay! Remain hidden! Don't come out! But it was too late and yelling would only give him away. Carston leapt to his feet, his arms and legs lunging into position to sprint.

All at once, time for Doc slowed. In the first blink, it was Carston rushing toward him. In the second blink, Carston faded and his face had become that of the kid from Afghanistan. He was about to lose him, all over again.

4

Doc had made it to the Black Hawk. The fresh team had grabbed him and stowed him away where he now sat, waiting. Only the pilot and two gunners remained with him. They had an idea how long it should take to make recoveries from the earlier wreckage and were ready to extract the team the exact moment it was complete. Both gunners were standing at the door with 7.62mm machine guns.

"I've got movement," gunner one advised.

"Something is coming this way," the second confirmed.

"Looks…small," the first gunner said. "A kid?"

Doc's head snapped to attention. A kid? Quickly, he shuffled on his hands and knees to the door. "Wait," he said, searching the growing darkness. *He was so tired he could barely tell one outline from the next.*

The second gunner said, "Whatever it is, it's coming fast. I've got a bead on it."

There! Doc saw the quick incoming movement of a person. A small person. It was the kid.

"There's something in the left hand."

"Hold your fire!" Doc yelled. "He's a friendly."

Gunner one confirmed, "It's not a weapon. Hold your fire."

Doc worked his legs over the edge as the boy raced excitedly toward him, arms and legs propelling him forward. Doc recognized the bracelet that hung from the kid's fist. It had been Ramirez's.

The kid waved the bracelet in the air, yelling, "*Rafiq!*"—friend.

Doc smiled, happy to see him. He'd thought he never would. This kid was the one living person on the earth who understood what he'd been through today. He'd miss this kid something fierce. No matter where life took him, he would be grateful for him. Doc jumped down, readying to catch the kid into his arms.

A single shot from a rifle rung out.

The kid stopped, frozen in place, looking like the Statue of Liberty with his arm over his head.

"No!" Doc yelled. Trying to close those last few steps, Doc felt unremarkably slow.

A dark stain materialized on the kid's shirt, growing larger and larger with each beat of his heart. Doc reached out, and the boy crumpled into his arms. It wasn't surprising how light he was, like a feather on a breeze.

"No..." Doc argued the logic. Gently, he laid the boy on his lap. "Kid...no. I'm so sorry." He looked to the sky and begged, "Take me instead! *Take* me, damn it!"

The sky offered no reply and no forgiveness.

The kid's breaths were short and draining. Yet, his tiny hand managed to fumble the bracelet he'd brought into Doc's palm. Without a word, and still without a name, the small brave warrior drifted away, like a feather on a breeze.

Chapter Twentyone

1

The half-melted window covering was ripped down by Jax and Seven, allowing Orson to step through the large glassless hole. Paine followed. After Hook Lip had showed Paine the problem with the numbers, Paine's suspicions had been confirmed. Both Dagger and Mailman had become mostly inoperative, though they'd continued taking their unearned pay in cash.

Due to the close proximity of each of their self-serving missions, Paine had briefly thought they'd teamed up, that a larger betrayal was in motion. The more he studied it, the more their wretched actions revealed that wasn't the case. They simply weren't that clever. They, each too obsessed with their own conquests, had both weaved themselves in and out of each other's disloyal trudgings without so much as knowing what the other was up to.

When Paine got a call from a trusted source about the start of another fire, he already knew who had started it, and why. It was time the cat caught the perfidious mouse.

Inside the building, a very surprised Mailman was butt down on the floor, gawking up at them like a broken puppet. To the left was a tied-up homeless man, and a boy, who strangely enough was not tied up. To the right, a tied-up old woman in her nightgown that Paine recognized as the owner of the store they were now occupying.

"Put out the fire," Orson ordered grumpily. "I have the Fire department and police on hold."

Jax and Seven hopped to it.

Orson clapped his hands together. "Mailman," he said, glowering down at him. "To what do we owe the pleasure?"

Mailman, still gawking up, replied nervously, "I was working." He pointed to the woman. "That's the lady that's been difficult in convincing." He was gaining confidence and added with a spit, "She's the one who dared give you that stupid button."

Orson rubbed his hands together. "So, you decided to teach her a lesson. For my sake?"

"Yes."

Orson took one large step, placing him directly over Mailman, and boomed so loudly the fire quaked, "I don't need the likes of a tiny creature like you acting for my sake! Do you think I'm so unqualified I can't do my own sake's work?!"

Mailman shriveled, and Paine noticed something else going on in the room. The boy who was not tied, was doing some untying of his own. He had the homeless man's hands almost free. Interesting. Paine knew of this boy. He'd heard about him from more than one front. And here he was, exactly as described.

Orson straightened. "You've been stealing. Not only from me, but from the people. You have broken the rules."

"Wait," Mailman pleaded, lifting a hand. "I—"

Orson looked at the fire. "Boys, don't let that go completely out just yet."

"No!" Mailman started shuffling backwards like a crab. "Wait!"

Jax and Seven got on both sides of Mailman and hoisted him to his feet. Mailman fought, kicking and screaming.

Orson looked calmly over at the boy, Carston. The boy froze, seemingly concerned that his untying efforts had been found out. "Close your eyes, lad," Orson advised him.

Carston obeyed, burying his face into the jacket of the man he was helping.

Speaking to Mailman, Orson said, "You're dismissed."

"No! No! No!"

Jax and Seven dragged the man who burned people alive for glee toward his rightful destination, jerking and shrieking. On count, they tossed him in, and he was caught up immediately, squealing like a pig having its skin ripped off. Not only the sound, but the smell was unbearable. The room of people bore it together.

2

Once the body of the man referred to as Mailman lay silent and motionless, almost undetectable through the blaze, the two men, Jax and Seven, commenced to putting out the fire once more. Everyone in the room had their nose either buried in fabric or pinched. Doc was no different. He'd stuck his nose as far into his jacket as he could. The window may have been exposed to the night, but the stench wouldn't be undetectable within these walls for some time.

"You're detestable," Mrs. Ellsberg croaked at Orson.

The large man turned to her. "Why say that, lady? If it weren't for my intervention, you'd be crispy bacon about now."

"No child should have been forced to experience what had just happened," she lectured, her voice raspier than usual. She ended the statement with a cough.

"I told the lad to close his eyes."

"Bull snot. What of his ears and his nose?"

Orson shrugged. "He wasn't tied." An attractive pale-skinned brunette walked in from the back room, escorting Chloe and the man with the knife—the knife no longer in his possession. "Aw, and here he is, the man of the hour. What say you, Dagger?"

Doc felt Carston tense right before he stood and called out, "Mama!"

"Stop," said Doc, reaching out and grabbing Carston by the arm, surprised to find that his hands were free.

Dagger had been looking around the room, pulling his face back in a grimace at the first whiff, then froze when his eyes landed on

Carston. Instant recognition registered in his hungry eyes. "What's going on in here?" he asked, distracted.

Orson laughed heartedly. "What a coincidence! I was just going to ask you what was going on out *there*!"

Dagger looked back at Orson, saying, "Nothing."

Orson stopped laughing. "Nothing. Hum. I'm not a praying man, but I prayed on the way here, asking, whom hath Dagger been concerning with? Why has thee ceased walking according to my law?"

Dagger swallowed. "I have not ceased walking…huh. You do not know—"

"I *always* know!" Orson bellowed, outraged. "I know when you piss on your shoe, and when you pick your nose upon exiting my place of authority. When your heart drives a dagger into my back, I see you smile!"

"No, I do no such thing—" His eyes flickered to Carson, the last element of the package that he'd been in need of.

Orson stepped up to the Asian man, at least four times the size of him. Looking down his nose at him, he growled. "Even now, your eyes deceive you. Your neck is mine, not your own. I fear you've forgotten the meaning of loyalty."

Dagger shook his head. "I've not forgotten."

"Who is she?"

"She is no one. I swear."

Orson took a deep breath that made his chest expand like a breathing mountain. He took one step back.

"Sir?" Chloe interrupted. Doc nearly choked when he heard her voice and had to hold the squirming Carston tighter.

Orson turned to her. "Something to add?"

"Yes, if I may. I know who he's working for."

Orson cocked his head. "How is this?"

"I once was held beneath Mitch Mateo, the Boa's, roof. A few years ago, I freed myself and my son, against his will. Boa hunts us.

That's why I'm here." Chloe dipped her head, not making direct eye contact with Orson's red-like eyes.

"Look up," Orson barked. "Look into my face when you speak to me." She did, though tentatively. "Explain."

"I heard that Boa would not dare cross into your territory. I came here to hide. Boa needed someone on the inside to look for us. That's who he is working for."

"She lies!" Dagger yelled. The pale-skinned brunette wrapped her arms around him, whispering something, and touched his own blade across his throat. He stiffened.

Orson turned to Doc. "Release the lad to stand."

Doc did, standing when Carston stood. Doc felt his body vibrating with adrenaline, ready for a fight. Carston seemed to be anything but afraid.

"Easy, Doc," a cool, low voice spoke into his ear. Doc jumped and glanced over his shoulder.

The dark gentleman who had been overseeing everything, yet saying nothing, had magically moved in behind him. Disheartened, he flexed his fists and concentrated on his breathing. He couldn't take them all, but he could try.

Orson asked of Carston, "Who in this room brings you and your mother the most danger?"

At first, Doc thought that a strange question, then on second thought, it was brilliant. Orson couldn't ask the boy right out if Chloe was lying. A boy would protect his mother's play, even though she wasn't playing at all. Orson didn't know that. He had to ask a question that a boy would not be able to predict the outcome to, and therefore he'd have no reason but to tell the truth.

Carston looked at the men fighting to smother the fire. He looked at Orson, towering over him. Then he looked at Dagger and the woman holding him. "I don't know that man," Carston finally said, referring to Dagger, "but I know that my mama is always scared. I know that even though her feet to go to work and home again to me, in her mind, she never stops running. She is scared of what could be behind her or what could be around the next corner. I know you are a scary man, sir, but I don't think you came here to bring us danger."

Orson's red mustache twitched as his lips moved thoughtfully. The huge man looked over Carston and Doc's heads. Doc sensed that the gentleman standing just behind him may have provided some sort of opinion, but Doc heard nothing.

"That kid knows nothing!" Dagger shouted. Then he directed his vehemence at Carston. "I will kill you kid! I will kill you a thousand times!"

Orson turned his attention back to Dagger and calmly stated, "No one is killed lacking my approval. You used to know that." Then he spun, addressing Carston, "Cover your eyes once more, lad." He glanced at Mrs. Ellsberg and added, "And your ears."

Carston turned to Doc and buried himself in Doc's abdomen. Doc wrapped his arms around his head.

"Coco," Orson said to the brunette woman, "Dismiss Dagger."

Without a breath of hesitation, Dagger's own blade was brought swiftly across his throat, slitting in clean through. His blood poured down his front and splashed over the floor. Then his body wrinkled like an empty dress blouse and collapsed to the floor.

Orson clapped his hands loudly again. "All right," he declared cheerily. "Show's over. My men will let the fire department in as soon as we get a few things cleaned up and out of your way. Not to fear," Orson said, pointing to the spot in the fire where a body lay, "they won't be asking you any questions about that." Then he calmly said, "It's hot in here. I'm takin' off."

Orson turned and exited the store the same way he'd entered—through the broken window. His men followed him. Last out was the black gentleman who'd stood behind Doc. When they were gone, Carston ran to Chloe, and they embraced one another while Doc untied Mrs. Ellsberg. Upon closer inspection, her fragile skin was worse than he'd thought.

"We'll get you to a doctor," Doc told her.

Mrs. Ellsberg only nodded, which told him that she felt worse than she looked, but he knew Chloe would see to it that she was well cared for. As though summoning Chloe with his thoughts, she and Carston came over and carefully wrapped their arms around Mrs. Ellsberg. Chloe opened an arm and extended it, motioning for Doc to join them. He shook his head. Instead, he turned away, exiting the store in the same manner that all cursed men exit the store on this dreadful night—through the broken window.

3

Hook Lip waited in the car outside the burning business. He wasn't entirely sure what was going on, or what it had to do with him, just that his presence had been requested. He felt sick to his stomach again. If this was a precursor to how he'd be feeling his entire career—however long that might be—he understood how the last accountant might have died of health reasons. At this rate, Hook Lip's health was on a rapid decline, and he wondered if he'd make it to the ripe old age of seventy-three. When he spotted Orson stomping across the sidewalk back toward the car, a scowl upon his face, Hook Lip nearly vomited.

Orson opened the door, slid in next to him, and plopped down onto the heated leather seat. "Hook Lip," he said, "you've done it."

Hook Lip swallowed. "What have I done, sir?"

Orson reached into his jacket pocket, and Hook Lip squeezed his eyes shut. This was it. He was going to die, and it wasn't going to be his health, so to speak.

"What are you doing?" Orson demanded grumpily. "It's not a birthday candle."

Hook Lip opened his eyes, one at a time, terrified of looking down the muzzle of Orson's pistol. All he saw was Orson's angry scowl, glowering at him. "Sorry, sir. I thought—"

"I was going to kill you," Orson finished for him. Orson slugged him in the shoulder hard enough to set his opposite shoulder against the door. The man laughed—at him? With him? Just at himself? "Are you always afraid of dying, or is it just when you're with me?"

Hook Lip swallowed the tiny bit of vomit that had slithered up his throat. "Just with you, sir."

Orson extended his fist, fingers closed, and held it there.

Hook Lip softly bumped Orson's fist with his own, afraid anything harder would be taken as a display of dominance.

Orson briefly closed his eyes as if calling upon a source of patience, then barked, "Put your hand beneath mine." The patience must not have arrived.

Hook Lip put his hand beneath Orson's and something feathery fell into his palm. He looked at it, curious. It was a stand of very short brownish-red hair. When it dawned on him what it was, he looked up suddenly, shocked. Sure enough, there was a spot in Orson's beard that was missing a chunk.

Hook Lip eyes widened, and he smiled the biggest smile he'd ever smiled.

"All right," Orson tapped the driver on the shoulder, "let's get out of here."

"Uh," the driver replied, if that could be considered a reply. "There's a problem, sir."

Orson leaned to peak out the front windshield, and Hook Lip followed suit. Sure enough, a gangly homeless man had danced into the street and was now belly dancing? He was ranting something about sweet beer and rotten teeth. Hook Lip figured the man might actually know something about beer and rotten teeth by the looks of him.

"Can't we just run him over?" Orson asked.

"Sir, I don't believe that would be advisable."

"Just tap him. A small harmless little tap." Orson tapped the driver's shoulder again. "Like that."

The driver sighed and crept the car forward, inch by inch, until the man belly dancing and ranting stopped. The man began howling and hopping on one foot. Then he toppled over, disappearing in front of the car.

"My leg!" Hook Lip heard the man holler. "I can't feel my leg! Boop! Help! I can't feel my leg!"

An unkept woman with dirt-brown hair moseyed up next to the front bumper of the car and looked down. Sticking her dirty hands upon her hips, she said, "I don't think you can feel your brain neither, Sam."

"I think he just wants money, sir," the driver calmly explained.

Orson sighed, rolling down his window. "Tell your friend, he's not getting any money. Move or become a speed bump. Ten seconds." Orson rolled his window back up. "Prepare to drive, Mr. Smith. Nine, eight, seven…"

"Gargantuan!" Boop yelled. "Get Sam out of the street!"

A monstrous man stood from the cradled position he'd been squatted in. He approached the front bumper, lifted the man from the road and deposited him onto the sidewalk. The moment the road was clear—one second to spare—the driver took off. As the store passed by Orson's window, he saw Paine standing on the sidewalk with the bystanders watching over the clean-up. He, always the persistent one, made certain that everything was performed and executed to a perfect standard. Paine was as loyal and obedient as he was wise and trustworthy.

The moment all of Orson's cars, excluding the one, vanished from sight a hand laid on Oscar's shoulder. He turned and was looking into the would-be identical face of himself, if they hadn't purposed to be so different.

Paine smiled charmingly. "Hello, brother."

Chapter Twentytwo

1

"Hello," Oscar replied politely. "Ought you be speaking with me?"

Paine retrieved a cigarette and commenced to lighting it as he watched the clean-up crew through the glassless window. He took a drag before answering. "No. Ought a dead man have reached out to me?"

Oscar rolled his lips inward toward his teeth, pressing them together. "I would think not."

"The boy and his mother, they have brought you too close to me."

Oscar ducked his head. "I have lived without living and have grown tired and old. They bring worth to my day."

Paine nodded solemnly. "They know this?"

Oscar shook his head. "Certainly not."

"Do they recall the night you met them?"

He shook his head again. "No," he replied. Then deliberately highlighting the importance of it to him, he added, "but I recall."

The night had been as dark and lonely as surviving for Oscar had turned out to be. He'd taken to an uninhabited alley outside two prominent red brick buildings well beyond Finlay territory. Even the bums didn't amass behind these buildings even though the dumpster behind them was always brimming with thrown-out food and drink.

Undoubtedly, it wasn't the dumpster that kept them afar—it was the management.

There were many a rumor, but no one knew what went on inside the smaller of the two buildings for certain. A very high-end night club most apparently, open only to select individuals. The top two stories were believed to be apartments, only, Oscar suspected, based on the constant barrage of transportation, it was no normal domestic housing. The back door seemed to be often guarded, no bum knew when or when not, but if you were caught outside of it, you would be swiftly, and painfully, reduced to a miserable version of repentance.

Oscar had had bad luck elsewhere this week. The leftover food that was daily thrown out by eateries and families was fast becoming far outweighed by sheer number of the hungry homeless. He'd decided to take his chances, hunched behind the dumpster of the formidable unknown. To his benefit, the alley was unlit, he just had to stay out of sight, and hope no one had trash to deposit, lest he be discovered.

A stomach full of stale crackers, discarded green olives, and the occasional half-empty bottle from a forgotten mini bar collection, Oscar settled down to digest his findings before departing for a safer slumbering site. He'd popped the last of a handful of peanuts he'd collected into his mouth when he heard a sudden loud thumping. Fearing a surprise beating, he stiffened, suspending even his chewing.

Listening, the swift Bam! Bam! Bam! made him jump. Was he wrong thinking there were voices accompanying the pounding? Female voices. Terrified female voices. Oscar stood, perplexed. Shouldn't he be making a run for it before someone busted outside and stumbled upon him? He stood there longer than he ought to have before he did something even more ridiculous.

As the pounding on the door continued, slowly, he made his way toward it. Why were they pounding on it from the inside? Were they too drunk to open it? They didn't sound drunk, they sounded desperate. What were the chances he would be able to open the door from the outside? None. Yet, he found himself reaching for the handle. He might die for this. He grabbed the cold metal. What did he have to live for anyway?

"*This*," *he told himself.*

To his surprise, the handle moved. The moment it did, the door flew open like all of hell had been trapped behind it. A young woman carrying a black child toppled out and would have accidently run him down like the dirty varmint he was for being in the roadway if he hadn't lost his balance and taken a step back to regain it. The second woman, she started to follow then she was yanked violently backward. She pushed something into the hands of the boy then seized the door with the last of her might and slammed it shut, locking herself in, and the young woman and boy out. The terror in that poor woman's scream behind the door was unmistakable and sent chills all over Oscar's body. It must have done the same to the young woman on the outside of the door too. She seemed petrified in stone.

Oscar wasted no time in telling her, "Miss, you best run."

Her tiny feet took her and the boy away as fast as she could.

"This is dangerous for you," Paine commented. "You ought to leave them and go elsewhere."

Again, Oscar shook his head. "I mustn't. They have no one, same as I."

Paine exhaled, and his breath came out as smoke, like a dragon that was done fighting. "You risk being found out."

"Brother," Oscar said, "I would rather be found out and killed than leave and die."

Oscar could see it in Paine's eyes that he wanted to argue Oscar's point, order it not to be, even, but Paine didn't have the heart to take this from him. It was the only thing he'd ever asked for himself after a lifetime of taking nothing, not even that which was his.

When they were but young boys, they were full of goodness and light. Their mother shared in their joy and sheltered them from all the evil that surrounded them. Until, on their twelfth birthday, it was ordered that they were to be cast into their father's world and to be molded into mere images of him—a lifetime of servitude and fortune. Their goodness was to be destroyed. Their father ordered that they would be dismantled then reassembled into creatures that would serve Finlay directly, without question and without fail. Many secrets were kept, and never written, and so it had to be carried on by blood. This was the first time that *two* advisors would be trained and brought in. For the twins, it was this, or nothing.

It seemed that Terrance had been broken almost immediately. He recited every word and obeyed every command. He'd learned fast that in order to exist he was meant to withhold himself and become a shadow of the image they desired. It hadn't been real in his heart, but he figured out a way to call a truce with himself, to be two different people, at the same time. Like living in the pages of one of Oscar's books. There was only one problem: he was scared he was losing himself, and he was right.

For Oscar, it had been different. Oscar couldn't be lost, and he wouldn't break, not even for pretend. He fought every command. He dug his heels into the dirt floor where his blood spilled from his lashings. No matter what they put him through, his goodness would not be swayed. All the more they tried to smother his light, the more it prevailed, the more it shone in their faces, like a ticking bomb. It was determined, a good man could not be trusted with age-old secrets that were kept and never written. The only way for those secrets to be kept safe was to kill Oscar.

Their mother could no more bear the evil she'd subjected her children to than she could bear to watch them accomplish it. It was her selfishness that had allowed her to believe they could escape it, and it was her selfishness that promised Finlay, and their father, that she'd kill Oscar herself, that very night. His body would be dumped in the river by morning.

They'd agreed.

All that night, she sat and planned as Terrance schooled Oscar how to act more like Terrance. To break the poisonous Finlay chain, it had to be Oscar who went forth. He was filled with good and strength; he wouldn't be overtaken. With practice, he would blind them with his wisdom, disguised as evil prudence, making a difference one small advisement at a time. The only way to fight back was to appear as though you weren't fighting at all. So, an hour before sunrise, their mother sent Terrance on his way to never be seen again, dressed in the clothing of the servants, then cut Oscar's hair and dressed him in Terrance's attire.

At dawn, Oscar took the position at his father's side as Terrance and Terrance was long gone, taking refuge among the homeless population. His mother had written a farewell letter that she was leaving to Paris to flee the horrid reality of what she'd done. In truth, it was her body that was seen floating by at the exact hour their father had demanded there be one. All had assumed the body had been Oscar. They never even bothered to fish it out and check. Because of the sacrifices their mother had made, Oscar and Terrance pledged to live out the promises she had spoken, exactly as she had spoken them. Some secrets are kept and never written.

"Let us be troubled for naught," Paine said, and he left, without any display of affection or acquaintance.

Chapter Twenty-Three

1

Fourteen years of practiced mountaineering, winter camping, and climbing and Carston still reached Denali base camp in awe from what he'd just witnessed flying over the Alaska Range. This world may have been relatively the same since the beginning of time and man, but it never grew old to Carston. Though he was only one man, he would remain more delighted than if he were millions.

Carston joined his small team in pulling his sled and belongings to a spot along the runway where they could pitch their tents for a time. While there, they each buried the supplies they would need upon return. No sense in hauling supplies for later up the mountain just to bring them down again. Between his sled, equipment, and pack, Carston would be managing about a hundred pounds of weight as it was, and he thought of himself as a light packer.

Inside his sleeping bag, Carston stared up at the ceiling of his white and red tent, willing himself to rest despite the sun never truly coming to a set. Like he usually did during such moments, he thought about all that had to happen for him to have made it this far—to this storm-driven, avalanche-plundered place of reverence just a few degrees south of the Arctic Circle.

One of the fellow students he was attending medical school with had once inquired, "People don't belong in most of the places you go. Why do you do it?".

To which Carston replied, "One day I'm going to be a very old man, lying in bed for hours on end waiting to die. I want to have plenty of memories to keep me occupied."

"Why do your memories have to consist of summitting a dangerous mountain, man?"

"A summit moment is just that, a moment," Carston said, reciting what Doc Winehouse had told him, years ago. Then he added a little something that Mrs. Ellsberg had told him during her time lying in bed for hours on end waiting to die. "A memory isn't measured by the size of the adventure; the adventure is measured by the pureness of all of the tiny memories along the way."

The student had looked at him like he'd just spoken Chinese and turned around to focus on the demonstration. Carston wasn't sure why so many young adults his age were so singularly focused. Usually, it was driving a sweet car and getting rich someday. Carston supposed, maybe it was because they didn't have people like Mrs. Ellsberg in their lives. He pitied them. Their eyes, though hungry for the world now, would eventually starve on the diet supplied to them. Carston, he didn't require a sweet car, and he wasn't becoming a doctor to get rich, he already had everything he wanted.

Carston had turned Mrs. Ellsberg's store into a homeless outreach, which he ran with Oscar, from the original "Under the Awning Hotel" crew, and a very dear friend of Doc's that had once been a singer named Natalia Hart, and Mama, when she wasn't nursing. He was also halfway through medical school, a torch Doc had unwittingly brought with him from his time in the military. Due to the unforeseen agonies of war, Doc couldn't hold the weight of the torch and had set it aside. Carston's admiration for Doc and love for helping people caused him to pick it up.

The next morning, Carston took his time drinking hot chocolate and munching peanut butter sandwiches. When the mountain called, he and his team packed it up and headed into a grueling week. This week would test the endurance of both his mental staying power when the winds were strong enough to wipe them off the mountain like toilet paper and his physical ability to withstand the cold, the effort, and the pain. In the toughest times, he reminded himself how impossible it must have seemed for Doc in Afghanistan. Of course, he didn't know all the stories. Doc had locked them away in a vault that only he accessed, but he knew they'd left Doc wrecked on an island of despair—an island that he was forced to drag behind him no matter where he went.

Hours and days later, Carston and his team arrived at Football Field. In front of that was a vertical open face of nothing but snow and ice that led to the summit ridge, where the team would climb in precarious and exposed conditions. Carston gazed up.

"Last thousand feet to the summit," Carston informed the team member who had joined him in gawking.

"Yep."

They each took out water and cheese in preparation for the last portion.

"Gonna make one hell of picture," his team member said, motivated.

Carston nodded, downing his cheese. "That's not why I'm doing it."

His team member looked at him. "Why are you doing it then?"

Carston tucked his water deep down where it hopefully wouldn't freeze. "Doing it for a friend," he said and started off, taking the lead.

"Not sure I got any friends like that."

Just as when Carston was young, he felt his heart being pulled forward—upward. This is what he'd been training for, what he'd been feeling in his soul for years. His legs burned, and his heart pounded until he feared they might give out completely. On the side of the mountain, he paused. Afraid to fall, afraid to fail. It was then that he called upon his most powerful tool, his willpower, his inability to quit on himself, his inability to quit on Doc. Even with the weight of his pack, again he began to rise. The mountain called, and Carston answered with each step. This was it.

When, at last, Carston's boot took the last step, there was no more mountain to climb, and nowhere else to go, he stopped and looked around. The world had changed. It was more beautiful and more peaceful than before. Nothing but clouds and a few snowy peaks existed here. No more pain. No more war. It was beautiful.

As his team filtered up and began taking hero pictures of each other, Carston knelt in front of his pack. From it he dug out an envelope, his name written plainly on the front. He knew that Mama had tucked there and from whom it was.

Most treasured friend,

I am proud of what you have done with your life and your outreach to people in your community, and around the world. If only I'd had your gift, maybe things would have turned out differently for me. I am grateful to have been able to know you and call you friend. You brought to my life more happiness than I could have ever deserved.

Just as we discussed, I visited the graves of my brothers. It took a bit to find them all, but I did. Every last one of them had a resting place, even if it was empty. I know you asked me to tell you how it went. I just can't. I hope you understand.

I finally delivered the black leather bracelet belonging to Corporal Ramirez to his parents. You were right. They didn't blame me as they could have. I told them how he loved them more than anything God has ever made. They thanked me, and his mother gave me a hug that I didn't want. You were right again; it wasn't as bad as I'd thought. His father told me it wasn't my fault that he'd died. If that were true, I wouldn't be writing this letter, because I never would have met you. So, for the first time in my life, I'm glad I bear this sin, because it led me to you.

I endeavored to linger with you, Carston, but I can accompany you no further in this world. My failures have consumed the last of me, and I can bear the sentence of my guilt no more. No strength remains within me to climb another mountain. Please forgive me. Please convince Chloe to forgive me.

Carston, my last request is this, please take me to the top of one of your mountains. I know that I will finally be able to rest there in the quiet, in the peace. I promise to watch over you and your wonders from there.

Your eternal friend,
Doc

P.S. You may be wondering about the account information and legal documents attached. I'm leaving you my savings that I accrued from my time in the military. I spent some but most of its still there. I know that You'll do better things with it than I ever could have. Please share it with Chloe. Don't tell her this, but I've always loved her. Love you too, Short Stack.

Carston pulled Doc's urn from his pack, holding it with his bulky gloved hands. He looked up when a hand touched him on the shoulder.

"The team is starting to head down," his team member said. "Do you want me to wait with you another minute?"

"No," Carston replied, removing the box's lid. "I'll only be a moment then I'll be right behind you."

His team member nodded and turned away to begin the descent.

Carston stood with all that was left of Doc in this world in the palm of his hand. The slightest breeze tickled his cheeks. Tossing the ashes into the sky with all of his might, the wind picked them up and swirled them about. They were carried away to land like snow wherever they may amongst the stillness of an unwavering mountain.

Carston thrust his arms into the air, just as he had been doing since his first summit with Doc. Using his index finger, pinky finger, and thumb, he signed, "I love you" to world. Then he whispered, "I hope you find your peace, Doc."

When the breeze returned to him, Carston felt a quiet sensation sweep over him. He could have sworn that he heard a soft voice say into his ear, *I found my peace. My brothers and the kid send their best.*

"What kid?" Carston wondered.

Grabbing his pack and axe, he started after his team. A summit moment is only meant to be just that, a moment. It was time to head back to the world beneath the clouds and let the dead rest and the living live.

More Books by
Lisa Slater
Visit
Website: www.slaterlife.com
Facebook: Slaterlife, Lisa Slater Author

CHANCING HOPE

A story of love and unpredictable suspense.
"I got way involved in the book. I laughed and cried. Got irritated. My stomach turned. I wanted to take matters into my own hands. I love it." – Janet

HOLDER OF THE HORSES

A family's legendary journey
"Lisa, you have done it again, and taken us on a journey of the heart. Holder of the Horses exceeds any expectations and once again I was up late because I had to finish the book. In the end tears were flowing from the emotions of the characters. Their loss was mine; their joys were mine. Thank you does not seem to be enough…" – Sandra

FOR THE GARDEN

A novel
Years ago, the unimaginable murder of eleven-year-old Samuella Rose left Sarina Rose, her twin sister, in a downward spiral and plagued by nightmares.
A cold shiver covered Becky's arms and legs with goosebumps. This was beyond superstition or hoaxes. This was actually happening. Graver still, she suspected, Sarina had no idea.
Could Samuella really be communicating over the gap of death, beseeching for justice? Or is Sarina losing her grip on reality? Either way, finding the killer was worth the risk, but if she succeeded would anyone believe her? What did she have to lose? Just her sanity. Maybe her life.

Made in the USA
Middletown, DE
27 July 2024

57900267R00198